What People Are Saying About

By Way of Paris

A new talent on the scene, dark, witty and believable —
Christopher J Newman takes you on a thrilling ride through
toxic landscapes.
Maggie Gee, OBE FRSL, acclaimed author of *The White Family,
Blood* and *The Red Children*

A heart-pumping ride with a wildcard protagonist. The seedy
streets of London and Paris shouldn't be this much fun. Buckle
up, Bruv.
C. McGee, author of *Owen O'Shea, Feral Chickens,* and *Exteriors
and Interiors*

Christopher J. Newman is a crime writer with a unique talent
for creating great stories and believable characters that you
can't help but care about.
Peter Kesterton, author of *Girls Don't Cry*

T0274631

By Way of Paris

A Novel

By Way of Paris

A Novel

Christopher J. Newman

**ROUNDFIRE
BOOKS**

London, UK
Washington, DC, USA

CollectiveInk

First published by Roundfire Books, 2024
Roundfire Books is an imprint of Collective Ink Ltd.,
Unit 11, Shepperton House, 89 Shepperton Road, London, N1 3DF
office@collectiveinkbooks.com
www.collectiveinkbooks.com
www.roundfire-books.com

For distributor details and how to order please visit the 'Ordering' section on our website.

Text copyright: Christopher J. Newman 2023

ISBN: 978 1 80341 608 3
978 1 80341 618 2 (ebook)
Library of Congress Control Number: 2023941821

A CIP catalogue record for this book is available from the British Library.

Design: Lapiz Digital Services

UK: Printed and bound by CPI Group (UK) Ltd, Croydon, CR0 4YY
Printed in North America by CPI GPS partners

We operate a distinctive and ethical publishing philosophy in all areas of our business, from our global network of authors to production and worldwide distribution.

Contents

For James and Annette Newman,
my loving parents.

Acknowledgments

Mom and dad, thank you for your love and support, your belief in me, and your unyielding patience with me as a wild, daydreaming child—now turned man-child. Creating Luke was easy—all I needed to do was imagine the person I would have become if you both were the exact opposite versions of yourselves. I'm thankful y'all are nothing like the parents in this story—I love you. To my sister, Mindi Schedel, for being my lifelong cheerleader and a perpetual ray of sunshine. Thanks to my girlfriend, Maggie Lawson, who gave me line-by-line notes on my massive first draft, helped me condense, brainstorm, and pull me from the depths of despair throughout this process—I love you. And thanks to Matt Ham for a lifetime of friendship and support and your inspiration for Cash and the whirlwind trip that created this story – thanks to you and Peggy for reading early drafts.

A huge thank you to the speakeasy crew in Bath, specifically: Chris Heath—a brilliant poet and the inspiration for Heath, to my favorite Aussie—Bec Jackson, and to my dearest fellow expat, Bev Kippenhan. Thanks to my 2019–2020 cohort at Bath Spa University. I was a world away from home and you were all so kind and welcoming – we really got a shit-deal with that pandemic. Special thanks for the hospitality of my fellow Yank, the wonderful Joanne Menon, and to my incredible writing group: James Banyard, Peter Kesterton, Freya McIvor and Ruby Bosanquet. Thanks to early draft readers, Katie Baleno and especially Annabelle Porter-Greenwood, the enchanting Mancunian who inspired Sophie.

And a huge thank you to David Moss for being my "English dad" and serving as inspiration for Daniel. I loved working with you and Joe at the pub and meeting your beautiful family (and Twiglet). And thanks to the City of Bath and all the fine British folks who inspired every single character. I promise I didn't break as many United Kingdom laws as this novel would have you believe—please have me back someday.

PART I

Chapter 1

A professor once told me I couldn't write the beginning of a story without knowing how it ends. That's good advice, but I'd say my ending is pretty damn close, since the banging inside my trunk is getting louder and it's drawing a crowd. I parked the stolen car in the heart of Paris, across from the Hotel de Ville, where I was inspired to do some last-minute writing. An author in Paris is dreadfully cliché, but I promise nothing about my time abroad has been normal. Hell, in the last twenty-four hours I've been beaten, kidnapped and blackmailed. And just this afternoon, I aided in the murder of someone I once called a friend.

I left North Carolina six months ago to travel Europe before my master's program started in London—a city I've been fascinated with since childhood. I was accompanied by my best friend, Corey Cash, a young entrepreneur who had seen the world twice over and firmly decided that Paris was his favorite city. He and his fiancé, Emma, had recently split and I thought some sightseeing would do him good. As for Cash, he saw my dysfunctional upbringing firsthand as kids, and he thought finally leaving the country would do *me* some good—my writing too. So, in late summer we set off to see what adventures Europe had in store.

In Munich, we had countless liters of beer from all six major breweries in a futile attempt to clear my writer's block. We toured a million museums in Rome and drank wine under the hot sun until I puked on the famous Spanish Steps—still couldn't shake a word loose. And in Barcelona, we lost eight hours of our lives when we were given roofied drinks meant for two hot Swedish girls. Cash woke up on the bathroom floor of our hotel and I woke up slumped over my notebook on the balcony. I'd written nothing but a losing game of tic-tac-toe on the page.

The last two weeks of our trip culminated in Paris, where Cash and I stormed countless cafes and bars with my notebook and pen. From Le Marais down to the Latin Quarter and back up to Montmartre, we saw the sights, met the people and yet I couldn't write a word about it. It wasn't until a particularly long session of staring at my notebook that I realized I needed to search for a deeper Parisian experience—go beyond that of the average tourist.

On our last night in Paris, we finally made a turn off the beaten path when we met a man named George Goodwin in a kitschy dive bar with American memorabilia on the walls. George was a dapper, young Englishman in a gray Armani suit. We spoke for an hour about all the authors he knew in Paris, and mentioned he was headed to a party brimming with writers and artists. "Mate, if you're going to make it as a writer you need to network," he said, poking my chest. "You've got to put yourself out there." Apparently, he and his weed dealer, Rémy, were quite chummy with the next wave of great Parisian wordsmiths.

"Screw this guy, let's get out of here," Cash said while George phoned Rémy. "I know you're looking for a story, but you'll be abroad for a whole year. There will be plenty of inspiration along the way. You're not going to find anything good with people like him."

That's not true, I thought. In fiction, sketchy people like George always make the best characters. The Englishman gave me a thumbs up as he reentered the smokey bar and smoothed down his hair. George's unpredictability was what my story needed—what my life needed. "Come on, let's check this party out," I said to Cash. "This year is my one shot and I've got to explore every option. If it gets weird, we can always leave."

Begrudgingly, Cash agreed. His business mind was more skeptical than mine and he thought George was a conman. As for me, I had never met other writers before and my blank page desperately needed whatever George was selling. Even if that meant maybe buying a little weed from this Rémy character.

The three of us downed our drinks and crammed into a tiny taxi that reeked of cologne and cigarettes. Cash was fidgety as we rode, stuffed between me and George. He and I grew up in the same shit neighborhood, but Cash's parents actually liked him and taught him never to get into cars with strangers. My mother didn't stick around long enough to pass along that gem, so I was happy as a clam watching a lamplit Paris stream by my window. My booze head buzzed with excitement, and I soon lost my bearings in the maze of gothic buildings.

The cab dropped us on God-knows-what side of town for Rémy's apartment—to pick up a few *party favors,* as George called them. Parked cars lined one side of the road, while a sea of mopeds lined the other. Distant honks echoed from the limestone buildings. George ushered us into a building with massive double doors, through a narrow hallway, where we made the laborious hike up five flights to the top floor. A dim bulb buzzed above us as we caught our breath on the landing. George approached an apartment with purple light pouring through the edges of the doorframe and keyhole. Just as he raised a hand to knock, the door swung open, revealing a messy-haired Frenchman with a patchy beard.

"Merde!" the Frenchman gasped, shrouded in purple light. "George, tu m'as fait peur."

George doubled over with laughter. "I'm sorry, Rémy. Are you leaving?"

"Oui, pardon," he said, closing the door a little. "Je dois y aller—très occupé."

George placed a hand on the door. "These are the blokes I phoned about," he said. Rémy examined us. "I understand my cousin sent you a shipment this week?" George tapped a finger against his nose.

The nose gesture was strange, but I was too focused on Rémy's hesitancy and the sweat shining across his forehead in the purple light. I hadn't met many drug dealers so I figured nervous and sweaty was how they always looked. Cash glared at me, primed to leave already.

As the Frenchman deliberated, I noticed a camera above his door with a solid red light that said it noticed me too. It was all getting too weird, and just before I said to Cash, *yep—let's go!* Rémy sighed and opened the door. "D'accord les gars, entrez."

We stepped inside a long corridor of doors with a kitchen at the end. Rémy marched over to the nearest door and slammed it shut, waving for us to follow. I took a wary breath and closed the front door behind me, where I discovered a second camera above the threshold overlooking the hallway. Whoever Rémy was, he was paranoid.

I followed them across the marble floors, gawking up at the arched glass skylight that spanned the length of the hall. Placed along the walls were four freestanding sculptures—asymmetrical modern-art nonsense. The only distasteful things about Rémy's lavish apartment were the purple bulbs installed in every light fixture. We came around the corner into the main sitting room, which looked like the ballroom of a French palace turned into a brothel. A large TV was mounted on the wall closest to me and at the far end of the room was a leather sofa and two armchairs encircling a glass coffee table. On the table was a bong about three feet high.

"Asseyez-vous," Rémy gestured for us to sit.

Cash and I sunk into the much-too-plush sofa and George grabbed the bong. He and Rémy rattled off in French. "Okay, wait here," Rémy said, disappearing down the hall.

George sparked up the bong. The device bubbled and churned as smoke filled the glass chamber. He yanked out the bowl and handed the bong to Cash. "Clear that, mate," he said, with a lungful of smoke.

Cash threw me a look that said, *I hate you,* but cleared the smoke like a champion. I choked when the bong was passed to me and my eyes throbbed as I sputtered plumes of smoke into the purple light. Cash and George laughed. I don't smoke weed often, since it makes me paranoid, but that night I was chasing my story and feeling adventurous.

Rémy returned with a bag of white powder tied up in a knot and a digital scale. Cash and I shot a look to one another. "Party favors," George said, chuckling. "You show up to the party with this, mate—you may leave with a book deal."

Cash elbowed my ribs. "Always a catch."

Not wanting to lose face with George, I pulled out a wad of Euros and paid Rémy, who nodded approvingly, then poured himself a drink from the liquor cabinet. Maybe it was the weed already messing with my head, but he looked more nervous than before. Sweatier too.

"Alright, mate. A bit of Charlie before we go?" George held up the baggy to me. "Don't let me do it alone."

Damn. My hand trembled as George took it upon himself to cut a few lines with his credit card on the table. He rolled up a twenty Euro note and snorted the first two lines, then handed it to me. Everyone watched to see what I would do. After a moment of deliberation and avoiding eye contact with Cash, I groaned and said, "Better get a damn book deal," then snorted two lines.

Holy shit—the drug delivered its punch quick. As if some warm, invisible force picked me up and set me on my feet. And the euphoria that followed, like whispers from an unseen voice saying, *anything is possible*. Minutes later, I was rattling off North Carolina stories and laughing with a stoned Cash. I forgot about Rémy's erratic behavior, and instead was intrigued by our new friend, George, and how he ended up in Paris.

"Let's just say I need a lot more money before I'm allowed back to London," George shrugged. "But I've made myself useful here, as you can see," he pointed to the cocaine.

Wow—a Londoner in the drug game, fleeing his home country—that's a hell of a character. My heart pounded, and not just from the drug, but from the excitement that my story was practically writing itself.

Time began to slip. It felt as if we had been at Rémy's for hours, and in the same second, like we had been there for no time at all. How was that possible? After what was probably my fourth line of cocaine, my heart fluttered as the drug mixed with the alcohol and weed. I closed my eyes. They felt jittery as I sunk further into the absurdly plush couch.

When I reopened them, the walls of the flat had drawn in closer. *That's ridiculous, you're just high.* My eyes landed on Rémy. He stared into his empty glass, looking like a man awaiting execution. Whatever pain he felt, it pulsed from him like WIFI. Cash and George joked about the artists we would meet later. There was a poet who detailed the genitalia of her past sexual partners in her recently published collection. Gross. A writer who used her own excrement to write a short story. Double gross. And a famous photographer who had taken nude portraits of his own mother. Unforgivably gross. *Maybe I don't want to meet these people.*

I watched their mouths as they spoke. There was static in their words which made them feel fuzzy in my ears. Why could I hear my own heartbeat? Like encroaching war drums. My breathing became short and shallow. My chest rose and fell like the breast of a panicked bird, trapped in the rafters of Rémy's purple hell. Oh, God. I'm in over my head. In a foreign country, smoking and snorting who-the-hell knows what with a possible criminal and a paranoid cocaine dealer. Gotta do something. Gotta get some fresh air or splash water on my face.

Why am I standing? I don't remember getting up.

George's wild, cocaine eyes leered at me behind a cigarette. "You okay, mate?"

"I'm swell, just need to piss!" I said, way too loud.

Then I was walking, but it wasn't something I told my legs to do. It was more like gliding—no, floating across the room to the hallway. I looked back to catch Rémy watching me, the creep.

The corridor was longer and had more doors than I remembered. I tried doorknobs on my search for the toilet, but each was locked. Really don't remember the hallway being so long. I was running out of rooms and stopped dead when I noticed the camera watching me—its red light beamed into my soul. Was Rémy watching me?

The last door opened with a low creak. The room was dark but my eyes were drawn to a dim lamp on a bedside table. A girl was lying on her back on a single mattress in the corner. Her legs hung off the bed with her boots still on. Like she had passed out where she stood and fallen onto the bed. I laughed, because it looked like she was dead.

A bubble of thought surged from the depths of my substance-rattled mind. This is a drug dealer's apartment; what if she overdosed? I decided to check on her. Afraid to wake her, I attempted measured steps toward her. But cocaine isn't a stealthy drug and I stomped over to the bed. She wore a black tank top and as her details came into focus, it looked like she wasn't breathing. My stomach knotted as I leaned over to see her face. But it was turned away from me.

"Please don't be dead," I said, under my breath.

My hand on the wall, I leaned over her and caught my reflection in a mirror on the wall. The harsh under-lighting from the lamp washed away all of my features I considered to be good-looking. My hazel eyes looked crazed and dilated like a nighttime predator. *If this chick wakes up, she's going to think I'm trying to feel her up.* I couldn't turn back now. I leaned over further and saw her eyelids were barely open, showing only the whites of her eyes.

She looked very damn dead.

"Jesus!" I fell back onto my ass.

I scrambled to touch her arm. It was ice cold. I yanked back my hand and a shiver ran up my spine. Frozen turkeys were warmer than this poor girl.

She wasn't just dead; she was *super* dead.

Chapter 2

This can't be real. This can't be actually happening. All I could do was stare at the poor girl. Bill was the only dead person I'd ever seen, but after thirty years of drinking he looked like a corpse long before he died. My mind couldn't compute a dead young woman. The room was quiet, and death hangs heavy in confined spaces. There was a stillness in that room I can feel to this day.

A tremble shot from my hands through my whole body. *Need to move—need to tell the others.* I bolted down the hallway and stumbled into the sitting room. The three of them were laughing, but stopped as I slid to a halt at the coffee table. My expression said it all. Their smiles evaporated.

"Dude, there's a dead girl in there," I pointed down the hall. Cash jumped to his feet. "What the hell?"

Rémy's eyes widened. "Non, non," he said. "That is Madeleine. She gets high, uh—and then sleeps. Elle va bien."

The tremble in my hand worsened, but this time as anger. "Rémy! That girl—Madeleine, *ne va pas* fucking *bien!*"

They were silent. Cash's eyes pored over me, but I didn't dare look at him. We wouldn't be in this drug den if it weren't for me. George stood up and tossed his cigarette into the ashtray. "Show me."

George, Cash and I hurried for the bedroom, while Rémy called from behind. "She's asleep!" he said. "Je promets!"

We poured into the room and halted at the foot of the bed. All the color had washed from Cash's freckled face. "I think I'm going to throw up," he said.

George took a direct approach in his inspection and turned Madeleine's face toward the lamp. Cash and I gasped. The motion opened her eyes, and the light revealed gray-blue irises under her pale eyelids. Cash covered his mouth and turned away. I patted him on the back, because sure, that would fix the dead girl.

Rémy's face was bright red as he paced, running his hands through his greasy hair and rattling off in French. Too fast for me to understand, but it didn't sound good.

George knelt beside her. "She's pretty."

My chest ached. I don't know why, but those two words broke my heart. I pressed my hands together to stop them from shaking. I scanned the room to make sense of everything but Rémy knocked me out of the way to grab George. "We have to get rid of her. Maintenant," he shook George by the shoulders.

Cash spun around. "Get *rid* of her?"

"We need to call an ambulance!" I asserted. "If it's an overdose, maybe they can save her."

Rémy faced me. Sweat clung to his lips. "Imbécile!" he said. "She's dead. There's nothing to save, she's already cold."

Why was Rémy so angry, and why didn't he want to call for help? I felt like an idiot for not putting it together sooner. George must have come to the same conclusion, because he jumped up and shoved Rémy. "Mate, there are bloody hand marks around her neck!"

Rémy stumbled back, his eyes welled with tears. Cash and I looked at Madeleine's neck and sure enough, there were bruises. Rémy, that bastard—he strangled her. Images of my battered mother came flooding back to me. This was all too familiar.

"We were having sex!" Rémy said. "She likes it rough. She kept saying, *étouffe moi. Choke me, harder!* But she stopped moving." Rémy put his face in his hands and wept French tears. "Elle ne bougeait pas!"

A voice in my head screamed *leave!* I should have yanked Cash out of that apartment and back onto the street. But the girl—I couldn't help Mom, but maybe I could help Madeleine.

"You need to call the police," I spoke up. "Tell them what you told us."

Rémy cried harder. "I can't. You know what I do here. I will go to prison for a long time," he stopped abruptly, wiping away his tears. His red eyes scanned our faces, before dropping the bomb: "*All of us* will go to prison."

"All of us?" Cash said.

Rémy took a breath. His hopeless expression faded into something eerily tranquil. His little mind tinkered with a plan. "You are foreigners, and have taken illegal drugs. And you do not speak French. I can tell the police whatever I want. Police in Paris do not like tourists causing problems," he pointed to Madeleine. "And a dead French girl, is a big problem for you. Unless you help me."

Look at that. He speaks perfect damn English when it comes to blackmail. The room dimmed. All I could see was Rémy's face, half-lit from the lamp. His beady eyes glared back at me. I shuddered with the urge to hit him.

"To hell with you," George said. "Clean up your own mess."

I balled my fists and stood with George. "You're outnumbered here, asshole," I said. "We're leaving now—try and stop us."

To my surprise, Rémy burst into laughter. He had a final card to play. He put a finger in my face. "And you—roi des cons. I have you, you stupid idiot. Viens ici." He pulled me to the hall and pointed to the camera above the front door. "That camera watched you come into this room. Maybe *you* killed her."

"Fuck you!" Cash said. "You're not putting this on him."

My eyes stung with tears in the purple light, and though I tried, I couldn't speak.

Rémy turned to Cash and George. "I will delete the film if you help me. If not, I will have to give it to the police. Nous sommes dans le même bateau, non?" he said, with a shit-eating grin.

A switch flipped and I lost control.

I slammed Rémy to the floor and pounded my fist into his forehead. Bad aim. My second blow broke his nose. Better. Before I could land a third, George wrapped me in a bear hug and we tumbled to the floor. I fought, but couldn't break free. Rémy laid on his back, stunned, with his arms stiff in the air like a toppled mannequin.

Cash rushed over to hold me back. "Jesus, chill out," he shook me. "Calm down."

"You can't just get rid of her," I yelled.

George and I struggled and panted, but he didn't dare let me go. All three of us watched Rémy sit up against the wall and tug his busted nose. He wiped away the blood with his palm.

"We don't have a choice," Rémy snorted blood. "We call the police and we are all screwed. Not just me, all of us."

All of us, the bastard. We were silent as Rémy produced a crooked blunt from his pocket. We understood what he meant, but none of us wanted to be the first to cave to blackmail.

"This is your problem, mate," George's voice rumbled against my back. "Not ours."

Rémy ignored him, fumbling with his lighter. "C'est facile. We get rid of her and...nous séparons."

Cash plopped onto the floor. He must have done the math in his head because he had a lost look in his eyes. "What do we do?"

George released me. Maybe he hoped I would kill Rémy and solve our problem, but I didn't. I examined Madeleine once more. She *was* pretty. And she deserved better than this, but Rémy was right. I was coked out of my mind. There's no way I could talk to French cops. We'd go to jail, and I'd be kicked out of my program before it even started. And there's no way I could go back home—I had no home. Everyone seemed to arrive at the same bitter conclusion; Madeleine's life was over, but ours wasn't.

"How would we do it?" I whispered.

Cash shot me a look. "Luke, you can't be serious."

"I can't go back, Corey," I said. "You know I can't go back—"

"We throw her in the Seine," Rémy's voice was stymied by smoke.

"No way," Cash said. "She's a human being."

I studied Cash and Rémy in the dull light. Two people from opposite ends of society, united in this room by one dead girl. And somewhere between them was me. The jury was still out on pretty boy George. Cash rubbed his face. The tremble that had been in my hands was now in his. He and Rémy were too opposite on the morality scale to lead us through this, but maybe I could bridge the gap between them.

I pushed myself off of George, who sat, dazed, against the nightstand. I rubbed my sore knuckles and an idea came to me. "We should take her back home," I said. "It might be a while before someone finds her. That'll give you some time to get rid of your drugs and put together an alibi."

George patted my back. "Attaboy," he said, finally speaking. "Rémy, you know where she lives, yeah?"

Rémy frowned as he considered the fledgling plot. "Ah, oui—not far."

"Do you have a car?" I asked, monotone and all business.

"Oui—Renault Dacia."

I shrugged. "I don't know what that is."

"It's a French car," George said. "A bit small, but it'll work."

I don't know how a vacation could turn to this, but if we were careful, maybe we could actually pull this off and get that footage deleted. Rémy took a long hit from his blunt.

"Stop smoking, asshole," I said. "You're driving."

Cash stared at the floor. I squeezed his shoulder. It's not that I was entirely calm, I was terrified of what could happen. But I got Cash into this mess and I was determined to get him out—but that meant moving a body through a city of two million people.

Chapter 3

Most people have speculated on how they'd get rid of a body if the situation were ever to occur. But I've gotta tell ya, when the situation *does* occur you can't think for shit. The four of us debated for a half hour in that dark room on how to transport poor Madeleine. Truthfully, we were stalling—putting off the inevitable.

First, I sent Rémy and George to retrieve the car, because evidently Rémy murders people when he's unsupervised. This gave me and Cash a chance to figure out how to move her. I yanked the shade off the bedside lamp for more light. Nausea rose from the pit of my stomach seeing the bruises around her neck, purple shadows of fingers.

I was ten years old again, crying into my mother's silk blouse. She rubbed my back while holding a frozen bag of peas to her neck. *Moms and dads fight sometimes, Lu,* she said. *He didn't mean it.*

Cash and I knelt onto the bed and sat Madeleine upright. Her torso had stiffed and her skin was ice cold. Cash's breathing stammered, as if he were on the verge of sobbing.

"I'm going to get us out of this, man," I said, wrapping her arm around my neck. "It's you and me, no matter what."

"*Get us out of this?*" his jaw quivered. "We're helping someone get away with murder. Don't you understand? This night is going to haunt us for the rest of our lives."

Tears formed in my eyes, knowing he was right. With her body against mine, I could see Madeleine had been dressed by someone else. Her tank top was inside out, her pants were only halfway zipped, and her boot wasn't pulled all the way onto her left foot. Feeling her in my arms, I finally got a sense of how small she was. Rémy wasn't a big guy, but there was no way she could have pried him off.

"Lay her back down, I'll just carry her," I said.

Cash guided Madeleine gently onto her back. "Are you sure?"

"Yeah," I forced a grin. "I'm way stronger than you, anyway."

He tried to smile but gave up. We were quiet for a while as the bare lamp bulb burned a black spot in the corner of my eye. I paced the room with a cigarette while Cash sat on the bed, staring at Madeleine's purse in his hands. Was he calculating our odds of getting away with this? There were so many points along the way we could get caught. We had to get her downstairs and into the car without being seen. If Rémy doesn't drive like a dipshit, we shouldn't have any trouble on the road. The risk resumes getting her into her building and apartment unseen. Oh God, what about neighbors or CCTV?

My body jolted from footsteps in the hall. "Oi," George called out. He stepped into the room out of breath. "The lift's broken. We'll have to take the stairs."

Cash jumped to his feet. "You left him alone down there?"

"Took his keys," George patted his pocket. "Do you need a hand with her?"

"No," I said. "We need hats. In case there are cameras."

We tore through Rémy's hall closet and found two baseball caps and a beanie. I pulled the beanie down to my eyes. The hats looked incredibly suspicious, but they were comforting. The three of us examined one another under the veil of purple light—three ghosts of the good-timers we were just hours before. I took one last hit from my cigarette and stubbed it out on Rémy's spotless wall, because fuck him. I dropped the butt into the hall light fixture.

I felt like crying again when I went to collect Madeleine, but I fought the tears back. "Come on, hon," I scooped her into my arms.

Cash tucked Madeleine's purse under his arm and opened the apartment door, peering onto the landing. He nodded and I followed him down the first set of stairs, George taking up the rear. Madeleine was heavy in my arms, and I could smell her shampoo. It was flowery and sweet, and it made me want to throw up. I probably would have if I weren't so focused on keeping surefooted on the stairs. Cash kept a hand on my arm and guided me down each flight, while also watching for any neighbors on the lower floors. I hoped he still wanted to be my friend after all of this. Step after step, the muscles in my arms and back started to burn, but I had no time to stop and rest.

When we reached the front door, I could hear faint city sounds. I was damp with sweat, imagining throngs of people on the sidewalk and an endless flow of cars streaming past.

"Okay, give us a sec," George said as he slipped past me. "I'll check the street."

He inched the door ajar and peeked outside, then swung it open. George ran out to Rémy's silver Renault and opened the back door. Cash went first and I followed. The pavement was wet and halos of mist clung to the streetlights. Not a soul in sight on the sleepy side street. A handful of cars and a scooter zipped by at the end of the road. What time was it? How long had we been in Rémy's flat?

Cash slipped into the backseat and I passed Madeleine to him, then took my place. George shut my door and jumped into the front seat.

Rémy turned from behind the wheel and scrunched his face. Madeleine's head rested on Cash's shoulder. "Are you crazy?" Rémy said. "Put her in the boot!"

One sentence from him and the hairs on my neck stood up. A wave of fear crashed over me. I was afraid of being caught and ruining mine and Cash's lives—afraid I'd never be rid of the scent of her shampoo. But most of all, I was afraid of how I could no longer control my anger.

I punched Rémy in his ear. His head slammed into the window. Even his yelp had a French accent. George grabbed me before I could hit him a second time.

"Everyone, calm down," George said. "She's not going in the boot, mate. Start the car, let's get on with it."

Rémy rubbed his ear, but took the keys and turned the engine over. Cash glared at me. "I didn't hit him *that* hard," I said.

Cash turned to watch the buildings pass by his window. I inspected Madeleine, but couldn't look at her anymore. Instead, I monitored Rémy's driving and surveyed the Paris streets. There were still people out, but not many. Stumbling bargoers headed for home and a few homeless people who had no home—the usual nightcrawlers. The clock on the dashboard read 3:17 AM and I realized how tired I was. My eyes struggled to focus as buildings blurred by my window like towering apparitions, judging us for what we were doing.

Most of my Paris exploration was by foot and in the car, I was completely disoriented. We were entirely at the mercy of an idiot murderer. We turned for a side street. Then another. Lightless, gothic buildings with darkened windows leered at our car. Old-world ghosts etched into the corners of the stone walls. Gargoyles perched high on building tops. I held my breath as the ghoulish figures stared at me with their hollow eyes and stone fangs.

I was relieved to see the Hotel de Ville. It was a massive building with ornate renaissance stylings which were lit up like a palace. We were on the Rue de Rivoli headed east toward the Louvre, where we turned north for the second arrondissement.

I have no idea how long we rode—five minutes? Ten? Time stands still when you're hitching a ride to hell with a dead girl's icy hand on your thigh. I had just reached down to move Madeleine's hand when we stopped in front of a tiny café ironically named Le Grand Café.

"This is it," Rémy ratcheted up the parking brake. "We need to be fast."

Rémy took her purse. I hated seeing him sift through her belongings; her lip gloss, wallet, phone, and finally her keys. We waited for a taxi to putter past, and in unison, shoved open our doors. Tugging the beanie down, I stepped out and lifted Madeleine from the car. Cash ran to give me a steadying hand, while Rémy fumbled for the door key.

"I'll stay with the car," George shut the backdoor behind me.

Cash and I rolled our eyes, but we had no choice but to trust him. We crossed the sidewalk just as Rémy got her door open. The entryway was dark but I could see from the streetlight there was a letterbox on the wall with about ten slots and a winding staircase at the back of the foyer. Cash flicked on a light and the hall and staircase illuminated. Dust had collected along the baseboards and the walls were a dingey white from years of passing residents. I stopped at the base of the stairs and waited for Rémy.

"Elle vit au sommet," he said, taking the lead.

Of course she lived at the top. I groaned, but started a steady pace up the steps. The car ride didn't give my muscles time to rest, and before I reached the end of the first flight they trembled under her weight and I was sweating again. Cash saw me struggling and placed his hand on the center of my back to push me all the way to the top floor. We were lucky. Her building was tomb silent.

Rémy slid her door key into the lock, and just before he turned it, Cash grabbed his hand. "Wait, I think I heard someone inside," he whispered.

Rémy bit his nail as Cash put an ear to the door. I felt my grip slipping and shifted Madeleine in my arms, clasping my hands together. It would buy me another minute, but not much longer.

"Does she live alone?" Cash asked Rémy.

"I think so."

I leaned toward Rémy so that Madeleine's head was next to his. "You better *know so,* asshole."

"Yes, elle vit seule," he recoiled. "It's a small place."

Cash gave me a sigh. We'd been lucky so far, but what if Madeleine had a houseguest who waited up all night for her? Just to be awoken by three strange men returning her body. The hallway was so quiet I could hear my own breathing echo between the walls.

Cash turned the key as quietly as possible, but despite his efforts the bolt clanked loudly. He grimaced and pushed the door open an inch. A faint light could be seen from inside. Cash pushed the door open halfway. He peered through the gap, blocking my view of the interior. Just as I shifted for a better vantage point, a voice called from inside and there was movement behind the door.

The three of us jumped back. I almost dropped Madeleine, but before we could run away, a gray and white cat darted into view inside. We stood for a moment sucking at the still air. Rémy placed his hands on his hips. "J'ai oublié qu'elle avait un chat." he panted.

Cash shook his head. "Asshole," he said, wiping the doorknob with his shirt.

Rémy and I followed Cash inside to Madeleine's one-room garret apartment. It had a single window at the far end with her bed underneath. I beelined for her bed, dodging the cat along the way. Her bed was a sea of pillows and I nestled her onto the fluffy, white duvet. I took a step back to survey the place.

A tiny kitchen by the door smelled faintly of her last meal. The apartment was lit by a single lamp atop her rolltop desk. The wall above the desk was plastered with still life sketches; Paris streets with people, pigeons on a park bench, a hound dog napping in the sun. She was creative, like me.

Her home was a cute place, decorated with posters of old French films like *Vivre sa vie, Lola,* and *Les Bonnes Femms*—titles I still remember. Looking down at her, it looked as if she were sound asleep and safe in her bed. My cheeks were hot with tears, because that wasn't true at all.

There were Polaroids of her and her friends making goofy faces, taped in clusters above her headboard. One in particular jumped out at me. It was Madeleine in front of a wall of squares and circles, all different colors of the rainbow. She had her hand on a yellow circle, looking over her shoulder at the camera with a wry expression that said *follow me.*

Madeleine seemed like someone who was particular about things in her life and home, and seeing her boots on the spotless white comforter bothered me. So, I unlaced her boots and set them on the floor next to the bed.

Cash and Rémy watched me wipe away my tears. I zeroed in on Rémy through blurred vision. I'd never felt so much hatred for another human being. My eyes darted around the room for something to kill him with, but I cried harder when I couldn't find a suitable weapon. I'm a screw-up. I couldn't even kill him for you, Madeleine. I'm sorry. Cash sniffled as Madeleine's cat circled through his legs.

He's the best person I know. When we should have been rushing to escape Madeleine's apartment, he searched her apartment for cat food. Cash tore open a big bag of cat food and refilled its water bowl. I guess he figured it might be some time before anyone discovered Madeleine and didn't want the cat to go hungry.

Chapter 3

None of us spoke as we descended the stairs to the ground floor. I took up the rear with a heavy heart, remembering Cash's warning about that night staying with us forever. He was right, because I could already feel it weaving into the fabric of my identity. How do I get rid of this feeling? Can I box it up and put it away—never to open it again?

I lagged behind the two of them, my steps labored. I felt the weight of her body still in my arms, bearing down on my soul. My head was too heavy to hold up and I looked down, watching my steps. Cash swung open the front door and I heard voices in the street.

When I looked up, flashing, blue police lights flooded the hallway.

Chapter 4

I had dreamt about London for twenty years, and should have been excited to finally be there. But over the span of thirty-six hours, a post-Paris fog had seeped into my head and left me numb. Cash and I lumbered from Paddington Station up to Praed Street through a torrent of people knocking against our luggage. Everything I owned was stuffed into a duffle bag, a backpack and a large rolling suitcase. Cash had his backpack and suitcase, but it was evident we were weighed down by much more than our belongings.

We dropped our bags at the busy corner, where I lit a cigarette and squinted into the late September sun. Cash was silent as he stared into the rush of traffic. I felt like a lost child, hypnotized by the voices and footsteps parading past us in the afternoon glow. A young woman was murdered and the world just kept moving. Would we ever move with it again too? It was hard to explain but I felt like Cash saw me differently after Paris. His mind had been planted firmly in the present throughout our European trek, but now his attention seemed elsewhere. We were in desperate need of cheering up, so I decided to put off meeting my landlady for another day.

"Let's get a drink," I said, hoisting up my bag.

"Do you think we should?" Cash frowned.

"I do. We've been through a lot."

He paused, then nodded. "I could use a drink."

"You could use ten. I'll just sign my lease tomorrow and we can grab a room somewhere tonight."

Cash agreed and we trudged south for the northern edge of Hyde Park where, suddenly, the townhouses took on a wealthy pedigree. Restored Victorians with ornate wooden trims and fresh white paint. Lush flower boxes and well-tended gardens behind polished gates. I laughed, seeing F *the Tories* spraypainted on an electrical box.

In Hyde Park we traipsed by joggers, walkers, and kids playing soccer, losing ourselves on the crisscrossed walkways. When the surrounding buildings were nearly out of sight, we collapsed onto a bench beneath a cluster of Maple trees. The sun was low and I closed my eyes, listening to the leaves sway in the breeze. The chatter of nearby park goers and the faraway hum of the city. Those sounds should have been pleasant, but they made me feel uneasy—feverish. My eyes were wet when I opened them and the park looked artificial. I had the oddest feeling that nothing was real. As if London was a wildlife preserve and I was some strange foreign animal dropped into the center of it. But was I predator or prey?

Cash led us through the park as I lagged behind. Blue skies above me and rich green grass below me—but still, nothing seemed real. It was impossible for me to know it then, but this feeling would cause me no end of trouble in London. It was a thread I couldn't help but tug at until it all unraveled.

Georgian terraces lined the tight streets of Mayfair and interspersed between them were upscale boutiques named for all manner of Giorgio's, Giovanni's and Pierre's. Sidewalks surged with tourists sporting tacky London hats and t-shirts. And I swear to God, Pret A Manger was on every damn corner.

Exhausted, we stopped at a pub called the Barley Mow. We dumped our things in the corner and stepped up to the bar, both of us pouring sweat. Afternoon light filtered through the windows, reflecting from the powder blue walls. Like the park, the pub didn't feel real either, like a set piece with antique furniture and tarnished brass lights in the rafters. The smell of fish and chips clung to the golden air.

The bearded barman gave me a nod. "You alright?"

I was winded and sweaty, but couldn't have looked *that* bad. "Do I not look alright?"

The barman cocked his head, confused.

Cash laughed. "Asking if you're alright is basically British for *hello*."

"Oh." I chuckled. "I thought you asked because you thought I looked like shit."

"You do," Cash added.

The three of us shared an awkward laugh, then ordered two pints of London Glory cask ale. The first round went down quick, and by our second we had cooled from the walk and were watching a rugby game on TV. Cash was quiet and his mood was hard to read, so I asked, "Have you decided where you'll go after this?"

"Already bought my tickets," he kept his eyes on the game. "I'm going to Marseille."

"Back to France?"

He nodded. "I like the food and the language—plus, some time by the sea will do me good. You know, try and put this all behind me."

Did he mean to put *me* behind him? "You said it yourself that we'll never be able to."

"I have to try." Cash took a sip of beer. "I miss Emma. All of this has got me thinking, you know? What's important in life."

"But you were miserable with her," I said. "You didn't even want to be in the same hemisphere anymore."

"Was I miserable? Or just afraid?" He looked at me, as if waiting for an answer. "Emma is a good woman and she loves me. And I love her too, I know that now. Love's not easy but it's worth fighting for."

I had hoped this trip would free Cash from Emma, not bring them back together. She was okay, I guess, but they had been together since freshman year and she had never held a job longer than six months. And to me, it was obvious she just wanted to sit back while Cash, and his thriving business, funded her complacency.

"I always thought true love would be easy," I said. "And wouldn't need so much deliberation."

Cash snorted. "Luke, you're my oldest friend and I don't want you to take this the wrong way, but you only love yourself."

"Jesus," I recoiled. "What other way could I take that?"

We were quiet for a minute, absently watching the game. I couldn't muster the strength to be mad, because honestly, I was hurt. I've loved people before—in my own way. For me, love is like a summer rainstorm. It happens often and intensely, leaving me renewed for the next one.

An ambulance came wailing down the street and got stuck in traffic outside of the pub. Cash waited for it to pass. "Listen, I understand better than most, your mom and dad weren't the best example of what love is supposed to look like. That's not your fault, but real love and real heartbreak teaches you things. Dating someone for a few weeks doesn't teach you anything."

I nearly gagged on my last sip of beer. We were supposed to drink and forget our troubles—not dive headfirst into mine. The barman returned. "Another round, gents?"

"Yeah, he's buying," I stood up. "I'm going for a smoke."

The pub had filled with well-dressed professionals having post-work drinks. I avoided my reflection opening the front door, certain I looked like a bum in my dirty t-shirt among a sea of suits and pencil skirts.

Rush hour traffic whizzed by the pub and passing pedestrians peppered me with fragments of conversations. I watched a young homeless couple arguing across the street while I smoked. Their hand motions were lethargic and over-exaggerated. The only words loud enough to carry across the street were, "You're such a cunt, Colin!" the woman shoved him and stormed off. I imagined not meeting the expectations of a homeless woman and decided Colin really must have been a cunt.

Between the cigarette and exhaustion, things got fuzzy and the world took on that dreamlike sensation again. I wanted to scream to see if it would wake me up. Was I actually standing in front of a pub in London watching Colin's dumb face, or was I making this up?

Cash came outside and brought me back to reality. "What's up, Freud?" I asked. "Shall I pay my therapy session in dollars or pounds sterling?"

He smirked and took a smoke from me. "You can play hard ass all you want, but I know where you came from," he lit the cigarette. "I know why you do the things you do. I'm confident you'll work the relationship stuff out when you meet the right woman, but Luke, you've got to work on your anger. You don't have to posture every time someone slights you. No one will think less of you for walking away from a fight—in fact, people will respect you more for it."

That's when I realized how much Paris had affected Cash. When someone starts speaking in proverbs they've been shaken to the core. I decided to tell him what he wanted to hear. A white lie. "You're right, man. Hopefully this year will be a growing year for me, you know? Finally do some maturing."

He took a drag. "I have faith in you."

"Sorry for being a dick," I sighed.

"It's okay."

"No, it's not." I said, rubbing his shoulder. "I feel like we should kiss now or something. Make-up sex?"

Cash flicked his cigarette. "Jackass," he swung the pub door open.

I followed after him. "Come on, dude, I'll let you be on top this time," I said, just as two women approached the front door. One of them was a striking brunette. "Bunk beds. At the hostel," I attempted a recovery.

"Whatever you say." The brunette laughed in my face, then slipped inside with her friend.

Well, that's just great.

***

Cash and I were pretty drunk when we left the Barley Mow a couple hours later. The sun had set over London and the sky was bright purple. We got lost in the labyrinth of theater marquees and restaurants of the West End. I whacked people with my luggage as they loitered for intermission under the lights of the Gielgud Theatre. We downed a few more pints at a few more pubs as we delayed the ending of the night. Although we said our sorrys, the conversation began to stall and the more I drank, the more I thought about Madeleine and the evil we were a party to.

In Chinatown, I stopped on Wardour Street to readjust my bags while Cash wandered ahead. The street buzzed with drinkers and tourists. Foreign languages and broken bits of English wafted by me. I suddenly realized I was alone. And without warning, I was struck with a familiar childhood anxiety. The feeling I got when my mother took me to the playground and the uncertainty of what other children would be there when I arrived. How would I fit into the jungle gym hierarchy?

Luggage in hand, I froze, staring at passing strangers bathed in a red glow from the Chinese lanterns. My heart raced as something violent simmered beneath my drunken exterior. Just when I thought I might scream out for Cash—*help!*—a group of girls stopped in front of me. They smiled as one girl snapped a group selfie. I thought of Madeleine and my stomach turned. She was around their age, and must have a group of friends who would be devastated to learn her fate.

As the girls gathered round to inspect their picture, a trio of twentysomething bros staggered over to them, reeking of light beer. The twerpiest of the boys, a dude with a Third Reich haircut, leaned in close to the girl with the phone.

"Fuckinell—lookin' fit, sweetheart," he flicked his tongue at her. His friends laughed.

Something inside me snapped—like with Rémy. I dropped my bags and lunged for him. "Eat a dick, Himmler," I shouted.

I uppercut him in the jaw. The kid's head snapped back, and he fell like a stiff board at his friends' feet. Passing pedestrians gasped. The girls shrieked. My chest heaved as I stood over the kid. I wanted his friends to retaliate, but they all cowered.

Cash ran through the crowd and shoved me. "Luke, what the hell!"

I looked down to see what I'd done. The kid must have bit his tongue. Blood gushed from his mouth. The group of girls clutched one another, expressions of horror on their faces. People stopped to gawk at the bleeding kid. His friends dragged him away.

"He was being an asshole," I told Cash. "I'm sorry—I just snapped."

"So, you hit him?" He pushed me again. "Let's go!"

I snatched up my bags as Cash dragged me past a Chinese restaurant. An old timer out front stood next to a sign, DIM SUM DAILY, shaking his head, as if he had seen hundreds of Lukes acting a fool in front of his restaurant through the years.

When I'd been pushed to a safe distance, one of the boys called out. "Watch your back out here, bruv!"

I shook my duffle bag at him. "Boy, I'll stuff you in this bag and ship you somewhere!"

"Knock it off!" Cash yanked me passed two money exchange kiosks and three more Chinese restaurants before stopping in front of a Dutch pub to catch our breath. A crowd stood outside smoking and drinking. Cash glared at me while I struggled to light a cigarette, still jittery with adrenaline.

"What the hell was that?" he said.

I shrugged, because I didn't know what to say. Simply put, I lost control. Hitting that kid felt like the right thing to do, but once the dust settled, obviously it wasn't. We decided not to stick around and Cash got us a room at the nearby W Hotel, whose lobby looked like a modern art installation with gold fixtures, neon lights and space black floors.

In our room, a ball of light hung in orbit above a sectional sofa that could have seated twelve. There was a swanky marble top bar in the corner and a glass wall behind it overlooking Leicester Square. Cash set his bags on one of the beds and grunted something about a shower and disappeared into the bathroom. I stood at the window, gazing down at Leicester Square. Tourists scurried about, gawping at the lit-up buildings as they came and went from a casino on the corner.

The exhaustion of Paris crashed over me and I collapsed onto my bed. I turned my head from the glow of Leicester Square and my breathing slowed. As my eyelids began to flutter, I saw Madeleine lying next to me. *There's something very wrong with me*, I told her, feeling her cold hand in mine. I stared at the gray-blue of her eyes in the dim light. The marks on her neck. Oh God, the marks on my mother's neck. A flicker of the kid from earlier. Blood in his mouth. And my hands around Rémy's throat and the look of acceptance on his face as I squeezed. Cash yelling for me to stop.

Then there was black.

Chapter 5

Bad dreams. Dead girls and bleeding Frenchmen. Police lights. Cigarette smoke in my eyes. George tells me, "Mate, if you need anything, see my cousin at his pub in Catford." Can't remember the names of pub or man. Think harder. I rub the sting from my eyes and find myself in my parents' kitchen. Looks different, brighter and modern like our hotel. My mother stands at the counter with her back to me, packing my lunch. I'm eleven again. My bare feet stick to the linoleum floor. "Lu, if you don't get ready soon, you're going to miss the bus," she says. I want to watch her for a little longer. She'll be long gone by the time I get home. I try to cry but the tears don't come. My voice squeaks when I call out for her and I can only manage a whimper.

She left me with him.

I woke up face down on my bed as daylight tumbled into my pounding skull. Rolling over, I remembered the fight from last night and scaring those girls. Cash's bed was made, but his suitcase was still in the corner. Glad to know he didn't just leave me. I stumbled to my bag for ibuprofen and a clean shirt. Outside, the sun was high in the sky and a new crowd of tourists meandered Leicester Square with shopping bags. My phone was dead so I couldn't know the time for certain. I grabbed my bags and stuck my head into the sitting room. Some old white guy was on TV talking about stocks.

"Morning," a voice called from nowhere.

I jumped. Cash was in the corner, sitting at the bar with his laptop and a coffee. "Dammit, man. You scared the shit out of me," I said. He didn't say anything. I plopped onto the sofa to put on my shoes. "Crazy night, huh?"

"Which part?" he asked.

"All of it. Like pub hopping and—"

"You hitting that kid," he looked up from his laptop.

Damn, I hoped he'd somehow forgotten. "Ah, yeah. He went down quick, huh?"

Cash frowned. "He was teenager, who said something stupid in passing. And you attacked him—on your first night in London."

I slouched on the sofa, squinting at him through the window light. "Well, when you say it like that it sounds bad."

"It's bad anyway you say it," he sipped his coffee. "I thought about it this morning, and I believe that Paris may have reopened some old wounds—deep wounds."

Doctor Cash the traveling therapist was starting to annoy me. "Oh goddammit, dude. Not everyone's as sensitive as you are."

Cash stood up. "I saw you in Madeleine's apartment. I saw what that did to you," he shook his head. "And Christ, what you did to Rémy? We were teenagers the last time you were this bad. I thought these outbursts were behind you."

Rémy. I was on top of him in the street, pinning down his arms. The orange glow of morning brought his split eyebrow into view. Blood streamed down his face and my hands were at his throat. Cash fought to pull me off. Calling out my name. George just stared, in shock.

I clutched at a sofa pillow, its white fabric jutting between my fingers.

"Luke, what's going to happen when I'm not here to talk you off the ledge?" Cash closed his laptop. "The UK is going to send your ass packing if you beat up their people. And you said it yourself, there's nothing for you back home. *This* is your future."

We call this a *Come to Jesus Meeting* in the south. When you're given dire advice and shown a fork in the road. You can take the tough road and try to change, or the easy road and just hope everything will work itself out. As that thought came to me, I couldn't help but think it would make a good story.

"Screw this," I grabbed my notebook and portable charger. "I'm getting coffee."

Cash pointed to an espresso machine on the bar. "We've got coffee here."

"I don't want your fancy self-righteous coffee." The words felt ridiculous leaving my mouth but I was hungover and not firing on all cylinders. I moved for the door.

"Don't forget to call your landlady," Cash added, the thoughtful bastard.

"Shit—thanks," I said. "I'm going to slam this door, since I'm mad at you."

***

Outside, Wardour Street was anarchy. Shoulder-to-shoulder foot traffic on the sidewalk. People dragging bulking luggage, tour guides struggling to wrangle their groups—there was a terrifying set of ginger twins by the M&M's store staring at me with melted chocolate around their mouths. Hangovers seem to heighten all of my senses—like the most nauseating superpower ever.

The crowds broke when I reached Charing Cross Road, where I saw Colin the cunt from the night before lingering by some trash cans. He frowned when I waved at him, but it was still nice to see a familiar, albeit dirty, face.

As if magnetically drawn, I wandered north to Bedford Square with my coffee. The square was quiet with a few book readers and lunch takers on benches. I stopped to look at a row of Georgian buildings—my university. For legal reasons, I can't mention my university by name, so let's just say it has *Royal* in the title.

I was proud for finally being there after so many years of trying. Like Cash said, *this* was my future. I wanted to call my mom and tell her I'd made it, but the thought made me nervous. What if she didn't care? Or worse, what if she did? That's just added pressure for me to do something with this opportunity.

I sat on a bench while my phone charged. Squinting in the sun, I flipped open my notebook and filled a page with nonsense about forks in the road. Then I wrote *Paris* on the next page, but nothing else followed. How could I have so little to say about what happened? Maybe I needed to see how my London chapters would play out, then go back and write the beginning.

My phone chimed to life with a voicemail from my landlady. She'd left my key and lease papers with my roommates. When I got back to the hotel, Cash was out front with our bags in a pile as tourists streamed past him. He was talking to someone on the phone, but when he saw me, he said, "I've got to run. Talk to you later?" then hung up.

"Who was that?" I asked.

"Emma. Did you get your coffee?"

"I did—are we talking to Emma again?"

"We are," he pointed to my notebook. "Are we writing again?"

"We are."

As our cab pulled away from the hotel, I scanned the tourists on the sidewalk. Gifts in their arms, phones in their hands—I felt an uneasy disconnect with them, as if they were just extras in the London story building around me. Just as the car picked up speed, I saw Colin once more in the crowd, leaning against the pristine glass of our hotel. He locked eyes with me through the moving bodies.

***

My flat was in a featureless apartment building on Wandsworth Road in South Lambeth, across the street from an Ethiopian restaurant and a kebab joint. The latter of which hired a droopy-faced man, Mustafa, to hand out coupons to pedestrians. He was a neighborhood celebrity because he called out to passersby what he liked about them. *Blue jacket, happy face, cool shoes — take a coupon!* Marketing at its finest.

My building was constructed in a pale, sickly colored brick with white windows. It must have been designed by an unimaginative, post-soviet architect who didn't believe in the luxury of elevators. Cash and I bitched and moaned, lugging our bags up four flights of stairs like pack mules.

The place was a tiny flat-share with a Latvian couple who rarely left their room. The floorboards looked as if they hadn't been polished in thirty years, and in the bathroom an actual mushroom, brown and gleaming, grew from the baseboard. My room was a Harry Potter-sized cupboard next to the kitchen with only a single bed, nightstand and armoire for furnishings. I did have a window, which afforded a great view of an abandoned courtyard in the center of my building. The rotting benches were overgrown by weeds jutting up between the cracked concrete. And a collection of bicycles rusted into oblivion in the far corner.

"It's rustic," Cash shoved my bags in the corner.

"You mean *rusty*."

"If you keep things along the wall, you'll have some okay space in here."

The mattress sunk when I sat on it. "I've seen the pictures, man — Anne Frank had more legroom."

Cash forced a laugh as he unpacked his bag. He no longer found me funny in those last days together, feigning laughter at every punchline. We did a little sightseeing the day before he left, but his mind was elsewhere. We walked wordlessly along the River Thames toward Tower Bridge. Glass buildings cast cool shadows across our path and the conversation, so we stopped at Potters Fields Park to people watch. Families and couples posed for selfies in front of Tower Bridge while kids galloped across the matted grass of the park. Where did these people come from, and were they as far from home as me? I should stop calling it home, since there's nothing for me to return to.

Cash snapped photos on his phone and began typing away — to Emma probably. And without warning, that uneasy feeling from Hyde Park leapt out at me from the shadows of the bridge and again it felt like nothing was real. I looked down at my trembling hand and discovered the remnants of a cut on my knuckle. Was it from hitting Rémy or the Soho kid? I didn't remember seeing it before, but there it was nearly healed. Does it matter what I do if the evidence just heals and fades away? Does that mean it never happened?

The sun was in my eyes and the gray stone and blue girders of Tower Bridge looked hazy; its edges blurred like watercolor. I was terrified I would wake up from this strange dream to find myself back in Raleigh on Bill's sofa, surrounded by boxes of his shit I'd rather burn than donate.

The urge to write all of this down came over me so strongly that I thought I would cry, until Cash nudged me, "I got us tickets to see Tower Bridge," he held out his phone.

I followed him through the crowds, pushing shoulder-to-shoulder up the steps to Tower Bridge Road. The sidewalk was at a standstill with strollers and tourists blocking our path, and the further we lodged ourselves into the masses the more anxious I got. Backpacks, selfie sticks and elbows jutted into our path. Then a small Spanish woman wedged herself between us and yelled in my face to her family behind me. Her breath was hot and her teeth unbrushed and I kept tripping on her heels as she moseyed along. Each time someone pushed against my body my heart leapt in my chest. I didn't want to be there anymore. I could see the goddamn bridge just fine from the park, but Cash pressed on.

The entrance to the bridge exhibition neared closer, but the lady kept stopping, blocking the crowd of walkers to wait for her family. Fed up with her shit, I placed my forearm against her back and pushed her like a cowcatcher on a train. Her brown eyes darted across my face and her mouth hung open. I felt bad for a second, violating her free will, until I saw the fading cut on my knuckle and realized in the grand scheme of things, her feelings didn't matter. For the sake of the line, she needed to walk faster and I was happy to make her. Soon, I'd be gone for good and like my cut, her trauma would fade. It would be like it never happened.

Cash entered the exhibition and I pushed the lady a couple more feet to do the same. "Lo siento," I called out, slipping through the glass door.

I was exhilarated rejoining Cash in the line. Jittery almost. Sure, it was mean to shove that lady, but haven't you always wanted to do something like that? Cross a line to right a wrong and put someone back in their place. Cash caught me grinning. "What's up with you?"

"I just pushed some lady forty feet down the sidewalk."

He spotted the woman outside, as she pointed me out to her family. "What's the matter with you?" he scowled.

What could I say? I was in a fantastic mood. Maybe I was onto something. I'm just a visitor, and maybe nothing I do in London has any long-term effects. Hell, I lived twenty-eight years back home with zero impact on anyone and no one gave a shit when

I left. I could spend this next year as whoever I wanted to be. Anything I did would heal and just fade away when I left.

Cash brooded at the top of Tower Bridge. Jesus, it felt like we were a couple and he was going to dump me at the end of the trip. Just do it already, say you don't want to be my friend anymore and let's get it over with. The two towers were connected by glassed-in walkways that overlooked the river from a hundred feet up. From that height, the sun transformed the murky brown Thames into a shimmering highway of boats and barges. Cash took pictures of the London skyline for Emma, while I strolled the glass walkway looking down onto traffic below. A long tour boat filled with sightseers slipped beneath the bridge at the exact moment I looked down, before reappearing on the other side.

"This is your city now," Cash said. "I know I've been giving you shit recently, and I'm sorry, but I want you to do well."

I was going to say something sarcastic, but instead I said something oddly truthful. "I just feel weird, man. Maybe you're right. Paris messed me up, and I'm trying to figure out where to go from here. How do we get back to normal?"

Another tour boat passed below us. This one was bright yellow and reminded me of those charter boats on the Carolina coast with jagged teeth painted on the hulls. I rode one once with Mom and Bill when I was nine. Our one and only family vacation, which I ruined by getting seasick. While other kids explored Lookout Lighthouse, I sat on the dock, puking into the water, while Bill berated my mother about me needing to *be a man*.

Cash stared out at the water. "I think we need to tell someone about Paris," he said. "That's how we get back to normal."

My body stiffened. It felt like the bridge shifted on its foundation. "Corey, are you nuts? We were two dipshits from nowhere North Carolina, in a city of millions," I said, putting a hand on his shoulder. "Swear to me you won't tell anyone—not Emma, not a lawyer, not your priest."

Cash ran a hand through his hair as he thought about his answer. "I swear."

Dead Parisian girls don't just fade away. You can get away with a lot of shit, but murders ain't one of them. Cash knew it and I knew it—Paris wasn't done with us yet. I wanted to reassure him everything would be okay, but just as I went to speak, a thought came to me.

Shane. George's cousin is named Shane.

The memory came vividly. Morning light broke over the Parisian roofs as I snatched up a napkin that tumbled across the sidewalk in the breeze. I needed to get Rémy's blood off my hands.

George was out of breath, "Mate, you're a writer?" he said. "I don't know what you write, but if you want London stories or maybe a job—if you need anything, see my cousin, Shane, at his pub in Catford. He'll sort you out."

Maybe I wasn't a writer—too caught up in the story to be writing it. The thought gave me comfort as I stood in Tower Bridge with Cash. We looked out at London. It was quiet, picturesque—almost fictional. If London was the next part of my story, then maybe this Shane character could help push my plot.

Chapter 6

I thought I would be relieved when Cash left—free to explore London without him moping to Emma at every landmark—but I wasn't. When I returned to my flat from Paddington, I realized it was the first time in twenty years my best friend wasn't just down the street. Hell—Cash lived in the dorm next to mine at college. I was completely alone for the first time in my life.

I stood in my kitchen with a ten-pack of Carlsberg beer and surveyed my new reality. The Latvians left a mass grave of pots and pans in the sink, along with a dense air of steamed cabbage. The floorboards wobbled underfoot on the way to my room, where I discovered a grain of brown rice stuck to the hallway wall. All I could do was crack a beer and shake my head.

Maybe I was depressed, but I didn't leave my flat for three days. Not until I dragged myself out of bed one afternoon when I had another dream about my mother—the third bad dream in a row. She'd been attacked by a burglar but I was too young to defend her. The frequency of those dreams seemed to increase the longer she and I went without speaking. I bet a therapist would have a lot to say about that.

Although my mom has always been miserly with her affection, I missed her and decided I should go to the most London place of all—Parliament—to video chat with her. She could finally see I made it to England after all the years of saying I would. Unfortunately, Mom didn't impress easily after her ascension to Venice Beach trophy wife, and the masochist I am decided Westminster would be the best setting for this episode.

I reached Westminster Abbey as the last round of visitors trickled from the Great North Door. Hundreds of saints carved above the doors watched as visitors shuffled to their next pilgrimage. And as I ogled Big Ben, draped in a reddish sunset glow, I realized I was stalling.

Deep breath, I hit the call button. My face looked tired in the camera and my hair needed a trim. On the third ring, my mom popped up on the screen. She sat on the sofa with her brown hair in a messy bun. California sun washed out the window behind her in an angelic glow. My mom had an uncanny way of looking thirty-five forever.

"Hey, Mom," I said. "Guess where I am."

"Hi, Lu," she tilted her head. "Guess where you are? I have no idea."

"You have no idea? Come on. Grad school—England." I spun around to show Big Ben in the distance.

"Oh that's right, the big move. How's that *goooing*?"

I hate how Los Angelenos always sound so insincere. "It's going alright. Cash left a couple days ago—that's been an adjustment."

I strolled past statues of important-looking men in Parliament Square. My mother nodded, and I could hear one of her kids calling out in the background. She looked off-camera. "Kaylee, I'm on the phone," she said, looking back to me, waiting for me to speak.

"Uh—did you get my postcards from Europe?"

"No, we've been up at the Big Bear cabin for a few weeks." She barely finished her sentence before Kaylee squawked again. "Kaylee, honey—I don't have your iPad—have you checked the car?"

Kaylee shouted, but all I could make out was, "Help me find it!"

"Okay fine, I'm coming," my mom said. "Lu, I'm going to hand you off to Braden."

"What? No, don't—"

The video blurred and I was plopped into my half-brother's lap. Braden barely glanced at me. He was thirteen and looked bored before I could say a word.

"What's up, man?" I asked.

"Just chillin'."

"I can see that," I said, crossing the street toward Parliament. It was strange how much Braden and I looked alike. Light brown hair, unkempt and wavy, except he had my mother's blue eyes. And the little bastard looked way cooler than I did at his age. He had California swagger and a Venice Beach tan. At thirteen, I was Carolina poor with a sunburn.

The sidewalk in front of Big Ben was dense with tourists. I stopped at the corner for a good vantage point. "Yo man, check this shit out. Look where I am," I panned the camera up to Parliament and Big Ben, and back to me. "You see that? That's Big Ben, I live in London now."

Braden barely looked at me. "Seen it."

"Yeah, in movies maybe. But this is real life—I'm standing in front of the damn thing."

"I've been there," he sighed. "We went last summer."

The swell of nausea told me everything I needed to know, but I'm a glutton for punishment and had to ask, "You did? Who's we?"

"Uh. Me, Mom, my dad and Kaylee," he said. "And Aunt Sarah and the cousins."

Seriously? I squeezed the phone so hard it shook in my hand. That's nearly ten people traveling across the world—a well-planned trip. And I never heard a goddamn thing about it.

"Wow," I said, my jaw trembling. "That's like, the whole family."

He shrugged. "Yeah, everybody was there. You should check out this sick rooftop restaurant, Aviary or something."

Everybody was there. I couldn't breathe, thinking about the little red double-decker bus my Aunt Sarah brought me as a souvenir when I was seven. She told me a million stories from her semester in London and I wept when I lost that bus in the Pullen Park sandbox.

My mother swished by in the background and the video blurred as she took her phone back and sunk into the sofa. "Sorry, Lu. Where were we?"

"London," I sucked in a breath. "Apparently you and the whole family visited last summer?"

Mom nodded. "Yeah, David had a conference there last June, so we tacked on a few days for a vacation."

"A vacation. For the *whole* family."

She paused. "Lu, we thought about inviting you, but you had a lot on your plate back then."

My legs went wobbly. I slumped against the iron gate of Parliament. "You're right, Mom. After Bill died, I enjoyed my lonely summer dealing with his fucking bullshit."

She stared so long I thought the screen froze. "Lucas, I don't like that language. The kids are around."

I snorted. "Grow up, Mom. You've heard *fuck* before. You don't get three kids without it."

"You're not in a good mood, so maybe I should go." She paused, waiting for me to release her.

If I'm the hysterical one, she could tell herself she tried and I was the antagonist. Normally, I'd oblige but I was hurt. And goddammit, I always hide when I'm hurt from her. London was the next part of my story and this version of Luke was going to be different.

"I just don't understand," I said. "I've always wanted to come here. I've told you about this school in London for years," I choked up. "You were the first person I told when I got in."

"Luke—"

"I'm not close with your new family—I get that. But I would have loved to come here with y'all."

I hadn't cried in fifteen years, but there I was, tearing up for the second time in a week. Nearly thirty and still a little boy crying on the phone to his mother.

"Lu, I'm sorry," she said.

To hell with this. "Great talk, Ma," I said, wiping my face. "I'll check in again soon."

I hung up before she could speak and jumped to my feet. My breathing stuttered and there were dark spots in the corners of my vision. Sometimes it's best to have a good cry, but all I wanted to do was scream. "Ahh!" I yelled.

It felt like traffic, pedestrians—the world came to a halt. All of them stared at the crazy man yelling on the street. A blond Nordic family in matching Nike tracksuits gawked at me.

"Be good to your stupid kids!" I shouted at the parents.

A cop at the corner scowled at me, with her hands stuffed into the sides of her Kevlar vest. The light changed and I marched across the street for a pub opposite Parliament and burst through the doors like a gunslinger looking for a challenger. The place was crowded and dim, and I beelined for the bar and plopped onto a stool.

The woman behind the bar was roughly my age. She measured out two glasses of red wine for an elderly couple next to me. I clenched my hands together to stop them from shaking and surveyed the pub. The joint was crammed with tourists and families—parents with their children.

Had my mother and family eaten here after seeing Parliament? I mangled a coaster into a twisted heap at the thought of retracing their steps. Even the pub's décor annoyed me. There were red phonebooth vases with flowers at the center of every table. I wanted to smash them onto the floor. Or better yet, chuck them into the giant Guinness mirror above the bar. When I was a pissed off teenager, I used to throw bottles at the dumpsters behind *Food Lion*. That's what I wanted; to destroy something. My liver would be a good start.

The barmaid raised a painted-on brow at me. "I don't imagine you want a food menu?"

"You've imagined correctly," I said, pointing to a beer called Badger. "Two pints."

She filled the first glass and placed it in front of me, then started on the second. "Who's the second for?"

"Me, in about three minutes."

She just rolled her eyes. I tapped my foot on the rung of the stool, waiting for an apology text from my mother. Seemed like I was always waiting for her—a phone call on my birthday, or our week together at Christmas as a kid. The older I got, the longer I waited for those moments with her, until they stopped entirely.

Bill and I had stolen her twenties, and I guess she was desperate to relive them in her thirties. That's why she moved to California and married David. I wasn't even at her damn wedding—some shit excuse about an issue with my plane ticket.

I'm done waiting for her, I thought, finishing my first beer. Never again. My future was London, and I was determined to find better people. I thought about George not believing I was a writer. Maybe I'm not a writer—I'm the story. Writers have control and I've never had any. So, I pulled out my phone and blocked my mother's number. It felt nice to have control over that at least. Then I rewarded myself with a gulp of my second beer and began googling pubs in Catford. My mind was made— tomorrow I was gonna have a Catford pub crawl until I found this Shane.

Chapter 7

I woke up the next day at the crack of noon with a headache and the vague memory of rambling to the bartender about being a character in my own story. I decided to keep those specifics to myself, because not only is it weird, but it might ruin the natural flow of the story.

When I went to the kitchen to make some lunch, I was hit with an awful musty smell. The Latvian dude, Juris, was shirtless and frying a brown blob in a pan on the stove.

He gave me an odd smirk. "You have late night," he said.

"Oh shit, sorry," I jimmied open the kitchen window. "Was I loud coming in?"

Juris shrugged and his shoulder blades jutted out like wings. "The floors—they creak."

"Ah."

He caught me staring at the sizzling globule in his pan. "Boletus—fried mushroom."

The science project growing in the bathroom made a lot more sense. I opened the fridge and dug out my sandwich meat. "Big mushroom fans around here, huh?"

"Traditional Latvian dish," he proudly pointed his spatula in the air. "It's good."

The sizzling grew louder, and the edges of the substance flapped in the pan, as if it were attempting an escape. "Well, it smells like ass."

"What? I don't hear."

49

"Smells really good, man," I feigned a smile.

Juris nodded, showing his crooked teeth. He pressed the spatula down onto the mushroom—which used its dying breath to let out a high-pitched whine.

I contemplated the sentience of mushrooms while I ate in my room and looked through a list of Catford pubs. My university was throwing a mixer for international students later in Central London, but I had no intention of going. I had a story to live. And when everyone in my program showed up on the first day with half-baked ideas for their novels, I'd already have the makings of a masterpiece.

The afternoon dragged as I waited to head to Catford, so I finished unpacking my bags, where I found my pocketknife. A gun-metal Kershaw with a four-and-a-half inch locking blade. It was worn, but razor sharp. My Kershaw was illegal in the United Kingdom, but back home I'd carried one every day since I was thirteen and never thought anything of it. As I went to put the knife in my drawer, I did a strange thing instead—I slipped it into my pocket.

That was the first law I broke in the UK.

When six o'clock came, I was beside myself to leave the flat. If not for my search, to get some fresh air, because fried mushroom is a persistent and hostile aroma. I hopped on a bus at Wilcox Road for Vauxhall Station, then rode forty-one goddamn stops to Catford, where I discovered my seasickness translated perfectly to bus sickness. London bus drivers have zero regard for the human life onboard, not to mention my Catford bus was well-past decommission age. It rattled worse than the Space Shuttle Challenger did before exploding on takeoff.

My nausea swelled at every turn, until I was happily distracted by an old man who hobbled onboard when we stopped at a massive Tesco. He plopped into the seat in front of me, pulled out a jar of green olives from his groceries, turned to face me and shoved olive after olive into his mouth. For seven stops, and maybe twenty-five olives, he didn't take his eyes off me—and I couldn't take mine off him. All I could do was stare into his gray eyes and marvel at his bushy white eyebrows.

When the old man hit the button for his stop, he capped the olives, rose shakily to his feet and said, "Same time tomorrow?"

I couldn't help but laugh. "Wouldn't miss it."

He nodded and shuffled off the bus, straight into a Betfred, where I imagined he went to gamble his pension for more olive money.

With my nausea subdued, I watched the endless urban sprawl from my window. Old brick buildings interspersed with new glass buildings—offices, trendy gyms, and fair-trade coffee joints. Like home, gentrification spread through London like wildfire. The further we traveled, the more rundown the businesses looked; broken windows, abandoned shopping carts, and entering Catford, there was a community of homeless people living under an overpass. Beer cans and debris scattered about, and on the wall above the huddled people, the name *Catford* was painted in postcard script.

I hopped off the bus and discovered a sea of black and brown faces. I was the only white person on the entire street. It was the first time in my life I was a minority. Every shop I passed was run by, and filled with, Black or Middle Eastern people. A Jamaican butcher shop, a Palestinian café next door, and a tiny grocery store with fruits and vegetables I couldn't identify. This was a side of London most tourists never see.

My initial culture shock dissipated by the time I found the first pub on my list. It was a trendy bottle shop, shiny and clean, and none of the bearded bartenders had heard of Shane. So, I downed an "artisan beer" for nine quid and continued my Catford quest. Dark clouds rolled in from the east and with them, came a cold breeze. I zipped up my jacket and started around a corner where I nearly collided into a group of twentysomething dudes loitering by a black phonebooth. Hoodies and joggers, gold chains and diamond stud earrings. They glared at me, sizing me up in a territorial stare down that could have been narrated by Sir David Attenborough. I held my gaze for a "don't you dare try me" amount of time but moved swiftly to my next stop.

Three pubs and three pints later—still no Shane. I had just discovered a tiny spot on the map called The Rifleman when Cash texted a sunset picture of the sea taken from his balcony in Marseille. What could I say back? 'Hey man, I'm looking for a shitty pub in the bowels of South London?' I decided not to reply.

The Rifleman had no pictures online, no reviews and no website—this *had* to be it. Ten steps into my journey and it began to pour soul-chilling English rain. I jogged down the high street, past an Argos, Specsavers and Greggs for a wide alleyway where local businesses were stuffed into cubbies with roll-down gates, scrawled in graffiti. The Rifleman was at the end of the alley in an old brick building that looked like it should have been condemned years ago.

Street water rushed across my shoes, and I was soaked when I reached the pub. I opened the front door and a squall of wind yanked the wet handle from me. The door was old and heavy with a large stained-glass window, and its rusted hinges locked up. Pelted by wind and rain, the roar of the weather died sharply as I slammed the door behind me. When I came through the second door, everyone in the quiet pub was watching me. The two bartenders, the three old men at the bar, and a table of guys in the corner—all staring to see the idiot who couldn't operate a door.

The pub was bright, with harsh fluorescent lighting. An odd choice for a pub, but scanning the room, I realized it was the type of place that probably didn't want any dark corners. Sky blue paint peeled from the walls in large patches, and where the ceiling wasn't stained from a phantom leak, there was a hole and a bucket underneath to collect the steady drips. Two buckets, by my count.

I dripped across the brown tile to the bar against the back wall. The barman was in his early fifties and tall, with dark hair and a widow's peak. He was well-dressed in a crisp white shirt, and he examined me as I planted myself onto the stool in front of him.

"It won't dry you, but a beer should help you care less," he said.

I wiped the wet from my face. "I think you're onto something." I nodded to a beer tap. "I'll do a pint of Henry's IPA."

The small girl behind the bar grabbed a glass and smiled at me with kind brown eyes. He and the girl seemed too normal for this dump. The place was quiet, save for a few laughs from the table of guys in the corner. I caught a glare from the three geezers hunched over their beers at the end of the bar. The barman leaned against the backbar. "From the States?" he asked.

"Yeah, North Carolina."

"Ah, Carolina. Lovely place, I hear," he nodded. "What brings you here?"

I met his eyes, deciding how personal I wanted to get. "Well, London for grad school. And The Rifleman, because I'm looking for someone."

"And who might that be?"

The wind and rain roared outside. I looked up to the ceiling, worried the storm would take the roof with it. "I'm looking for a guy named Shane." I watched his reaction. "Do you know him?"

He rolled his eyes. "Please tell me you're here to kill him?"

"What? No, I just want to talk to him."

"Hmm. Pity."

The girl handed me my beer. A thin layer of bubbles lay across the beautiful toffee colored liquid. "That will be-a four pounds, my love," she said, with an Italian accent.

I shook water from a fiver and paid her. "So, Shane. Is he here?" I asked.

The barman glanced to the table of guys in the corner. "The wanker with graffiti tattooed on his neck."

The man he was referring to had his back to me. And of course—the table of guys was the group of miscreants who mean-mugged at the phonebooth earlier. *Shit. This ought to go well.* I stood up and took a long sip of my beer.

The barman tossed me a pound coin and said, "If you change your mind and decide to kill him—drinks are on me."

That was my first introduction to Daniel Ross, who inherited The Rifleman from his uncle. I liked him instantly. "I'll keep you posted," I raised my glass.

My shoes squished with each step. Time slowed. Was it wise to approach the cousin of a guy I hid a body with? Shane was a stranger covered in tattoos in a shitty pub, in a shitty town with a table full of juvenile delinquents. I was suddenly afraid, but not for my life like a normal person. What if this was a dead end—what next?

My waterlogged Vans caught the attention of the table long before I arrived. The delinquents glowered at me; two black kids, a middle-eastern kid, and a tall lanky white boy—all with the same death stare from earlier.

I cleared my throat. "Are you Shane?"

Shane didn't turn around. Instead, the black kid next to him, who I learned was named King, set his drink down. "And who the *fuck* is askin'?" he said, looking me up and down.

It was a badass response and I made a mental note to remember it. "My name is Luke," I said to the back of Shane's head. "I helped your cousin, George, out of a not-so-chill situation in Paris last week."

The table was quiet. Their eyes darted between me and Shane, who had a tattoo of a burning Union Jack on his neck. Next to it was a St George's flag, intact and luffing in a permanent breeze.

"He said I should come by once I got to England," I added. "Said you'd have some London stories. You see, I'm a writer and—"

"W-what's your accent?" the white boy, Kieran, stuttered. "Are you I-Irish? Cause we don't do no IRA here, bruv."

I studied the boy, trying to determine if he was mentally sound. "No, it's American...from America."

My mind blanked. I was about to mumble *neat tattoos*, when Shane finally looked at me with his dark green eyes. He wore a spiffy gray suit, sans tie. "George mentioned a Yank helped him with a spot of bother," he said, in a shockingly proper English accent.

A goofy smile spread across my face. "That's me. I'm the Yank."

Shane rubbed his flattened nose. "You see, mate, the problem is—George is a tit," he said. "A tit who often finds himself in these pickles with other tits who are just as pickle prone. So, what's that say about you?"

While I thought of an answer to his rhetorical question, a drip fell from the ceiling and splashed loudly into a third bucket in the corner. "Uh, that I'm handy in a pinch?" I fired back.

Shane laughed, and as if by cue, his table joined in. He had big white teeth and a missing upper canine. "That you may be. But this table doesn't like pinches, pickles or tits. At least not the kind of tits you can provide."

The table erupted with laughter. I was hot with anger, being made fun of by five jackasses in a pub. I wanted to hit Shane, but I'll be damned if I didn't hear Cash in my head. *You don't have to posture every time you think someone slights you.*

I gave a polite nod. "Well, this was a huge waste of time."

Shane and company stopped laughing. He stood up to face me. My scalp prickled with fear. He was shorter than me but built like a rugby player, with broad shoulders. I stepped back, staring at his flattened nose. How many times do you have to break the thing before it looks like that?

"Now, now," he put a hand on my shoulder. "While I don't always like my cousin, he *is* my blood. So, whatever you did to help him, I believe thanks are in order."

Shane steered me toward the bar. My thigh knocked into the arm of a chair, but I pretended it didn't hurt, because the entire pub was watching. All three geezers at the bar stopped mid-sip to see what would happen. Both bartenders were wide-eyed as we approached. They were worried for me. Which made *me* worried for me. A spark of adrenaline shot through me and I remembered my knife. Could I reach it in time? And more importantly—what do I do after I pull it?

Just when I thought he'd hit me, Shane called out to the barman, "Hey, Danny!"

The barman groaned. "Daniel."

"This young man," he waited for me to fill in the blank.

"Um, Luke."

"Luke, has earned himself a few pints on me," he pulled out a wad of cash and slapped a twenty-pound note onto the bar. "Have a few drinks and a laugh with Danny here," he said, whispering. "But don't hit on the little Roman—Kieran's got his eyes on her. You can tell the folks back home about the dodgy little pub in Catford, then go back to being a writer—or whatever you are."

Shane clapped me on the back and returned to his table. He and his crew picked up their conversation as if I had never interrupted. I looked at Daniel, speechless. What the hell just happened?

"That went better than I expected," Daniel said.

"What were you expecting?"

"To call you an ambulance."

I bought a few more pints with Shane's money and thought about what Daniel said. Being in danger only reinforced my theory I was in the right place. Catford, The Rifleman, Shane and crew—this could be one hell of a story. I borrowed a pen from Daniel and jotted some notes on bar napkins. It's funny, thinking about it now, though, because Daniel was right.

An ambulance would be called to The Rifleman.

Chapter 8

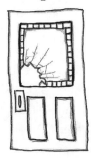

The next day I woke up to the animalistic sounds of the Latvians fucking on the other side of the wall. I like a nooner just as much as the next guy, but the walls of my flat were practically paper mâché and it seemed inconsiderate to go that hard. Grumbling, I got up to scramble some eggs and transcribe my napkin notes into my notebook.

Around three o'clock I went for a shower but the Latvians slipped into the bathroom seconds before me. When they reemerged an hour later, the hot water was gone and they left their wet towels on the floor. During my cold shower, I decided to take revenge on my flatmates, but I would need to play it cool until I determined my method of attack.

Notebook in hand, I left for Catford at exactly six o'clock, and same as yesterday, the old man shuffled onto the bus with his groceries. He decided to step our friendship up a notch and sat next to me. We locked eyes as he produced a new jar of olives and unscrewed the lid with a loud SHMOP! As the bus rolled along, he chucked olives into his mouth while never breaking eye contact with me. Fourteen olives later, he hit the button for his stop and capped the jar. "Watch yourself, it's a hard bus to quit," he said, hobbling off and into Betfred.

I thought about that line all the way to Catford, certain that once I figured out what it meant, it would be pure genius.

Outside The Rifleman, I stood looking at the stained-glass window on the front door. Yellow and blue squares created a border along the edges, and pinks and reds made up the floral pattern in the center. It was a lovely piece of artistry, and quite delicate for such a dive—surviving decades of ruffians slamming that rotting door on its piece of shit hinges.

Daniel was wiping down a table when I came inside. He seemed surprised to see me. "Of all the gin joints in all of London," he turned for the bar. "And you choose to spend your time in this one?"

"I like this place," I said, seeing a couple familiar faces from the night before, but no Shane. "It's interesting. Which is good for a writer."

I hopped onto a stool while he washed his hands behind the bar. "Interesting is a polite way of describing The Rifleman. I don't believe the regulars even like being here, but they don't have a choice, do they?"

Daniel always injected these bits of wisdom into our conversations and I regret not writing them down. He flipped the switch on an old radio on the shelf that was stuffed between a few dusty champagne glasses, and rolled the dial to a jazz station.

"No, I guess they don't," I opened my notebook to a blank page. "Can I ask why you're at this pub?"

Daniel ran a hand over his widow's peak and opened his mouth to respond but stopped. "IPA's fresh on—first pint on the house?"

I nodded. Only one of the geezers from yesterday was hunched at the bar. He flipped through a newspaper a little too quickly, as if he were just looking at the pictures.

"This was my uncle's pub for many years," Daniel filled my glass. "It was a Catford staple for the locals. As his health declined, the pub fell into disrepair. He left it to me when he passed in the spring. So, I came up from Bath to fix it up and sell."

The small Italian girl, Chiara, emerged from the cellar with a few bottles of wine in her arms, smiling at me as she unloaded the bottles onto the bar.

Daniel gave me my beer. "And the first thing I did was sack the drunks who worked here and replace them with a couple of hardworking uni students." He nodded to Chiara.

"I don't know how hardworking we are," she shrugged. "But at least we don't steal from the till or get drunk at work." Chiara tied a black apron around her waist. "Tell me, is *Caro-leena* a nice place?"

"Nice enough," I shrugged. "But as my hometown got more popular and people flocked to it, it began feeling less like home and more of just a place I was from. Ghosts on every corner— memories I was tired of reliving."

It felt weird talking about North Carolina, since they were both from much cooler places. But they were intrigued by the ruggedness of my home and I was happy to answer their questions. It felt nice being listened to. By the end of my second pint, the pub had filled with regulars—then came Shane and his crew.

"Fam, if you'd seen how shook he was, I'd swear he shat himself!" one of the boys said as they entered the pub. The group burst into laughter.

They boys draped themselves onto the bar quite comfortably. Chiara and the white boy, Kieran, spoke in whispers. I referred to my notes on the boy's names and exchanged glances with the Arab dude, Ibrahim, who wore a blue Chelsea football tracksuit. He nudged Shane to look in my direction.

Shane showed his big teeth. "Danny, mate, tell the Yank there are better pubs than this one."

Daniel rolled his eyes, incapable of hiding his disdain for Shane. "Already have," he shrugged, as he and Chiara poured beers.

If I wasn't determined to weasel my way into Shane's graces, I probably would have been annoyed too. He stared me down with his green eyes, then raised his glass. "Cheers, then."

Shane and crew retired to their corner table, left empty, as if the regulars knew those seats were permanently reserved. Three more nights went on like that and my encounters with Shane were much the same. But I enjoyed those few days and setting my mind to a goal, no matter how dumb the goal was. I was just happy not to think about my mom, Madeleine or Cash—anything that would distract me from my story. That week, I slept through orientation events at my university, wrote in the afternoons, then rode with the olive guy for Catford. I'd have a few pints and talk to Daniel and Chiara, until Shane showed up with a snide remark and sauntered off to his table. Who doesn't like a tight schedule?

On the fourth night I wore out my welcome. The pub was busy and I was already a few pints deep when Shane cruised over to the bar in a brown tweed blazer. "Spoke with George," he said, sipping his beer.

It was hard not to stare at his flattened nose. "Oh yeah?"

"Naughty boy, that Rémy. Shame about the girl."

That got me focused on his eyes. "A goddamn shame."

He studied me, as if he was trying to match George's description with the person in front of him. "Apparently, you *are* quite handy in a pinch."

I gave a humble shrug.

"I don't know exactly what it is you're after—and you seem like a good lad, but my instincts tell me it's best you don't come back."

It felt like I'd been hit in the stomach. I didn't know what to say. "Ah, come on, man. I like this place."

"I don't care. No tourists at The Rifleman. Once more, we'll get your pints paid for—thanks for your service, mate—but don't come back, yeah?"

"I don't need—"

Shane stood up, his stool screeching across the floor. "If I could have everyone's attention," he yelled, silencing the crowded pub. "I'm sad to say that this is Luke's last night at The Rifleman. So, as favor to me, buy him a pint to wish him well. And if you ever see him in this pub again, please be sure and tell me." The playfulness vanished from his green eyes.

My face was hot with embarrassment—anger. Shane returned to his table where the boys laughed at me. Daniel gave me a comforting smile from behind the bar, but it felt like I got dumped in the middle of the schoolyard. I looked down to my beer and decided the only thing I could do was to drink my feelings. A few lonely minutes passed until a drunk dude with a gray ponytail and leathery face stumbled up and set a pint in front of me.

"Oi, mate," he spilled beer on the bar. "Gonna miss you round here. For all the years I've known you—you've been aces."

"Sure, thanks, man."

He patted me on the back, "And I was sorry to hear about your aunt, by the way—good woman she was."

What the hell could I say? I raised my glass. "To my aunt."

The man clinked glasses with me and swayed back to his friends at a corner booth. An hour went on like that; people bringing me beers to get in favor with Shane. And every time someone handed me a pint, Shane and his table would burst into laughter. I think they kept count—I sure as shit wasn't. The drunker I got, the madder I got, which has always been a bad combination for me.

When I took the first sip of what was probably my ninth pint, a middle-aged woman with fake blonde hair approached Chiara at the bar. "Hiya, lovely. A man has wandered into the ladies'. I think he's a junkie, because he got aggressive when I told him to leave. Is Daniel round to sort him?"

"He stepped out for more crisps," Chiara said. "But I'll take care of it."

"Thank you, love," the lady said with a smile.

Finally, something more entertaining than my free pints. Chiara slipped from the bar and into the ladies' room in the back corner. I sipped and watched intently to see how things would play out. After a moment, a tall white guy in his mid-twenties stumbled from the bathroom. He looked homeless, in a dirty gray hoodie and tattered sneakers. He had a droopy face, but not in a sad way like Colin the cunt. This man looked angry and oddly familiar. Chiara reemerged and guided him toward the front door. I looked around, seeing I was the only one in the joint watching this unfold. How had no one seen this guy stumble in off the street and into the women's bathroom? The pub roared on with conversation and laughter.

Chiara corralled the man through the tables and chairs. He'd stop to mumble something and start off in another direction, but she patiently redirected him to the entrance—the little Italian saint. She swung open the first door and placed a hand on his back to nudge him along. But in that moment, everything changed.

The man yanked his arm away from her. His posture shifted from hunched—to upright and annoyed. The man's eyes looked wide and lucid as he shoved Chiara. When he raised a fist to hit her, I realized who he reminded me of.

My dear ol' dad, Bill.

I bolted across the room before he could land the blow. So close, I could taste his body odor. I punched him in the throat. His breath stopped short with a gag. That should have been enough. But the word *mommy* popped into my head. Weird. I shoved him into the outer door. His arm crashed through the stained-glass. The door swung open and he toppled into the street. He rolled onto his ass. The pub fell silent behind me. He sat on the sidewalk with his legs out straight. He looked at me as a river of blood gushed from his arm. His face was scrunched like he didn't understand what was happening. People rushed behind me to gawk. I should've stopped, but I couldn't.

Bill never learned—this guy would.

A running start. I kicked his face as hard as I could. His head thudded off my foot with a hollow THONK. His bloody arm flailed through the air. He fell onto his back, where his head hit the pavement.

Knocked out, cold.

Chapter 9

I did a bad thing, but Jesus, I did it well. I stood with my back to the pub, praying the man wasn't dead. A crowd gathered around me. Their words were hot on my neck and stunk of alcohol. I'd lost control again. Was this my story—my character taking over? I couldn't think of any other way to explain it.

My eyes were wet and my vision blurred. The alleyway looked two dimensional. The boarded-up chippy across from the pub—just a facade. The curry place next to it, with the Indian woman watching from the doorway—a paid extra. It was all an elaborate set piece.

There was a single drop of blood on my wrist—the homeless man's blood. He laid at my feet snoring. Guess he's alive after all. I felt hands on me, a playful shove, a pat on the back. Shane and crew were by my side and laughing. "Handy in a pinch!" Shane said. "Well done, mate."

Chiara mustered the strength to see the damage for herself. "Oh my God." She clasped a hand over her mouth.

"Okay, the kick was too much. I know that now," I said. "But he was going to hit you."

"I know. I know," she put a hand on my arm, but pulled it back.

I felt sick. She was afraid of me, like those girls in Soho. But that feeling faded as Shane and his boys celebrated me. King even gave me a high five. Their acceptance was a beach that felt warm and good, but it was beaten by the icy waves of guilt.

After the attack, I chain-smoked on the bench out front and drank another pint someone donated me. A thick drizzle coated me in a watery fuzz, and I shook from nerves and the cold until the cops showed up. Shane strode over to the officers, waving his arms while he spoke to them. He pointed to the door and, as his eyes skimmed over the shattered glass, he looked as if he were about to smile at me, but he turned away before he did.

I was afraid of being arrested, but mostly I worried about upsetting Daniel. The ambulance screamed onto the scene just as he returned with his groceries. If I had a tail, I would have tucked it and hid, seeing the sullen look on his face as he crunched through the broken glass to see someone loaded into the ambulance.

Daniel seemed to sigh in relief when he saw it wasn't me, but then frowned. I had only gotten disdain from Bill. Disappointment was an alien feeling that somehow hurt more.

When the authorities left, Daniel came outside with a broom and dustpan, sweeping up shards of colored glass. I watched him from the corner of my eye, a cigarette trembling between my fingers.

"Apparently, the young man tripped and fell," Daniel said. "His arm went through the window and he hit his head on the pavement. Poor bastard."

I shot a look to Shane, who was still outside talking to one of his boys with dreadlocks, Llanzo. "That sounds about right," I said, meeting Daniel's eyes.

"When I first saw the ambulance, I thought it was for you. Glad it wasn't," he smirked.

It's lame, but even in the cold drizzle I felt warm. "Thanks, Daniel."

Daniel left to empty his dustpan, and Shane sauntered over with a spliff dangling between his lips. "You alright, mate?"

"Yeah, I'm alright." The drop of blood on my wrist was still wet from the rain. "Thank you for talking to the cops for me—I guess I owe you one," I said, wiping the blood onto my jeans. The blood was gone from my skin, but forever mixed into the denim.

Shane nodded as he seemed to consider that. "I'll have to think of a way you can repay me," he turned to leave. "In the meantime, you can forget about not coming back."

I shot him a look. The burning Union Jack tattoo on his neck glistened in the rain. "For real?"

"You do liven up the place," he said. "And I'm certain we could find a use for you—since you *owe me one.*" Shane swung open the skeletal remains of the front door. Its hinges squawked in protest. "Welcome to The Rifleman," he said.

Welcome to The Rifleman. I left the pub feeling oddly proud of what I'd accomplished. Yes, I lost control, but I weaseled my way into Shane's graces just as I'd set out to do. But as I rode the bus home, I couldn't help but wonder—what would it mean to be in Shane's debt?

Chapter 10

[handwritten notes: Sophie / What's her accent? ~~Scottish~~ ~~Newcastle~~ Welsh?]

On the day before my first class, I spent the entire morning packing and repacking my bookbag with binders, my laptop and assorted pens. Strange how the first day of school feels the same no matter your age. A stomach full of butterflies and a head full of possibilities. Despite wanting to be rested for my first day, I couldn't stay away from The Rifleman, and so I returned to the scene of the crime that afternoon.

The pub door was boarded up with plywood, an aesthetic often found in that town. Colored bits of glass, too fine to be swept, gleamed between the paving stones. *I am such a dick.* I hoped Daniel had insurance for the repair. He seemed fine last night, but what if there was CCTV footage—what if he didn't want me back at the pub? I worked up the courage to go inside, where he leaned against the bar reading a worn copy of *Crime and Punishment*.

"Hello, my friend." Daniel said, chipper. "How are you?"

"I'm good," I sighed in relief. "Almost recovered from last night." The pub was empty, save for Shane at his corner table with his face buried in a newspaper.

Daniel took that as a cue to serve me an IPA. I was hesitant to start drinking again, but decided a single pint couldn't hurt. "Hair of the dog," he smiled.

"Have you heard anything about the guy who fell? Is he okay?"

"I've not heard a thing," he said. "Are you concerned?"

Did he just give me a smirk? Did he know? "Er—not as concerned as I am for that door. That thing was a classic—" I'd barely finished the sentence when a beautiful girl emerged from the backroom and slipped behind the bar.

"Your mother ever teach you it's impolite to stare?" she said, in a thick northern accent.

"Oh, sorry," I said. "I was expecting Chiara"

She tied her hair into a ponytail and surveyed me with piercing blue eyes. "I'm sorry to disappoint you."

Her voice sang sweetly in my head, like the hum of a violin. "What's your accent?"

"Am I the one with the accent round here?"

Daniel grinned and stood back to watch. Apparently, her ball-busting was notorious.

"I mean, you sound different than Daniel," I said.

She locked onto me with those intense eyes. "That's because Daniel is a completely different person, not to mention he's a man."

I stared at her, confused, and looked to Daniel who was chuckling. "I don't understand what's happening," I said.

"This is Sophie," Daniel laughed. "She's taking the piss."

Before I could say anything else stupid, I felt a hand on my shoulder. It was Shane. "Come on, mate. Have a seat over here," he pointed to his table. "Alright, Soph?"

Sophie gave a nod. The devilish look faded from her face. Guess she didn't like Shane. "I'm going to figure that accent out sooner or later," I said.

Life returned to her face and she gave me the faintest smile. "Not if I have anything to do about it."

Right there. That was the exact moment my obsession with Sophie began. Sometimes people catch you off guard. You don't know you need them until you've met them, and by then it's too late. Once you know someone exists you can't unknow it.

I sat down at Shane's table, smiling to myself. Happy I met Sophie, and happy to finally be sitting at that damn table after a week of trying.

"Careful, mate. You're Sophie's type," Shane said. I stole another glance at Sophie and wondered what he meant by that. "So, tell me about Paris. I want to hear it from you."

Damn. I'd gone twenty-four hours without thinking about Paris, and there it was again. It was a wound that never healed. Like chapped lips that split with every winter smile.

I remembered saying to Cash—tell no one about Paris, but all Shane had to do was ask and I spilled my guts like a schoolboy sent to the headmaster's office. Told him how we met George in the American bar and how I tried cocaine—cocaine George said was Shane's. Then I confessed about finding Madeleine, and how Rémy blackmailed us into returning her body to her flat.

"Mate, let me get this straight," he said. "You three cunts step out of a flat where you've left a body, the police are there— how the bloody hell did you get away?"

"It's stupid, really. But George had double-parked. Rémy finally pulled himself together and told the police we were leaving."

Shane fiddled with a newspaper on the table—it was *Le Parisien*, a French paper. "I bet they regret letting you go now," he said.

It took a moment to understand what he meant. Nearly a week had passed since I'd laid Madeleine to rest in her apartment. I'd been so focused on The Rifleman that I didn't think about how she had probably been discovered and an investigation was underway. My fingers trembled against my pint.

We are going to burn for this.

My heart hammered at the inside of my chest, like a fist trying to burst through the bone and cartilage. Beer gargled up into my throat and while I fought to stop from puking, footsteps came shuffling in behind me.

"And what the hell is this?" King smacked a hand onto the table.

I flinched and looked up to see him staring at me.

King broke into laughter, showing the gap in his teeth. "The look on your face, bruv!" he collapsed into the seat next to me. The others joined us. I cringed at their chairs screeching across the tile floor. These were the least comforting people to have around while contemplating the most traumatic experience of my life.

Kieran stood with his crotch in my face. "The u-usual, lads?"

Ibrahim ran his hands through his curly hair. "N-n-no," he mocked his stutter. "We've got work later. Get us some Cokes, you eedyat."

The big guy, Llanzo, shook his head. The beads in his dreadlocks clicked. "Screwin' up today, Kier. Jesus."

"Screwing up, how?" Shane's grip tightened on his newspaper. "What've you done?"

"Sorry, Shane, can't hear you, fam," Kieran said. "Gotta get them Cokes," he trotted to the bar.

"What's he done, now?" Shane persisted.

King sat back and unzipped his Nike hoodie. A thin gold chain glimmered around his neck. "The genius was caught by them Soho boys, selling to day-drinkers at Zoo Bar. They about jacked him for his food, 'til we came round," King said. Shane groaned. "It went bad, Shane. We almost threw hands with mandem from Charlie's crew in the middle of Charing Cross. Traffic whizzing past, and all that."

Shane squeezed the bridge of his nose. "We're not like them, remember? You boys are smart—we make smart moves. Not rows in the bloody street."

The way they talked was fascinating. Madeleine was far away again. Back in her flat, with the front door shut and locked. These guys and this table—this was what I needed to focus on. I flipped open my notebook and wrote what they said, noting the intonation—the slang.

King sighed. "I know, Shane, but if they catch him on his ones again, they'll wet him, fam."

"Then you lads sort that boy out, before they do!" Shane slammed his fist onto the table.

The table was silent, except for the scratching of my diligent notetaking. I had just finished writing *sort that boy out, before they do* when I realized they were looking at me.

"You some sort of writer, yeah?" Ibrahim stroked his peach fuzz mustache. "What you write?"

Their eyes followed as I set my pen down. "Uh, mostly fiction," I said. "But recently I've been writing about the things that happen around me."

King touched the corner of my notebook. There was a gold signet ring on his pinky of a lion wearing a crown. "You gonna put *us* in a book, or something?" He flapped my pages with this thumb and looked to Shane. "Is that wise?"

Uh oh. The future of my story was in jeopardy and I needed to think quickly. "I can change the names and locations—I won't write anything incriminating."

Kieran returned with a tray of Cokes and set them on the table. "Interesting," Shane said, putting his hands behind his head. His shoulders were as broad as a truck. "Names and details should absolutely be changed, but I think Luke and I have a mutual understanding of discretion, since I know his dirty little Paris secret," he smirked.

Despite that making me sweat a bit, it seemed like a fair exchange. I gave Shane a nod. We had a deal. Kieran shot me a look. "Ooh, you n-naughty boy," he said. "What'd you get up to in Paris?"

Ibrahim grabbed a pint of Coke. "He took ya mum for the weekend—dogged her at the Eiffel Tower."

Everyone at the table laughed, even me. Kieran scrunched up his face. "Fuck me, bruv."

"That's what she said!" Ibrahim hooted, spilling Coke onto himself.

***

When I went to refill my beer, Sophie was alone behind the bar and looking through a white binder—some kind of accounting ledger. She slammed it shut when she saw me. Sophie had a way of glaring at me like she could read my mind, and her expression always made me think whatever she saw wasn't worth the read.

I handed her my glass. "Okay, so your accent is from up north—it's definitely not Scottish."

"You think I'm Scottish?"

"No, I said you're *not* Scottish. Just saying it out loud— process of elimination."

Sophie rolled her blue eyes as she filled my beer. "Well, if it seems like I'm living my life as usual while you figure it out—I am."

I gave a big dumb grin. "Newcastle?"

"No!" she smiled and stuck out her hand. "Four pounds."

As I dug into my wallet, Shane drummed his hands along the bar up next to me. "Chatting up our resident ice queen, eh?"

Sophie scowled. "You got the queen part right."

Her response made me smile, and I stared at the hint of freckles on her nose as she delivered that white binder to Shane. She caught me looking, so I tossed my money onto the bar and grabbed my beer. The four boys were laughing and horsing around at the corner table. Kieran threw a bottle cap, lodging it in Llanzo's dreadlocks.

"How did you meet those guys?" I asked.

He took a deep breath. "Long story short—I saved them."

"Like from a burning building, or like you would a basket of puppies," I laughed.

He smiled, tapping on the white binder. "What do you know about gangs in London?"

"Next to nothing."

Shane nodded. "There's a never-ending turf war on every street corner, throughout every borough. Sometimes, it's as simple as whatever council house you live in—that's your gang, but not always."

I sipped beer as I listened, wishing I wrote that down.

"There are a lot of street kids who slip between the cracks, and the weak ones fall prey to the strong, as it is with nature. Those boys seem tough now," he pointed. "But not when I found them. I gave them protection—gave them goals, and a chance to make a bit of dosh for themselves. Now look at them, they're like brothers."

Shane smiled like a proud dad, or a creepy uncle. Whatever he was doing was either admirable or scummy. "So, it's like an internship program?"

"Ha! I may use that," he laughed, revealing the crater from his missing tooth. "Take Kier, for instance. I found him nicking bags of crisps from a Co-Op in Battersea a few years ago. He'd been living off stolen junk food for two weeks while his mum was on the pipe somewhere. He's got a new family now, and he never goes hungry."

Kieran reminded me of when Bill was on the bottle, and Mom was gone with her new family. How many times did I eat cold SpaghettiOs from the can for dinner? Or day-old McDonald's Bill dragged home on a bender. I realized I was one of those kids who fell between the cracks in my own neighborhood. Me and Cash got our asses kicked bi-weekly for years. Sure, Shane giving the boys drugs to sell, or whatever they did, was slimy— but oddly, I was jealous. Where was a Shane when I needed one?

Shane studied me. You could feel when his mind worked, as if it gave off a low, vibrating frequency. "What's up?" I asked.

"Come with me. I've got an idea."

The boys snapped to attention when Shane and I returned to the table. He pulled out my chair for me and stood next to me, scratching his chin and putting the finishing touches on whatever idea he was cooking up.

Finally, he said, "Tonight, lads, I want you to take Luke along with you."

I froze as the boys hissed in protest. "Shane, no. He's a tourist," King said. "He'll stand out like a sore thumb."

"Yeah, I'm with King on this one," I said. "Whatever it is you guys do, me standing out sounds like a concern."

Shane patted my shoulder. "That's the point, mate. I know you'll stand out," he said. The boys fell silent, their brows furrowed. "After the row with Charlie's crew, having a guest might keep you lot on your best behavior. Give Luke our product and he's just another tourist with a backpack."

Sirens went off in my head. "Wait, hold up—you want me to go with them *and* carry illegal shit?" I asked.

"I do," Shane said. "As soon as you open your mouth, all suspicion is gone. And worst case—and I mean the absolute worst case—apparently, you're handy in a pinch," he grinned.

Sweat clung to my forehead. "I'm beyond flattered by your confidence in me, but my first day of class is tomorrow at nine in the morning," I stood up. "Come to think of it, I should be heading home."

"You owe me, mate. Remember?" Shane's smile vanished.

Oh yeah, that old chestnut. I melted back into my seat. Five pairs of eyes were on me, all wanting something different. Shane; for me to help. The boys; for me to go away. I'd never felt so torn. On one hand, the hint of danger that came with chasing my story was enticing. But on the other hand—I really, really didn't want to get arrested or die. Could I trust these kids to have my back?

Shane sat next to me. "Consider this repayment for the cops—for letting you write your story." He gave my shoulder a friendly pat. "How bad do you want it, mate?"

Chapter 11

Apparently, I wanted my story pretty bad. The next thing I knew I was carrying a backpack full of drugs onto the train. Was this the third law I broke in the UK? I was already losing count.

The train pitched side-to-side as the boys perched themselves on the car railings like parakeets. Other passengers—professionals in Oxford shirts and blouses, slid to the opposite end of the car. Like a kid with his teddy, I hugged the backpack in my lap as we rocketed through the tube deeper into London. While I fought off another panic attack, the boys chatted casually.

"Yo, get this," Ibrahim held out his phone. "The manager at the Comedy Store said I could do ten minutes on stage next Thursday."

"Alright, mate!" They congratulated him, tousling his hair.

King grinned at me. "Don't be nervous, bruv—look, he's sweating," he pointed at me. The rest of them laughed.

"Look, I'm just a little uncertain about this plan," I said.

And why shouldn't I be? It was concocted thirty minutes ago in a pub by a majority vote of twenty-year olds. The brilliant plan went like this: I mule their drugs into a club, then hang out while they sell said drugs—that's it. The train squealed to a halt at Tottenham Court station and Llanzo nudged me. "This is us," his face was expressionless.

My pulse throbbed as I followed them through the mass of late dinner goers and club hoppers. Noxious cologne and perfume handily overtook the stale platform air. Girls in tight dresses, guys in tight shirts. They stepped aside for the four boys in the same way schools of fish do when a shark swims past. When we got to the escalators, I caught sight of a colorful mural of squares and circles on the wall and froze. I had never been to this station, so why did it look familiar? I was pulled by it. The boys were halfway up the escalator before they realized I wasn't behind them.

"Oi," one of them shouted. "What's his name again? American guy — shit!"

The echoey steps and voices of the station faded into silence as I stood before the wall. I placed a hand on a yellow circle and remembered being in Madeleine's apartment, seeing the sun rise like an orb over the Paris rooftops. The first day of the end of her life. There was a polaroid on her headboard — a picture of her standing at the exact spot with her hand on the same yellow circle.

Someone shoved me from behind. It was King. "The hell are you doing?" he pulled me to the escalator. "Let's go!"

We met the others out on the street. Traffic buzzed behind them and pedestrians crisscrossed between us. The boys weren't laughing anymore — they were pissed.

"Sorry, I was checking out that mural down there," I said.

"It's a rainbow wall for like p-puffs or something," Kieran shrugged. "Who cares?"

King got in my face. He was just as tall as I was. "Listen to me, fam. You knocked out a nitty — wotevs — that don't make you a roadman," he poked my chest. "Do as we say, and guard that bag with your goddamn life — because it will be your life if something happens to it."

Deep breath. The bag straps tightened against me. The traffic of Charing Cross hummed in a dizzying blur of engines and wheels, but all I could see was King's gap teeth. I thought the boys liked me, but clearly, they only saw me as a tourist. If I screwed this up, I'd just go back to writing novels on my course with all the other middle-class kids who were too special and creative for a nine-to-five. *To hell with them — they don't know shit about me.* I needed this just as much as they did. I stepped up to King. The brim of his hat touched my forehead, as the rest snapped to attention.

"Listen here, slick," I said, in a heavy Carolina drawl. "I'm the guy you want in your corner. I'm smart and I'm swift, and if I flip the switch—I'm a goddamn pit bull."

He sucked his teeth.

"Personally, I think this is a stupid idea," I said. "But Shane dealt the cards. This is your jungle and I'm trusting you, just like you're going to have to trust me. Our futures are strapped to my back and I don't know about you, *bruv*, but my back ain't gonna break easy."

The four of them stared at me as the crowds pressed past, until King's shoulders jerked upwards with laughter. Smiles spread across the boys' faces and they looked like kids. The dipshits who used to fling food across my high school cafeteria—but still kids.

"*A goddamn pit bull,* he says," King grinned. "I like that, fam."

I couldn't help but smile too. "Are we cool for now?"

"Yeah," he gave me a fist bump. "For now."

I nodded. "Following your lead, *slick.*"

We crossed Charing Cross as a group, ignoring the honking surge of black cabs. Despite the task at hand, it was nice to be back in Soho. The sidewalks were filled with different people from a week ago, but they were all high on the same energy. Voices, laughter and shouts whooshed past me. The aroma of pizza, curry, kebabs, stale beer and weed mixed in the air.

We stopped at a row of neon nightclubs that pulsed bass music into the street. The faces of passersby were shrouded veils of pink, purple and blue light. Twentysomethings loitered in loud groups, their voices clambering over one another. King stopped on the sidewalk and faced us. "We're going to The Roxy—but be careful. Charlie's crew is out tonight and shit can pop off in these ends—fast."

My eyes wandered to a group of women in tube tops, huddled together in varying stages of drunkenness. It was nice to see tube tops were back in fashion.

"Luke, you listening?" King said. "This info is for you."

I whipped around to face him. "Shit can pop off—got it. Wait, why can shit pop off?"

Ibrahim turned to me. "Cause we're not the only ones who shot in these ends."

"So, be alert. Watch our backs," Llanzo added.

I wanted to write all of this down, but they stuffed my notebook into the bowels of the drug bag. "Totally—can do," I rubbed my sweaty palms together.

"Luke, you go in first," King said. "Then me and Brahim. Llanzo and Kier—a bit after."

I took a deep breath and tightened the bag straps. "Guess I'll see you on the other side," I said as I squeezed past them. Everyone on the sidewalk looked so young, fresh faced with chubby baby cheeks. I was only twenty-eight, but I felt ancient. And with my five-day stubble, I probably looked it. My body went cold as I approached the pink *Roxy* sign, glowing in stencil lettering. *Just be cool, Luke,* I told myself. *You're from out of town, stopping in for a drink. No one cares.*

Inside I found were stairs with neon arrows pointing to the basement. There'd be no easy escape from a basement. Nevertheless, I plopped down the steps and passed a couple making out on the first landing. The girl shoved her hand down the front of the guy's skinny jeans. Nothing like a public handy on a night out.

Dance music thundered up to greet me as I passed a second couple struggling to summit the steps, like it was Everest. She wobbled in her high heels like a baby deer. "Justa fewrmore shteps, baaabe," the guy slurred out.

The basement floor shook beneath my feet from the music. Two massive bouncers in all black stood guard of the neon hellhole, inspecting two girls and their IDs with flashlights. The joint was packed, shoulder-to-shoulder. Strobing lights shimmered off one of the bouncers' bald head like a disco ball as he waved the girls inside. I held out my passport and flashed him a grin, but he didn't smile. Just nodded for me to enter without so much as looking at my bag.

I bulldozed into the crowd for the bar. My bag whacked elbows, tits and drinks all along the way. I thought I'd be much cooler under pressure than that, but give me a break—it was my first night as a drug mule. I paid fourteen pounds for an Old Fashioned which I took to a high-top table overlooking the dancefloor. I sipped my drink with two shaky hands, like hot soup on a cold day. Eventually, King and Ibrahim emerged from the dancefloor and stood next to me without a word, too busy scanning the crowd for customers.

"Now what?" I yelled.

"We paid off the bouncers to let us work," King said. "But they won't help us if anything gets fucked. I'll be back," he said, then slipped into the crowd.

Ibrahim watched King moving through the dancefloor. "Yo! Why would anything get fucked?" I asked him.

"Look mate, play it cool, have ya drink—but don't get drunk."

A river of condensation ran from my glass onto the table. "I'm not sure I know how to do that," I said, taking another sip.

Ibrahim spun around, "Oi, open the top zipper and give me two baggies in the red rubber band."

Oh shit, it's happening. I unzipped the bag and saw how serious it was. The bag was separated into a bunch of cubbies with bundles of baggies tied up in different colored rubber bands—for each of the different drugs. I could have thrown up right there into that bag.

I yanked out a roll of baggies with an orange band. Each baggie had two pills inside. I'd been prescribed enough Xanax to know what an anti-anxiety pill looked like—these guys had enough for forty Lukes with mommy issues. I pulled out another roll, this time it was red. In the bags were about a half teaspoon of white powder. Cocaine.

I freed two bags and placed them in Ibrahim's palm, my sweaty hand smothering his. "I said, hand them to me, not finger bang me," he said with a laugh, then slipped into the crowd after King.

My eyes darted across the blurs of sweaty zombie faces on the dancefloor. Did anyone see my handoff? Would they even care? My nerves were getting the better of me, so I downed my drink. If I was going to do this job well, then I'd need more booze.

A cocktail waitress in a skimpy dress came slinking through the crowd and I waved her over. "Can I have an Old Fashioned brought to me every fifteen minutes?" I asked. "I'll tip you five pounds for every drink," I handed her a fiver.

She nodded and snatched my money, then disappeared into the strobing nightmare. I know, I know, I know. They said don't get drunk, but I needed sedation.

But Luke, what about class tomorrow? Shut up.

The only way I was going to make it to class was if I did a good job at the club and didn't get arrested. And by the time my second drink arrived, along with Kieran and Llanzo, I felt cool as a drug dealing cucumber. I have to admit, it was impressive watching the boys and their work ethic. They gave each other hand signals, exchanged money and handed off different colored bags. Blue, orange, red and yellow like Madeleine's subway wall.

Our process was a well-oiled machine until my third Old Fashioned turned up and I noticed a guy in the crowd staring at me. He was a head taller than everyone on the dancefloor and the only one not moving with the music. He just stared at me with dark circles around his eyes. Under the blue and purple light, I could see he was a bit younger than me, and maybe mixed race. I thought I was just being paranoid, so I went back to surveying the club. But when I looked again, the son of a bitch was still locked onto me.

He mouthed something to me across the room. What the hell? I squinted through the strobe lights to read his lips, but only caught the word *fucked*.

A shadowy figure appeared next to me. I jumped, rocking the table, nearly spilling my drink. It was Llanzo. For Christ's sake.

Llanzo threw his head back and laughed. It was the first time I'd seen him smile. I laughed too—to keep from crying. "Wagwan, you alright?" he said. "Lemme get a double ecstasy bag, yah?"

I caught my breath and dug into the bag. "Llanzo, there's a dude standing in the middle of the dancefloor, a Tall Guy, and he was staring at me. I think he knows what we're doing."

Llanzo stopped smiling. "Where at?"

"He's in the center of the dance floor. Super tall. He's over—"

But Tall Guy was gone. Vanished. "He was just there, man. Super tall, curly hair and dark circles around his eyes."

Llanzo nodded. He seemed to believe me. "Keep an eye out," he stuck his hand out. "Gimme the food. I'll hand it off to Kier and come right back."

Here's where things got dicey. Whoever packed this roll, in their infinite wisdom, stapled some of the ecstasy bags together. And when Llanzo tugged on a bag, a few of them ripped, scattering bright yellow pills across our table. We froze in horror, before palming at the pills to stop them from toppling to the floor. We snatched them up and scooped them into Llanzo's big hands. Llanzo and I took a second to catch our breath as I dug out a loose baggie from the backpack.

"No one's got to know that happened," he grinned, then disappeared in a gap between dancers.

As for me, I was trembling. I grabbed my drink and took a long sip and scanned the dancefloor in thorough sweeps while tonguing down the bitter aftertaste of my Old Fashioned. Tall Guy was nowhere to be seen.

After a couple minutes of throbbing music and a few *really* bitter sips of my drink, Llanzo and Ibrahim returned. Ibrahim asked me to describe Tall Guy, and when I did, he and Llanzo consulted for a moment, stopping every now and again to scan the crowd. They both nodded in agreement. "Get the bag," Ibrahim said. "The lads will meet us at the next place."

Thank God. I nodded at Ibrahim and my head moved in slow motion. *That's a new development.* My nerves were playing with my mind. I slung the bag onto my shoulder and slapped some money down for the waitress, then finished my drink off in one final gulp. The club lights strobed through the bottom of the glass as I swallowed the last of it. The ice shifted and at the bottom of the glass I saw a small yellow ring of residue.

The dissolved, bitter remnants of an escapee ecstasy pill.

Oh, shit.

Chapter 12

The three of us clambered out of The Roxy and onto Rathbone Place. The consensus was we'd been spotted by a rival gang, and they seemed pretty worried about some guy named Charlie. "I think it was Charlie's boy, mate," said Llanzo as he tied up his dreadlocks.

"It had to be, blud," Ibrahim agreed, out of breath.

I had my own problems to deal with, because once we were on the street the ecstasy started kicking in. The night air felt liquid, cool against my skin and I was hyper aware of everything around me. Two girls shared a bottle of Coke—one wiped her mouth with the back of her hand. A group of costumed men on a bachelor party were chanting. The groom was dressed as a banana. *For he's a jolly good fellow* hollered in drunken unison.

We stood under the buzzing pink Roxy sign while we got our bearings. Two police officers strolled by, staring at my backpack. Could they tell I was high? I gawked at the glowing pink sign. Its glory was overwhelming, like the second coming of a pink Christ. "Come on," Llanzo nudged me. "We're going toward Chinatown."

"Gonna take you down to Chinatown," I said, for no reason at all.

My feet felt heavy and loud as I plodded behind them. After a few minutes of trying to coach myself through the early effects of the ecstasy, I decided maybe I should tell the guys. But just as I went to speak, Ibrahim said to Llanzo, "If that's who we think it is, and they catch Kier—they might kill him."

"Mate, it won't get to that." Llanzo shook his head.

On second thought, the ecstasy was more of a *me* problem than a *we* problem. We scampered through Soho Square Gardens and came across a guy and girl arguing. "I don't give a shit, Claire!" The man stormed off. Claire burst into tears, burying her face in her hands. My empathy levels were through the roof, so I stopped and watched her sob while Llanzo and Ibrahim kept on.

Claire was smashed and looked at me with makeup running down her face. I must have looked insane—clenching my jaw with one eye shut, trying to stop from seeing double. I pointed at her date and said, "You can do better."

She cried through her tears and from across the square, her guy called out, "The 'ell you say, mate?"

Time to go. I jogged after Llanzo and Ibrahim but not before I yelled to her, "Remember, he made you cry in the street!"

Claire's date cleverly yelled, "Yeah, you betta' run!"

Llanzo and Ibrahim shook their heads when I rejoined them. We powerwalked for ages toward Chinatown. Cars passed and clips of music zoomed past. A loose bumper rattled on an ambulance. A mystery liquid oozed from a pub dumpster into the street. "Where are we going?" I asked.

"Club Soho." Ibrahim said.

"Would you say it's more or less clubby than the last place?" He didn't answer.

Shit. I'd never taken ecstasy before and the thought of mixing it with another busy club terrified me. I wanted to go somewhere quiet and relaxed where I could do a million jumping jacks— because holy shit! Where did this burst of energy come from?

Finally, I was hit by the full strength of the drug as I jogged after the boys. My eyes jittered back and forth in my skull. My teeth were grinding in my mouth like a cow chewing cud. Christ I was thirsty—and why hasn't my mom reached out to me somehow? Did she not care at all?

We reached a bright intersection of pubs where the sidewalks were packed with life. Pride flags flapped in the breeze. Smokers in our path with drinks in their hands. Oh my God, that's what I wanted, a cigarette. I stopped to light a smoke and my mother came to mind again. It had been a few days since our argument. Sure, I'd blocked her number, but why didn't she shoot me an email? I was alone in a foreign country for Christ's sake!

"This is it," Llanzo stopped next a pillar box. "King and Kier should be right behind us. We'll wait here."

Club Soho was a monstrous club. Stupefied, I gawped at its multiple stories and metallic facade. Waiting in line out front was a crowd of tailored suits and cocktail dresses. I took a drag of my cigarette and peered at the three bouncers at the front door. They were bigger and meaner looking than the ones before, with bulging muscles and bulldog faces. Even the patrons at this club looked mean as they waited in line. Perfumed, cologned and coiffed—stunning but ruthless.

Was this my generation? Like a mortician's handiwork, beautiful on the outside and dead on the inside. Yeah, Luke, but I bet they all had mothers at home that cared and worried about them. Oh no, why did I have to think about that?

My eyes stung with tears, which didn't help my already janky vision. I was a wreck. Drunk, rolling on E, hanging with gang members and carrying their drugs. And there I was, about to cry in the street like poor Claire.

I rubbed the tears from my eyes. Think of something nice. Something good. Sophie, from The Rifleman, popped into my head. She's so pretty and I love her accent. I'm going to figure it out eventually.

"There they are," Llanzo called out.

I spun around to see King and Kieran emerging from the crowded sidewalk. I was so happy to see them that my cheeks hurt from smiling. Their skin looked soft and dewy from sweat. I wanted to touch it, but that would have been weird.

"Alright?" King called out.

"I've been better," I said, before anyone else could speak. "Nice night though."

King narrowed his eyes at me but said to the group. "It was definitely them boys from Charlie's crew. Looked like they're headed this way."

"Fuckinell, bruv." Ibrahim kicked at the pavement.

"It'll be fine," King said. "But we should probably go into the club."

I had no inclination of going into that godawful place, so I stepped up. "Guys, I'm not really in a club mood right now. Could we maybe head to a chill cocktail bar or—ooh! I saw a *TGI Fridays* close by."

The four of them looked at me like I was insane. King stepped up for a closer inspection. "Mate, what's a matter with you?"

Yep, I said too much. I pointed to myself, *who me?*

"Bro, are you high?" he asked.

My mouth was dry. I swallowed the lump in my throat. "I've been meaning to mention something about that. One of the ecstasy pills fell in my drink," I looked to Llanzo. "When the bags tore."

"Shit!" Llanzo put his hands on his head. "You joking me?"

"Naw, unfortunately I'm rolling my dick off right now."

The whole group groaned. "Look, we can't deal with this right now, fam," King shook his head. "We need to get inside. Can you hold it together enough to get past the bouncers?"

I took a hit from my cigarette and flicked it into the street. "Yeah, no problem—but please don't leave me. I don't know which train to take to get home."

King sucked his teeth and pushed me toward the door. "Come on, man."

We got in line and one of the bouncers nodded to King as if he recognized him. We waited for either three minutes or twenty, I don't know, because I was too busy staring at the neon lights moving and shifting inside the club, like a kaleidoscope. At least there'd be a lot of shit for me to stare at inside this club.

"Th-they're here," Kieran pointed to the pub across the street. In front of that pub there was a group of guys searching the crowd. A head jutted up, taller than the rest of the group. It was Tall Guy, with those dark circles around his eyes. My knees shook and my palms were sweaty. Tall Guy scanned the crowded road, and finally, as if he could feel me watching him, he locked eyes with me across the street.

"Shit, he saw me," I grabbed King's arm.

"What?" King looked across the street.

Tall Guy pointed us out to his friends. On cue, his group of guys fanned out as they inched from the curb into the street toward us. There were more of them than there were of us.

The line shifted forward as two girls ahead of me were let into the club. "IDs," one of the bouncers said to King and me.

I could see King's mind working. He and I could go inside where the backpack would be safe, but that would leave Kieran, Llanzo and Ibrahim outnumbered on the street. They'd get their asses kicked, or worse. I had only known them for a couple days, so my initial reaction was, eh—good luck! But those were King's friends, and I knew he wasn't going to bail.

"IDs," the bouncer said louder.

The other crew was in the street now. A red Honda slammed on its brakes and honked at them. I jolted from the horn.

King grabbed my shoulder. "Don't fight. Just take the bag inside."

"Yeah, man. Way ahead of you."

King stepped out of the line and the other boys followed. Loud bass music from the club pumped into the street as my four guys fanned out, just as the other group had done.

"Pussio!" Tall Guy shouted at King. "You in the wrong ends, blud." Another notebook moment. The slang was just superb.

"Nah, cuz," King shrugged. "Me and the boys just out for a dance."

"Fuck that!" Tall Guy said. "Think I'm stupid, ya?"

I slinked back into the line of people, who all watched with intrigue as to what would happen next. As for me, I was not in any condition for conflict. When I drink, I have a short temper, but on ecstasy I'm a big softy.

"Oi!" A bouncer yelled. "You wankers can't fight here. Do it somewhere else, ya puffs."

But they weren't going to do it somewhere else.

Both groups started shouting and maneuvering, anticipating their next moves and sizing one another up. Hiding behind two girls in the line, I felt guilty for not helping the boys. We kind of had fun in the last club, like we were friends. And I didn't have any friends in London yet, except for Daniel and maybe Shane. And I've always been protective of my friends.

That's when I got a really dumb idea—this was all sort of my fault, and maybe I could play up the tourist thing and convince Tall Guy we were just out having a good time? Not selling drugs on his turf, or whatever he was pissed about. So, I slipped from the group of girls and knocked between King and Llanzo and walked straight up to Tall Guy and said the stupidest thing of my entire life.

"It's okay, man," I put a hand over my heart. "I'm an American."

Tall Guy and his entire crew stared at me. There was an odd second of delay where all I could hear was the bass music from the club. The haze of the streetlights splintered into golden sunbursts above me. Amazing, the pretty things you can notice at ugly times.

Tall Guy snorted. "Don't care who you are, blud. You're with them. You're dead."

Dead? I thought. Dead like Sly, my childhood cat? Like Bill, dead? Like Madeleine, dead? Only a moron could want death for such a tiny disagreement. I both pitied and hated Tall Guy, which led me to say the second stupidest thing in my life.

"Hit me then, bitch," I spread my arms out wide.

Without hesitation, the bastard clocked me with his right fist, sending a jolt of pain through my cheek. Then he jabbed with his left. Busting me in my big, fat American mouth. I tumbled to the ground onto my back.

All hell broke loose in a blur of shuffling feet. Grunts. Expletives. And before I could even taste the blood in my mouth, my brain shot a flare into my adrenal system—the exact process it takes to override the effects of drugs in the body.

Above me, King and the Tall Guy scuffled, landing a few hits. Until King tripped over me and fell onto the pavement. Fortunately for me, and unfortunately for Tall Guy, the only thing Bill ever taught me was how to fight. And his weekend benders taught me how to take a punch like an absolute champion.

Before Tall Guy knew what happened, I sprang to my feet. Livid, I slipped the bag from my shoulders and raised my fists. He put up his guard. Guess he's boxed some before.

Good for him, but fuck a fair fight.

I faked a jab. Up went his arms and I swung my foot. The point of my toe rocketed into his dick. Tall Guy dropped to his knees, grabbing what was left of his cock. I lunged, shoving him onto his back. His head thudded onto the street. Like a crazed chimp, I slammed my fists into his face. His nose clicked and sunk. Countless more blows. I think I chipped his tooth on my knuckle.

Two sets of big arms pulled me off. The bouncers. I swung my torso hard. My elbows shot into their ribs and shoved them away. King was up now. The street was chaos. Bodies moving and flailing. People filming on their phones. Were they cheering? My generation.

Who next? Where do I go? Tunnel vision.

Llanzo fought off two. Two more were on top of Kieran. King and I bolted for them. We spear-tackled them to the ground. I landed my knee on the neck of some black kid. Put my weight into it. He scratched at my arms and neck and took blind desperate swings. I waited for a break in his strikes and pummeled his face. Then again. Until the fight had left him. King had a guy's head pinned against the wall as he battered his stomach. There were sirens in the distance. Close and closing in.

"Luke, the bag!" King shouted.

Damn—forgot about the bag. I pushed myself up, hearing a gargle from the kid's neck beneath me, and bolted for the bag. Tall Guy crawled over to it. Blood poured from his nose and mouth. Still on the ground, he gripped at the left strap, while I tugged at the right. A bouncer fell to the ground beside me. Good work, Llanzo. Tug of war with Tall Guy, the bag's seams splitting. King rushed to my side. Tall Guy yanked a blade from his sock. A kitchen knife—sharpened to a daggered point. He sliced at the air between us—WHIT-WHIT.

But I remembered—I've got one too. Yanked the Kershaw from my pocket. The blade flipped out CLICK. And I said the third stupidest thing in my life, "This is going to hurt."

I swiped my knife across the veins in the top of his hand. Blood spurted like a sliced water balloon. Bet your ass he let go of the bag.

And that was the fourth law I broke in the UK.

Chapter 13

My phone alarm blared on my pillow, jolting me awake. Somehow, I was back at my flat with golden sun seeping into my room. Ugh, it was seven in the morning. I killed the alarm and just laid there as pain pulsed through my body. My skull throbbed from being hit or hungover, and my heartbeat kicked like a drum in my ears. This was bad—every muscle in my body was on fire and every joint felt rusted over.

I closed my eyes and slipped into a dream—no, a memory. I was fourteen years old and sneaking into Bill's apartment one evening while trying to hide my busted face. It was the work of Derek Hardaway from down the street. Bill believed that a son who couldn't defend himself was a poor reflection of his father.

I slithered through the kitchen but Bill spotted me while working at his easel. He was painting a collapsed tobacco barn in deep shades of red and brown. He'd gotten it into his head long ago that he was meant to be a great painter, and he was rather good—he certainly mastered the drunken, tortured artist schtick.

"Lucas," his voice rumbled like distant thunder. "Get the hell over here."

There were a few Miller cans at his work-station. No whiskey yet, so maybe he'd be manageable. He grabbed my chin with his big hand and inspected my face. His fingers were covered in dry paint, dark blues and reds. "That Hardaway kid again?" he asked.

"We were just dicking around," I mumbled.

Bill squeezed my chin. It hurt. "No, *he* was dicking around—and you just took it."

Bill's hazel eyes, which I inherited, were set firmly on me. His cheeks were flushed from the booze. "He's a southpaw, ain't he?" Bill let go of my chin. "Hard for righties to block. But once you learn, you can light his ass up—won't know what hit him."

Liking the sound of that, I nodded. That's when I noticed the bottle of Jim Beam peeking out from behind his canvas.

"Put your bag down," he said. "Let's see your stance. 'Member what I showed you?"

I lowered my eyes. "Yeah, I remember."

Bill raised his hands and squared up into a fighting stance, and I did the same. "'Member to move a little," he said.

And so, I did. I bobbed and swayed.

"You need to work on your jab," he pointed. "'Cause you'll be using your right to block his left hook."

We did the motions a few times. Slow left hook from Bill, block with my right, then jab with my left. We repeated the movements, and for a moment—just a single goddamn moment—Bill was being a dad. I couldn't help myself—a smile spread across my face.

Bill's eyes went dark and he punched me in the gut. I fell back into the metal shelves behind me, it grated the flesh along my spine and I crumpled to the floor. Clutching my stomach, I fought for breath I felt would never return.

"You ain't a punching bag for white trash!" Bill shouted. "I'd rather you die fighting that Neanderthal, than come home lookin' like that! You hear me?"

Hit first and hit the hardest, Bill always said. *Fuck a fair fight.*

My alarm rang again at seven-forty-five. My room was brighter now and I noticed a smudge on my wall in the profile shape of a man's face. If only I hadn't skipped every orientation event I could have just gone back to bed. But no, I had to go.

My face stuck to my pillow when I sat up. Brown-red, crusty blood splotches stained my new pillowcase. The room swayed with a lack-of-sea-legs feeling as I stood. I was in my clothes from last night. I had no recollection of coming home and setting alarms but—*holy shit*—I ran from the cops through Soho. I cut a guy with my knife!

No time for a shower, I chewed a handful of aspirin in the kitchen and chugged a pint of water. Running a hand through my cowlick, I hobbled down the stairs into the crisp morning. The air was too fresh, it made me sick. I limped across the street to a cubbyhole coffee shop next to the kebab joint where the smell of cooking meat sent me dry-heaving on the sidewalk. Nothing came up, just the sounds of my retching to set the mood for people walking to work.

Mustafa, the coupon guy, sat out front, giggling at me. "Sad face, black hoodie," he said. "No coupons yet—come back later!"

I smiled, but the thought of a kebab made me gag. "Sure thing, buddy."

I got a huge Americano from the café—black like my violent soul, and staggered off for the tube. My train ride was a struggle with breakfast food smells and the morning breath of the man leaning over me with his morning paper. Luckily, I made it out to the street before puking vinegary booze all over my shoes.

At eight-forty-five I reached my university, where an old man fed pigeons in Bedford Square. Every urban park seems to have a resident elderly person to feed the birds. But what happens when that person dies and the pigeons show up one morning met by no one? The thought of confused pigeons made me sad and even more nauseous.

My class was on the third floor, so I wound up the narrow steps and slipped into the bathroom, where I finally saw the wreckage of my face. My lip was swollen and split down the middle, and I had a purple shiner and a puffy cheek. Hot water nipped at the cuts on my knuckles as I washed my face.

I put up my hood and slithered into the bright hall, praying my classroom was large enough for me to hide in the back. But when I poked my hooded head into the room, I discovered it was a tiny boardroom with seven people crowded around a conference table. They all stopped talking to look at me. Every seat was taken, except for the professor's at the head of the table and mine next to it.

Great.

Six women and one other dude watched me, the human punching bag, limp along the tiny space between their chairs and the wall. I groaned as I fell into my seat. I must have remembered to get my notebook from the drug bag. The entire table gawked when I flipped it open on a page of indecipherable scribblings of a drunken lunatic. Maybe I should say something. How about a joke?

I cleared my throat. "My girlfriend gets a little punchy when she drinks," I pointed to my face and chuckled. "Swears she loves me, though."

Not a domestic violence joke! No one at the table laughed except for the guy, but he stopped once he realized he was the only one. The room was painfully silent. A large modern clock ticked on the wall, the hard-to-read kind with no numerals on the face. I counted the minutes until the door swung open and a tiny, white-haired lady swished into the room. "Hellooo," she said. Everyone's face lit up.

Our professor wore a white blouse and a brown cardigan, with a long, gray pleated skirt. A round pair of black glasses sat on her little nose. Everyone pulled their chairs in to let her by—a courtesy I was not shown.

She set a floral-patterned Mary Poppins bag on the table and scanned our faces, recoiling when she saw me. "Everyone, take a breath," she said. "This is a big day, yes, but there's no pressure at all. Just getting everyone acquainted with the course and with each other. I do hope you know who I am?"

Everyone nodded. I'm not allowed to give specifics, but our professor—let's call her Ms Smith—was an accomplished writer, who amassed decades of writing credits in literature and film. Of course, we knew who she was. Ms Smith prompted my classmates to give their names, where they were from, and their genre. All things considered, I decided my genre was crime.

So, it went; English person—forgettable place, English person—forgettable place, Bhavani—Delhi, English person—forgettable place. Then an enthusiastic American chick. May—from Boulder, Colorado.

"I'm sooo happy to be here in the UK," May added, flipping her scarlet hair. "Connecting with my Celtic roots."

Kill me. I zoned out until Ms Smith pointed to me. "How about you, Robin Hood?" she giggled. "You *have* to tell us what happened to your face. I'm sure that's an exciting story."

May, already the teacher's pet, leaned forward. "Apparently, his girlfriend did it."

What a nightmare. I should have stayed in bed. "No—no, that was just a lame joke. I'm afraid there's not an interesting story behind this."

"Well, that's unfortunate," Ms Smith said. "So, who are you and what do you write?"

"I'm Luke, from North Caro-liiina." Shit, why did I sound so southern? "And I write criiime." So impossibly southern!

Ms Smith seemed intrigued, maybe by my stupid accent. A closed-mouth smile spread across her face. "What kind of crime stories do you write?"

"Umm," I said, thinking I might puke again. "Well, right now I'm writing a story about a guy, uh—," *Come on, think dammit.* "Who met a crew of criminals in London, and accidentally becomes a part of their gang."

Wow, Luke. That's a little on the nose, ain't it? Apparently, it wasn't enough description for Ms Smith, who encouraged her students to *dig deep*.

Ms Smith studied me from behind her thick specks. "But if there's no mystery to solve, is it really crime? What else could it be?"

I gave her an eye roll. "That's what I'm here to find out."

She narrowed her eyes at me, but eventually smiled. "Luke, I'm going to let you off the hook, since it's the first day." Ms Smith talked about genre as the class muttered on. Meanwhile, I looked through my phone to stop from falling asleep. Apparently, I sent Cash a text at three in the morning, saying: *just had the craziest night lol I effing love London bro.*

What would possess me to send that? That night was the worst! I drugged myself, got beaten up, cut a dude, and cherry on top—I ran from the cops. Was drunk Luke confessing to enjoying those things?

"How about you, Luke?" Ms Smith said.

My eyes shot up to her. "Oh shit, could you repeat the question?"

"We were discussing what got us into writing," she stated. "What's the first story you remember writing?"

How the hell should I know? The whole table examined me, and I began to sweat under my hoodie. I looked to my classmates for help, as if they could somehow answer for me.

Ms Smith saw I was struggling. "I've often found that the first story you write finds its way, by some small piece, into everything you'll ever write," she pushed her glasses up on her nose. "So, what was your first story?"

Bill came to mind. And the night I came home beaten up by Derek Hardaway. I had tried to forget that night, but it was in fact the first time I wrote a story. After Bill sucker punched me, I locked myself in my room and wrote a story about an orphan boy. A shiver shot up my spine when I remembered the story was actually meant to be a letter. Beaten to hell and at the end of my rope, I had locked myself in my room to write a suicide note.

Hell, no. I couldn't share that. "It wasn't a good story," I said.

Ms Smith grinned. "Whose first story ever is?"

Sweat poured now. Eight pairs of eyes watched for the busted-up idiot to spit it out already. I hadn't thought about the orphan story in ages, and I didn't feel like reliving the process of writing it to a room full of strangers.

Just give her a little bit, Luke, I thought. *She's not going to quit.* "It was about a boy living at an orphanage."

"What adventures did you write for this orphan boy?"

I felt myself getting angry — or sad, maybe both. "The bigger kids were mean and he got hit a lot." The room was so silent that it felt loud. My ears began to ring. "But he would sneak to the chalkboard and draw himself a mom and dad, who came to life at night. The three of them would run around the orphanage, pranking the people the boy hated."

"Ooh that is brilliant!" she clapped. "I love that. Very good, Luke."

Ms Smith leaned back, satisfied. My fingers turned white from clenching them together. She looked to the blonde girl next me and the room's attention was finally pulled away. "And what about you, Audrey—"

"Luke, what made you write about an orphan?" Bhavani smiled from across the table. "I was actually adopted myself."

Ms Smith lit up that Bhavani was *digging deep*. "Great question," Ms Smith said. "Back to Luke. Why write about an orphan and his imaginary parents?"

I know Ms Smith and Bhavani weren't trying to pry, but my temper has a mind of its own. A flash of heat shot through me as the room waited for an answer. I buried that story years ago, pretending it didn't save my life. The ringing in my ears grew louder. My vision funneled, narrowing on my pen on the table. The orphan story was the first thing I'd ever written, but it was meant to be my last. Page after page, I scribbled while trying to remember where Bill kept his revolver. That pain stayed hidden for fourteen years.

Until those two had to pry.

Something deep inside me spoke up, completely out of my control. "I wasn't really going to end it," I choked out. "Just liked knowing I had the option. Control of my life for once."

Ms Smith's little eyes widened. "Oh goodness," she touched my forearm. "You're not talking about the story—are you?"

Sweat or tears blurred my vision. The ringing in my ears was deafening. "Lady, what do you want me to say?" I yanked my arm away. "That my parents didn't love me? That I was gonna blow my goddamn head off, but I got distracted writing about some stupid orphan."

The room fell silent. So silent, I could hear the fluorescent lights humming above me and the tick of that stupid faceless clock on the wall. I wanted to yank it off its hook and smash it with my heel. I was burning up, so I yanked off my hood and glared at the table. "How's that for an ice breaker, assholes?"

Chapter 14

Class came to a screeching halt after my outburst. I bounded down the stairs for the front door and draped myself on the railing outside to light a cigarette. As my lungs filled and my head cleared, remorse poured over me like ice water and I began drafting an apology to Ms Smith in my head. That was until I heard shouts from across the street.

Construction workers in yellow vests were unloading a massive glass panel from a truck. Six of them shouted at one another in some foreign language, all straining under the weight. Maybe I should quit writing and work construction. Spend my days building things with a team, then clock out and go home. The working class was in my DNA after all. Maybe it's best to leave writing to affluent kids who could *dig deep* without unearthing childhood trauma.

"Hey, man," a voice called behind me. It was the guy from my class, Heath. "You alright?" he plodded down the stairs.

"Yeah, I'll be alright." I said, watching the workers.

"That was rough in there. Sorry, that happened."

Heath had a kind face and was my age but with older, wiser eyes. He stroked his beard, catching sight of the workers too.

"I feel like an idiot. Torpedoing myself on the first damn day—hope they don't kick me out," I said.

He and I watched the men hoist the glass panel over the curb. "I doubt they'll kick you out for something like that," he chuckled. "After you left, Ms Smith told us how terrible she felt forcing you to share something so sensitive."

"*She* felt bad?" But I was the one who yelled at *her*. Cursed at *her*. I was relieved, yes, but I felt like I should be punished somehow. I think I wanted to be punished.

He nodded. "Don't go packing your bags just yet. And silver lining—it's only the first day and you've done a lot of self-exploration as to why you write. So, maybe it was a good thing?"

Heath had a point. If turning your thoughts and feelings into words was easy, then everyone would be writers.

"Good to meet you, mate," he said, shaking my hand. "See you around?"

I nodded and watched him cross to Bedford Square, feeling better already when I realized Heath was my first ever writing friend. Maybe I didn't have to quit after all.

Across the street, the workers' shouts crescendoed. I looked just in time to see the men drop the panel, as it shattered into a trillion pieces on the concrete. Glass fell for ages, scattering across the sidewalk into the street. I never saw anything more satisfying in my entire life.

***

A black Audi followed me to Warren Street tube station. I first noticed the car on Bloomsbury when it crept behind me for two blocks. So I jogged the rest of the way and slipped into the station.

I told myself I was being paranoid, but considering I now had more enemies than friends in London it seemed wise to be wary. I kept a watchful eye on the train but by the time I reached my flat, my body ached for a nap and the Audi, with its darkened windows, was far from my thoughts. So far from my thoughts that I didn't find it strange the door to my flat was ajar. I chalked it up to idiot roommates—until I jumped when I saw someone sitting at my kitchen table.

Shane glared at me over a cup of tea.

"Jesus, you scared the hell out of me!" I said.

"About time you showed—your foreign housemate let me in."

I stood up straight. "Wait, was that you following me?"

Shane nodded and took a sip of his tea. Steam rose to meet his freshly shaved face.

Oh shit. He was probably mad about Soho. We were supposed to be on our *best* behavior. I was about to explain myself, until I noticed Shane looked more dapper than usual. He wore a James Bond quality suit; navy blue and well-tailored, with a new haircut. But something else about him looked different and I couldn't place it. "Things went smoothly for a while. But uh—"

"For three years, my modest operation has chugged along quietly, not so much as a blip on anyone's radar—particularly Charlie's. Then you come along and send one of Charlie's top lads to the A&E."

I realized I had no idea what Shane was capable of. Was he there to hurt me? "Well, I hear your health coverage over here is pretty great so—"

Shane wagged his finger. "No jokes."

"Right, yeah."

"I admit, my initial reaction was anger, but the rumors I've heard today," he flashed his big grin. "Grandiose notions I'm working with a cartel from America and such. Well, it's given me some unexpected leverage. So, maybe I should thank you."

My face scrunched up. Thank me?

"I've got a meeting with Charlie in half an hour and I'm not sure that would have ever happened if it weren't for your cock up," he said.

"Phew, you had me worried, tracking me down like this."

Shane checked his watch. "I tracked you down because I want to know who the bloody hell you are, and why you've forced your way into my life? And don't say some story, mate. What do you *really* want?"

My eyes darted around the silent kitchen for an answer. I thought my story was all I wanted, but last night in Soho I felt myself wanting something more. I remembered what I told

Ms Smith about control. "I want control of my life," I said. "And the power and respect that comes with it. For once in my damn life."

Shane gave a nod. "I thought about what you said yesterday about the boys. And I'd like to help you get that power and respect through an internship—as you called it. In return, you'll help me get what I want."

My transition from notetaker to gang intern was happening a little fast, but there were butterflies in my stomach and I forgot to ask what Shane wanted in return.

He stood up. "All you need is discipline and a specific role."

Probably not a role I could put on LinkedIn, but I was intrigued. "Can I have some time to think about it?"

Shane shook his head. "I have my meeting in twenty-five minutes, so I'll need an answer now."

Whatever this tactic was, it was working on me. Shane knew it and I knew it. All I had to do was say the words. "Under one condition," I said. "This role can't affect my writing program."

"Of course not," he stuck out his hand.

When I shook his hand, I noticed the edge of his forearm tattoo creeping out from his sleeve. The handle of a knife or sword. *That's* what made him look different. With his tattoos covered, he could chameleon into the normal world. There were many secret layers to Shane and he was much more than just a guy from the shitty little pub in Catford.

Shane opened my front door. "Now, let's get to that meeting."

Me—go to a gangster meeting? In the movies, gangsters always met in some warehouse where there's a gunfight and everyone dies. Police would show up and draw an outline around me, lying in a pool of my own blood and piss. And they'd all be stumped. Who the hell is the dipshit in the hoodie with dried puke on his shoes?

Despite that horrific fantasy, I followed him downstairs to the front of my building where Shane's black Audi was hidden between two work vans. I trudged over to the passenger side, eyes down like a man off to the gallows.

Shane laughed. "Stop worrying, mate. You're just going as back up. You're not to say a single word. Are we clear?"

"Crystal," I crammed into the tiny passenger seat. The Audi was low to the ground and my knees were up to my chin, but the Moroccan leather interior was impressive. The engine started with a throaty purr and, without warning, Shane slammed on the gas. We shot through my lot and into traffic on Wandsworth. He dumped the car into second gear and slid us around a corner.

"My dad was a London cabby for twenty-seven years," he shifted into third. "And I learned every street in London riding with him. And by studying his passengers I learned about people—what they said and how they said it. It's where I discovered that every person wears a mask—the face we want the world to see, and we rarely take them off for anyone."

I couldn't focus on his pseudo-psychology, because my stomach shot into my throat when he nearly clipped an old lady and her Pomeranian crossing the street. Probably should have told him about my inclination toward motion sickness.

Shane took his eyes off the road to look at me. "Some people—like you—don't have the ability to hide behind a mask. Who they are on the outside is who they are on the inside."

"Are you saying that I'm dumb?"

"Ha! You see? Normal people would have said something polite to skirt the accusation, but you said exactly how you felt."

The road slipped beneath us like a raging river of tarmac. Couldn't help but notice he didn't answer my question. Shane downshifted and the engine roared as we jettisoned through a stale yellow light toward the London Eye.

"I was like you, you know?" Shane said. "But I taught myself how to wear a mask—for them," he pointed at people on the sidewalks. "Then I learned how to wear different masks for different people, and that's worked greatly to my advantage."

I thought about my quick temper, my outbursts, and a lifetime of erratic behavior. Was what Cash called posturing just my inability to hide the scared, bruised kid beneath it all?

He braked hard when we hit traffic and I slid forward in my seat. The engine dulled to a tame purr as we cruised behind a sooty bus. "What made you create different masks? Why go through all that trouble?" I asked.

Shane was silent for a moment. Just kept his eyes on the bus. "My dad," he said, in a softer tone. "Christmas Eve, 1990. He always drove Christmas Eve night. Lots of drunk, happy people leaving big tips. Us kids would wait up for him to come home, because then it would finally be Christmas," Shane smiled as he shared the memory. "But on that particular Christmas Eve, two thugs knifed him in the neck and gut, stole his fares and his car. He died on a cold street in Brixton. Since they'd taken his ID, he lay in the morgue all alone until Boxing Day. Needless to say, I'm not so keen on the Holidays anymore."

"That's awful," I shook my head. "I'm sorry."

Traffic let up and Shane put the car in gear and rumbled off. "It is what it is," he said. "But because of it, I can always tell when other people haven't come from great starts."

I sucked in a breath. "So, like the boys? Like me?"

Shane gave me a strange, nurturing look. Almost fatherly. He must have been the greatest mask wearer ever, since he could adapt himself for every person he met. It's what made him a successful gangster and negotiator.

It's also what made him a psychopath.

We barreled across the Thames in silence, as Shane navigated us through City of London traffic toward the skyscrapers ahead. "That's where we're going," he said, pointing to a building that looked like a walkie-talkie. "There's a restaurant at the top."

Not only was I immensely relieved we weren't going to a warehouse, my inner-child was amped to see London from the top of that ugly building. I nearly forgot we were going to a gangster meeting. Shane whipped a sharp left and cut a cyclist off to zip us into a parking deck. The tires squealed around the tight corners. My weak stomach found me again. *Happy thoughts, Luke,* I thought. *Cash, Daniel, Olive Guy, Sophie.* Shane slid us into a parking spot. The Audi skidded to a dramatic halt and he killed the engine. We were silent as I swallowed down the sick in my mouth.

"If you're not serious about helping me out, tell me now," he said, watching me pant. "No more Rifleman, no more story — we part ways. No hard feelings, mate."

It would have been wise to just walk away, but Shane and the boys interested me. They were like a family, and I know how ridiculous that sounds, but it appealed to me. Maybe because I never had *real* siblings, since Braden and Kaylee don't count. Cash was as close as a brother, but he was gone.

"I wasn't entirely honest with you before," I sighed. "I just want to belong to something. To have people watch my back as I watch theirs. Power and respect — we can grab that along the way."

A smile spread across Shane's face. Which I thought was from mutual understanding. "I'm glad you mentioned watching each other's backs," he said. "Because that's what being a part of my crew means. Now, could you grab the newspaper that's in my glovebox?"

I pulled out the French newspaper he had yesterday, *Le Parisien.* The headline read that France's elderly population were living in poverty. I began to quiver, knowing, but not knowing where this was going.

"Turn to the second page," he said.

My fingertips trembled and I struggled to flip the page. My eyes darted across the different sections. The endless French words could have been hieroglyphics. Finally, I spotted a column on the left side of the page that led with a photo of a woman.

Madeleine.

It was the photo of her in Tottenham Court Road Station. There she was, in ghostly black and white, staring right at me in front of the yellow, but now gray, circle.

The newspaper shook in my hands as I read the headline out loud. "Touristes soupçonnés du meurtre d'une Parisienne: L'enquête est en cours."

Shane held up a finger. "En anglais, s'il vous plait."

"Tourists suspected in the murder of a Parisian woman," I nearly gagged. "An investigation is underway."

Jesus Christ. We are going to burn for this.

Chapter 15

Walkie Talkie Building

Shane and I rode the elevator in silence to the rooftop atrium, called Sky Garden. It was a massive botanical garden with three-hundred-sixty-degree views of London. It's the kind of place where social media influencers take pictures while sipping glasses of overpriced champagne. And it's a stark contrast to the parking deck downstairs where I just had the worst panic attack of my life.

My chest heaved as I sucked in dank parking deck air. Shane handed me his hip flask of whiskey. "Mate, relax—*I'm* the one who told Paris police to look for tourists."

"Why the hell would you do that?"

Shane gestured for me to take a drink. It burned on the way down. "Because once again, I had to protect George," he said. "And though you hate him, Rémy too. They're important for my business in France and I needed to make sure Paris police never looked in their direction."

"Neat story—don't give a shit. Me and my friend are going to prison!"

Shane gestured for me to drink again. "Mate, how many tourists visit Paris each day?"

I gulped down some whiskey and shrugged.

"The Louvre alone gets fifteen thousand visitors per day," he said. "The city—one hundred thousand." His words were as soothing as his whiskey. Shane put his arm around my shoulders. "That's twice now I've saved you from the police. Now, give us a fag before we're late."

A posh young couple rode the elevator with us in silence. The girl had a handbag worth more than any car I've ever owned. I pretended not to notice her staring while I rubbed dirt off my hands from stashing my knife in a planter box outside.

"Try not to look so nervous," Shane said as he watched the floor numbers flicker higher. "Just be quiet and look mean."

My nerves finally did settle when we came into the atrium and I looked out at the panoramic view of London. It was a clear blue day with a few chunky clouds loitering in the distance. Colorful plants spilled from every edge of the atrium and filled the air with a familiar floral aroma.

It reminded me of that funeral home in North Carolina and studying a shelf of urns for Bill's stupid ashes. The smiley undertaker insisted the Folgers coffee tin I brought was *absolutely* not legal to use. I told him he could keep the ashes, since Bill was *absolutely* not worth a three-hundred-dollar urn. Before I could reminisce on the storm drain I eventually dumped Bill into, Shane called me over to a staircase for the restaurant that overlooked the atrium.

We were intercepted by a skinny waiter in a tie. "Here to see Charlie," Shane said, before the man could speak. The waiter gulped when he spotted my bruised face. At least someone thought I looked mean.

We came through a narrow corridor and out into the open restaurant that overlooked the South Bank. It was eerily empty, as if the entire restaurant had been booked for this meeting. There was a table at the far end of the restaurant where a black woman sat alone. "That's Charlie," Shane said, over his shoulder.

Charlie is a woman? The waiter led us to her table, where I took my seat across from Charlie, who looked about my age.

She had a pretty, but stern, face, with long and neatly-tied braids fanning across her shoulders.

"I'll have a gin and tonic, with a squeeze of lime," Shane said, without meeting the waiter's eyes.

The waiter turned to me. "And for you, sir?"

"Um—a water."

"We have a sparkling from Vergèze, France, a mineral water from the Pyrenees, and a still from—"

"He'll have tap water—from London." Shane said.

The waiter nodded, spun on his heels and strode away. I nodded at Charlie as she pored over me from behind her teacup.

"So, this is him, then?" she said in a posh accent.

Shane helped himself to some tea. "In all his glory," he said.

Charlie leaned back, revealing a large, pregnant belly. "Rough night?" She narrowed her eyes on my busted lip.

"Could have gone better," I said.

"I'll say," she said. "Do you know how much money I lost with an entire crew off the street?" Her voice echoed through the empty restaurant.

My heartrate sky-rocketed. *Don't say anything stupid, Luke.* "Last time I saw 'em, they were still laying in the street."

Shane groaned through a sip of tea.

Charlie pushed her cup aside. "Another cute statement like that and I'll have you thrown from the roof of this building. Do you understand?"

My fingertips went tingly, thinking about my body splattering on the sidewalk forty stories below. I nodded.

"Charlie, if I may," said Shane.

"You may not," she glared. "I've tolerated your mutts in Soho for quite a while, because up until last night they've never caused any trouble." She rested a hand on her pregnant belly. "What do you have to say about that?"

The waiter returned and delivered Shane's gin and my water. He opened his mouth to speak, but seemed to sense the tension and backed away slowly. Shane sighed. "What can we do to make up your losses?"

"Good lad," she nodded. "What are you capable of offering?"

Despite only knowing him for a few days, I could tell Shane didn't like being talked down to, but he calmly sipped his gin. "I hear you have a problem in Camden Town."

"Camden is thriving—you've heard wrong."

Shane gave a close-mouthed smile. "Charlie, I know that over the course of this past year, your priorities have changed," he nodded to her belly, to which Charlie frowned. "And rightly so, of course. You've been clever to put more emphasis on the legitimate branches of your organization. But periods of transition are risky. Pulling away too soon from your— unsavory dealings—makes you look weak. And the vultures are circling."

"Spoken like a true vulture," Charlie said. "And I'd be careful who you call weak, Shane. Your cousin, George, got too big for his boots too. And where's he these days?"

Hey—I know George. Before I could speculate on how George got stuck in Paris, Shane leaned toward Charlie. "You're not weak, just taking on risk. Instead of being enemies, I wonder if we can find a mutually beneficial arrangement?"

To my surprise, Charlie laughed. "Are you suggesting you would take up the *unsavory* side of my business?"

There was a glint in his eye. "What better way to help you make the transition?"

"Hmm." Charlie leaned back in her chair. She looked out at the horizon just as a lumpy cloud blotted out the sun.

The rest of the conversation went over my head, but one thing was clear—Shane was definitely some kind of mastermind. Was it his intention all along to take over her business? And did he just finesse her into thinking it was her idea?

Shane refilled Charlie's tea, and she took a long sip. "If we do this, what becomes of my problem in Camden?" she asked.

"Well," he grinned his big grin. "It becomes my problem. And you'll be happy to know I solve my problems swiftly."

Charlie gave an amused smile. "I imagine you'll be using him, yeah?" she glared at me. "He seems to have a knack for destruction."

Okay, bitch. That was an unfair assessment, but I held my tongue. Pregnant women scared me. My mom snapped at me once when she was pregnant with Braden. And ever since, I've treated the knocked-up as I would a bear or lion—keep them well-fed and at a distance.

Shane chuckled. "I've begun drafting a to-do list for the Yank."

My mouth went dry from the talk of solving problems and destruction. I took a shaky sip of my London water and thought—what if he wants me to kill someone?

Footsteps shuffled into the restaurant behind me, but before I could look, Charlie spoke, "Alright, but you keep out of my crew's way," she pointed at me. "Or you'll end up in the Thames—now, bugger off," Charlie waved a hand at me. "Your boss and I need to discuss details."

"Wait at the bar," Shane said.

My chair made an awful screech through the cavernous restaurant. Sweat dripped from my forehead and just before I turned to leave, Charlie said, "He looks like shit."

Without thinking, I shot back. "You should see the other guy."

Shane groaned. Charlie's lip curled. "You mean him?" she pointed behind me.

Oh no. I whipped around to see Tall Guy sitting at the bar between two bulky goons. His nose was taped-up and his hand was mummy-wrapped with gauze. He was seething.

"That'd be him," I croaked.

The three thugs stared as I sat at the bar a few spaces away, feeling my pocket for a knife that wasn't there. A tiny bartender with a big nose slinked in from a backroom. "Can I get anything for you, sir?" he asked, shakily.

Screw it—I ordered a beer. The three mouth breathers gawked while I sipped a Moretti. "Can I get you boys anything?" I said.

The two bulky guys, one black, one white—both ugly—snorted. I looked into Tall Guy's bloodshot eyes. Purple bruises blotted his swollen face, and wet stitches gleamed above his eyebrow. "How 'bout you, slim? Maybe some ice for that face?"

Tall Guy shot out of his seat after me. Luckily, the big white goon caught him and shoved him back onto his stool. I didn't even have time to flinch.

"Let me go—right now!" Tall Guy snarled, with a chipped front tooth.

"Can't do that, Profit," the white guy said, in a Cockney accent. "Not 'ere, not now."

Profit. What a stupid name. I chuckled into my beer as the bartender slithered into the backroom. "To your health, *Profit,*" I raised my glass.

Profit jumped up again. "Pussio! I'll fuckin' wet you—"

This time, both bulky guys shoved Profit back down into his seat. The Cockney dude's bulbous nose turned Rudolph red. "What's your name, then?" he asked.

My hangover brain fought to think of any other name than my own. And for some reason, still unknown to me now, I blurted out the one name that came to mind. "Uh, Cash."

"Okay, Cash," the Cockney said, his forehead glistening with sweat. "I don' fink your boss would 'pO I mean—'ppreciate you takin' the piss at a mee'in like this, would he?"

He had a point. I nodded and went back to nursing my beer until finally Shane came over, his meeting concluded. "A beer sounds good," he said, setting his empty glass on the bar.

The three thugs hopped to their feet when Charlie waddled past. Profit took her laptop bag and slung it over his shoulder. He must have sensed me looking at him because as he walked by, he reached his long arm out and swatted the pint out of my hand. My glass went clanking across the bar and smashed at the feet of the tiny bartender, just as he'd reemerged from the backroom. I lunged for Profit and snatched his shirt in a bunch. But the Cockney dude grabbed my arm and twisted it behind my back. The other bulky guy did the same to Profit, yanking him from my grasp.

"Profit!" Charlie scolded him.

"Watch your back, white boy," Profit ignored her. "Got eyes all over this city!"

I fought to free myself, but the Cockney shoved my fist further up the center of my back. Pain sliced through my shoulder. Didn't stop me from talking shit though. "Good!" I gritted my teeth. "More people to see me kick your ass again."

The Cockney guy squeezed my throat to shut me up, and the big black dude dragged Profit away. Shane stooped down and handed Charlie her dropped bag.

"Keep your dog on a short lead, Shane," she pointed at me. "Or I'll put him down."

Charlie stormed off and just before things went black, the Cockney released my throat. I gasped, seeing spots in my vision. The big guy looked at Shane and smothered my face with his sweaty gorilla palm, shoving me onto my stool. "Stupid git, this one," he said, lumbering off.

My head spun as the blood came rushing back. Shane tossed a twenty-pound note at the bartender, who stood trembling, with the shattered pint at his feet.

"Well done, mate," Shane shrugged. "In town for only a week, and one of London's most ruthless cunts wants you dead."

"That dude can eat a dick," my voice rasped. "London's huge. We can ignore each other like adults."

"I don't think you understand London yet. These things escalate—never dissipate." He nodded to the exit. "You're an experiment I think could pay off, so don't let that pissant stick a knife in your gut when your guard is down."

A knife in my gut? Shane continued down the corridor as the craziness of the past twenty-four hours washed over me. Between the street fight, the world's worst hangover, my outburst with Ms Smith, Madeleine's article, and now this meeting—I didn't know how to start processing it all. Shane stopped at the end of the hall. His face was lit red from the exit sign above. "Come on, I'll buy you a pint."

And I decided to do that instead.

Chapter 16

Shane's Audi thundered past the Tower of London and its weathered turrets. We crossed Tower Bridge and I scanned the faces of tourists as if I could look through time and see myself with Cash sifting through the mob. Funny—I'd only just remembered Shane's name the last time I was on that bridge, and there I was in his car.

Shane skidded onto Tooley Street. Nausea churned the beer in my stomach while I planted my eyes on the road ahead. "Where are we going?" I asked.

"The Rifleman. We've got work to start on for Charlie."

Go ahead, Luke. Just ask him. "I'm not going to have to kill anyone, right?" I gulped. "'Cause I don't wanna do that."

Shane laughed and we stopped at a red light. He pointed at a corner store just outside his window. "Mate, if you had to, how would you rob that shop?"

"I wouldn't."

Shane rolled his eyes. "If you *had* to."

I sighed and gave the off license a better look. It sat at the busy corner of Jamaica Road and a quiet side street. Graffiti was scrawled on the white brick by the front door. Ads for the lottery, vapes and money transfers in the window. Just as I was about to say *I don't know,* I remembered a shoplifting phase from my teenage years. I stole everything but cash from those kinds of places and never got caught.

Shane turned to me. "It's not that hard—"

"It *is* that hard," I said. "People don't get caught from overthinking it, but from under-thinking—if that's a word."

He smirked. "How would you do it, then?"

I pictured myself hanging out across the street, smoking cigarettes and staking out the shop. "I'd note the busy times.

Buy something cheap days before to get the layout, check for CCTV and size up the employees. Then mask up, glove up—hit 'em hard and fast."

I'm no criminal mastermind, but I was shocked by how possible it seemed, and worse—how planning it was kind of exhilarating.

"Well, Mr Writer," Shane smiled. "Using that imagination for more than just stories."

***

The Rifleman was a graveyard at two in the afternoon. Daniel and Sophie were behind the bar and Chiara sat at a table with a book. I crept in behind Shane, gathering my courage to show myself. The three of them gawked at my beat-up face as I dropped onto a stool.

"My God," Daniel said to Shane. "What have you got the man into?"

Both Sophie and Chiara stared, open-mouthed.

"Who, the Yank?" Shane laughed. "Why he's the terror of Oxford Street. I wouldn't worry about him. Any messages, Danny?"

Daniel scowled and gave a single nod. "That mumbling moron, Stumpy, phoned for you an hour ago."

"It's as if he could read my mind," Shane smiled. "I'm off to make a call, get us a round."

He set some cash on the bar and sauntered to the backroom. I scanned the pub, trying to ignore the three of them staring—especially Sophie. A few pensioners sat quietly at the far end of the bar, with a couple more scattered about in the booths.

"Are you okay?" Daniel asked.

"Honestly, I'm fine." I said, ignoring the new pain in my shoulder.

"Yes, you're a vision of health," he snorted.

Chiara stood next to me. "What happened? Are Kieran and the others okay?"

Her asking about Kieran first made me smile. "He's fine. They're a little bruised up too, but they're okay. It was just a misunderstanding with another group—stupid male bullshit."

Chiara seemed convinced, but Daniel and Sophie weren't buying it. Sophie raised an eyebrow as she finished filling my beer. Daniel shook his head. "Watch yourself."

"I will."

"Hmm," he grunted. "I'm going for a fag."

Daniel grumbled to himself all the way out the front door. Chiara gave my arm a pat and returned to her table and book. I sipped my beer as Sophie crossed her arms and stared at me—through me. "You're in it now," she said.

"I can handle myself, thank you."

"Clearly," Sophie rolled her crystal blue eyes. "We're used to seeing the boys come in banged up, but I've never seen an idiot purposely put himself into a lifestyle like that."

Was this flirting? I can never tell. "I didn't know you cared so much about my wellbeing."

"I know writers are imaginative," she laughed. "But you're taking too much creative liberty."

I smiled my goofy grin. "Look at us banter—the back-and-forth."

She groaned, trying not to smile. "So stupid."

It really seemed like we were flirting. Then I noticed the white binder on the back bar. "What about you, huh? I saw you pass that binder off to Shane yesterday."

Sophie's smile faded. "Like the boys, some of us don't have a choice," she said, as Shane returned, looking at his phone. She leaned close, lowering her voice. "He's a blackhole. He will pull you in, and there's no climbing out. Get away while you can."

"Sophie," Shane called. She spun around to face him. "Pour us a pint, love." His eyes still on his phone. "Luke—table. We need to talk."

Sophie's blue eyes lingered on mine for a second before she grabbed a glass. I took my pint and sat down at the corner table. Afternoon light fought through the layer of dust coating the high windows. I ran my hand across the faded gloss finish of Shane's table. So much had happened over the last twenty-four hours since I'd sat there—so much to write about. Like, what the hell was Sophie being forced to do with that binder?

After a few minutes of daydreaming, the boys burst into the pub and beckoned me to the bar. King, their veteran commander, stood among them relatively unscathed. A raised bruise on his cheek and a dashing cut through his eyebrow. He smiled his gap tooth at me when we shook hands. "Roadman!" he laughed. "A goddamn pit bull! You was right about that, bruv."

Sophie glared at me, so I tried steering the guys away from the bar, but it didn't work. "Ha, unfortunately I was," I said, feeling my face get hot.

We all looked a bit ragged, except for Llanzo, with a few knicks on his knuckles. Ibrahim wore big *Dulce & Gabbana* sunglasses to cover his bruised face. Kieran threw his arm around Ibrahim's neck and dragged him to me. "Brahim g-got it the worst, look 'ere Luke," his speech slurred through his busted lip. "Sh-show him, Brahim. Don't be bashful, mate."

Ibrahim begrudgingly removed the glasses to reveal deep purpling around both eyes. He looked like a racoon that had been hit by a car. "Oh, man," I said. "I'm sure it'll clear up in no time."

It didn't.

When the boys got their drinks, and Kieran stole a couple minutes with Chiara, we all settled down at the corner table. Shane rolled up his sleeves to reveal his tattooed forearms and regarded his sprawl of misfits. "Well done, lads. You fought hard and held your ground. Showed Charlie's lot your true mettle."

Despite the praise, I sensed something was brewing—and with me in mind. "Had a meeting with Charlie earlier," he said. "She and I came to an agreement. Our crew will now be able to sell at Club Soho and The Roxy unmolested by her people. For the time being, we're now in alliance with Charlie and her crew. While she expands her legitimate business, we will start selling product in her territories of London."

Furrowed expressions spread across the bruised faces at the table. "Shane, this all sounds Gucci," King said. "But I don't like that Profit mandem. Can't trust him, fam."

"I understand, but there's more," Shane said. "In return for giving us room to sell, we've been given a task to do for Charlie, which will take some careful planning."

"A task?" Ibrahim asked. "Cooking and tidying up her flat?"

The boys chuckled, except for Shane, who cleared his throat, cuing the table's silence. "Her shop in Camden Town—near the markets—there's a rival shop across the street with a cheeky little operation that's cutting into her profits. She wants it stamped out."

King spun his pinky ring. "She can't use her own people?"

"It could start a war," Shane said. "However, we're unknown in Camden and the men who run the shop won't have time to react," he looked at me. *"Hit 'em hard and fast,* as they say."

A cloud must have slid over the pub because the moment my words left Shane's mouth, the light that fought through the dirty windows died across our table. What have I gotten myself into?

Shane explained how we'd ransack that shop in Camden Town. King would lead us and I would help plan an attack. The boys approved of my promotion by giving me a smile or a pat on the back. Although I was nervous about my involvement, I remembered smashing glass bottles against the Food Lion dumpster. Wanting to chuck phonebooth vases into the Guinness mirror, and shatter Ms Smith's modern clock. Before I knew it, I was already planning our attack in my head.

Sophie believed I had a choice and should get out while I could. But sitting at the table with those guys—my new friends, I realized I didn't have a choice. If it weren't that dodgy little pub in Catford, it would have been another one.

"I'll get the next round, boys," I excused myself from the table.

Behind the bar, Sophie packed the white binder into her oversized purse. When I strutted over, she gave me a look like, *what the hell do you want?*

"Yorkshire," I said. "Like the pudding. Or the tea."

"Wrong again, but closer than bloody New Castle," she said, pulling on her jacket. "I'm off now. If you want another beer, ask Daniel."

I looked at my table, trying to think fast. "Do you want to come hang out with us for a bit? I'll buy you a shift beer."

She darted her blue eyes over to Shane and laughed. I was just about to compliment her pretty teeth when she shook her head. "Absolutely not. But you have fun. I've got to pick up my daughter." She slipped from behind the bar.

"Well, I'll see you later," I called out after her.

Sophie walked to the front door and threw up a hand without looking back. As the front door shut behind her and her silhouette passed by the front windows, what she said finally sunk in.

Wait a second—Sophie's a mom?

Chapter 17

Just as my new friend Heath predicted, I discovered an apology email from Ms Smith when I returned to my flat that evening. She CC'ed a man in to the email—let's call him Mr Doe. He was the head of my creative writing program and a notorious hard-ass.

Although her email contained familiar keywords found in apologies like, *heartfelt sincerity* and *deepest regret*, there was a line I didn't quite understand:

> *...I have asked that Mr Doe audit our next few class sessions in a strictly observational role, in the hopes of procuring vital feedback on my teaching methods...*

Was she afraid to be alone in a room with me? The shouty, suicidal guy with questionable extracurricular activities. Exhausted, achy—and a little drunk—I grew angrier each time I reread the email. So, I replied to them both, thanking her for her apology and asked:

> *Is Mr Doe the guy on the website who's heavyset with rosacea or the one with bird lips and a giant mole on his forehead? Guess I'll find out next week.*
> *Thanks, Luke*

If they were going to treat me like I was crazy and unpredictable then I didn't want to disappoint them. Tomorrow, I had an afternoon class on novel settings, so I cracked another beer and sat in the kitchen and thought about Sophie. God, I really am a therapist's wet dream. The dude with mommy issues was enamored with a young mother who wants nothing to do with him.

Practically textbook.

I decided to go to bed when the Latvians made a rare kitchen appearance. The girl, Estere, shuffled into the kitchen wearing a towel and slammed pots around like an ape who'd just discovered tools. Meanwhile, Juris wandered in wearing only a large t-shirt. The tip of his uncircumcised penis swung like a pendulum just below the hem.

"What happen your face?" He bent over to look in the fridge.

I sucked beer into my windpipe. "Tripped and fell," I croaked through a string of coughs.

I bolted from the kitchen into my room. *Focus, Luke.* No more emails, no more Sophie, no more Latvians—just school and Camden Town. I collapsed onto my bed and opened my notebook and wrote: *Camden Town To-Do List.*

Under that I wrote, *Go to Camden Town.* I needed to see this shop for myself to know how to start. Soon enough I got sleepy and found myself fantasizing about Sophie. What would it be like to look into her crystal blue eyes and not see annoyance? To hear her laugh with me, instead of at me. As my room grew dark and the aches in my body faded, I felt warm. Held tight in the arms of a fantasy, I fell into a deep sleep.

***

The next morning, I discovered it was the first time in a week I wasn't hungover. So, I made bacon and eggs, and drank an entire

French press of coffee—all without seeing one naked Latvian. I left for class feeling very sore, but altogether refreshed.

It was early October in London, and the trees that lined the streets had exploded overnight into oranges, reds and yellows. I zipped up my blue bomber to combat the cool breeze rushing off the Thames. I decided to pretend that day one never happened; the hangover, my outburst, the gangster meeting—day two was my blank slate.

The professor for my settings class, Mr MacDougall, was a handsome man with dimples and a jaw that could have been chiseled by Michelangelo. He also had a charming dash of a Scottish accent to top it off. He talked about settings and the novels we'd read in the class, and things went well until he stopped abruptly and said, "Let's talk about Paris."

"No!" I said.

Everyone looked at me. "No?" MacDougall smirked. "You don't want to talk about Paris?"

"I meant—*no way*. I love Paris," I chuckled. "Carry on."

Can I go one damn day without being reminded of Paris? I seemed incapable of escaping that city. People shared favorite Paris moments and how it's been used as a setting for novels— romance, memoir and comedy. I nearly suggested true crime, but decided that was too dark.

I tuned out of the conversation to think about Camden Town. The weather was nice and it would be a good idea to begin planning for Shane. Just before I completely zoned out, MacDougall said the term "stake out," which caught my ear.

He discussed Georges Perec's novel *An Attempt at Exhausting a Place in Paris*. Perec sat in a Paris café and wrote down everything he observed in the street. That was the entire novel. No plot, no characters—all setting. Before Mr MacDougall could assign us the same task, I decided I should attempt the same thing—to exhaust a place in Camden Town. I thrust my hand into the air to volunteer to turn in my observations for our workshop. MacDougall was excited to see me excited, and I was excited because I was killing two birds with one stone: bang out my first assignment and conspire to commit a crime.

***

After class, I trekked to Camden and snagged Perec's novel from a Waterstones on the way. Camden Town High Street was elbow-to-elbow with tourists coming and going from souvenir shops and clothing boutiques. By chance, I stopped to lean on a post box to observe my surroundings, and I discovered I was standing in front of Charlie's shop. A clothing store named Wicked.

It was sandwiched between a pub and a shabby currency exchange. There were mannequins in the window, donning oversized hoodies, shredded jeans and bulky sneakers in gaudy neon colors. *Underground Fashions by London's Hottest Designers* was printed across the glass in goofy-ass font. Although I doubted the veracity of that statement, Charlie's store was packed with tweens rifling through the racks.

So, if this is Charlie's shop, I thought, the place we're supposed to hit was across the street. I spun around to find a souvenir shop with a giant garage door opening. It sold tacky London trinkets, cheap sweatshirts with glittery Union Jacks, and racks of key chains and coffee mugs were rolled onto the sidewalk to entice passersby.

This is what we're making such a big deal over? I lit a smoke and confirmed my texts from Shane. The place was aptly called Chaos, and not only did it sell cheap souvenirs, it offered a variety of services, like phone and computer repairs, tattoos and piercing, and my personal favorite—palm reading.

Chuckling, I went inside for a closer look. Airbrushed t-shirts filled the shelves, hippy tapestries hung on the walls, with glass cases packed with pipes and bongs. All Chaos needed was a stack of Confederate Flag beach towels and it would have fit perfectly in redneck Myrtle Beach, South Carolina. A few employees huddled behind the front counter, watching what sounded like porn on one of their phones. They were all brown dudes, maybe Pakistani, and seemed relatively normal to me— all except one.

One guy stood off to the side, about my height, but with broad shoulders. He had thick black hair and a sculpted beard. He wore a black cashmere sweater and gray slacks with a gold Gucci belt. Boss Man—he ran the show.

He glared at me while I perused plastic Big Bens and Prince Charles masks, so I decided to buy a stack of London postcards to get him off my back. Five pounds later, I stepped outside to discover all my postcard photos looked to have been taken in the 1980s.

What was Charlie's issue? Chaos was a shithole and hardly competition for the "high end" apparel sold at Wicked. I stopped into Buck's Head pub next door to Charlie's shop and sat at a window table with a beer to observe Chaos and the high street while I read my Perec novel. By my third beer I dug out my notebook and began jotting down the things I observed:

Camden Town High Street, 4:47 PM.
White van parked illegally—flashers on. Bike chained to sign post; front basket askew. Father pushing empty stroller, toddler lagging behind—picks up discarded pink lighter. Dude with mohawk holding hand of girl with green hair. Cop car passes, silhouette in backseat. Chalk Farm 27 bus; old lady in window makes brief eye contact with me. A man in blue windbreaker, shoelace untied. Woman in yellow cardigan texting, nearly trips over man tying shoelace. Tall black kid runs across street, scares group of girls, they all laugh, group goes into Chaos.

My observations went on like that for some time, until I thought about Sophie again. I wondered who her daughter's father was, and if he was still in the picture? Camden slipped by my window as I daydreamed, until I clocked a pattern across the street. I narrowed in on two youths, an Arab kid with a red hoodie and a white kid with a black hoodie. They skulked in front of an abandoned storefront a few shops away from Chaos. Questionable characters were always putzing around the Camden High Street, but these two looked particularly suspicious.

After a few seconds I realized they were propositioning passersby, mostly younger males. And it wasn't long before they stopped a trio of guys in their early twenties. They talked for a minute, until the white kid pulled something out of his hoodie to show the trio, while the Arab kid kept watch of the street.

Holy shit, a drug deal in broad daylight. The three customers paid the two youths and, as quickly as it began, the trio merged back into the masses of unaware pedestrians, leaving the dealers in front of the abandoned shop.

It was incredible. I watched the pair make four more sales in only thirty minutes. I felt like a National Geographic photographer observing a kind of urban food chain. Just as I was about to get another beer, the food chain went a link higher, and I discovered why I was there in the first place.

The white kid handed his cash over to the Arab kid, who then ambled down the street and disappeared into Chaos.

Chaos was a front.

My knowledge of "fronts" came entirely from movies but it had all the telltale signs. A shitty store hocking useless tchotchkes in mostly cash transactions, with a Gucci-clad Boss Man who looked too clean, mean and out of place. I scribbled what I'd observed into my Camden notes and by the time I looked up, the Arab kid had returned to the abandoned shop and the process began again.

Over the next couple weeks, I discovered Chaos employed nine different youth dealers, working in shifts along the high street. They sold in front of KFC, in front of the Two Feet shoe store, and a BDSM shop, Heather's Leather. And one time, when I was out smoking, I saw two dealers waltz into a Pret A Manger and sell to some teens having coffee. Chaos had a simple, but effective, operation and business was booming.

No wonder Charlie wanted them dealt with.

Chapter 18

By the end of my two-week stakeout, I had collected pages of notes for Mr MacDougall's workshop. He praised my observations and found my focus on the criminal underbelly of the high street "particularly interesting." Shane was also eager to hear my findings, so we met at an American bar in Fitzrovia called Yank Tank, to discuss our next steps.

Between class and Camden Town, I hadn't spent much time at The Rifleman so I was a little disappointed when only Shane and King showed up to Yank Tank.

"Just us three?" I said.

"Best to keep it light for the planning stages," he said, gawping at the bar. "Is this where we're going?"

The place was a dive, with a bunch of Philadelphia team banners on the walls and five massive TVs blaring football. "Google said they've got Philly Cheesesteaks and good American beer," I said.

Shane laughed, "No such thing as *good* American beer."

The three of us sat down at the bar, where I discovered my Carolina Panthers were playing against the Philadelphia Eagles on the TV. I bought us a round of Boston Lager, which to my surprise, Shane didn't hate. He drank and silently read my Camden notes while I explained the rules of American Football to King. And when our beers got low, I called the bartender over. "Hey man, can we get another round—yes!" I cheered, seeing the Panthers score.

The American bartender was chunky and probably in his late thirties. "Panthers fan?" he scowled.

"Yeah, bro. I'm from North Carolina."

"Damn," he scratched his man boob. "You might be the first country boy—or redneck—we've had in this bar." His stomach bounced as he laughed. "Not many southerners make it across the Atlantic, I guess."

Maybe it shouldn't have pissed me off, but it did. I wanted to smack that sweat-stained Phillies hat off his head, but I was there on business and I needed to stay cool.

"These notes are thorough, mate," Shane said. "The bastards at Chaos are running quite an operation. Are these tally marks the number of deals you counted?"

"The ones I saw for myself, yeah."

King flitted his fingers as he silently counted. "Depending on what they're shotting, could be twenty to forty pounds per sale—look at that. Wednesday alone could have been up to three thousand pounds. They're moving mad food."

King's quick math made me wonder why he wasn't in school, but the bartender returned with our beers, and when he got to me, said, "Surprised you're drinking Sam. Would have thought you'd go for something a little more southern, like Budweiser." He put a hand on the Bud tap. "We get Busch Light in here too sometimes—NASCAR beer!" He laughed at his own joke.

Before I could tell him to kiss my ass, Shane lasered in on him. "Maybe it's because I'm English, but what would you imagine a southerner to drink? Homemade moonshine? A six pack in the car park?"

The barman's smile faded. "I was just being funny. You know, southerners and stereotypes."

Shane glared with his piercing green eyes. "Since I'm unfamiliar with the stereotype, I'm forced to take what you've said to my friend as an insult. Do we look like people you want to insult?"

The smile washed from the barman's face, finally realizing we were not in a playful mood. The three of us stared at him, waiting for another stupid comment.

"Sorry, it was meant as a joke," he said to me.

"Your job isn't to tell jokes. It's to serve beer," Shane volleyed back. "Learn your place, mate."

There's nothing more soul-crushing than a quick-witted insult from a snarky English person. The poor slob just stood there, eyes darting for something to do or clean until he turned and slipped into the back room.

"Fuckinell, Shane!" King burst into laughter. "Think he's gone to the cellar to hang himself."

I felt a little bad, but King made me laugh. I'd probably hang myself too if a British gangster told me to *know my place*. Shane held up my notes, "Back to the task at hand, lads."

We hammered out the details of our fledgling plan. Shane's driver friend, Stumpy, would drop off the four boys a few blocks from Chaos where Shane knew a CCTV blind spot on the high street. The boys would destroy Chaos while Stumpy drove to the rear of the shop, on a tiny street called Early Mews. This would be pick-up spot A.

"But if something goes wrong, the boys will need an alternate pick-up spot," I said.

We huddled over the map on my phone and found a park a few blocks north of the Camden Lock, called Castlehaven Community Park. "Right here," King pointed. "We'll meet at the north end of the park. It's close, but far enough to shake anyone who'd follow."

Shane tongued at his missing canine with a glint in his eye. "This is good, lads. Get us another pint, yeah? I'll phone Stump to find a vehicle."

Shane went outside and I found myself smiling, thinking about our plan. Yeah, it was scummy, but oddly, I was having fun.

"What's with you, fam?" King showed the gap in his teeth.

"It's kind of like putting a puzzle together."

"Pfft," he finished off his beer. "But I'm just a piece of that puzzle, mate. You get to sit back while *we* get up to the madness."

King smiled as he spoke, but there was a weight in his voice when referring to himself as a puzzle piece. He had a point too. I didn't have to be in Camden while it all went down. I'd be safe at home or The Rifleman. King held up three fingers to the bartender who returned, un-hanged, from the cellar. The man sighed and grabbed glasses for our next round.

"King, you're a smart dude. Ever think about going to university?"

King laughed. "Schoolin' was never for me. Too distracted by football—and girls."

"Soccer," I said with a nod. "Did you play a lot—were you any good?"

King's eyes went wide. "Was I bloody good? I was a forward on the Chelsea Youth League, mate!" he said. But a somber veil draped over him. "Until I proper shredded my ACL. Career ended before it started."

The bartender set three fresh beers down. By the time I finished paying, King had a glassy, faraway look in his eyes.

"You're young, bro," I slid him a beer. "Athletes tear their ACLs all the time and bounce back. I'm sure you could get it worked on and get back to where you were."

King nodded. "Loosely that's always been the plan. Shane knows a geezer who does therapy for Tottenham. He promised to get me in with him. But if I'm being honest—"

Before King could continue, Shane returned. "Stumpy's keen to drive. He'll find us a van, and we'll brief him on the plan. And to top it off—we landed on a go-date—Halloween night." Shane gave a devious grin.

"Spooky," I said. "Why Halloween?"

"Camden will be mad on Halloween," King said. "It'll be chaos."

Cheers for the wordplay. I ignored the Panthers fumbling the ball on TV and raised my glass. "I guess it's all coming together."

King clinked glasses with me, but Shane just put a hand on my shoulder. "All except one final piece, I'm afraid. We'll need a lookout. And since you're the most acquainted with Camden and Chaos, I want you to be there on the night."

Chapter 19

Camden Checklist

☒ All-Black Clothes
☒ Walkie talkie
☒ mask?
☒ get away driver
☐ motion sickness
    bands

Halloween came and I was a nervous wreck. Not only did I need to help commit a crime, but my writing was scheduled to be workshopped in Ms Smith's class that same morning. And because God hates me, Mr Doe had returned to audit our class again and was taking notes in the corner. I know it sounds crazy, but it felt like the mole on his forehead was looking at me.

Our workshop began with an awesome sci-fi piece from Audrey, a flawless excerpt from Bhavani's detective story, and three poems from Heath that left us in awe while Ms Smith read them aloud.

"Now, on to Luke's work," Ms Smith said. "A pacy piece about a gang-fight in Soho."

Shakily, I flipped open my notebook and regretted my choice in subject matter. I was relieved that Mr Doe had stepped out of the room, but then Heath volunteered to start the assault on my work. *Dammit, Heath! I liked you.*

His eyes darted across the pages in his hand and he smiled. "Luke, I really enjoyed reading this. It pulled me in straight away, and it was a rollercoaster to the end of the chapter. It's so over the top, and yet there's an authenticity in your prose that's convinced me this fight actually happened. It's a very fun piece of fiction."

My jaw trembled as I smiled. Heath liked my work? He then listed some of the things he thought I could improve, and

I happily wrote down every word. Other classmates joined in, giving me their good and bad feedback and for the first time in my life, I enjoyed being in a classroom. I didn't even give a shit when Mr Doe barged into the room while Bhavani complimented my dialogue.

I was proud of myself for not taking offense to the critical comments. I just nodded and wrote them down. If I wasn't hours away from committing a serious crime, I'd have thought I was maturing. I even laughed when Ms Smith described my protagonist as a lovable asshole. You hear that Mom and Bill? I am lovable.

Once the room paused in silence, so the tick of the modern clock was the only sound, an unfamiliar voice chimed in, "I do have a small issue with the piece."

It was the class mole, Mr Doe.

"It's the believability of the entire scenario," he said. "I find it hard to believe a London street gang would want anything to do with this American stranger. Especially when he seems incapable of doing anything right."

The jab at my intelligence stung, but moreover I was hurt. Up until this needle-dick, everyone had been so helpful. The silent seconds felt like ages until Bhavani huffed and turned in her seat to face Mr Doe. "But they didn't accept him at first," she said. "It wasn't until he stepped in and fought alongside them that they approved of him."

Hell yeah! She gave me a smile. Now I had two writing friends.

But Doe wasn't done. He shook his head. "These groups have a strict honor code. I don't think a single fight would guarantee his acceptance. My point is, if we have to debate the believability of the work, then the author has already lost credibility."

Heath came to my rescue and pretended to nod off to sleep as Mr Doe spoke, then jerking his head upward as if he'd jolted awake. Everyone at the table laughed, and instead of anger, I felt warm with affection.

Mr Doe's mole seemed to pulse with anger and he was silent for the remainder of the class. With the help of my new friends, my bad feeling had retreated. I took my time packing my things when we were dismissed, wanting to linger in the moment.

"What's everyone doing for Halloween?" Bhavani asked the table.

I didn't look up—I knew what I was doing.

"Hadn't planned on anything," Heath zipped up his bag. "Maybe watch a horror film."

"I always watch *Scream* on Halloween," Audrey said.

May, the annoying American chick, stopped at the head of table, her books held against her chest. "I'm going on a little pub crawl later with my flatmate. You're all welcome to join, if you'd like."

There were a few mutters of approval, but I knew the invitation wasn't for me, so I grabbed my bag for the door.

"What about you, Luke?" Heath asked.

"Uh, I don't want to impose."

"Oh, come on," Bhavani chimed in. "Just a couple drinks."

Heath and Bhavani seemed to be the only ones who wanted me there. I wouldn't be able to join them, but May annoyed me, and if I agreed then maybe she'd spend the whole night dreading my arrival.

"Where does this pub crawl start—what time?" I asked.

May sighed. "We'll meet up around nine o'clock at the Oxford Arms. Don't be late—we *will* leave without you."

"Sure, Oxford Arms—see you there."

"You better be, mate," Heath smiled. "I want to hear what happens to your character next."

"Probably nothing good!" I darted into the hallway.

There were two things I had dreaded doing that day, and I had completed one of them. Now I needed to focus on Camden Town. But by the time I passed by Madeleine's mural in Tottenham station, my bad feeling returned and twisted my stomach into a knot. The closer my train zoomed toward Catford, the more I worried about the plan and my involvement in the whole damn thing.

My walk to The Rifleman was clear blue skies with a slow crisp breeze at my back, which reminded me of a day when I was little and my folks took me to Fletcher Park in Raleigh. It was the first time I saw Bill hurt my mother. He brought his Pentax to attempt a family photo and they bickered about how the timer worked. When Mom reached for the camera, he snapped her wrist and she tumbled to the ground as the camera clicked away.

When I stepped inside The Rifleman, Sophie and Chiara jumped from behind the coatrack and yelled, "Boo!" with ghoulish paint on their faces, pale with dark circles around their eyes.

"Holy shit!" I clutched my chest. "Woman, what's a matter with you?"

Sophie rolled her crystal blue eyes at me. "Come off it. It's Halloween, innit?"

I felt bad for overreacting. "I know what day it is. Americans invented this holiday—right after we stole it from you guys." I tried smiling.

"You're highly strung today," she said, brushing past me. "'Cause of your silly boys club meeting in the office? Go on—they're waiting for you."

She heckled me some more, but I was too busy noticing how the gray face paint made her eyes sparkle. And how the white lipstick couldn't hide her plump bottom lip.

"You're pretty," I said.

Oh shit. Did I say that out loud?

Sophie touched her cheek. "The paint's supposed to be scary."

"It's scary how much I'm into it," I snorted.

Thought I could see her cheeks flush from under the face paint. "I have to go—to the cellar," she turned right, but stopped to go left.

Sophie beelined for the cellar and that's when I discovered the entire pub was decorated for Halloween. Fake cobwebs hung over top of the real ones. Flickering blacklights in the booth fixtures. A jack-o'-lantern on the front bar and a bubbling caldron on the back bar. The place looked awesome.

Chiara smiled. "You have a crush on her."

I knew my secret would be safe with her, but I switched topics. "Speaking of crushes, how's it going with Kieran?" I asked.

Chiara smiled as if she were in a beautiful place, far from The Rifleman. "Falling in love is like travel." Her words were so Italian they were practically sung. "The journey can be just as beautiful as the destination."

"Romance is a first language for you people, huh?"

I left Chiara in deep thought and made for the back hallway where Daniel was grumbling while he swept. "That bastard thinks he owns the place." He shook the broom at me. "But has he ever dusted, mopped or paid a bloody bill?"

"Everything okay, Daniel?"

He gave an almost smile. "I'll survive. How are you—how was your class?"

"It was good." I pointed to the office door. "But I'm running late, so I'll have to tell you about it later."

Poor Daniel. He was my best pal at The Rifleman, and not only did Shane commandeer his office, but I didn't have time to talk. Nevertheless, he stepped aside and gave a congenial smile. "I look forward to it."

The voices fell silent when I poked my head into the office. Five pairs of serious eyes locked onto me, but Shane and the boys smiled once they saw me. "What's up fellas?" I said.

The office was bigger than I expected, but with a low ceiling that made me feel like I needed to hunch over. There was a desk scattered with papers, a filing cabinet, and some kind of TV screen on my left. The boys absorbed the light in the room, dressed in ominous black, but they were in good spirits, albeit a little nervous—especially Kieran, who botched our handshake. Shane looked a cool breeze in a brown tweed blazer. He shook my hand, squeezing it a little hard.

"Glad to see you didn't get cold feet, mate," he said. "We're just going over everyone's roles once more. Putting bits and bobs in order."

The thought of going over the plan again bored me. "Sounds good, let's do—" I stopped abruptly, catching sight of the TV behind Llanzo.

It was a live shot of the pub's interior. The entire main room was visible from the bar to the front door. Sophie and Chiara were busy behind the bar, and Daniel swept between the tables. My shirt clung to my back with sweat.

Daniel knew I beat up that homeless guy.

He must have reviewed the footage. Oh God, and I had plenty of chances to tell him the truth. He just went on being my friend and letting me lie to him. Hell, he even invited me for a weekend in Bath with his family.

"Oi!" Shane said. "You stopped talking mid-sentence."

"I did?"

Ibrahim sniggered. "Seen my uncle do that when he had a stroke."

The boys laughed, but Shane rolled his eyes. "Focus, lads— let's start from the beginning."

The plan began with me leaving early to scope out Camden, then Stumpy would drop off the boys. I'd radio with an all-clear and the boys would do their worst to Chaos. Stumpy would pick them up from either A or B locations, and I'd bail for home. But as Shane talked, my mind raced back to Daniel. He'd been nothing but kind to me since I'd washed up at The Rifleman and how had I repaid him?

"Any questions?" Shane asked, pulling me back to the room.

Kieran put up his hand. "Shane, I'm sorry mate, I know this is a p-proper serious meetin', but I'm mad hungry, fam. A-Absolutely gaggin' for some KFC or somethin'."

We all burst into laughter and the tension dissipated. Not even Shane could stop from smiling. King shook his head and patted Kieran on the shoulder.

"Yes, Kier," Shane nodded. "We'll get some food before everything kicks off."

"Thank bloody 'ell," Kieran said, then turned to me, "Do you have KFC in America?"

The little office roared so loud with laughter I thought Daniel would come knocking. We were all in tears. Ibrahim laughed himself into a heap on the floor. "Kier, you eedyat," he said. "The K in KFC stands for Kentucky—it's a bloody state."

The meeting never recovered from that outburst, although we did cover some minor details, like how King and Llanzo were to be on the lookout for any hero bystanders who might intervene. And I was to keep a vigilant eye for any of the Chaos dealers that may show up to ambush the boys.

Meeting adjourned, the boys went for food, leaving me and Shane in the office. He scrawled into the white binder and I tossed my black clothes onto the desk. "All-black—as requested," I said.

"Let's hope they don't come in use."

"Yeah," I paused. "So, what's in that binder you and Sophie always pass back and forth?"

Shane gave a mischievous grin. "Do I ask you to read what's in your notebook?" he asked. "You're writing a hell of a chapter tonight, mate," he stood with a stretch. "Not many authors can say they've actually lived the stories they've written."

Ain't that the goddamn truth.

***

Everyone stared when I came into the pub dressed in all-black. Like when the black hat cowboy pushes through the saloon doors, regulars looked up from their pints and conversations trailed off. Even a game of darts paused in the corner. Sophie shook her head and went back to drying glasses. Daniel leaned against the bar, watching TV. Bath's rugby team, in their blue home kits, took the pitch against Exeter.

"Hey, Daniel," I said, in a tone much softer than I was dressed for.

He gave me a doubletake. Then, as if he didn't like what he saw, he looked back at the TV. "Out with the lads, I see?"

"Yeah—I just wanted to say I'm sorry."

"For?"

"For breaking your front door."

Daniel was quiet, but eventually smiled. "How was your class today?"

I hoped the topic change was his way of saying he forgave me. "I feel like I made real connections today with some of my classmates."

"That's excellent." He looked at me. "You know, those writers will be the ones you take with you for the rest of your life and career. It would be wise to cultivate those friendships."

"I never thought about it like that."

Daniel said in a whisper. "That lot you're with now, as interesting as they are—you're still a visitor in their world. And there's no future in *just visiting*." He looked at the TV as Exeter kicked off to Bath. "And whatever that wanker's got planned for tonight, you be careful. Look after those boys. They're tough, but that's all they are—boys."

I hoped my conversation with Daniel would relieve my conscience, not cloud it further. How could there be no future in the exact thing I was investing my future in? I went outside to think over a cigarette. The sun was low in the sky, and the makings of a blood red sunset clung to the chunky clouds drifting in the distance. Was a red sunset a good or bad omen? And why was everything good in one direction and bad in the other—always black or white and never gray. For once, I wanted a third choice—can I please have gray?

Halfway through my smoke, the boys returned from KFC and King sat next to me on the bench, handing me a takeaway bag and a Pepsi. "You know, Pepsi was invented in New Bern, North Carolina," I said.

King searched for something in his pocket. "I prefer Coke— if I'm being honest."

"Blasphemy."

King handed me a black piece of fabric. Printed on the cloth was a ghoulish face, but scarier than Sophie's Halloween makeup. The face had black pits for eyes and sharp fangs. Examining it, I realized it was a mask—a balaclava.

King's brown eyes were as spooky as the mask. "Got you a bally, mate—you know, just in case."

Chapter 20

KFC chicken ain't so tasty when you're sitting with a table of gangsters with a balaclava in your pocket. I managed a few bites, but spent most of dinner fighting back my nausea while the boys tucked in to their chicken. King sat next to me after dinner with a black Jansport backpack, the exact bag I had in fourth grade, and pulled out a silver walkie-talkie.

"It's got an earpiece to put in your ear," he said. "Just click this button to talk—channel two."

We powered on our walkies and when I clicked the call button, a loud burst of static went off in my ear. My walkie's power light flickered then died and the static went silent.

"Right, yeah, it does that." King smacked my walkie. The light flickered on and the static returned to my ear. "Just gotta give it a proper smack sometimes."

Nope. Didn't like that, but it's all we had. I shoved the walkie-talkie into my jacket and stood up unceremoniously and gave everyone a nod. Shane joined me outside for a cigarette.

"There's one more thing you should know." Shane's green eyes looked black in the early evening. "There's a small task I've asked the boys to do once they're inside Chaos. It won't take long, but it does raise the stakes. So be watchful."

"I swear to God, if you say it's murder..."

"Nothing of the sort." he laughed.

"Then I don't want to know anything about it."

Shane nodded and shook my hand. "Good luck, mate. You'll do great."

That's what I was afraid of—that I'd do great. After weeks of planning, I discovered I had a knack for less-than-legal kinds of work. Have you ever suspected in another life maybe you'd have made a good assassin, thief or baby seal clubber?

I set off for the train station, fiddling with the balaclava in my pocket until it felt damp with sweat. When I got to the station, there were a lot of grumbling people standing about. Pushing through the crowd, I discovered my seven o'clock train had been canceled.

Frantic, I called Shane and asked him what I should do. He was quiet for a moment as the commuters' grumbles grew louder around me. "Stay there, Luke," Shane finally said. "I need to make a call."

The phone clicked and I stood there like an idiot. Our schedule was busted—I wasn't going to have enough time to survey the Camden High Street. The station eventually cleared and I paced the sidewalk alone, chain-smoking cigarettes for forty-five agonizing minutes. Just as I was about to call Shane again, a white windowless Ford Transit van screeched to a halt in front of me. A man with salt and pepper tangles of hair stuck his head out the window and called out to me in gibberish, "Awritetheremate—whetsyername?"

"Huh?"

"What's *yer name*, ya daft cunt?" he said in a thick Scottish accent. He turned to someone in the back of the van. "Have we got the right Yank, lads?"

King's head popped into the front seat. "Yeah, that's him—come round the back, fam."

Stumpy, the seemingly insane Scotsman, had come early to take us to Camden Town. I opened the back double doors and a wave of rap music spilled into the street. The van's interior had been stripped, save for two parallel benches running front to back, where the four boys stared at me in all-black. A Bluetooth speaker blared Dizzee Rascal from Kieran's lap. Christ, they looked scary.

I was settling into the van when Stumpy rocketed us around a corner, sending me tumbling into a heap at the boys' feet. They all laughed but helped me up. "Ay, don't tell me that was the Yank!" Stumpy cackled. "Be awful hard to find another one at this hour!"

I stuck my head through the shoddy plywood barrier into the front seat and watched Stumpy drive. That's when I realized how he got his name. He was missing his middle, ring and pinky fingers on his gear-shifting hand. Ibrahim whispered that he lost them while freelance bombmaking in the eighties. It didn't stop him from flying through the gears, lurching the van over curbs and scraping past lampposts. My stomach began to lose its fortitude.

"Hey, uh—Mr Stumpy," I said. "Any way we could tone down the speed?"

"Feeling a wee bit peely wally?" he called over his shoulder.

"Yeah, sure."

"Hm," he said, then burst into wheezing laughter. "Do your worst, lad! I'm burning the van at the end of the night!"

"Gee, thanks!" I sat back onto the bench.

Twice—that's how many times I opened the back door to puke into the road during our forty-minute descent into hell. By the time the van rocked to a stop on Camden High Street, Kieran had also thrown up his KFC dinner from the side door of the van. The other three guys pushed themselves as far away from us as possible. I shoved open the back door, as cool air rushed into the van, churning up the vomit smell. I stumbled onto the pavement, desperate for a cigarette.

We were parked under the sterile white glow of a Superdrug, and people skirted past me along the high street. I finally got my bearings seeing the red brick of the Camden Town underground, which looked like an old fire station. At that moment, a drunk Boris Johnson, complete with a disheveled blond wig, staggered past me. Through the horrors of my journey, I'd forgotten it was Halloween.

Go-time was less than an hour away, so I powerwalked north toward Chaos, clutching the balaclava tight in my pocket.

Masked people filled the sidewalk. A handful of Spidermans, two Jokers, even a Donald Trump, and hundreds of football jerseys. Every pub along the way was packed with drinkers. Who knew the UK did Halloween like this?

I turned my radio on when I saw Chaos in the distance, stepping off the curb to allow the Spice Girls to pass by me. "Guys—can you hear me?" I called over the radio. "This is uh—*pit bull*." I probably should have chosen a more imposing American call sign, like bald eagle or student loan debt.

"Pit bull sounds *aboot* right!" Stumpy chuckled in my earpiece. "Me mate's pit bull likes to boak in the backseat too!"

I heard King laughing. "Oi, pit bull—you alright, roadman?"

"Yeah," I said. "I'm almost at my position. Just wanted to test the radio. I'll call back with any developments."

"Do that, fam," King said. "Lates."

The radio went silent, save for the buzz of the empty channel in my ear. Alone on a crowded sidewalk, that little radio was now my only tether to the guys, since Shane collected their phones in Catford. I planted myself in front of the Buck's Head, the pub where I'd observed Chaos for weeks. The pub was crowded, with condensation on the windows. I lit a cigarette and listened to the murmur of people inside and the banter flowing by me on the pavement. All those people were enjoying their night and none of them knew what was about to happen.

I was startled by a loud knock at the window behind me. I spun around to see it wasn't coming from the pub, but from Charlie's store next door. Her shop was dark, save for a purple neon glow of the words *Wicked* on the back wall inside. My eyes adjusted and staring back at me from between the mannequins was Profit.

My heart thudded in my chest. Profit scared me and pissed me off simultaneously, and I never knew whether to hit him or run away. The front door swung open and he stepped out onto the sidewalk, glaring at me with those dark circles around his eyes. He wore a bulky black puffer, and coupled with his height, it made him a very intimidating presence.

"Yo, wasteman," Profit called out. "What ya doin' muckin' about? You got work to do for me tonight."

I tried playing it cool by lighting a cigarette. "Didn't know I was going to have an audience."

Through my lighter flame, I watched him look across the street to Chaos. He licked his bottom lip, as if his appetite for something wicked had swelled. "Not an audience, blud. A witness—to make sure you pussios do your job." Profit snarled at me, showing a glittery mouthful of bloodred gems in his teeth. "And if you don't do your job, you get fired." He pointed a finger gun at me, and laughed like a hyena.

I flicked my cigarette at his feet and walked away. With a half hour to go, I needed to focus on Chaos, and not get drawn into some altercation with Profit. Watching the store, I saw two familiar dealers—a skinny black kid and a skinny white kid. I was relived it wasn't the Arab kid and taller white kid—of all the Chaos dealers I had observed, they looked the toughest.

The skinny dealers shared a bag of gummy bears as they crossed the street into Chaos. The crowd became more grownup as the clock ticked. Three adult Harry Potter's and two Iron Man's later, the two skinny dealers left Chaos, heading north for the canal. I called on the radio. "Fifteen 'til go-time. Only two dealers on for the night." My voice was tinny and delayed.

There was a crackle of fuzz over the line, "Copy that, pit bull," King said. "Moving that way. Keep us updated."

Another group of Spice Girls passed by Chaos. An ambulance siren in the distance, or was it police? UK sirens confused me. A drunk group of white dudes, too cool for costumes, catcalled the Spice Girls. Distant rap music from somewhere carried across the cool breeze. Finally, I saw the Chaos Boss Man step out onto the sidewalk. I recognized his broad shoulders, long beard, and that gold Gucci belt. He surveyed the street as if he owned it. Like Profit, that guy made me nervous too. He wasn't going to take our plan lightly. I needed to be vigilant in monitoring him.

After a moment, Boss Man stuck his chin in the air and strode south. Bingo! I clicked my radio button and there was a long delay. "Boss Man has left," I said. "I repeat, Boss Man has left the building and is walking south."

There was a crackle of fuzz then Stumpy's distorted voice, " — good. Two minutes from our drop off."

Then an even longer delay before I could say, "You've got the all-clear. Stay on the radio for updates."

Eventually I caught sight of the white van chugging up the street. The butterflies in my stomach gave way to what felt like a swarm of bees when the van stopped in front of the Superdrug — the CCTV dead zone. As quickly as it stopped, the van continued north toward me. The pharmacy had closed for the night and the boys would wait there until Stumpy gave notice. The van followed the flow of cars toward the canal, a Chalk Farm bus whined closely behind it.

Stumpy glanced my way as he passed but made no gestures or nods. A crowd of people slipped between us, and when they dispersed, the van was gone. Just when I thought I would throw up again, a sharp crackle came over the radio and through the garble Stumpy said, "Position A — all clear."

Go-time. The boys moved down the street in unison, pulling balaclavas over their faces. A black mass surging across the pavement. There was another TAP-TAP-TAP behind me. I had drifted in front of Charlie's shop and Profit stared at me through the glass. Four more faces of Profit's cronies emerged from the darkened store as they gnashed their gemstone teeth at me. The details of their eyes were lost, ghostly, in the night. A group of passing girls shrieked seeing them, then giggled, thinking it was all part of the Halloween fun.

I moved away from Profit's little shop of horrors like a fish upstream against the flow of drunk walkers. Stopping at a post box out of the way, I caught sight of another pub just a few shops down from Buck's Head. Its sign swung in the breeze — the Oxford Arms.

"No goddamn way!" I said, out loud. "This can't be happening."

My classmates were probably inside, while I stood out front as the lookout for a soon-to-be crime. Were there two Oxford Arms in London? Or was I just *that* unlucky? I backed away toward Charlie's shop, my radio earpiece dangling silently in my ear. I moved parallel with the boys across the street as they approached Chaos. No one seemed to notice four guys in ski masks. I stopped abruptly when I sensed a figure in my path. Profit.

My shoulders tensed as the street noises swelled — the hiss of another Chalk Farm bus, the jeers from the passing voices — everything made noise except the radio in my ear.

Profit's guys filed out of the store. They were the boys we roughed up in Soho. "Oh, come on, jackass," I said. "I need to focus —," the words barely left my mouth when I saw my boys enter Chaos.

They pulled out their clubs and started swinging. One of them clocked the rack of sunglasses at the entrance, which collapsed and toppled onto the pavement. Profit looked across the road. His cackling sounded like distant machine gun fire. I backed away from him in big strides toward the Oxford Arms, keeping an eye on Chaos.

And that's exactly what it was — chaos. Four dark figures reigning terror, like the horsemen of the apocalypse. Glass shattered with every club swing. Scared shoppers bolted from the shop into the street. People stopped on the sidewalk to watch the destruction. To film it with their phones.

Llanzo, big and broad, pushed the onlookers back, while Kieran smashed an entire shelf of glass bongs onto the floor. More gawkers stopped to watch, obstructing my view. One of the boys, maybe Ibrahim, clubbed a Chaos employee's legs until the man fled, limping down the street.

They'd been to work for mere seconds and the place was destroyed. Clothes and knickknacks scattered about, shelves tipped over and broken, even a few light fixtures dangled flickering from the ceiling. Meanwhile, the four horsemen loomed, dark and ominous in the bright store. It was like something from the last chapter of the Bible, or a nightmare. Or maybe it was that Johnny Cash song I'd heard a million times about a man going round taking names. *The one who decided who to free and who to blame.*

When I looked up, I was standing in front of the Oxford Arms. I could see people carrying on inside, but could they see me? The murmurs of onlookers pulled my attention back to Chaos and I saw Boss Man running down the sidewalk. Behind him were two familiar faces, the Arab kid and the white kid. I scrambled for my radio.

"King—get the hell out of there! You're gonna have company," I yelled, but the radio was silent. "Get out of the store. You've got three dudes coming up behind you!"

Something was wrong, there wasn't even static in my earpiece. I pulled the radio out and smacked it. The little light flickered, then went dark. Boss Man and his dealers closed in on Chaos.

Profit stepped to me. His lip curled over his jeweled teeth. I wanted to smack those fronts out of his mouth. *Focus, Luke!* I turned away from him and that's when I saw Heath's bearded face through the shifting crowd only twenty feet away. He'd just stepped out of the Oxford Arms to put on his coat. Bhavani was there too. She was talking to Audrey and May, who was dressed as Hermione from *Harry Potter*. I froze when she pointed past me to the Buck's Head.

Across the street, Boss Man and his dealers pushed through the crowd of onlookers at his shop. Warn the guys. Deal with Profit. Avoid my classmates. I couldn't figure out where to start. And to top it off, I couldn't remember that Johnny Cash line because Daniel's voice was in my head, telling me to take care of those boys.

Join my classmates or help my boys. Two paths laid before me while Daniel's words waged war in my head. Always black or white, never gray. I locked eyes with Heath through a brief opening in the crowd. There was a glimmer of recognition in his eyes and the start of a smile before he was eclipsed by another group of walkers.

Feeling for the balaclava in my pocket, I chose my path. I turned my back on my classmates and yanked the mask onto my head. Profit's shit-eating sneer faded. Maybe he saw a hint of Bill's evil staring through the holes of my mask. I saw it in the mirror when I discovered Madeleine. Cash saw it when I nearly killed Rémy. Mom saw it long ago and that's why she loved her other kids more.

I was the man in black and I'd picked my side—the forgotten Johnny Cash line came screaming back; *and behold a pale horse, and his name that sat upon him was death.*

And hell followed with him.

I bolted into the street. My classmate's voices faded behind me, as if shut behind a door I'd never be able to open again.

Chapter 21

My Vans landed POCK-POCK-POCK on the pavement. Tunnel vision on the shop. There was a sudden blinding light and screeching tires as I slid across the hood of a hatchback. The breath of its engine hot on my thigh.

Full speed, I crashed through the crowd of people at the shop entrance and skidded to a halt on a patch of shattered glass. A dangling light flickered above me. *Baker Street* by Gerry Rafferty blasted on overhead speakers. Ibrahim and Kieran smashed TVs on the back wall, unaware two dealers headed for them, tossing aside debris along the way.

Where's King and Llanzo?

Adrenaline pumping, I slipped on the wreckage, clutching a clothes rack to keep from falling. A clatter to my right. Boss Man rummaged behind the till; his Gucci belt shimmered under the store lights. He stood up from the counter with a goddamn machete.

Don't think, just move. I launched for him from a heap of t-shirts. Boss Man looked up in time to see my demon mask descending upon him. I rammed my shoulder into his side. His head slammed into a shelf of Big Bens. I caught myself on a column. Searing pain shot through my shoulder as I struggled to breath.

Boss Man fell into a crumpled heap as blood streamed from his head. I stomped his hand to free the machete, a crunch of glass and finger bones. I tomahawked the blade into a gap of missing ceiling tiles. It landed with a faraway thud.

Kieran and Ibrahim! The two dealers were only feet away. My Vans squeaked in Boss Man's blood as I jumped over a shelf. A rack of incense caved under my weight. My clumsiness disguised by the badass sax solo of Baker Street. Like a pro wrestler, I dove from the shelf for the tall white kid. Wrapped my arms around his head and rode him to the floor. His knee bent wrong, with a sinewy snap. He shrieked until his head put a dent into the wall. He fell silent in a plume of drywall dust.

Pain zapped through my shoulder again. There was commotion above me as Ibrahim and Kieran kicked the shit out of the Arab kid, who collapsed into the fetal position.

The room spun as I stood. The crowd at the entrance encroached on us. Chaos employees had all returned and were climbing through the rubble. We needed to get the hell out of there.

"Where are the other two?" I yelled, not wanting to use names.

"Th-the booth!" Kieran shouted. His blue eyes bulged through his mask.

We scrambled over the debris to the back corner staircase that led to the tattoo parlor upstairs. Underneath those steps was a fortune teller booth, curtained like a church confessional. I yanked back the curtain, seeing Llanzo with his club pressed against the face of a tiny Pakistani man who was dressed as a fortune teller. Silk robes and a purple turban. King was crouched over an open safe and was stuffing stacks of cash into the Jansport backpack. This wasn't a vandalism job.

It was a goddamn robbery.

Ibrahim, forever the comic, skidded into the booth and spotted the fortune teller. "I think a real fortune teller would have seen this coming."

Maybe it was the adrenaline. Or anger love being kept in the dark about the heist—but I doubled over with laughter. We were so screwed.

The entrance was overrun. The crowd shouted as someone winged a souvenir plate at us. The red and blue blur of a porcelain Union Jack whizzed between Kieran and me, and smashed against the back wall.

"Pack it up faster, slick!" I dropped to my knees, helping King grab cash. A sea of Queen Elizabeths stared up at us, silently judging. More sounds of things shattering around us. And worse—sirens in the distance.

"M-m-mates!" Kieran called out. "We need to g-go!" He chucked a metal shelve like a spear. Someone returned fire. A pink shot glass shattered at Llanzo's feet. Finally, King jumped up with the bulking backpack, grinning his gap teeth through the mask hole. He and I slipped from the booth into the store as Ibrahim chucked a lava lamp into the crowd.

"Backdoor!" King tugged Llanzo and Kieran. The three of them bolted down the back corridor of the store while Ibrahim pelted people with porcelain coasters.

"Dude, let's go!" I yelled at him.

The crowd attacked us with a barrage of picture frames, drinking glasses, ashtrays—you name it. Ibrahim trailed behind me just as a goddamn coffee mug cracked him in the head.

Ibrahim howled, grabbing me for balance. "Fuckinell—a tea mug?"

"Come on, I got you!" I yanked him toward the back door as shit shattered along the narrow walls of the hall.

I pushed Ibrahim through the Chaos backdoor, just as some asshole got a lucky throw with a bong. It shattered on the door frame, sending shards of glass into my eye.

The world went dark as I crashed into Ibrahim and we toppled onto the back-alley pavement. Through the wet blur of either blood or sweat, I could see the silhouette of a dude sitting on a trashcan smoking a cigarette. He saw me too.

Llanzo pulled me and Ibrahim to our feet. The mews was quiet, save for distant sirens. No Stumpy, no van. Just the narrow canyon of grime covered brick. King and Kieran sprinted from the amber streetlight toward us. Behind them, the giant gate to the mews was closed. Our only way out.

"Stumpy had to move," King said, the radio in his hand. "The bloody gate's shut, fam. We need to get to pick up B."

There was a collective groan. Castlehaven Park was five minutes away at a full sprint. My Marlboro lungs burned at the thought.

Llanzo pushed a small dumpster against Chaos' backdoor. The angry crowd beat on the other side like a zombie movie. The boys finally noticed the guy sitting on the trash can a couple doors away too. Fake blond hair, an unfazed expression, artsy rings on every finger. He wore an apron that read *Nan's Tea Snug*.

"That door unlocked?" King pointed at *Nan's* door.

Trashcan guy nodded. Not giving a shit five dudes in balaclavas had encircled him.

"Cheers," King whipped open *Nan's* door.

We funneled inside after King. Ibrahim and I took up the rear, staggering through the trendy little tearoom. The herbal aroma hit me through my mask as we barreled down the corridor— colliding into glass shelves of porcelain pots.

Couples on dates, tourists on a girl's trip, shop employees— they screamed as our masked horde crashed through the shop. We knocked over tables and smashed tea sets bolting for the door. I thought about the construction workers and that glass panel. The bottles I used to fling at dumpsters.

King hit the front door hard, knocking it from its hinges. We all tumbled onto the sidewalk after him. A group of dudes jumped out of our way, shouting *woah*! My eye still burned and my vision was hazy. I dodged the crowds of walkers, not daring to look back at the sirens swooping down the high street. Déjà vu. My first night with the boys in Soho.

Shops blurred past as we darted after King, headed for the Camden Lock. Arms pumping, my breath was jungle hot in my mask. Halloween fun over. Only sirens and concerned onlookers. My vision narrowed on the back of Ibrahim's masked head. It was wet with blood.

A side stitch pulsed in my gut and my shoulder ached as I swung my arms to keep up. We crossed the bridge over the canal and thank God—the sidewalks thinned when we reached the railway bridge. Camden Lock painted in gold above us. The commotion of the night faded and the sirens became distant.

And that's when I heard it.

Footsteps pounding up behind me. Over my shoulder I saw Boss Man sprinting toward me. Blood gushed from his face—and Jesus Christ—he had the stride of an Olympian. He was closing the gap between us.

The harder I pumped, the more my shoulder clicked. My breath felt like fire in my throat. Just need—to get—to the park. But Boss Man neared closer, and on a quiet stretch of Chalk Farm Road, he caught me.

Betrayed by southern food, he tackled in front of a chicken and waffles joint. I landed with a THUD. My already-busted shoulder took the brunt, then my chin on the sidewalk.

Flash of white.

Things were foggy. Boss Man was on top of me, pinning my arms. His eyes were dark pools of hate. Blood dripped from his face onto mine. Ew. He punched my head with his broken hand. My brain went fuzzy. Things went dark as the street sounds muffled. Only the sound of my breathing and the thud of my heart. My vision returned, and sounds followed. Boss Man clutched at his hand in pain. It looked gnarled, twisted like vines. This was my chance to shake him off. Time for that wily, Luke whit!

So, I humped him from below.

Didn't work.

He jammed his elbow into my face. *Okay bro, I'm starting to get mad.* What's his goddamn deal anyway? Then I remembered the safe—the money. We just destroyed this guy's livelihood. He wasn't going to kick my ass.

Boss Man was going to *kill* me.

My scalp prickled with fear I'd never felt before. Death. He elbowed my head harder and grabbed at my face to unmask me, luchador style. My legs! Brain still foggy, I forgot I had legs. I kicked. I flailed. I dug my heels into the pavement to move and twist. My hands found his stomach. I hit him weakly in the gut and grabbed his Gucci belt. The buckle was undone.

I freed the belt from his beltloops. He elbowed me again, fighting to stay on top of me. Chicken and waffle employees watched from the windows. I twisted his Gucci belt around my hand and WHACK! I knocked the bastard in the head with his own belt buckle. He stopped, stunned. I did it again. WHACK! His skull sounded hollow in the quiet street. I did it again, and again.

Boss Man jumped off me. Blood poured from his head like I'd never seen before. I fought to stand, but he lunged for me. This time, I spun and fell on top of him.

"It's over, bro," I punched his face with a handful of Gucci belt.

Wobbling, I saw the boys running half a block away. Clueless to my plight. Boss Man faded but still grabbed my legs as I stood. Chicken and waffle people yelled at me from inside. I gave them the middle finger while Boss Man kept struggling to hold onto me. I thought of the glass bottles again. The glass panel and shattered tea pots. There's an art to destruction.

I raised my leg and stomped his face.

Oh, chill out, he didn't die. I checked the newspaper the next day. I stumbled down the sidewalk, desperate for breath. My speed reduced to a limping trot and I could hear the sirens again, only closer.

I tried swinging my arms but there was something wrong with my shoulder. It dangled at my side as I ran. The lights of the approaching park streaked into starburst flares ahead. I could feel I was just moments behind the boys, chasing their shadows. What do I do if I get left behind?

The street got residential and quiet. Just the sound of my shoes pounding the pavement as streetlights whooshed above me in a tired rhythm, set by my fading pace. The sirens were over the bridge now and heading my way. The fight with Boss Man cost me precious time. I would have to cut through Castlehaven Park instead of going around it.

At the park there were three little soccer pitches under the stadium lights. No sight of the van, but I spotted where I needed to go. Police lights danced against the buildings as they trolled along the west side of the park, while I ran along the east. Two of the three pitches had games going. Red versus blue, white versus black. The players stopped to watch me huff past like the dregs of a stampede. Most players just stared. But I heard a few laughs, cheering me on. *Fuck the feds, mate, run!*

I could see the two police cars. Their flashing lights ran parallel with me on the other side of the park, but they stopped moving. Tunnel vision on the sidewalk, which unfolded ceaselessly before me. Each step harder than my last. At the north end of the park was a church on Clarence Way. The stone bell tower rose into view above the high fences of the park. I dumped my last bit of energy into the fire. The church is where the van would be—if they hadn't left me.

Please, please be there, I begged God or whoever gave a shit to listen.

Running out of the park, the sirens moved north again to intercept me. My legs burned and my breath was ragged. I hurled myself around the corner to see the van.

Thank Christ, I pushed the words through my teeth.

Brake lights on. Engine puttering. I flung myself over a railing into the street for the van. Just as the back doors opened, the church bells rang high above me, marking the longest half hour of my goddamn life.

King materialized from the darkened van. "Come on, Luke— you've got it, fam!"

The van lurched forward. A moving target. The police lights neared the northern corner of the park. Their sirens reverberated against my body as I chased after the van. King put a foot on the back bumper and stuck out his hand while Llanzo, Kieran and Ibrahim anchored him. I'd either make the jump or miss and land in the street right in front of those cops. The church bell struck again as I leapt with the last of my energy.

King let go of the van, his faith in the boys. He clasped onto my wrist and yanked me into the van and I tumbled onto the metal floor, with a sharp jab of relief as my shoulder snapped back into place. My face pressed into the flooring, and the smell of my vomit from earlier greeted me like an old friend.

"Shut the bloody door, yeh cunts!" Stumpy yelled.

Llanzo slammed the doors shut just as the cops rounded the corner of the park. The two patrol cars screamed past us, sirens and lights blazing, and screeched around the next corner. It was their turn to chase a shadow.

PART II

Chapter 22

Stumpy parked the van in an ancient industrial complex along the Thames. I hobbled from the vehicle as the buildings of Canary Wharf bullied into my eyeline, with Central London glittering in the distance beyond. The boys left me with two big beers and a few Vicodin, both of which worked in communion to dull my aches. Stumpy sloshed petrol onto the floorboards and crevices of the van, and I beheld the process with an odd funeral reverence. A Ford prepped for the pyre.

Stumpy filled my empty beer with gas, stuffed it with a rag and handed it to me. Guess he knows a bottle breaker when he sees one. I lit the concoction and flung it, shattering into the van. Flames engulfed the vehicle, first blue then yellow. Black knuckles of smoke curled from the van, putting a burnt plastic taste in my mouth. And as I watched the Ford burn, felt the heat of its flames on my face, I had that strange feeling again that none of this was real.

And nothing I did mattered.

Deep breath, I rolled the burnt taste over my tongue and swallowed it down. Microscopic particles of the Ford forever with me. Embraced by the warmth of the flames, I felt free for the first time in my life and I decided never to question the process again. Shane was right—Camden Town was one hell of a chapter. Wherever this endeavor was headed, I wouldn't stop until I filled my pages. There was only one path now, and that was to write the rest of my story.

***

The boys stopped by my flat the next day with a sling for my shoulder and twenty more Vicodin.

They all sniggered at my face when I came outside to greet them.

"You gotta keep up with us, old man!" King dapped me up.

"I'm sorry, bruv," Ibrahim lowered his eyes. "If I'd have known, I'd have stopped to help."

"It's okay, man," I pointed to a cut over his eye. "That gash might be an improvement to your face."

"It's quite dashin' innit?" he smiled.

"It's something," I said, realizing we were down a man. "Hey—where's Llanzo?"

"Big man's at Uni," King said.

"He and B-Brahim study finance," Kieran said. "Gon' be millionaires, them two."

I nodded, impressed. "I thought you were a comedian?"

"I'll be on stage in a few weeks, actually," Ibrahim said. "You're invited."

King pointed at me. "And speaking of invited. We're having a kickback at Brahim and Llanzo's yard this weekend. We'll bun zoots, get faded. Gon' be some peng tings there—you gotta come through, fam." I had to Google *peng tings* later, but I accepted the invitation.

***

Later, I was jarred awake from an afternoon nap by a text from Shane. "Meet me outside your flat in 10 mins."

Outside, there was a brief break in the London gray and the sun warmed my face as I stepped out onto the front stoop. Shane leaned against his freshly-waxed Audi, wearing a charcoal suit with a red tie and pocket square. Weirdly, I was both happy to see him and instantly angry. You know, about unwittingly planning a robbery.

"You alright, mate?" he eyed my arm in the sling.

I nodded, then getting straight to the point, said, "So you kinda left me in the dark about the goddamn robbery. I'm digging the internship thing, and I'm getting a lot of great material, but I didn't appreciate walking into that."

"I understand your frustration, mate, but I didn't know if I could trust you yet. Clearly, you more than proved yourself."

"That guy almost killed me," I snorted. "He would have killed me. Had to stomp the poor bastard's face."

Shane looked around and pulled out an envelope from his jacket. "How's a grand and a half for your troubles?"

"Fifteen hundred pounds?" I snatched it from him. "I mean, shit, I didn't die, right?"

That big grin spread across his face. "No, you didn't."

"Last night was pretty high stakes," I said. "How'd you know I wouldn't mess it up?"

There was a glint in Shane's eye, like he savored how quickly I'd come around. "Let's just say, I've always had a keen eye for talent," he said. "Plus—you're handy in a pinch."

When Shane left, I felt proud of my story and the cash in my pocket. But mostly, I was proud I finally had his complete trust. With just a smidge of fatherly warmth, Shane could always pull you from the brink of desertion and back into the fold.

***

I was eating a sandwich in the kitchen later when Cash attempted a video call. I don't know why, but I panicked and stared at my phone until it stopped ringing. Cash was my best friend, but I'd been so busy doing sketchy shit with my new friends

I'd not been checking in as often as I should. I imagined his life had returned to normal, if not a little boring, ever since he'd returned to the States. But for me, every day in London was new and different, and I simply forgot to keep up with him.

While I wrestled with a wad of whole grain bread stuck to the roof of my mouth, he sent me a follow-up text. "Call me back, I've got some news."

In my experience, no news is good news, but I figured I should hear him out. I took my sling off, grabbed a beer and went to my room and killed the lights. I pulled my hoodie over my head so he couldn't see my bruised face and rang him back. He was walking down a busy sidewalk when he answered, sporting a fresh haircut.

"Nice, hood, Darth Luke," he chuckled. "How are you?"

"I'm good, man," I said. There were tall buildings over his shoulder. "Is that New York?"

"Good guess," Cash smiled. "That's why I called. Surprise—I landed a new consulting job up here—just signed a lease for an apartment this morning."

"Wow, that's sudden, but I guess I should say congratulations?" I realized if he moved to New York, then he would probably leave Emma behind. I smiled ear-to-ear. "When do you move up?"

"I fly home tomorrow to pack up the apartment, and Emma and I will drive up next week."

"Ah," I said, unable to mask my disappointment. "That's still a thing, huh?"

There was a slight pause where I thought maybe the video had frozen, but nope, I'd pissed him off. "I texted you a couple weeks ago to let you know the engagement was back on, but I never got a reply." He arched an eyebrow.

Shit. I remembered getting that text while I was in Betfred with the olive guy. I won £100 on a horse named Trident and went to The Rifleman to celebrate and forgot to text Cash back. "I meant to reply, but things have been busy here."

"No, I get it. Just wanted to keep you in the loop." We were quiet for a few seconds until he spoke up. "How's everything— the course, your writing? Been exploring?"

Maybe because of Emma or because I'm a shit friend, but I felt like antagonizing him. "Yeah, a lot of exploring. Lots of writing—and you won't believe this, but do you remember George?"

Cash frowned. "From Paris? What about him?"

"I got up with his cousin, Shane. Been hanging with him for some stories—inspiration. Lots of things to write about."

Cash stared at me, as if lost for words. "Luke, there's like nine million people in London to get stories from. I told you, you don't have to go find *those kinds* of people. You didn't tell him about Paris, did you?"

Okay, bad idea. "Did I tell him about Paris? Of course not."

"You told me not to tell anyone, not even my own fiancé," his voice was firm, teetering toward anger. "So, don't go getting drunk and blathering to strangers."

"Corey! I'm not an idiot."

Cash sighed and ran a hand through his expensive haircut. "I know you're not, but hanging out with George's cousin? That's bordering on self-destructive, brother."

I grit my teeth because he was making some damn good points. "Look, you're right. It is pretty dumb, but I'm making smart decisions and focusing on my schoolwork," I lied again. "Didn't mean to make this call stressful for you. Congrats on the job and the move—I mean it."

"*And* the engagement?"

"Yup." I gave a contorted smile.

"Right," he nodded. "Well, I'm in New York now—one flight away if you ever need anything."

Before we hung up, Cash mentioned the possibility of visiting for my birthday in the spring, which seemed far enough away for me to agree. Anything to get him off the phone and his pulpit. After we said goodbye, I took the last swig of my beer and felt the strong urge for more. Lying is thirsty work, and I decided to make for The Rifleman.

Chapter 23

It was early evening when I reached The Rifleman, and the last bit of sunshine added a rich orange glow to the forever dinge of Catford. A chilly breeze seeped through the fresh tear in the elbow of my bomber jacket, which looked as battle torn as I did. But this time I wasn't embarrassed to show up to the pub bruised. Both my scrapes and the £1500 in my pocket were well-earned.

A new front door had been installed on the pub. Instead of stained-glass, it had a thick frosted window and in the dull light, my reflection looked dark and distorted. Daniel must have seen the same, because he didn't greet me with his usual cheery, *hello my friend*, but a solemn, "Heavens," as he surveyed my damage.

Sophie was behind the bar and glanced up from her binder to give me her famous crystal blue eyeroll. When I couldn't think of an explanation for my face, I pointed to the IPA, "A pint, please, Daniel."

He opened his mouth to speak, but instead poured me a beer. I worried he saw me as a lost cause and would give up being my friend, but I should have known Daniel didn't believe in lost causes. I discreetly searched my giant wad of money for a tenner. Daniel didn't clock the stack of bills, but Sophie did. Daniel slung a rag over his shoulder and went to clear tables of glasses and crisp wrappers. Like a sixth sense, I looked at the corner table and met Shane's eyes over the top of his newspaper. He gave a nod hello.

"First time you've had dirty money in your pocket?" Sophie asked. "It's like you don't know how to hold it."

I shot her a look, feeling my face flush. "You know what the best thing to do with dirty money is, right? Spend it."

She smirked and shook her head. As someone who presumably worked with numbers and budgets, Sophie probably thought that was the stupidest thing to do with dirty money, but seeing her smile sent a surge of confidence through me. "Help me spend it—let me take you out some time. You're single, right?"

Sophie's mouth hung open. Her icy exterior came down briefly, and I caught a glimpse of the tenderness behind it. She liked me too—even if it was just a little. "You're mad—whoever gave you those bruises has knocked something loose in your head."

"Or knocked something into place."

She lifted her binder, as if to hit me. "Shall I knock you again?" There was a flirty tone in her voice not even Sophie could hide.

"Is that a no? You won't go out with me?"

"Will you bugger off if I say *maybe*? I'll think about it."

"Yes ma'am," I smiled so hard my face hurt. "Maybe ain't a no."

"You're very perceptive," she shooed me.

She opened her binder and her icy exterior went back up, but this time with a piece of me left inside. I sauntered over to Shane's table and sat down at my usual chair, grinning like every idiot with a crush does.

"You're in a good mood, mate."

"I am," I sipped my beer. His sleeves were rolled up and I saw the dagger tattooed on his forearm and the inscription *Put it in their heart, before they put it in your back*. Big yikes. But even that couldn't ruin my good mood. "I'm just eager to get to work. What do we have planned next?"

Shane beamed, like a proud dad. Or psycho uncle. "I'm glad to hear you say that," he said, folding his newspaper. "We've gained Charlie's trust with Camden Town. Now we build that trust as high as we can—that way it has further to fall."

That dagger tattoo was starting to make sense.

***

In Ms Smith's next class, I had a whole new set of stories to go with my new bruises. And while the class discussed themes and motifs in literature, I studied my classmates' faces, trying to determine if they'd seen me on the Camden High Street. I was certain Heath spotted me, but he had been his normal friendly self that morning, so was I mistaken?

After class, Heath and Bhavani, followed by a reluctant May, approached me while I packed my things. *Oh shit—here it comes.*

"Hey, Luke," Bhavani said. "May is hosting a Thanksgiving dinner at her flat, and since you're the only other American on the course, we thought you'd like to come."

I stared at them. "Thanksgiving?"

"Yeah," Bhavani nodded. "Are you free?"

Thanksgiving was my favorite holiday—not for the gathering of family, but the food. "Thanksgiving sounds good." I searched their faces. Maybe they didn't know about Camden after all? Bhavani and Heath were smiling, but May didn't look so pumped.

"You better actually show up this time," she scowled. "Because everyone who's invited has to bring a dish. You and Heath are in charge of desserts."

Heath smirked at me, with a knowing look in his eyes. He *definitely* saw me. And he didn't say a word—what a mensch! I could have hugged him.

"Is there a particular southern dessert you could bring?" Heath asked. "That could be fun."

My eyes glazed as desserts flickered through my head. Only one dish made my stomach growl with just a thought. "Sweet potato piiie," I said, with an extra helping of southern drawl.

After class I walked to the tube, elated that Heath was pal enough to keep my secret. But that feeling soured when I remembered the sweet potato pie recipe I agreed to bring belonged to my late Grandmother Lillian. And I'd have to call my mom to get that recipe.

Dammit.

Chapter 24

"A Goddamn Pitbull"

When the night of Ibrahim and Llanzo's party came around, I agreed to meet King at The Rifleman beforehand. He thought it was best if we walked there together, at least until people in their ends got used to seeing some random white American guy. I got to the pub early in the hopes of stealing a few minutes with Sophie before the end of her shift.

"Have you given much thought to going out with me?" I asked.

Sophie rounded the bar. "I'm mulling it over—what about my daughter?"

"I don't date kids," I said, fighting to keep a straight face.

Sophie broke character and laughed. "I'm being serious." She gave me a shove. "Most lads don't go for single mums—kids running around, and all."

She had a point, but for better or worse, I'm not like *most lads*. Sophie let me buy her a beer, where she revealed she was working on a bachelor's degree in accounting, which explained the white binder. Shane must have decided a single mother would be a safe choice to maintain his books.

When I asked about her daughter's father, she said, "It's complicated—but we can't be together."

Sophie finished her beer and collected her bag. Before she left, she locked her blue eyes onto mine and touched my forearm. "Tell me something. When you packed your things for London, is this where you imagined you'd end up?"

"We've got shitty bars like this back home."

"I don't mean the pub." She neared close. "You don't have to answer right now. Just think about it."

***

I met King and Shane out front. King was in all-black, with his gold chain hanging on the outside of a new Nike hoodie. Shane smoked a spliff. "I hear you boys are off to do a little celebrating." He offered me a hit.

I waved him off. "We are. Are you coming?"

"No, no." He passed the spliff to King. "I've got some things to arrange, but you boys enjoy. We'll be working weekends from now on. So, make the most of tonight."

"Oh?"

"Don't worry, we always find downtime." Shane smirked. "Work hard, play hard."

I despise that saying, but we said our goodbyes to Shane, and King and I walked east. "How do you feel about working weekends?" I asked as we passed a Greggs.

"The way I see it—either make Ps with Shane on the weekend, or work at this bloody place." He nodded to the shop. "Better for my wallet and my image to work for Shane—until I get back to football, you know? Cause it's not just about *being* a footballer, but making sure you look like one."

"Social media? Yeah, I get it—there's a lot of pressure."

King groaned. "Seems like all I've got is pressure these days, fam. Got a kid brother and sister to take care of, a dad who's poorly, and my mum who works too much. The usual story, innit?"

I didn't know how to respond to King's unprompted disclosure, so I nodded. The street quieted and turned residential. I caught myself looking into the windows of each home we passed, briefly tuning into the channels of the lives inside. Finally, I asked, "Your folks don't ask about the money you bring home?"

"I was a good kid coming up. So, when I bring home a few extra Ps they just assume it's from football somehow. Think they're afraid to ask." He sighed. "Allow it, fam—bringing me down. Supposed to be gettin' faded."

"You're right," I laughed. "I'm sorry."

Gradually, the townhouses got shabbier and the streets grimier. The quiet road burst to life and eyes were on us from every angle. People in doorways, sitting on stoops, glancing through their windows in the glow of their TVs. Hooded men with blunts, glowing cherry red in the night. King seemed to know most groups in varying degrees and they'd dap him up or give a passing *wagwan*.

We arrived at a particularly dark street with bulking concrete apartments that King called *the Block*. We made for a building draped in a dulled orange streetlight glow, where the drone of hundreds of lives inside grew louder as we got closer. A group of men stood at the entrance, smoking and scrolling through their phones.

"Wagwan, Oba?" the tallest one said to King. He studied me with his good eye, the other clouded gray.

"Wagwan, Sleepah, you alright?" King dapped the man.

"When I'm gonna see you back on the pitch? Been too long, brudda."

"I know, I know," King put a hand over his heart. "Real soon, Sleeps. On God, bro."

"That's what I wanna hear—" Sleepah's smile faded when he saw me watching him.

King opened the front door. "This is Luke—he's mad cool."

Sleepah stuck out a hand. "Wagwan."

I shook his hand, but didn't know what to say back. "And also with you," I said, defaulting to my brief stint in Sunday school.

What an idiot.

To my surprise, everyone roared with laughter. King hooted, waving me into the building. "See what I mean?" He and the guys laughed. "Lates, Sleeps."

King chuckled to himself down the main corridor that seemed to narrow in on us. The cinderblock walls were painted in a sickly pale blue. The air tasted stale and there was a rust-colored puddle that had dried on the floor. When we passed the broken elevator for the stairs, I asked, "Oba?"

"My name—it's Nigerian for *King*."

"That's a cool name," I huffed, out of breath. "When *will* we see you on the pitch again, Oba?"

King sucked his teeth. "Not you too—I'll talk to Shane about that trainer, promise."

The third-floor hallway was painted in hospital green, which reminded me of visiting Bill at Wake Med when he first got sick—because if I didn't, who the hell would? I could almost hear the beeping machines and see the tubes that pumped good things into Bill's body and the bad things out.

We stopped at apartment twenty-eight—my age—which made me a little embarrassed about showing up to a party of early twentysomethings. Llanzo answered the door, big and broad in the threshold with blue light glowing behind him. His stoic face lit up with a smile. "Wagwan, boys?" he dapped us up.

The hallway swelled with rap and girl and guy voices— conversations and laughter. There were twenty people jammed into the two-bedroom flat. The partygoers smiled and called out to King, which was nice, since I'd never shown up to a party with the cool kid before. I got appraising looks from people as I followed him to the kitchen, where we were greeted by Kieran and Ibrahim. Kieran was stoned, his eyes bloodshot.

"I'm glad you're here, Luke," he squeezed my shoulder, which was still tender.

I hadn't been to many parties where people were happy to see me, so I uncapped some Henny and poured a shot into each of the boys' glasses for a toast. The boys introduced me to their friends, and there were so many names that I forgot most of them, except Swift and Jamie. Swift was a short, chubby black dude who was into anime and was almost as funny as Ibrahim. Swift's best friend, Jamie, was a tall, athletic white kid who knew King from football. Swift and Jamie would eventually be brought in to sell Shane's product part-time for us, and so I got to know them fairly well.

An hour and four drinks later, I found myself smoking a cigarette on the rickety balcony with a cute Korean girl, named Sun. I was explaining to her North Carolina was not Northern California when I caught sight of Chiara inside the packed party. Her face lit up when Kieran came over to hug her. I looked over the top of Sun's head, hoping to see Sophie follow in after, but she never did, which made me sad. Something about me kept pushing Sophie away.

"Will you excuse me for a minute," I told Sun, weaving through the party for the kitchen.

I threw back some more Henny as King and the boys piled into the kitchen, smiling like little kids who'd just made me a mud pie on the playground. Kieran had something behind his back.

"Luke," he said, his stutter apparently improved by weed. "We've got you a little somefin.'"

I placed a hand on my chest like a southern debutante. "For me?"

"It's twice now you've helped us," King said. "Saved our arses in Camden, fam."

"Well, I like you guys," I cracked a beer. "Didn't want y'all to get hurt. You didn't have to get me anything."

"We did, anyway," Llanzo nodded to Kieran.

Kieran snapped open a ring box and inside was a gold signet ring, just like King's. Instead of a lion in a crown, engraved on the ring was the beefy head of an American pit bull.

I was speechless. When was the last time someone gave me a gift? Bill never did, and my mother stopped sending gifts as far back as high school.

"We was going to cop you one like ours, you know, with the lion," King said. "But Llanzo saw this and we decided you had to have it—it's fuckin' criss, innit?"

It fit perfectly on my right pinky finger; the same place King wore his. I stuck my fist out for them to see. *Yeahhh*, they said in unison, pulling out their necklaces and rings to match.

"This is so awesome, guys," I smiled. "Thank you."

I poured them all refills of Henny. And as we all clinked our glasses, I caught sight of my new ring glimmering in the blue strobe lights as Sophie's question echoed through my head.

Is this where I imagined I'd end up?

Chapter 25

The boys and I spent most of November selling in the Soho clubs, and each morning I'd drag my ass to class with only a couple hours of sleep—or sometimes with none at all. Good thing I had access to knockoff Adderall from Spain.

In the afternoons before we'd work, I wrote at The Rifleman and hung out with Daniel. The pub was quiet, and if I really focused, I could complete a week's worth of assignments in a couple afternoons. Meanwhile, Shane and King worked logistics at the corner table, but those conversations didn't interest me. I preferred the parts of the business that promised adventure, like sneaking drugs into clubs, or the hit of adrenaline seconds before a fight.

By the end of November, I made a habit of visiting Mustafa at the kebab joint on his lunch break. His uncle, who owned the shop, told me a group of thugs were harassing him—one guy even threw a bottle at Mustafa's head. So, I stopped in quite often, hoping those guys showed up.

Thanks to global warming, Mustafa and I sat in the sun in front of the shop one afternoon when my phone rang. It was Heath. "What's up, man?" I answered, concerned he'd bring up Camden.

"Just out, enjoying the weather," Heath said. "What about you?"

"Same here. A few weeks of gray can take a toll on you."

"Oh, just wait until February. You'll be longing for home."

I forced a laugh. How could he know I had no home? I'd gladly take gray skies in London over sunny skies in Raleigh.

He continued, "I'm calling because I've still not decided what to bring for dinner tonight. What sorts of desserts are expected for Thanksgiving?"

Shit! I lurched up in my chair. I'd completely forgotten about dinner. It was a few minutes after four o'clock and dinner was at eight. There'd be enough time to make a pie but only if I called my mother now for the recipe. I gave Heath some suggestions; cakes and pies or ice cream, assuring him he couldn't go wrong with sugary foods for an American holiday. I gave Mustafa a high five and bolted for Sainsburys.

No one should ever be nervous to call their own mother, but I was. I told myself I had changed since we last spoke, and I wasn't the same whiny kid, desperate for mommy's approval. Near Sainsbury's was a park where people from my building walked their dogs. I sat on an old bench and ran my fingers over the names *Jim & Annette* carved into the wood. I repeated the motions until I felt at ease enough to call.

Mom answered on the third ring. "Hi, Luke. How are you?" she already sounded distracted.

"Look, I know you're probably busy with Thanksgiving, so I'll be quick—do you have your recipes handy?"

"Recipes?" she paused. "I'm actually in Santa Monica this morning with Braden. He's got sailing lessons."

I couldn't help but laugh. "Cultured little fella. He must get that from David's side of the family—all I wanted was a BB gun at his age."

"I remember you shooting Kyle Miller with it on the first day," she laughed.

"He shot me first!" I chuckled. "I still plead self-defense."

Our laughter fizzled into silence. Maybe as we contemplated how twenty years passed by so quickly. "So, what's up?" she asked. "You were pretty upset the last time we talked."

"Sorry, I was stressed with the move. I'm calling because I'm going to a Thanksgiving dinner tonight, and I need Grandma Lillian's sweet potato pie recipe."

"Oh," there was a long pause. "Here's the thing; the kids studied the Native American holocaust and so we decided as a family to no longer celebrate Thanksgiving."

I didn't understand. "No one celebrates Thanksgiving because they're happy about what happened to Native Americans."

"Right, but that's not the point."

My comment sounded dickish, so I tried backtracking. "I understand. Do your thing. Just shoot me the recipe, then y'all go enjoy *sailsgiving*."

Mom sucked in a sharp breath of air. I felt disappointment coming. "Luke, when we moved to Venice Beach, we purged most things from North Carolina."

Yep—there it was. "And let me guess; you threw the recipes out?"

"I'm sorry, Lu, but we don't eat like that anymore."

"Yeah, but I do. I love Grandma's food. You always cook it for me when I visit."

"Except, you've not visited in a few years."

My anger boiled over and I couldn't stop myself. "I haven't been invited, Mom—big difference." We were silent. Sweat formed between my face and the phone. "Mom, you moved west eighteen years ago, and it's like you forgot North Carolina ever happened. How do you delete everything and everyone like that?"

"Lucas, you cannot comprehend what I suffered through," she raised her voice. "The evil that I shielded you from —"

"What you shielded me from?" I practically screamed. "That shit came down on me ten-fold when you left—I know that I remind you of him, but I'm *not* him. It's okay to like me! I won't hurt you."

My eyes were wet. I could hear her sniffling. "Luke, I do like you. I love you. And I'm sorry. I know I've not always been a good mother —"

"You are a good mother," I said, unable to stop my tears. "Just not to me."

She sobbed into the phone, which honestly wasn't my goal, but it was nice to hear she actually felt something. "Our calls never seem to go well, do they?" I laughed through the tears. "Surprised you still answer."

"You're my son, I'll always answer."

My mother never called me first, but it's true, she always answered. I nodded, as if she could somehow see me. "I gotta go, Mom." I hung up.

I didn't block her number this time. Instead, I let the tears fall. In my younger years, I hid my blubbering from the world, but I hadn't felt normal since Paris, and to hell with the world. Bill used to say, "Knock it off—crying ain't gonna bring her back."

Why are the worst people always the most fertile?

In the end, I googled sweet potato pie recipes. I decided if I ever had kids, to just pass off internet recipes as old family secrets and pretend the customs I created had been passed down for generations.

***

May lived on the western edge of Soho, in a flat above a shoe repair shop. I was pretty drunk when I showed up with my ugly ass pie. I'm not saying the difficulties I had baking the pie had anything to do with me being drunk, but it would be unwise to say they were unrelated.

May answered the door in a green velvet cocktail dress, which I would never admit to her, complemented her red hair. We both realized how underdressed I was in my hoodie, and she looked even more disappointed to see me than usual. "You're late." She let the door hit me as I entered.

Fairy lights were strung across the exposed brick of May's flat and chunky candles flickered on every ledge. Chattering voices filled the room, where all the furniture was pushed against the walls to allow for a large dinner table at its center. Heath sat at the end, with Bhavani across from him next to two girls—May's roommates. Audrey sat across from them, with May placed at the center like Christ. There was also a guy and girl I'd seen at uni but had never met. "Hey!" the room said in unison. May took my pie and dropped it onto the buffet table.

"Happy Thanksgiving." I waved to everyone.

"The turkey is cooling for another twenty minutes." May eyed my lip, which had been freshly split by a banker bro who didn't want to pay for his drugs. The nerve of some people.

"So, not late, then?" I smirked.

"No, you missed pre-dinner cocktails."

"I had them before I came over."

May rolled her eyes and pointed to the chair between Heath and Bhavani. "Sit there. Feel free to pour yourself a drink—or a glass of water."

I cannot stress how much May hated me. I sauntered over to the wine table and poured a big glass of a pricey looking Bordeaux.

Heath grinned when I sat down. "How'd your pie turn out?"

"I crushed nine Xanax into the batter," I whispered.

He and Bhavani laughed. Heath's teeth were stained red from his wine. Thank you, Jesus. It's not fun being the only drunk person at a party.

"What did you end up going with?" I asked him.

Heath pointed to a stunning chocolate cake, in a fancy glass container. "I binned the box it came in," he said. "Then took a wet knife to the icing to give it a homemade look."

Bhavani confessed, "I got the mashed potatoes and gravy from KFC." The three of us burst into laughter. We were definitely the cool end of the table.

Eventually, the dinner party entered into political discussions—my least favorite subject. They discussed the Labour Party, the Tories, the Liberal Democrats, and in the US; the Democrats and Republicans. May spoke on behalf of everyone in the western states and their unanimous beliefs. Then everyone looked at me, the supposed spokesperson for the southeastern states.

"Do I look like someone who votes?" I laughed.

May didn't find that funny. "Being apolitical is morally apprehensible," she said. "Especially at a time when so many are in need."

"When haven't people been in need?" I drained my wine. "Call it selfish or privileged—but I've hated politics since the hall monitor election in second grade. And no matter what asshat lived in the White House, my life has always kinda sucked."

The table chuckled and luckily the turkey timer went off— my cue to refill mine and Heath's glasses. He'd just got a poem published, so the table toasted him. After everyone filled their plates, we discussed Bhavani's detective novel and whether or not her main character should have a love interest. Some said it could strengthen the story, others worried if it were forced, it could weaken the novel.

Naturally, it made me think about Sophie. I'd asked her a few times about going out with me, and each time she said more or less the same thing; "I'm still mulling it over—now, what would you like to drink?" Maybe I was forcing things, and she wasn't actually my love interest at all. Maybe she was my turning point, or plot twist?

By dessert, Heath and I were pretty drunk and working on another glass of wine. Bhavani and Audrey sniggered. "The bromance is adorable, you guys," Bhavani said.

"If the writing doesn't work out, we could start a dessert shop together," Heath said. We both giggled.

"I will say, Luke," Audrey said. "You have a particularly interesting writing style."

"Why thank you." I said, spilling wine on my jeans.

The others dinner guests brought plates into May's little kitchen. "Where do you get your story ideas?" Audrey asked. "London gangs and all. They seem very—"

"Authentic?" I said.

"Well, yes," she said. Bhavani nodded too. Heath—my secret keeper—glared at me.

My face felt warm from the wine. Examining the three of them, I decided to trust them. "It's because they are." I leaned back in my chair. Heath shook his head. The two girls looked at me blankly. "They've actually happened to me."

The girls still looked puzzled. Heath patted my arm. "He's joking."

Like an idiot, I pointed to my busted lip and the two girls gasped. "You're mad," Audrey said.

Heath shook his head. "Mate, you sure the bruises aren't from skateboarding, or a boxing club, maybe?"

Too drunk to realize he was trying to help, I explained how I tag along with a gang for stories. Heath tried dressing it up by calling it research. Bhavani was concerned, but eventually approved of my process as long as I promised to be careful. Audrey just stared with a hand over her mouth.

Confiding in them felt nice, because it's not like I could tell Cash or my mom—or anyone. I drained my wine and contemplated whether I should refill my glass or go home. I stood up for the toilet and looked into the little kitchen just feet away.

And there was May, packing away leftover food and staring right at me.

Chapter 26

No city does Christmas like London. I felt childlike excitement, marveling at the lights on Oxford and Regent Street, and losing myself in the market stalls of Covent Garden. People were bundled in scarves and hats, carrying shopping bags and hot drinks. The pubs were full, with fires in the chimneys, and every nook in London was made cozy with holly and twinkling lights. The boys and I worked double-time *shotting food* with all the Christmas parties and tourists around. And I did all of this while working on my end of term assignments.

In early December, the boys and I sat at our corner table at The Rifleman, exhausted and drinking coffee or tea instead of booze. I was putting the finishing touches on a piece where my main character and his friends got into a fight with another rival group at the Goodge Street tube station. A couple of the rival guys being thrown down the steps of the station, bystanders were horrified and screaming. Figured it was best to end the semester on an action-packed piece.

"Alright, lads," Shane closed the white binder. "You lot should take the weekend off." The boys and I smiled like Santa came early. "We'll be working hard from here until Christmas. Plus, Brahim, I know you've got your gig Saturday."

Llanzo gave Ibrahim a proud shove. "You coming, Shane?" Ibrahim asked. "I'll reserve us all a table."

Shane packed some weed into a spliff. "I'll try to be there, mate. But I've got a meeting that night with a supplier. Need to keep the wheels churning."

The excitement left Ibrahim's face, but he gave a brave nod. My face felt hot as I stared at Shane, wondering if he knew how the boys looked at him as a pseudo-father figure—King especially. Shane smirked at me as he rolled his spliff tight.

Chapter 26

***

Those knockoff Adderall pills worked wonders to help me finish my assignments by my Friday deadline. I wrote one essay on the development of my protagonist and whether I thought he was evolving or devolving. Another essay was for Mr MacDougall's setting module, where I discussed whether I believed London had a positive or negative effect on my protagonist, and vice versa. And I even submitted a last-minute piece for the Hammer & Brunswick Literary Prize that my university hosted. Why not?

Once everything was handed in, I sat in my kitchen, sobering in the gray morning light and reflecting on how much I'd changed in the past few months. Spending Thanksgiving with my so-called peers, I felt like I could see things they couldn't—I had a more grounded view of the world. Maybe that's why I struggled to give a shit about politics, and snooty literary discussions. Throughout dinner, I just wondered what King and the boys were up to. What was our next move, and when was my next high from the fight?

I closed my laptop to make myself some breakfast, but the Latvians had dirtied every pot and pan and piled them in the sink. So, I ate two cans of tuna, then slept for the rest of the day.

***

That night was my coldest yet in England and my walk to Ibrahim's show in Soho was brutal. I'd grown wary of riding the tube alone since the Goodge Street incident. The loud-mouth white boy who initiated the altercation, lost his tooth on the steps and me—the sick bastard—thought it would be funny to keep it as a trophy. So yeah, I didn't want to be caught alone on the train when that guy and his pals came looking for his front tooth.

Crossing the Lambeth Bridge, the wind whipped across the Thames so intensely that it took my breath. Things had gotten blustery after Thanksgiving, so I upgraded my bomber jacket to a bulky Superdry parka, which helped combat the river wind. A police boat spotlighted the river as black waves lapped its hull. If they were looking for someone then they were doing so pretty casually. As if whoever had fallen into the Thames didn't have much chance of coming back out.

The boys waited in front of the comedy club. Breath steamed from their red noses. "Is Brahim already inside?" I asked.

"Y-yeah,' Kieran stuttered. "C-can we go inside now?"

"How is it, the southern boy is handling the cold better than you, Kier?" King said with a laugh.

"Kiss my arse, I'm going in!" Kieran threw himself inside.

Inside, a smiley girl escorted us into the main room and sat us at a small table right of the stage. King left an empty chair for Shane. The girl took our drink orders and when she returned, she brought along five shots of tequila. "Ibrahim said to make sure you boys were good and pissed, so you'll laugh louder at his jokes," she said, all smiley.

We thanked her and gagged down the shots and I asked the boys, "Have you ever seen his act before?" They shook their heads. I began to sweat. Ibrahim was funny in conversation, but being funny for an audience was a different animal. I flagged the smiley girl down for another round of shots to stave off my secondhand embarrassment.

"Just four this time," I whispered, eying Shane's empty seat.

The room filled, the house lights dimmed, and the crowd applauded. Then from the darkness, Ibrahim sprang onto the stage and into the spotlight. He was in a hoodie and joggers, like he'd just wandered in from Oxford Street. He grabbed the mic and said, "Good evening, ladies and gents!"

The audience wooed and Ibrahim went straight into a few jokes about the difficulties of being one of the few Arabs in

London who wasn't a rich prince, then he did impressions of his father's thick accent begging him not to go into comedy, followed by one of his mother trying to set him up with a third cousin. In short—he was hysterical and the audience adored him. No more tequila required, I beamed with pride watching him introduce each act, filling the gaps with his jokes.

All the while I kept eying Shane's empty chair, feeling the vines of anger growing between my pride and laughter. All his talk of how he and the boys were a family—he was like their father—he *saved them*. Ibrahim was chipping away at his dreams and Shane couldn't give shit to be there.

Chapter 27

King texted me the next morning to see if I would join the boys at a swanky club in Soho called Caldera. He said: *I'll be bringing a couple birds round. Someone's got a crush on the ol' pit bull.* Apparently, Sun, the cute Korean girl I spoke with at Ibrahim and Llanzo's party, liked me. The thought of a last-minute date made me nervous, but I agreed to come.

But Luke, what about Sophie? She and I had a weekly appointment where she turned me down for a date. So, despite being nuts about Sophie, I was still human and hanging out with a girl at a club sounded fun.

Sitting in the kitchen, I scribbled into my notebook with a cup of coffee. The semester was over, but I still had so much to write about. Juris came in to make tea and shocker—he was fully clothed. As he waited for his kettle, he looked at me with weirdly sympathetic eyes.

"What we going to do about your bad dreams?" he said.

"Huh?"

"You don't remember? Five this morning, I woke you up? You yelling in your sleep, *momma, momma!*"

Was he making this up? I knew I was prone to bad dreams but I assumed I suffered through them silently.

"This seem to get worse," he continued. "Third time in two weeks I wake you up. Really, you don't remember?"

I shook my head. I had been working more and sleeping less in the past few weeks, so maybe it was stress? Or was the increase of violence taking some unknown toll on me? I shuddered at the thought. No, that's ridiculous. What I did in the UK didn't matter.

I apologized and thanked Juris for helping. As soon as he returned to his room, I ran to the fridge and rifled through his bin of mushrooms. Got it! I found the little shiny fungus I'd snipped from the bathroom and tossed it in the trash. Maybe Juris wasn't so bad after all.

***

As the day went on, the more I grew nervous about seeing Sun. Men are in serious trouble if beautiful women ever figure out how terrifying they can be. I took one of Kieran's Vicodin while waiting for my Uber and washed it down with a shot of Jameson, and soon enough, I felt anxiety-free but sleepy. So, I followed that up with an Adderall.

My Uber seemed to float through a glimmering London, still wet from the day's rain. I felt damn good when I reached Caldera, which was two stories and oppressively Romanesque. Massive columns propped up the exterior facade, with gaslit torches bolted to each of the four pillars. Their flames licking the wind in unison. Below them, throngs of people braced against the wind, waiting to get in. I sauntered passed the blurs of faces with confidence and cut straight to the front of the line. There was a big red-faced bouncer in a puffer jacket, sweating under a propane heater. He gave me a strange look.

"I'm on the list," I said. "Luke."

He barely glanced at his clipboard. Just nodded and I shook his hand, slipping him a twenty-pound note. "You 'ave a good night, sir," he said.

Another bouncer opened the door for me and once inside, I had to ask myself; was I actually on the list? Or did I seem like someone who could be trouble if you told no. I've got to be honest, I enjoyed that feeling.

I came into a long torchlit hallway to check my coat. The bass music throbbed the foundation beneath my feet like a passing train. The hallway opened up to a massive dancefloor where blips of lasers and colored strobes flickered across an ever-shifting sea of faces. The fog, the bass, the perfume—I'd spent a lot of time in clubs with the boys and I always longed for a quiet pint at The Rifleman.

The club was a huge rectangular space with an upstairs level overlooking the dancefloor. There were long bars on each of the ground floor walls, with liquor bottles glimmering high on the shelves. A squad of women paraded past me in cheeky shorts and black corsets. They held champagne bottles with sparklers overhead. Through the madness, I caught sight of King walking toward me.

"You alright, fam?" he shook my hand.

"Yeah, feeling good, bro," I said, looking around for Sun and the boys. "So, where's—"

King laughed and threw an arm around my shoulder. "She's upstairs. Let's get a drink first—talk business, yeah?"

People stepped aside for us as we strolled through the club. "So, what's this business talk?" I placed a hand on the bar. The club lights danced across the shiny surface.

King held out his arms. "This place."

I glanced around to the four bars, the massive DJ booth, and the nest of flashing lights in the rafters like a movie studio. "You want to sell here?"

"This place is lush, fam. We could make mad Ps."

Caldera was nice, for a club, and the clientele had money—or at least they liked to be seen spending it. We ordered two vodka and sodas and soon the excitement seemed to fade from King's face.

"Why do I feel like there's a *but* coming?" I asked.

Just as King went to speak, someone smacked the drink from my hand, spilling vodka down the front of my shirt. The glass smashed to the floor.

Profit.

Without thinking, I flipped out my blade. He grinned at me with those stupid red gems in his mouth. I wanted to plunge the blade into his gut and twist, but King grabbed my arm. Profit burst into laughter, seeing me restrained.

"Can't touch this pussio," King said. "It'll start a war, fam."

Profit cackled, shouting to his buddies behind him. "Look how mad he is!"

My hunger for violence spiked and the thought of not satiating it killed me. I took a breath and thought of my story. If Profit was the antagonist, then he would surely get his comeuppance. I slipped my knife back into my pocket.

"Another double vodka soda, please?" I called to the bartender.

"You was never gonna do nothin'," Profit shouted at me.

I wiped my shirt with bar napkins. "We've got a saying back home; fuck around and find out."

The idiot grinned and then motioned for his boys to follow him back into the crowd.

King handed me more napkins. "He's why we can't shot here. It's the jewel in Charlie's crown. They don't want to lose it."

My shirt clung to my chest and my mind raced with plots of revenge. The club strobed in columns of light, like the Pantheon in Rome, and I remembered what Shane said about building Charlie's trust just so it has further to fall—like Rome.

"Charlie and Profit can kiss my ass," I said. "I say we snatch this crown jewel."

King studied me, then cracked a smile. "Psh, you're mad, fam—let's go."

Taking Caldera from Charlie would be an act of war, and King wasn't ready for that. I dropped the subject and followed him through the shifting bodies and upstairs to the VIP section. Our booth was a semi-circle of large white leather sofas with a low table in the center, scattered with drinks and bottles. Our booth was dead center in the club, overlooking the DJ below.

Sun sat by the railing with Nandi, a girl King had been seeing who could have been Naomi Campbell's daughter. Sun wore a black lacy halter dress and smiled at me while Kieran talked at the two girls with a weed pen in his hand. Ibrahim and Llanzo were on the opposite couch with Jamie and Swift. I greeted everyone and explained what happened to my shirt, and then we all went to the railing to see if we could spot Profit—but we couldn't.

King directed me to sit next to Sun. She smiled politely as Kieran rambled about his friend from school, Big Brudda, who was "going to be the next Stormzy." Llanzo beamed proudly that Kieran was excited about something, and after a couple drinks, agreed to invest in Big Brudda's next album.

The champagne girls came with a few bottles, and our group clinked glasses, which finally afforded Sun and I the chance to talk. "I like your dress," I said.

"Thank you," Sun smiled. "It's Dior."

"Oh—it looks black in this light."

She threw her head back and laughed. "No, Dior is who made it!"

I'm an idiot, but we both laughed and after a couple glasses of champagne, Sun put a hand on my thigh and whispered, breathy in my ear, "Dance with me?"

Sun had a lot of energy and she danced for ages, grinding her ass into my crotch. By the fourth song, I didn't even try to hide my erection. Life in that moment was good, almost euphoric. I snuck away from our booth to take another Adderall and returned to flowing champagne and more of Sun's grinding.

Everything was perfect—then Sophie showed up.

She and Chiara appeared at our booth out of the fog and lights. She was in a black leather skirt and a blood red sweater. Sophie gave me a weird smirk seeing Sun dance on me, but she sat down on the sofa with Chiara and Kieran and ignored me. It didn't take long for my erection to go soft. Apparently, there's no lying to a penis.

I put my hands on Sun's waist and guided her to the sofa for a refill. Sun had that sweet smell of sweat as she sat with her body pressed against mine. All the while, my betraying eyes wandered back to Sophie.

"Are you having fun?" Sun asked.

"Absolutely," I nodded, eying Sophie.

"Who's she?"

I took a long sip of my champagne. "Oh, that's Sophie. She's a friend."

"She's very pretty."

"Hmm, hadn't noticed."

For the next hour, Sun and I labored through awkward conversation and uncomfortable bouts of dancing. What the hell was wrong with me? Sophie wouldn't even let me take her on a date. And here was beautiful Sun, who by some miracle liked me, and I couldn't even bring myself to do the one thing men do best—think with my dick.

Sun wasn't stupid, and eventually whispered in my ear, "You really like her, don't you?" She searched my face.

I couldn't bring myself to lie. "I do."

She nodded. "At least you're honest, Luke," she attempted a smile. "It's getting late. I think I might go home."

I felt sad for both Sun and myself. "Sun, you're like the nicest—and objectively, one of the hottest people I've ever met."

She laughed. "You're sweet," she said, glancing at Sophie. "If you're just as sweet to her, then it'll all work out."

I escorted Sun through the crowded club for her coat and I stepped outside to hail her a cab. I've never done that for a woman, and once I had, I wished it was done under happier circumstances. Sun kissed my cheek and I waved goodbye as she slipped into the car.

Both relief and remorse washed over me as I trudged back inside. Hands in my pockets, I felt my knife. The metal was warm and heavy, as if it were alive. Maybe it was the Adderall high wearing off, but I felt sad. I chewed my next pill and washed it down with a shot of tequila at the bar. The booze and pills hit me as I stepped out into the throbbing dancefloor. Forgetting my agoraphobia, I closed my eyes and exhaled the sad business of Sun. Another breath, I exhaled the constant rejection from Sophie. And on the third breath, I opened my eyes and saw Profit through the sway of the crowd.

He was in the VIP section next to the DJ booth. And directly above him were King and Kieran talking at the railing. The rat bastard sat directly beneath us the entire time. Some idiot white dude with cornrows in Profit's group stood up on the edge of the booth and flicked cash out onto the dancefloor like a cunt.

The champagne girls returned for a fourth time. They marched to our booth with the bottles hoisted in the air, golden sparklers blazing away.

And I was struck with a stupid idea.

One that would set off a chain of events I could have never imagined. I pushed through the people and back up to our booth. Sophie was the first to see me. She seemed surprised I'd returned alone.

I sprang onto our table. Everyone jumped from their seats and put their hands out to coax me down. I stepped carefully between the glasses, phones and purses and yanked the two full champagne bottles from their buckets and hopped over to the railing.

King grabbed my shoulder. "The hell are you doing?"

"Getting us kicked out of this club." I laughed like a lunatic. "But don't worry—we'll be back."

King peered over the railing and spotted Profit below, talking to some girl. That idiot white dude chucked more money into the crowd. King let go of me and I turned the champagne bottles upside down, dowsing Profit, his girl and the white boy in a fizzy waterfall.

"Holy shit, fam!" King laughed, pouring his drink too.

Profit slipped and skidded trying to clamber off the leather sofa. And by the time he got to his feet, he was drenched, and I was all out of champagne. Kieran, Llanzo, Ibrahim and the rest of our group charged to the railing to see what we'd done. Profit finally got his bearings and looked up to see my pilled-up American face, laughing at him with all my friends.

Chapter 28

Days after the champagne incident, I was at the post office shipping my mom an antique tea set I'd found in a shop near Kensington Palace. It was her Christmas gift and my way of extending an olive branch after our Thanksgiving call. I spent hours the night before wrapping each of the twenty pieces for international shipping. By happenstance, I ran into Heath at the post office and informed him that Ms Smith had called me into uni for something important.

"Could it be the Hammer & Brunswick Literary Prize?" Heath's eyes lit up. "What a Christmas surprise that would be!"

There were butterflies in my stomach. "Don't get my hopes up!"

We agreed to meet at the American bar in Fitzrovia after, where I figured I'd get more respect by going with a writer instead of gangsters. The streets roared with that countdown to Christmas buzz on my walk to uni. Charing Cross swelled with lights and activity. It was cold and steam poured from every vent, as if London was a living, breathing thing. But it was hard to enjoy, because since the Profit incident I'd felt the need to constantly look over my shoulder. Especially in Soho.

Profit didn't take his champagne shower gracefully, and in a surprising turn of events *he* was thrown from the club. Profit and his boys retaliated by throwing bottles and glasses up at our booth. It took a team of bouncers to remove them from Caldera. But Sophie was the only one in our group unamused by what I'd done to Profit and what she said to me afterwards put me in a funk all week. But I told myself not to think about that on my hike up to the university. Instead, I speculated — *had I won the prize?*

Bedford Square was gray and breezy, and only a few hardy pigeons pecked beneath the benches. My building was much quieter at the end of term. I took the winding staircase to the professors' offices at the top floor, and marveled at how their hallway even smelled academic. Like Bill's set of *World Book Encyclopedias* that he never allowed me to read.

Ms Smith said to meet in Room 429, a massive office at the end of the faculty hall. Standing before the door, I realized it wasn't the office of an assistant professor. It could only be one person—Mr Doe. I locked eyes with my reflection in the big brass doorknob and knocked.

"Come in," a voice called from inside.

A big breath, I pushed open the door. The office was lamplit with a wall of bookshelves to my right, and a table covered in papers to my left. Mr Doe sat at the far end behind a large wooden desk that looked built for signing presidential orders. And in one of the two chairs before it, was Ms Smith.

"Please shut the door behind you, Luke," Mr Doe said.

I did as I was told and flashed a nervous smile to Ms Smith. "How are y'all?"

"We're fine, Luke," he answered, mechanically.

A large oriental rug muffled my steps as I eyed an ominous grandfather clock standing against the wall. *Maybe this isn't about some prize?*

"Please, have a seat," Mr Doe gestured to the armchair next to Ms Smith—who never returned my smile. "Luke, we've asked you here today because we've received some troubling information about some of your possible activities—outside of the classroom—which may or may not be represented in the work you've submitted to the course."

I stared at the mole on his head. "Oh?" I said.

"As you're aware, I audited a few of Ms Smith's classes, making note of your particular writing style, and your demeanor, to ensure you wouldn't be of harm to yourself or others. Although my assessment concluded you had no proclivities toward violence, I did note a certain correspondence to your physical appearance and the violent acts in your writing."

My hands shook. I wanted to speak—deny it, but no words came.

He continued, "Quite simply, there are many similarities between your work, which you claim to be fiction, and your personal life. And if it's proven you are participating in organized crime while enrolled on this course then it would be a breach of the university code of conduct—not to mention illegal in the United Kingdom and therefore, a breach of your visa."

It was shocking how quickly I was ready to deny and lie. "Let me get this straight," I said. "All of the crime and violence I write about—you think I'm doing that for real? You said my work had believability issues, does this mean I've improved?" I looked to Ms Smith and thought I saw the makings of a smile.

But Mr Doe didn't smile. "Luke, serious evidence has been levied against you."

"Like what?"

"Similar wounds to your main character."

"I'm clumsy."

Mr Doe glared. "Vivid and intimate detail that corresponds to recent London crime scenes."

"I watch the news—try again."

He held up the notes in his hand. "Your protagonist is called *Duke*, an American writer who moves to London and joins a gang."

Okay, I'll give him that one. "I'm not great at coming up with names."

Mr Doe huffed and looked at his notes. "And a report from a fellow student, stating: at an off-campus gathering you confessed to classmates that your work was not fiction, but in fact true."

A flash of heat shot through my body. May—I *knew* she overheard me in the kitchen. She just soaked it all up, waiting for her chance to report me. No one likes a snitch, May.

Still, I tried to deny it. "You're going to come at me for hearsay? I can't help it if I'm a convincing crime writer and someone misconstrued my methods," I slapped my knees to stand.

"Luke, wait," Ms Smith finally spoke up. "We are very concerned—"

"Your concerns have been noted. And thanks for having my back, teach."

"Luke, I *do* have your back," she said, raising her voice. "If anything, I believe you may be a victim here."

Ten-year-old me screamed inside my head, while twenty-eight-year-old me trembled with anger. "I'm not a victim of shit, lady!"

Mr Doe sat up straight. "You are suspended from the program, pending an investigation. We shall inform you of our findings before the start of the second term."

"Fuck you, don't care—twerp!" I shouted, then spun around to leave.

"Luke, please wait," Ms Smith touched my arm. I nearly hissed. "It's about your story. You see, I believe this Duke character and the other boys may be in real danger."

I scowled at her. What's her angle? "For the sake of my story, *how* are they in danger?"

Ms Smith took a deep breath. "The character, Sean, the leader of this gang—he's manipulating these young men to do his bidding. They take all of the risk while he earns the rewards. He's a Fagan-type character and it's all wonderfully Dickensian, but I wonder if Duke will ever realize he's being taken advantage of?"

The three of us were silent as I stared. Was she trying to pull some kind of reverse psychology on me? I was too angry to place it. "Haven't figured out the end of the story yet," I said with a shrug.

"I want you to know, suspension or not, given Duke's family history—how alone he is in London—if you need guidance for his story, please do reach out to me," her eyes were wet behind her thick glasses.

I didn't give a shit about her little gesture. "Well, that's mighty Christian of you," I said to her, and to Mr Doe. "Let me know how your investigation goes—can't wait to find out if I'm a gangster or not," I gave him the middle finger and stormed out of the room.

Stomping through the building, I burst out into the cold. I could have breathed fire into the rain-drizzled air. *Suspended*—what do I do now? Christ, and I was supposed to meet Heath. I should just call and say something came up—but no, Heath was smart, maybe he'd have some advice.

Goddammit! I powerwalked through the cold, shaking my fists at the wintry air. I'd never felt so foolish, thinking I could actually earn praise for my work. But, no—they'd seen through me. Saw the violent, childish screw-up I've always been. My mother saw through it and Sophie did too. Shane was right. I'm incapable of wearing a mask.

My black Vans pounded the pavement for Fitzrovia. The BT Tower reflected the last of the orange sunset like the flaming torches at Caldera. I remembered my heart fluttering after I poured the champagne on Profit. King and the boys cheered, but Sophie looked disgusted.

I was steaming hot when I reached the American bar. Heath sat at the bar watching NFL highlights with a puzzled look on his face, like he was trying to learn the rules on the fly. He smiled and watched my face for the news.

"I didn't win," I said.

"Oh...that's unfortunate." His smile faded.

"Remember at Thanksgiving, when I said my stories were authentic?" I asked. Heath nodded. "Someone told the administrators and now I'm suspended—*pending an investigation.*" I felt like crying as the words left me.

"That's bloody awful," he covered his mouth. Heath was silent for a moment. "I bet it was May. You know I would never—"

"You can bet your ass it was May."

The chubby bartender, who called me a redneck, pointed a finger as he approached. "Hey—the Panthers fan, right? What can I get you both?"

Heath ordered a Philly cheesesteak and a pint of Boston Lager and I ordered a Modelo with lime, since I'd lost my appetite. Heath ate while I drank, and eventually he asked, "What will you do now?"

"I'll just keep writing. I wrote long before this program, and I'll write long after."

"I hoped you'd say that," he said. "You've got a talent for it, mate."

I finished my fourth Modelo and smiled. "Thanks, man. I just feel so stupid, thinking I won that prize."

"If you're stupid, so am I. 'Cause I thought you'd won it too."

The bartender slapped a hand onto the bar in front of me. Heath and I jumped. "Looks like your Panthers aren't going to make the playoffs this year," he said.

"Luckily, I don't give a shit," I held out my empty bottle. "Bring us another round."

The idiot had the nerve to look offended as he fetched us another round. Heath and I spent the rest of our time together talking shit about May until he checked his watch and sighed. "Man, I hate to leave you, but I've got an early train to Surrey in the morning."

"Don't apologize," I put up a drunken hand. "Do your thing."

"I'm at my mum's for Christmas, but I'll be back in a couple weeks—we'll meet for some beers," Before he left, he shook my hand and said, "Happy Christmas, Luke. Let me know if you need anything, yeah?"

"Thanks, bro. I'll be fine—promise. Merry Christmas."

When Heath left, it was just me, my thoughts and the moron bartender, which I decided would be the title of my second novel. I ordered a few more beers to drown out the bartender talking at me about football and I thought about my conversation with Sophie. When the dust settled and I plopped down next to her on the sofa.

"The guy I poured champagne on is an asshole," I said.

"I know the type," she put her crystal blue eyes on me.

"I'm not *that* guy—I'm not what he is."

"And what are you?"

"A writer."

Sophie set her glass down. "You keep saying that, and I even see you write in the pub, but are you writing fiction, or the truth?"

"Life is a fiction," I said, grinning. "We're all making it up as we go. All just characters in each other's stories."

She laughed. "You've rehearsed that line before, I think."

"I really haven't."

The club music pulsed and the lights flickered between us in purples and blues—still her eyes shown through it all. "So, is that what all of this is? You're just playing a character in a story? How long before this character becomes who you are?"

To Sophie, I was translucent. With just a bit of light, she could see all the pieces that made me. I licked my lips and asked, "Is this your flirty way of telling me to try harder to ask you out?"

I was jarred from the memory by a shove from the American bartender. He was wiping the bar. "You know what the Panthers' problem is?" he spat on my face a little. "It's your offensive coordinator—that guy's gotta go!"

Without thinking, I snatched the musty rag from him and threw it into his face. "I don't give a shit about football, you dumb prick!" I held up my empty bottle. "Get me another beer or I'll burn Philadelphia down next time I'm home."

The bartender stood up straight. I'd crossed the line and he wore the frown of someone who had no intention of serving me another beer. The handful of people left in the bar stopped talking to watch us. I should have tossed some cash on the bar and left, but the club scene with Sophie played on a drunken loop in my head. An icy look swept across her face. "I loved a gangster once," she said. "Then, I was left to tend to the wreckage he left behind. I won't do that again."

I'm a gangster? I asked myself once she said it, then a thousand times since. I asked myself in Mr Doe's office. And sitting at the American bar, with my tenth empty beer in my hand, I asked myself once more. The rage building inside me was sobering. I scowled at the bartender, who took a step away.

If they all want a gangster—give them a gangster.

Heart pounding, I flung the empty bottle at my reflection in the big Yuengling mirror behind the bar. It shattered and crashed to a thousand pieces. Chubby bartender and the bargoers gasped.

I caught my breath and said, eerily calm, "Another Modelo, please." He scurried to the fridge and handed me a bottle. I used the old oak bar top to uncap my beer and chipped the wood. I tossed him a wad of cash. "That should cover a new mirror."

I left the bar, beer in hand, for the drunk walk home. Dark clouds billowed in the sky and remorse washed over me, like cold English rain.

Chapter 29

The boys and I kept busy in the days leading up to Christmas. We sold in the Soho clubs and picked up a few more violent chores for Charlie along the way. I was thankful for the work, because it didn't leave me much time to think about Sophie or my suspension. Bill used to say something about idle hands and the devil. Can't remember it just now.

Averse to all things Christmas, Shane left for Paris on the twenty-third to meet with George and Rémy about *something important*. He gave me and the boys the night off to hang out at The Rifleman, where I hoped to explain myself to Sophie about the Profit incident. But although the pub was packed and joyful, Sophie wasn't there.

"Sorry, my love. She went home for the holidays," Chiara said, then pointing to some purpling on my right pinky, above my pit bull ring. "What happened to your hand?"

"I'm very clumsy—are you going to miss Kieran over Christmas?"

"He'll be with King's family, but I feel bad still."

She was sad that Kieran would have a parentless Christmas, but so was I, and I was doing just fine. "Sometimes, the family we're given doesn't cut it, Chi," I said. "And you have to create a new family—he's got you and the boys." I felt wise saying that and it made Chiara smile. We snuck a shot of Amaretto together and I think I left her happier than I'd found her.

I made the rounds with Daniel as he visited the regulars. He invited me to Bath for Christmas with his family but the thought of spending Christmas with a happy family made me uncomfortable. So, I lied about getting ahead on some schoolwork.

"Well, anytime you want to see Bath, let me know. I usually drive, so we could stop at Stonehenge if you'd like."

"Maybe this spring?"

"Of course. My schedule will have opened by then," he said, quietly. "Between you and me, there are parties interested in purchasing the pub."

"Really?" I frowned.

Daniel laughed and slapped me on the shoulder. "Don't worry, you'll still have your local. The regulars would rather see it burned than turned into a Wetherspoons or something."

Despite that news, the night went on happy and loud. For the first time, I could see how different the pub was without Shane. The boys and I visited with other tables and bought folks rounds. It was my favorite night at The Rifleman, surrounded by friends. I wanted to hold onto that feeling, because soon I'd be alone.

I see that night like a movie. Christmas lights glowing in the rafters, the warm flicker of a fire in the hearth. People laughing and clinking glasses. The camera pans over Daniel, me and the boys and our table. Then the camera glides through the front door as one of the regulars comes inside from a smoke, shaking off the cold. The camera pulls back across the wet paving stones as our cheery voices muffle behind the front door. The frame stops and holds for a while on the merry glow of the shitty little pub in Catford.

And, cut.

***

When I woke up on Christmas Eve, my flat was cold and gray and silent. The Latvians had gone home for a few weeks, the boys were with their families and I was all that remained. Christmas Eve and Christmas Day, I walked an empty London, listening to Christmas music and taking in all the decorations and lights. Those days dragged and every hour felt like ten, until finally London came back to life after Boxing Day, and I came out of my holiday funk.

A couple days before New Year's, I moseyed down Wandsworth Road, with a solid buzz for five o'clock, when Shane called. He had returned from Paris.

"You have a good Christmas, mate?"

"My Christmas was quiet," I said. "Didn't do much."

"What are you doing now?"

The streetlights had just flicked on in sequence ahead of me, like a runway. "On my way to get a kebab."

"The place across from your flat?"

I stopped in the bright glow of a gym on the corner of Wilcox, where I made eye contact with an older gentleman on an exercise bike inside. He had a unibrow, like Bert from *Sesame Street*.

"How do you know everything?" I looked deep into the man's eyes.

Shane laughed. "I'm nearby. I'll meet you at the kebab place and we'll get a drink."

"Sounds good," I gave the old man a thumbs up, and continued my walk.

Traffic had picked up to nominal levels on Wandsworth, so I didn't think much about the ambulance that screamed past. It stopped at the shops across from my flat, where a small crowd had gathered at the kebab joint. There was a flutter of worry in my stomach. *Please, don't be Mustafa.*

First responders pushed people away with their med kits and that's when I heard someone hollering. I muscled through the onlookers and saw Mustafa on the ground, wailing. His hand was pressed to the side of his head and blood ran down his face, staining his white apron.

His uncle rubbed his back as the EMTs tried inspecting his wound. I dropped to my knees and saw a shattered Kronenbourg bottle at his feet. "Mustafa, who did this?"

"Some *yout* did," an elderly black lady said, above me.

"Alright, that's enough," the male EMT put a hand on me. "Get back!"

I shoved the man away. "What did they *look like*?"

Mustafa looked at me, sobbing. "Sad face — Yeh-yeh."

"Yeh-yeh?" I repeated.

"Yeh. Yellow jacket," Mustafa said. "Yellow jacket, sad face."

"Which way did they go?" I asked the elderly lady.

She pointed south. I shot to my feet, darting through the people and ran smack into Shane.

"What's all this?" he asked, seeing Mustafa. "Jesus." He looked disgusted.

"Give me a ride up the street." I pulled him by the arm.

Shane sighed, but jogged with me for his car and we tore down Wandsworth Road. "We're looking for a group of teens," I said. "One of the dudes is in a yellow jacket."

"All this trouble for a retard?" he laughed, shifting gears.

"No! Don't call him that," I growled. "He's mentally challenged. You call assholes or douchebags retarded — but not him."

Shane grinned, watching me search his car. "I don't have any weapons in the car," he pulled out an issue of *The London Magazine* from the door pocket. I looked at him bewildered. "You roll that up proper, and mate, you'll see," he said.

I rolled it up tight, and to my surprise, it made a solid improvised club. We cruised a few blocks as I kept a watchful eye. When we stopped at a red light, I looked down a narrow side street slicing between apartment buildings. A group of dudes hung out under a flickering streetlight. I saw the sleeve of a yellow jacket under the flashing cone of light.

"There!" I pointed.

Shane ran us through the red light, down into the narrow street. We screeched to a halt and the teens jumped back, staring at me when I hopped out. The magazine wound tight in my hands.

"Hey—retard!" I yelled at the white kid in the yellow jacket.

He frowned but stood his ground. The group looked more confused than outright brave. That's when I saw Mustafa's neon green fliers at their feet, balled up and scattered about. And I lost it.

I swung that magazine so hard across the kid's jaw, I thought I broke it. Everyone in the group lurched into defense mode. But my magazine had momentum. I caught the lanky black kid next to him in the throat on my back swing. He bent over, gagging. A fat black kid fumbled with a butterfly knife from his joggers. I swung on his knife with the magazine and the blade folded on his fingers. He screamed, catching his heel on the curb and falling onto his back. Wop—wham—whap! I railed his chubby cheeks with the magazine.

The other boys scattered, bolting for the main road. The boy in yellow wobbled to his feet and I walloped the back of his neck. And again on his spine. He snapped like a balsawood plane and fell to his stomach.

Shane got out of the car, cackling. "Jog on." He kicked the kid with the bloody hand in the ass. The kid ran away, whimpering.

I rolled yellow jacket onto his back. His forehead bleeding. He was just a boy and was crying. I slapped his hands away and shoved the magazine into his cheek. "Mess with the kebab guy again, and it'll be a lot worse, you hear me?" I said. He just whimpered. "Say you understand!"

"I understand!" he said in a weird accent.

Satisfied, I stood up to leave, but Shane had a strange look on his face. He knelt down next to the boy. "What's your name?"

The boy cried. "Dieter."

"A German with a Polish accent?"

"My-my mum's Polish, and my father's German." Dieter trembled.

Shane inspected the narrow street, and seeing no one around, he pulled out a very old, but well-polished revolver.

I froze.

The boy tried to wriggle away, but Shane grabbed him and shoved the barrel into the kid's mouth. "This is an Enfield," Shane said. "And unlike you, Dieter, it's British. It was my grandfather's in the war, and I wonder—how many Germans has it killed?"

The kid bawled. "Pwease—pwease," he looked at me, with true fear in his eyes. "I'm sowwy—I'm sowwy."

Shane grinned. The Union Jack tattoo, ablaze on his neck. He removed the gun from Dieter's mouth and put it to his forehead, above his left eye. "You're only half German, so maybe I'll shoot this half." Shane laughed.

I'd seen enough. "Okay, man." I grabbed Shane's shoulder. "He already got his ass kicked—he's supposed to die too?"

Shane slipped the pistol into his jacket and stood. Dieter scrambled to his feet and clambered up the side street, his yellow jacket dirty from the alley. I stood in a daze, as he disappeared around the corner, unsure of what I'd just been a party to. Did we steer the boy away from violence, or did we push him harder toward it? And was this cruel side of Shane new, or was this just my first time seeing it?

"Kids." Shane chuckled. "Let's get that drink."

***

Shane was talkative in the car, seemingly energized by the encounter. I was silent as he told me how the pistol was his grandfather's, an RAF pilot in the war. His grandfather was shot down twice over occupied France, captured twice, and escaped twice back to Britain, where he eventually took part in the D-Day Invasion.

"I feel like I'm channeling the warrior my grandfather was when I carry it," Shane said, driving us toward Catford.

I'm a southerner, so I understand how a gun can make you feel badass, but I doubt Shane's grandfather ever shoved that revolver into a teenager's mouth. The scene with Dieter replayed in my head as we passed through Catford.

"What will you do after your course?" Shane asked. "Stay in the UK?"

People had asked me that question before, but never Shane. "I know I'll keep writing, but I haven't thought about where I'd work or live if I stayed."

"Hmm," he said, as we passed The Rifleman. It was lifeless and dark until Daniel's return in the new year. Maybe it was the realization I had no plans for the future, the sight of Daniel's absence, or the events with Dieter, but I didn't feel like hanging out with Shane anymore. I wanted to go home and check the mail to see if Mom sent me a Christmas card.

Shane parked on a modest lane a few blocks from the Catford High Street in front of a brick house with white windows and a faded red door. I followed him inside where he set his keys on a hall table in front of a small Tiffany lamp. To my left was a very twee sitting room, with an upright piano, and pea green carpet from the 1960s.

The decades passed before me in the photos in the hallway. Marriage portraits, newborns, elderly couples, even family dogs. There was a somber energy in the house, and I realized it was Shane's childhood home—to him, it was a holy place.

At the rear of the house was a study that overlooked a small garden. I perused Shane's bookshelf, spotting hackney taxi repair manuals peppered between the classics—Dickens, Eliot,

Brontë and Forster. And on the wall was a painting of a derelict barn that Bill would have loved. Taking it all in, I realized Shane had sealed his family home up like a tomb. Left it the way it had always been.

He poured us two glasses of whiskey, which isn't my thing, but I needed something after Mustafa and Dieter. Shane's live-in mausoleum was also a huge downer. I sat down on a worn leather sofa, Shane at his desk. He removed his jacket, exposing the pistol in a shoulder holster.

"I hear the rivalry between you and Profit may be getting out of hand," he said. Oh crap, I'm in trouble. "I don't need you to explain. Just letting you know the timing needs to be right, and then you can drop him in the Thames for all I care."

Nope, not feeling the murder talk. "I don't think that's necess—"

"Once this thing with Charlie is sorted, we won't have to worry about wankers like Profit anymore." He grinned. We took a couple of silent sips, until he groaned, "I wasn't going to worry you with my troubles, but I feel like I can trust you, Luke."

"Sure," I nodded. "What's up?"

Shane placed his pistol in the top drawer of his desk and pulled out the white binder from the bottom drawer and looked me straight in the eyes. "Someone in my organization is stealing from me," he said. I began sweating. "It's been done quite cleverly. Sophie and I can't seem to find the hemorrhage. She's brilliant, but so far, she's been unable to track it down. That worries me."

"I can promise you, it's not me," I said, my voice breaking.

Shane burst into laughter. "I know, mate. Relax." He sipped some whiskey. "I just need more people I can trust. You've got a good work ethic, and mate—you're bloody brutal when you need to be."

Still ashamed about Dieter, that didn't feel like a compliment. "Feels good to be useful. It's been great for my writing."

"That's well and good, of course, but I'd like to give you a chance at something with a bit more responsibility—payment collector," he handed me the binder.

"Payment collector—that doesn't sound so bad." I said, looking over the binder.

"It'll be your job to collect, then deliver all payments to Sophie, along with the ledger." He finished his whiskey. "And do me a favor? You're close with Sophie, pick her brain on who she thinks is stealing. Sometimes, I think she holds back because she's afraid of getting someone in trouble."

I frowned, unsure of his request. "What *would* happen if you caught who was stealing?"

The jovial expression left Shane's face. He reached into the drawer for the gun and pulled out nothing—aimed a finger gun at me. I flinched, like a little bitch.

Shane roared with laughter. "You think I'm going to gun them down in the street?" he chuckled. "Come on, let me show you something."

I followed Shane into the hallway with my whiskey, as he stopped in front of a family portrait that screamed early 1980s. Big hair and a soft focus. "I'm showing you what's under my mask. Do you remember that conversation?"

I nodded.

Shane pointed to the portrait. His father was plump with a bushy mustache, rosy cheeks and a familiar big grin. His mother had poofy blonde hair and green eyes; his older sister next to her looked like a miniature copy of her mother. The oldest, his brother, looked just like Shane, but with freckles and darker hair. Shane was the youngest and front and center, but with no tattoos or broken nose yet.

"This is the last bit of happiness I've ever known." He wiped dust from the frame. "Dad was dead later that year. Theo was diagnosed bipolar three years later—eventually taking his own. Vic has three children with two different men and has battled addiction since nineteen. Eventually, we lost mum to cancer and almost lost the house too—blah, blah—a sob story." He rubbed the dust between his fingers.

Strange seeing a picture of mostly dead people smiling back at you. "That's rough, man. I'm sorry."

"Don't be. Evolution says *adapt or die*. Adversity flamed the forges of who I'd become," he said. "I once studied at Cambridge, you know." Shane's posh accent finally made sense. "I studied business—head of my class. But those lads never let me forget I was just a cabby's son. So, I left and started my own business instead of learning to run someone else's. No matter the masks you wear for the world, you must never lose the face you have under it." He looked me in the eyes. "Writing is a fine hobby, mate. But your true skills lie in this business."

I looked down at my whiskey, wishing it was a beer. "I thought you said this was just an internship? Cause me and the boys—we all have dreams beyond this kind of work."

Shane laughed a smug laugh. "Mate, it's important we have dreams, but we all can't be—astronauts, famous actors or footballers." That hurt, thinking about King. "My goal has always been to aid the boys in seeing their potential, as well as their limitations." He steered me to the study to refill my glass. "Be honest, with me and yourself, where do you feel most comfortable? In a classroom or at my table at The Rifleman?"

With one hand he gave me my drink and with the other, the binder. And for the life of me, I still couldn't remember that saying about the devil and my idle hands.

Chapter 30

Lambeth
Bridge

I dreamt that I drowned. Cold water flooded into Bill's apartment and rose to my chest. I clung to a table, desperate to keep afloat, but water kept surging. It churned, black and brackish, and floating in the debris I saw a painting of me and my parents. Kicking to stay afloat, I grasped the painting, the colors smearing in my hands. The canvas and I were battered by the rush of water and as the paint washed away it revealed a pencil sketching underneath of straight lines and geometric shapes. A Y-shaped lattice work of lines—no, girders. The canvas and I sunk to the dark depths and in the last bit of fading light, the picture spun upside down. The Y-shape was the Eiffel Tower and it was the last thing I saw as the final breath spasmed from my body.

Paris, and the past, forever grabbing at my ankles from the darkness below.

***

I woke up in my bed, drenched in sweat. A shadowy figure stood in the doorway wearing only a pair of briefs. I rubbed my eyes, but it was only Juris.

"Jesus!" I shouted, catching my breath, "I'm sorry, man."

"It's okay," he turned to leave, but stopped. "You know, my grandmama used to say, bad dreams can only be healed while awake."

My head spun, trying to process my dream and the Latvian proverb. Juris sat on the foot of my bed. "Dream is like mirror to our life. Whatever is happening out, will also happen within. See?"

"I do." I wiped my brow. "And again, I'm sorry."

Juris nodded and gave my leg a friendly pat. When he shut my door, I began to wonder if *I* was the shitty roommate all along?

It was four forty-five in the morning and there was no going back to sleep. Which was unfortunate since my follow-up meeting with Mr Doe and Ms Smith was later that day and I wasn't going to be fully rested. I had drifted through the doldrums of January into early February, and by days end I'd know for certain if I was kicked out of my program.

I crept out of bed to make some coffee and to transcribe my dream. And when the sun rose orange through the kitchen window, I decided to make some bacon. I moved a giant stack of mail from the counter and a small package dropped to the floor. The return label read, *Venice, California,* written in my mom's perfect looping handwriting. The postage was from before Christmas, but the UK customs stamp was from a few days ago—what the hell?

Tearing into the package, I found a black and gold Cross pen inside. It was beautiful and heavy, and it eased into my hand. The more I studied it, the more touched I was by the gesture. That pen and my pit bull signet were the best gifts I'd ever gotten. I took a picture of the pen and sent it to my mother in a text, thanking her and explaining the mail fiasco.

After breakfast, I flipped through the white binder, reviewing the shops I would collect from that day. It was a little concerning how quickly I adjusted to payment collection. But despite having to break an occasional shop owner's nose or finger, it wasn't that hard of a gig. Most people were eager to pay and get me out of their shop and back into the car with Stumpy. There was only one rule for collecting: I never delivered Charlie's cut. Stumpy made the drop in Soho alone, because Charlie, Profit and their entire crew despised me.

When Stumpy called that morning to say he was outside, I left the white binder in my room for Sophie to collect later. The last time she picked it up, she agreed to come up for tea but insisted it wasn't a date. I think she just wanted to see where I lived.

It was a cold February morning, and I sunk into the heated leather seat of Stumpy's BMW 545 saloon. "Check out this bad boy," I handed him my pen.

He gave it a once over and tossed it back to me. "Too nice of a pen for whatever jobby you're writing, ya spazzy bastard!" he cackled.

"Prick," I stowed the pen in the breast pocket of my coat

As the day chugged along, I grew increasingly nervous about my uni meeting and I worried my drowning dream was some kind of premonition. Our collection route dragged and I became incapable of hiding my emotions, which made shop owners twitchy. Once they saw my sullen face, they scrambled to get me Shane's money.

Even the Sikh guy, Taranjit, who always tried haggling seemed put off. The bell clanged overhead as I stepped into his shop by Farringdon tube station. Taranjit stood behind the counter, and instead of yelling at me, he frowned and said, "You look sad today."

"Just some uni stuff—it's been weighing on me."

Taranjit handed me a band of money, then pointed to the little rack of candy bars next to the till. "You may choose one candy."

***

Stumpy and I got our last collection at four o'clock from a cocktail bar in Shoreditch and I needed to be at my university by five. "I won't have time to take you to uni before I make the drop to Charlie," Stumpy said. "You should be safe if you stay in the car."

"Sure, whatever," I said. Profit had been so far from my thoughts, I nearly forgot he existed. Surely that idiot couldn't still be mad about the champagne?

I stuffed Charlie's money into an envelope as we pulled up to her luggage shop on the north end of Carnaby Street in Soho. You know, those knockoff Samsonite's where the zippers break after one use? Stumpy locked me in the car and I scrolled through my phone looking at a new pair of Vans. But soon I had that feeling that someone was watching me. I looked up and made eye contact with Profit, walking down the street. He squinted at me, as if he couldn't believe I had the balls to show myself near his headquarters.

I jumped when the driver's door swung open. Stumpy poured himself into the driver's seat. "Jesus!" I yelped.

"A right wee feartie, aren't we?" Stumpy started the car.

Profit stopped dead in his tracks and as he passed my window, he nodded emphatically. Signaling he read my presence loud and clear. In the mirror, I saw him pull out his phone as he watched us drive away.

Stumpy dropped me off at Bedford Square with fifteen minutes to spare. I gave the park and my building one last look, worrying they'd scheduled our meeting for the end of the day on purpose. Like when a job fires you on a Friday afternoon so you have all weekend to talk yourself out of returning with an assault rifle on Monday.

I paced the top floor hall, rehearsing my speech of why they should let me stay, and how I planned to improve my behavior—although I had no plans of actually improving my behavior. With a couple minutes to go, my mom phoned me. She never called first.

"Hello?" I said.

"Lu, how are you?"

"I'm okay. This is quite a surprise."

"Well, I saw that you finally got the pen, and figured I would give you a call."

"Thank you. I really love it," my voiced echoed through the empty hall. "Mom, full disclosure; I'm about to go into a meeting with my university to determine whether I've been kicked out—ha!" It was so ridiculous I couldn't help but laugh.

"Oh, Luke."

"Yep—you know me. I'm going to get it figured out, though," I said, eying Mr Doe's big door. "Maybe you could call me back in an hour?"

"I can do that," she said. "Good luck with your meeting—and no matter what, keep calm."

I felt better after we hung up. Why couldn't all of our calls be like that? I knocked on Mr Doe's door, and like last time, a voice called from the other side. "Come in!"

Keep calm played on a loop as I stepped inside. Ms Smith stood by the presidential desk, while Mr Doe leaned an elbow on his armchair.

"Hello, Luke," Ms Smith said. "Please come in."

Big breath. The grandfather clock struck five, with cinematic timing, as I crossed the room. I studied them both, trying to read their expressions.

"Have a seat," Ms Smith smiled.

I gulped and did as I was told.

"Saving you the theatrics, I'm delighted to inform you the university has decided not to remove you from the course."

Screw my stupid dream! I nearly leapt from my chair with joy.

"Under certain conditions, however," Ms Smith added. I sat up straight. "Conditions that I have informed Mr Doe you would be more than happy to abide by."

"Yes, absolutely," I said.

Ms Smith opened a folder and read from a sheet of paper. "There can be no more outbursts in classes, peers and professors must be treated with respect, and there can be no more indications you are participating in distasteful activities."

"I can do that," I said. My eyes felt wet.

"There's an agreement for you to sign, placing you on academic probation through the end of the course," Ms Smith set a document on the desk. It looked official, with the school seal and everything. "Furthermore," she held up a folder. "I have your first term marks. Would you care to see them?"

The clock ticked as I stared at the folder. "Yeah, let's see 'em."

Mr Doe frowned as she handed over the folder. Inside was a cover sheet for Mr MacDougall's class with a checklist for grading criteria, and a box with some handwritten notes. I scanned the paper, seeing the number 69 written in a blank. She smiled when I flipped the page to her class. She wrote the word "moody" and the phrase "violent but emotive," and she wrote the number 70.

I scrunched my face. "I don't know how grades work over here—is a seventy good?"

Mr Doe rolled his eyes. "Yes," Ms Smith chuckled. "Anything 70 or above is distinction level work. In academic terms, that means your writing is publish-worthy."

Utter shock. I went into that office expecting the worst and instead I was reinstated to my program and earned high marks. I was on the brink of tears—I worked hard for those grades. I bled for those stories and my professors saw it. I feasted on Mr Doe's silence and I washed it down with a glass of praise from Ms Smith.

"My offer still stands if you need any advice on Duke's tale," she said. "I believe it's a story worth telling."

We concluded our meeting as I signed the list of conditions, where I proudly pushed Mr Doe's pen away and brandished my beloved new pen to sign my name. I shook both of their hands and I was off.

Out on the street, London sang to me in a way it hadn't in months. There was a big guy with dreadlocks milling about in Bedford Square and I thought it was Llanzo. I jogged over to say hello, but it wasn't him. The man glared at me, so I did an about-face for home. There was music in my commute—percussion as tires beat the street, brass in car horns, and woodwinds in the whine of passing engines. I stopped at Tottenham station and I thought about visiting Madeleine's mural, but decided she'd prefer me to walk. I put some music in my headphones and sauntered south.

Pedestrians and traffic flowed past me like a Sonata. I did a touristy stroll through Trafalgar and that's when the wind picked up, leaves and Costa cups whirling by. It was the coldest wind I'd ever felt, but with my thick parka and sunny disposition, I felt great. The temperature dropped and the sidewalk thinned. South of Parliament and along the river, I strolled alone, with the exception of a few hardy Londoners, scarved up like mummies.

The wind was so brutal at Lambeth Bridge, that I seemed to be the only pedestrian who dared cross it. I put my hood up and braced against the sting of river water nipping at my face. Ten feet across and my mother called, an hour on the dot.

Her voice was in stereo in my earbuds. "How did it go?"

"It went really well," I said. "It was kind of a misunderstanding, and anyway—I got my grades back. From what they explained, they were above average."

"Luke, that's incredible! I am so happy for you."

My tears felt like ice on my cheeks as I neared the halfway point of the bridge. The Thames churned below, black and brackish. Cars passed in waves. A rush of twenty for a minute, then almost nothing for another minute.

"I wanted to call and tell you—shrrrrsshhh—," she said, a gust slashed into the phone.

The blustery weather hampered my progress under the amber lights of the bridge. I threw off my hood and pressed the earphones into my ear. "I didn't hear what you said, Mom. I'm on a bridge and the wind is insane."

And suddenly, the wind died all at once. My face tingled as the feeling returned. A fellow pedestrian was walking toward me, so I stepped to the railing to let them pass. "Go ahead, Mom, the wind stopped."

"I said, David and I want to visit you this summer."

I was stunned. "You do?"

"Yeah. I thought a lot about our last two calls and I'd love to see you. The kids might come too, if that's okay?"

I remember thinking, *today is my lucky day*. "Of course," I said. The wind and traffic were silent as I stood alone on Lambeth Bridge. The London skyline brightened the more I stared at it.

The man walking toward me was a white boy with cornrows. He picked up his speed. Tires screeched on the bridge. My body tensed and I turned to discover a Mercedes G Wagon stopped in front of me. All black. Its subwoofers blaring rap music.

Wait a second.

The doors opened and guys jumped out. Profit towered above them. The cornrow dude charged at me. Behind me was the guy with dreads like Llanzo. He'd followed me and was now sprinting at me.

"Mom, I gotta go," I yanked the earbuds from my ears.

I dropped my bookbag and put up my fists as they rushed me. I hit one of them, but stumbled on my bag. Dreadlock dude punched my jaw. I saw a flash of white. They slammed me against the railing. Sharp pain in my spine.

I hit the dreadlock dude with a right hook. He fell back, but someone else punched my face. My knees buckled. I fought to stand. I thrashed. My elbow made contact with someone, but they pinned my arms against the rail. Then there was Profit. He punched me in the stomach. Then pulled out a blade. It was long, and shiny. Shimmering in the dull lamplight.

"Fuck you, pussy," I said. The only creativity I could conjure.

He didn't say shit. Just grunted as he sunk the blade in my gut.

Down feathers spurt from my parka as he pulled out the knife. I gritted my teeth as he sunk the blade in again. Then again and again. Sharp jabs of pain on the fourth and fifth stabs. I wrenched my leg free. Kicked Profit in the abdomen. Hands grasping at me, I lifted myself onto the railing. Rather take my chances with the Thames. I kicked another guy to free my arm.

"I'm going to kill you," I grunted at Profit.

"Me first," he said, aiming the knife high. For my neck—or face.

I kicked him in the mouth with my heel. His head flailed back. And I flipped backward over the railing.

London spun, then steadied. I saw my feet in the air and the skyline above me. Time slowed. The twenty-foot fall lasted forever. The brightness of the city pooled in my peripheral vision. I saw everything and nothing at once. Instinct kicked in and I took a deep breath. The holes in my gut burned. My back hit the water, solid and cold like pavement.

And that's how I died.

Chapter 31

Just kidding. I'm still alive.

It was a long fall. Things went black when I hit the water. When I came to, I was far below the surface and moving with the current. Icey water rushed into my parka, and when I kicked, I went nowhere but down.

Panic.

My legs were above my head and I thrashed at the water to right myself. It was a hard fight against the current and the weight of my coat. I struggled, but managed to peel it off. Felt the frigid water against me. I released my parka into the darkness. My mother's pen sinking with it. I kicked and fought for the surface. Pain shot through my side. The Thames is a bastard of a river. With each stroke, my progress was halved. My dream of drowning came to mind and a voice in my head called out, "No, not yet!"

My heart stammered in my chest. Like my old Volkswagen years ago, when it died one block from the gas station. *Just a little bit more, please.* I slammed the gas before everything faded. One more shot of fuel in the lines. My heart stuttered back to life before it pumped death through my veins. One last kick, one last thrash. I clawed for the surface.

By a goddamn miracle, I found it.

I broke through and sucked in a lungful of beautiful city air. A tinge of diesel in the taste. I faced the river wall on the South Bank, where voices shouted at me.

"There he is!" a woman shouted.

"I see 'im! I see 'im!" a man answered.

A row of darkened faces looked down at me from the ledge. Something was thrown. It landed in the water with a PLOP.

"Grab it, mate!" one of the heads called.

"Come on, you've got it!" another called out.

It was an orange life ring, tethered by a yellow nylon rope. I'd seen them along the embankment and often wondered what poor asshole would ever need one. I hooked an arm through and felt myself being towed to a dock of moored boats. Police boats often patrolled the Thames and I figured it wouldn't be long before one arrived. There'd be too many questions. I needed to get on that dock and home before the cops showed.

I chopped at the water with my free arm to speed up my tow. A couple men ran down the gangway to meet me on the dock. They heaved me out of the water and onto my knees. Water poured from my clothes and squished from my shoes. I was so numb I could barely feel their hands on me.

No time to rest—I staggered to my feet, feeling a stab of pain in my gut. *Nope. Ignore that, Luke.*

"Hold on, take it easy, mate," one of the men steadied me. A black guy, maybe my age, in a suit and tie and thick wool coat.

The other man was an older white man with a snowy beard. He coiled up the nylon rope. "You're alight, my boy," the old man patted my back. "We'll get you to hospital."

"No!" I shimmied past them. "It's uh—an emergency. I've gotta go."

They frowned at me like I was crazy.

"Are you quite sure?" the businessman asked. "Mate, you've been thrown from a bridge."

"I live nearby. I'm good, thank you!" I hobbled up the gangway with numb legs.

A crowd gathered at the river walk, their faces coming into detail under the streetlight. All types, young and old. They stared with wide, concerned eyes. "Are you okay, darling?" a blonde woman, my mother's age, asked. I recognized her voice as the lady who called to me in the water.

"I'm fine," I reassured her. "Thank you all, but I need to go."

My stomach burned white hot. I clutched a hand to my side and ran to the bridge for my backpack, but it was gone. Bastard!

A flash of heat shot through me, but the blistery wind dowsed it. *No time. Home—now.* I left the bridge just in time to see a police boat put its search light on the boat dock.

Profit, that piece of shit. I had everything in that bag. My laptop, and all of my coursework—my story. Yes, I'd backed up my documents but what about my notebook with five months of notes?

Fantasies of killing Profit fueled my wounded jog home, but soon my thoughts shifted to hypothermia. Most North Carolinians know nothing about that, but I figured I'd be okay if I kept my body temperature high. I scampered by commuters in Vauxhall Station, their faces in their phones, unaware of the bleeding sewer rat scuttling past. Blood soaked through my hoodie, staining my hand red. I couldn't help but see my passing reflection in parked car windows. My eyes were dark and panicked like a wounded animal.

A side street spat me, limping, back onto Wandsworth. My Vans squeaked under me. Tunnel vision on my building, I galloped. My throat was sore, as I fought for breath. My legs sensed their proximity to home and began to falter. I stumbled to my front door. My sight blurred and I didn't notice the person sitting on the front steps.

"My God," Sophie said. She had come for the binder. I was both relieved and embarrassed to see her. "Are you alright?"

"Totally fine," I wheezed, struggling to pull the keys from my wet jeans.

She spotted my bloody hand. "You are *not* alright! You need an ambulance."

"No!" I shouted. She took a step back. "I'm sorry—I just can't do that. Please, help me inside?"

Sophie glared, but grabbed my arm and guided me into the building. We labored up the four flights. The closer I got to my flat, the more my muscles gave up. But Sophie dragged me up the last flight. My flat was dark and there was a glow from under the Latvians' door, which meant they'd not resurface until the morning.

"Bathroom," I pointed.

Sophie pulled me down the hall where I collapsed onto the floor against the tub. My body shook violently. Sophie's crystal blue eyes were wide with fear. "What happened to you?"

My throat was dry. "Water—please," I said.

She left and returned with a pint of water. I drank until my sides hurt. "Remember—champagne guy?" I asked. She nodded. "Stabbed me—I fell off the bridge—into the Thames."

Sophie's eyes went glassy. I wasn't looking for her sympathy, but it was nice to know I had it. "We need to warm you." She turned on the tub faucet. "Let's get you out of your clothes."

"You first." I gave a painful chuckle.

"Do you want my help or not?"

"Yes, ma'am," I said.

My blue fingers trembled as I untied my Vans. A river of brown water poured from them onto the white tile. With Sophie's help, I shed everything but my boxers. I was concerned about the damage we'd find on my stomach, so I didn't look. Just felt the warm stream of blood from my side and pointed to my towels behind her. "The white ones are mine."

She dabbed at my side to inspect the wounds. "How do you feel?"

My teeth chattered. "I should mention, I'm prone to nausea."

Sophie chuckled. The white towel reddened as she sopped up the blood. "How bad is it?" I asked.

"You've got two wounds."

"Only two? Prick stabbed me a million times."

"Lucky for you he missed," she shrugged. "One's wider than it is deep, and the other's nicked your love handle quite bad. Both need stitches."

I braved a glance and saw one long gash and another the shape of a crescent moon. It was only a couple inches deep into my pudge. I was still nauseous, but relieved. "Can you stitch it? I can't do the hospital. They'll call the police."

Sophie's lip curled. "What makes you think I've ever sewn anyone up?"

"Who the hell has? But I'm screwed if I go to the hospital. Please—help me, Soph."

Those piercing blue eyes. If she had a knife, I swear she'd have given me a few more holes. "Hold that." She pushed the towel to my side. Pain shot like lightning from my gut into my chest. She rinsed her hands off in the tub faucet. "Get in and clean the wound as best you can. I'll find something," she said, leaving the bathroom.

"There's a sewing kit in the kitchen," I called after her.

I looked at the muddy, bloody state of the bathroom and eased into the tub. The water greeted me, white hot. It took everything in me not to scream in pain. If only the Latvians were as noise-conscious when it came to their bathing rituals.

Sophie returned with a small first aid kit and a tube of super glue. "If you're too stupid for hospital," she groaned, "then I'm sure as hell not running some dirty needle through you and having it go gangrene."

The super glue seemed like an expert move, but I didn't mention it. Once my bathwater turned pink, Sophie helped me onto a towel on the floor. Pain shuddered through my torso as she glued me back together. I closed my eyes and I saw myself below the Thames and drifting in the darkness. Two paths were placed before me. One with God; spare my life and I vow to do good things with my life. And one with the devil; spare me and I vow to have my revenge. Once again, the choices were only black and white.

All I wanted was to save my mother's pen.

"There," Sophie said, perched on her knees. "All done."

A doctor would have been hard pressed to do a better job. "I thought you hadn't done anything like that before," I said. She didn't look at me. Just rubbed a thin layer of ointment on my wounds until they were shiny. "Sophie," I said.

"I never said that," she snapped at me. "Do you have any pain medication? 'Cause you're in for a long night if you don't."

"I have some Vicodin."

"You'll want to take those." She helped me sit up. "And tomorrow, you'll want to get on a course of antibiotics—with all the drugs you boys have access to, please tell me you can get those."

"Kieran's basically a pharmacist." I smiled through my burning side.

I hobbled to my room while Sophie cleaned the bloody mess in the bathroom. I changed into some dry clothes, took my last two Vicodin and laid down. By the time she returned with my ruined towels in a trash bag, I felt the pills and not much else.

"How are you feeling?"

"Good." I smiled, closing my heavy eyelids.

"Glad to hear it. Now, where's the ledger? I need to pick up my daughter from my neighbor."

I opened my eyes. "Will you stay with me for a bit? Just until I fall asleep?"

"There's nowhere for me to sit."

Carefully, I wriggled across my bed to create a space for her. "Only if you think you can keep your hands off me," I said, closing my eyes.

She huffed, but eventually the bed shifted and I felt her next to me. Our arms touched. Fingers, centimeters apart. We were quiet for a while and when I opened my eyes, I found her blue eyes locked onto mine. "What's up?" I asked.

"Strange seeing you drop the tough guy act."

"Pfft, I'm not tough," I slurred. "In fact, I must look like the biggest pussy ever. People always mess with me. Kids picked on me. Teachers critiqued the shit out of me, and Bill—my dad..." I trailed off.

"What about him?"

"He wasn't a very caring single parent."

"Oh," she said. I felt numb and warm, floating in that narrow space between sleep and awake. "What about your mum?"

I'd never taken Vicodin on an empty stomach before—let alone two. I saw visions of my mother on a beach playing with a little boy. Sophie was there too somehow. Like I'd foreseen her visit, and left the door open to this memory.

"She left for California," I pointed to my young mother and the boy. "To escape."

"To escape what?"

The waves crashed on the beach, and I felt very distant from my mother. "I was too little—small like him," I pointed to the boy.

"I don't understand. Too little for what?"

"Couldn't protect her," I said, a sob in the back of my throat. "I was just too little, and Bill was so strong. Couldn't stop him from hurting her."

Sophie sucked in a sharp breath, held my hand. "You know, that's not your fault. That wasn't your responsibility."

I shook my head. The waves rolled in gray-blue behind my mother and little Braden. Teenage me sulked in the distance, tossing my cigarette butts to seagulls. "Therapists—family— they all said that. Wasn't my fault—wasn't my responsibility. But no one could ever help me feel like it wasn't."

The memory grew dark as sleep came for me. The waves receded from the beach and I was all alone once again. "Warned me," I mumbled. "He warned me."

"Who warned you, Luke?" Sophie asked. Or was it my mother.

"Don't be me. Don't be—"

***

The next morning, I woke up on my good side. Golden light filled my room. Sophie stood next to the bed, putting on her coat. "You're leaving?" I asked.

"I shouldn't have stayed in the first place."

My side was stiff and I was slow to sit up. "I'm glad you did, though," I said. Sophie forced a smile. "Soph, it's no secret how I feel about you."

"Luke, please don't."

"And I think you feel something too." I put my feet on the floor. "We've had a couple of almost moments."

"*Almost* is the keyword," she picked up her purse. "Where's the ledger?" I pointed to my wardrobe. She crossed the room for it and I stood to face her.

"Are you telling me you don't feel anything for me at all?" I asked. "Because that's bullshit, and I'm not buying it."

"Well, that's your problem." Sophie snatched the binder and threw open my bedroom door. She bolted down the hallway for the front door, but I was right behind her.

Morning light reflected from the hanging pots in my kitchen like a shitty disco ball. I caught Sophie by the arm at the door and spun her around. I pulled her close. She didn't resist. She pulled herself tight against me.

"Tell me that you don't feel anything when you're with me." I looked into her pretty eyes. "I want to hear you say the words."

We gazed silently at one another. Her eyes were wet and her lips began to part. I wanted to kiss her. It's all I had wanted for months. I leaned in but she put up a hand to stop me.

"Pain," she said.

I pulled my head back. Did I hear that correctly?

"I didn't know what I felt until last night," she said. "But after stitching you up and hearing about your life—you make me feel pain. What I feel for you is a shadow of a copy of what I feel for another man. My daughter's father."

Speechless, I let go of her. The light from the pots pulsed in my peripheral vision, matching the throb in my side.

Sophie's breath trembled, with her on the verge of tears. "You remind me of him," she said. "The same impulsive, rash behavior. Both of you caught in the same cycle of bullshit and violence. Too stupid to see the consequences of your actions. I can't be mum to both a little girl and a man—sewing him up in the bathroom for the hundredth time." She shook with anger. "No, not again. *Never* again."

The words hung in the air as I tried to process what she'd said. Every vibe I got from Sophie, from the first glare to the snarky comments, what I perceived as flirting or a mutual attraction was only pain. I couldn't even be heartbroken, since love was never on the table.

Sophie's glare softened. "I'm sorry, Luke."

"I get it." I put up a hand. "I hate how much I get it, but I do."

She looked like she wanted to hug me, but instead she swung open my door and left. It slammed shut, and I was left with nothing but pain in my side and emptiness in my heart.

Chapter 32

After Sophie left, I went back to my room, but couldn't sleep. I had no more pills for the sting in my wounds, and even if I did, I wouldn't have taken them. I wanted to feel the pain. I needed to live in that pain, because it was better than the sunken feeling in my chest. They should have never pulled me out of that damn river. I should have done everyone a favor and gone down with my mother's pen. Instead, I pushed Sophie away for good.

I clutched my bedding as I thought about how I got there—Profit. If it weren't for him, maybe I could have salvaged things with Sophie. I sat up in bed. Profit, and his boys, stabbed me and forced me to jump into the damn river. I was so concerned with Sophie that I hadn't thought it all the way through.

What Profit did couldn't go unanswered. And he had my story—I bled for that story and he couldn't have it. I changed my bandages and threw on some clothes. Then I lit a smoke right in the middle of my kitchen. A burnt offering on the altar of retaliation.

***

It was eleven in the morning when I rocked up to The Rifleman, and dark clouds came with me. Wind rushed in behind as I pushed open the pub door. Everyone was huddled around the corner table: Shane, King, Kieran, Ibrahim and Llanzo. Hell, even Jamie, Swift and Stumpy were there. Daniel sat at the next table with his newspaper.

They all stood up from their seats like they'd seen a ghost. *Holy shit! Fuckinell!* The boys rushed me.

"We heard this mornin', fam." King put a hand on my shoulder. "Profit's mandem were bragging online about jumping you."

People on Twitter know who I am? The boys grabbed at me. "Careful, careful." I raised my shirt, showing my bandages. *Ooh*, they all hummed. Shane was silent.

"Profit stabbed me," I said, trembling. "He and his boys jumped me on the Lambeth Bridge. He stuck me twice and I ended up in the Thames."

There was a collective gasp. Daniel's face twisted to something between disbelief and disgust. "We can't stand for that, Shane," King said.

"Fuck that pussio," Llanzo growled.

"Let's get that cunt," Ibrahim said. The rest of the boys joined in.

Shane put up a hand. "Moving against Charlie has always been a part of the plan—" He looked at Daniel. "Danny, mate, could we all speak alone?"

Daniel's shoulder rose and fell in defeat. His business had been overtaken by a gangster, he couldn't help me or the boys, and now he'd been asked to leave his own pub. He snatched his paper from the table and grumbled down the back hallway for his office.

"I wasn't planning on moving against Charlie this soon," Shane said. We all groaned. "But! Profit *did* cross a line. King is right, we can't stand for that." We all hissed, me the loudest. "Stumpy!" Shane called out.

"Way ahead of you, lad," Stumpy said. "I've got a van close by. It's grim, but she'll haul this lot."

Shane ordered Kieran and Ibrahim to go with him. He sent Swift and Jamie to fetch us masks. And lastly, King and Llanzo were sent for a cache of weapons stored nearby. I told myself not to think about that, afraid I'd talk myself out of our violent plot.

Before the boys returned, Shane pulled me aside. "I told you, mate. These things escalate. This is all on you now. If it goes well, I'll claim it and we'll cut Charlie's legs out from underneath her. But if it goes poorly, I'll have to denounce it. And you'll be on your own, just you and the wolves. And they *will* come."

I nodded, understanding the risks. Just as I turned to leave, Shane grabbed my arm. "When the time comes, you'll be tempted to kill him." His green eyes went dark. "I know you want this story bad, but if you kill him like this—it'll be the only story you ever write."

"I understand, but forget the story," I said. "I'm doing this for me."

Shane grinned his big teeth. "Good man. Keep that level head."

***

The seven of us jammed into another busted-ass work van. Stuffed between Llanzo and Swift, I closed my eyes to visualize my hands on Profit's throat and feel his pulse fade beneath my fingers. *No! Don't kill him.* Maybe I couldn't kill him, but I was determined to untangle our two paths that day.

King dropped a duffle bag at my feet, unzipping it to reveal a nest of weapons. There were aluminum bats, police batons, asps, even machetes and daggers.

"You pick first," King said to me, stoically. I wondered if he'd done this sort of thing before.

I rifled through the bag and felt the cold touch of steel, rubber grips, blades edges, until eventually I found the only piece of wood and pulled out a rounders bat. It was dark-stained and nicked—it served its previous master well.

"I'll take the fish bat," I turned it in my hands.

"W-what's a fish bat?" Kieran asked across from me.

"When you go deep sea fishin' and you pull in a big ol' fish and it's flopping on the deck for dear life," I said, looking him in the eyes. "You beat its ass to death with this."

Kieran gulped. The rest of the crew gave a solemn nod, then dug into the bag, snatching up clubs and knives. My pulse quickened as the van rocked over the narrow Soho streets, but I wasn't nervous, just anxious to get this over with. I felt the sting in my side and wondered what Sophie was up to—

No! Don't think about that.

The dark clouds followed our van into Soho and blanketed us in brief silence as Llanzo handed out masks. He handed me the demon mask from Camden Town. It was strangely calming to be reunited with, like seeing an old friend.

"Two minutes!" Stumpy called from the driver seat.

King knelt in the center of us as the van thudded over uneven pavement. "Alright, fam. The shop is small. Only one or two mandem up front—they all hang in the back room, ya?"

"How many in the back?" Jamie asked, shakily.

"No more than five," King said. "We'll go in fast, catch 'em off guard. Don't let any customers leave until we're done—they'll bring the feds."

"One minute!" Stumpy called.

The road got bumpier over a stretch of cobblestones, and I thought about Sophie again. If I was going to get through these next few minutes, then I needed to live in that pain. Feel the coldness of her rejection, like the sun had set on me. *I've dated a gangster before—I won't do that again.* Her words echoed. Live in that pain. The ache in my side. I let the blade sink in again and again.

"Thirty seconds!"

"Most importantly," King added. "Save the tall one for
Luke."

I was a teen again, watching my mother with her new son.
The motherhood she actually wanted. Not the pregnancy she
was forced to keep, or the marriage she was forced to have.

Live in that pain.

Sophie, her blue eyes wet, staring through me and seeing all of
the evil I was before I was even born. *You make me feel pain,* she said.

If pain was all I had to give, then I would give it well.

The boys and I pulled on our masks. The van lurched to a halt
and the doors opened, filling the cab with light. We poured onto
the street, a mob in black, and I followed the masked marauders
into the store. A cheery doorbell sang its hymn seven times
as we filed in. The shop walls were crammed with shelves of
luggage. The only customers were a Chinese couple, who froze
when they saw us. There was a struggle ahead of me—a solitary
clerk swung his arms. A tall African man with a long reach.
King hit the man's thigh with a pipe, POCK! The clerk yelped
and dropped to the ground in surrender.

Where do I go? I rang the bat in my hands. Jamie and Swift
grouped our three prisoners together. "Don't move," they said.
"If you know what's good for you."

Llanzo kicked the backroom door open. Kieran followed,
smashing the camera overhead. I yanked my mask off. I wanted
Profit to know what this was all about. To live in the pain
with me.

I charged into the room after the boys. There was thrashing
and hollering, "Fuck you! I'll kill you!" Followed by fists, then
clubs. The groans of struggle. The room was small. Shelves of
luggage, wrapped in plastic. The boys clubbed people I couldn't
even make out. Just arms and legs in the air—ill-fated defense
against the iron.

Profit stood, untouched in the middle of the chaos. A bruised
forehead and the dark circles round his eyes. He scrunched

his face, seeing me. "Cash!" he shouted. He rifled through the workbench behind him.

"No!" I shouted. I came for blood, not money.

The room moved in waves of club strikes, then stopped as Profit's boys were beaten senseless. I charged for him. He spun around and swiped at me with a machete. Adrenaline shot through me, electric. I swung—broke his hand with my bat—CRACK! He yelped, but took another swipe at me. I lunged back—he swung again. Everyone watching. The loser would lose bad. *Life or death, Luke.*

Live in the pain.

Profit was there with me now. We were all hurt boys in this room. I could take a bit more. So, I charged him. Profit chopped down for my head, lodging his machete into my bat. I ran through it and crashed into him. The bat and machete fused, fell to the floor. We tore at one another. Twisting and slashing, nails dug into flesh. The stitches in my side ripped.

Live in the pain.

We kneed and kicked one another. We spun and thrashed. The boys dove out of our way as Profit's and my legs interlocked. Falling, we grasped a tall shelf, which tore from the drywall. Profit and I crashed to the floor under the shelf. Maybe I'm lucky, or maybe I'm better, but I wriggled free from the heap of metal. Profit didn't.

The room hissed for me. Profit fought but couldn't free himself from the hefty rack. I stood on the shelf, put my weight onto it. The shelves dug into his stomach and neck. The air squeezed from his body. He gritted his ruby teeth but couldn't free himself.

I picked up my bat and kicked the machete free. A ring of masked faces watched in silence. My wounds pulsed with pain. A trickle of hot blood ran down my side into my jeans. I whacked Profit in the cheek with my bat. He whined, and the boys took a step forward. I hadn't decided what to do next, but the boys seemed to have their suspicions.

"Get off me," Profit growled. "You pussio, faggot-mother-fucker!"

I glared at him with Bill's insane hazel eyes.

"You're dead," he moaned. "Charlie's gonna kill you—you're done!"

I stepped on his neck. He gargled in pain.

"Luke, come on," King said. "Can't kill him, fam."

"Who the hell says I can't?" I faced him. "Shane? He ain't here, slick! We are! We're always the ones!" I thought of Ms Smith. About Sean and Duke. The young men in my story.

"Bruv, what're you saying?" King said.

My body shook with rage. "I don't know what I'm saying—but this asshole stabbed me and tossed me off a bridge. And I can't kill him?"

Profit kicked at the floor with his free leg, trying to wriggle free.

King shook his head. "No, you can't kill him. It's not fair, but that's the rules, innit?"

Profit looked up at me as he struggled. Like Dieter in the yellow coat, he was caught in the same cycle of violence I was. No, I couldn't kill Profit, but I could free him from that cycle.

"You're right," I said. "It's not fair to kill him. After all, he didn't kill me."

I took a breath and exhaled my anger like smoke from my lungs. The room gave a collective sigh. Although he was stuck, Profit looked relieved too.

Until I went for his free leg.

Smashed my bat into his knee. Profit screamed, blood curdling. I went for the knee again. He screamed louder. The shelf shifted, but he remained trapped. I lifted the bat high above my head and put every ounce of my strength into each blow. Until the bone was no longer solid. Until Profit passed out from the pain. Until my fish bat snapped in half. Until the boys pulled me off of him.

Until I freed Profit from the cycle of violence he desperately needed freeing from.

No need to thank me, Profit. See you on the other side, brother.

Chapter 33

I left a piece of myself in that backroom. Something vital and human, but for the life of me I can't place what it was. The shop was silent when I came out. Stumpy was there, with a pistol in his belt. I set my broken club on a shelf next to a knockoff Victorinox suitcase.

"L-Luke," Kieran said. "This your bag, mate?"

Inside was my notebook, laptop and pens—all of it untouched. Didn't think I'd see it again. I looked at Kieran, tall and lanky like a Great Dane puppy and gave him a hug. Just felt like I needed it, maybe him too. His chest spasmed as he laughed.

"Aye, ya bampots!" Stumpy grabbed us. "Let's get *oot* of here!"

I threw my mask on cockeyed as Stumpy pushed us outside and into the van. King slammed the doors shut, and we rumbled off, leaving any onlookers bewildered in a cloud of black exhaust.

The boys chattered away on the ride back to Catford—who they hit and who went down easy. But no one spoke of the horror I inflicted on Profit—a guy who had the exact same job they did. Maybe they believed it was justified. That balance was restored. "Roadman tings" as King said. But I don't think any of them ever stopped to think; *could something that brutal ever happen to me?*

Rumors flew around London. Strangers knew my name and what I'd done to Profit, with all kinds of barbaric variations. Some claimed I used a sledgehammer or a crowbar, but no matter the version, Shane instructed us to just let people talk.

Shane and Charlie met a couple days later to discuss the brutal removal of her top boy. It must have been an intense meeting, because Shane and Stumpy looked disheveled when they returned to The Rifleman.

Shane drank two helpings of whiskey before telling me, "She's gone now," his sea green eyes churned. "Er—took her baby to some quaint market village. Somewhere in Wiltshire. Right, Stump?"

"Um, Corsham, I believe." Stumpy threw back his drink.

The story was oddly reminiscent of that "farm" people sent the family dog to when it got old. But I didn't have time to interpret what really happened, because as soon as Charlie was gone, the vultures descended on what was left of her empire. For the rest of February and well into March, the boys and I were sent all over London to stomp out any of Charlie's former crew who attempted to pick up the pieces of her business.

All the while, Shane grew increasingly desperate to find who was siphoning from his burgeoning empire. "I'm taking you out of the clubs, mate," he said, over a pint, a week after Profit. "We've got to capitalize on this rumor of yours, and we have to do it now."

"Shane, what the hell?" I said. "The boys and I crush it at the clubs and—we have fun."

"Fun?" Shane snorted. The boys cowered behind their beers. "Mate, I don't give a damn you're having fun. The point is to make money." Shane pushed himself from the table. "Come with me."

Head down, I followed him to the bar. He gestured for Sophie to grab the white binder and come too. She and I stood side-by-side in the alley as Shane paced. Sophie's sweet smell hung in the air. It was the same scent that had been slowly fading from my pillow for days, as if she'd never been there at all.

"Mate, pay attention," Shane opened the binder. "We're on a razor's edge with cashflow and that's dangerous when we're on the verge of an expanse like this." He showed me a gridded page, scrawled with numbers. I nodded as if I didn't take college statistics twice.

"Sophie checks our numbers against these businesses once a week," Shane said. Sophie stared at her feet. "And each week, someone's numbers don't match our takings. And as soon as we catch it, the difference shows up somewhere else. And it's the same with Paris numbers. She's doing her job to sort it, and I need you to work exclusively with Stumpy," he said.

I groaned and Shane got in my face. "You take your bad attitude and that rumor, and keep these shopkeepers in line," he said.

Embarrassed, I didn't look at Sophie again. Just followed Shane inside and quietly drank my beer. Working for Shane was beginning to sour, but I told myself to look on the bright side. I was being paid well and he still looked out for me and the boys. Plus, there was never any shortage of stories.

***

My first day back at uni was Valentine's Day. My stab wounds were nearly healed, but gossip of me being a gangster hadn't. I felt the curious glances from my new classmates. All of them wanted a look at the program's problem child. Whatever, man. I let their imaginations run wild as they ogled the fading cuts and bruises on my hands. I lived an adventure they could only dream to write about.

Ironically, one of my new classes on Valentine's Day was called the Love Story. The module covered romance novels, which we discussed in excruciating detail in order to apply them to our own writing. Considering Sophie's recent rejection, the will-they-won't-they premise of books like *Pride and Prejudice* didn't make me swoon. There were no funny or brave heroines in my story, just scared and violent men.

Stumpy and I stopped into The Rifleman later that night to meet with Shane. A few ugly couples cozied up in the booths and the whole place was decorated in red hearts. Kill me. Sophie and I barely exchanged glances as she handed me the binder.

Chiara served me a sympathy pout. "I know you're sad, so I don't want to gloat."

"I'm not sad."

"I'm a woman, and Italian. I can sense these things."

"Please, just gloat away," I said with a sigh.

"Kieran and I made it official," she said, beaming.

I wanted to be annoyed, but I loved her and Kieran. "The kid's crazy about you," I said with a smile. "And you're a good influence on him. Maybe you can convince him to go back to school."

"We've actually been talking about it." She handed me an IPA. "He wants to study business, like Llanzo and 'Brahim. Says he wants to manage rappers."

Couldn't knock the kid for aiming high. I called Kieran over and the three of us snuck a celebratory shot of tequila. I bought one for Sophie too. She rolled those pretty eyes at me, but knelt down behind the bar and threw back her shot.

Unfortunately, I couldn't stay. Stumpy and I had more shops to visit. The rest of February I spent less time with the boys and more time in dusty bodegas, smacking immigrants for missing money they probably didn't steal. I felt myself spiraling into depression.

Shane said it was "probably just a vitamin D deficiency — everyone in the UK gets it in winter. Just work through it."

My wounds healed, but the pain moved into my chest and grew heavy like a cancer. It shortened my breath when I got too sober or asked myself — where is all this going? And one day in March, I finally got my answer.

I was in the backroom of a vape shop, washing the clerk's nose blood off my hands when I got a text from Cash; *hey buddy, I've got a few days off at the end of the month. I booked tickets to London for your birthday!*

Was that where this was headed? I'd spent months convincing Cash my time in London was completely normal. That I was growing from the experience. Cash knew exactly who I was when I last saw him in September, but what would he think of the Luke he found when he returned?

Chapter 34

As soon as I got a reputation for hurting people for Shane, it felt like I left traces of myself across London. I noticed the turn of every CCTV camera, or the sideways glances of cops I passed — as if some criminal case was being built against me from some backroom. When you do enough bad shit, it feels like the world is watching.

I stood in the Heathrow terminal, wondering how I was going to hide my new life from Cash for the next six days. As my best friend, he knew twenty years of my secrets, but I'd accrued much darker secrets over the past six months. If he found out the truth it would mean the end of our friendship.

Cash looked at me funny when he came through customs, like he didn't recognize me. But his eyes looked happy and he gave me a brotherly hug. "Man, it's good to see you," he said. "You look — sturdy! Been hitting the gym?"

"No," I laughed. "A little boxing, though." I mean, it wasn't a complete lie.

"Boxing is a great stress-reliever."

We concluded our reunions and I took Cash's laptop bag and led him to the Heathrow Express. We small-talked about some turbulence on his flight and the snoring man next to him. Eventually, he pointed to a Costa, "You mind? I'm dying," he said.

While we waited for his Americano, I asked, "How's Manhattan and your new place?"

"It's great." He drummed on his luggage. "We're in the Upper West Side, our street is nice and quiet. It's a short walk to the eighty-sixth street station on Broadway."

I oohed, pretending I knew where that was. "And the job?"

"It's challenging — but I'd be lying if I didn't say the pay was worth it." He grinned. I grimaced when he poured almond milk into his coffee. "That's the only caveat to my visit. We can sightsee, but because of the time difference I may need to work late some evenings."

"We can do whatever you want."

Cash sipped his almond-coffee soup and smacked my arm. "Hey—it's your birthday week, we'll do what *you* want to do!"

I didn't want to celebrate my twenty-ninth birthday in the first place. I thought I'd have life figured out by twenty-nine, instead I'd never been more confused, and I'd lost the blind confidence of my early twenties.

Déjà vu hit me like a gut punch when Cash and I got to Paddington. It had only been six months since Paris and it seemed like he'd become more Cash-like, channeling his trauma into productivity. He landed a killer job in Manhattan and locked down a fiancé. Whereas I became more Luke, and built an unstable wall, high around my wounds.

"Tube?" I asked.

"Let's get a cab. I've got a surprise," he said.

We schlepped his luggage out to Praed Street like we did in September and piled into a cab. Cash gave the driver an address and we rode toward Hyde Park, past the Wellington Arch, through Belgravia and into Pimlico. White Regency homes, and their sterile columns, were copied and pasted along the way until we stopped at a large townhouse on Saint George's Square.

"Perks of the new job," Cash said, paying the driver.

He hopped up the steps to the massive white door and punched in a code to buzz us in. Gawking up at the place, I lugged his bags into the foyer. Despite its nineteenth century exterior, the interior had been gutted into a modern open concept. Polished marble floors, and pure white walls, with long dangling light fixtures. The corridor illuminated when we passed through, as if the place had a consciousness of its own.

Noon sun poured in through the rear of the house, which was made entirely of glass. And directly off the kitchen was a greenhouse, brimming with jungle ferns and red orchids, dwelling thousands of miles from their native lands. The place was more of an art gallery than a home.

"What do you think?" he asked.

"Surprised there wasn't a credit check at the front door," I said. He laughed. "Is this—yours?"

"It belongs to my company. It's for their executives when they're in London and—" he paused dramatically. "For the company's top earners."

It took me a second, but I pointed at him.

He nodded. "I landed a string of clients this quarter—a company record hot streak. So, they let me stay here and said I could bring whoever I want."

Cash ran his hand across a wall, which turned out to be a fridge. He pulled out two bottles of sparkling water and cracked one for me.

"Not to sound ungrateful, but maybe you should have brought Emma?" I said.

"No way, bro. I'm here for *your* birthday. She understands." He hopped up to sit on the counter. "Plus, I promised to take her somewhere tropical for the honeymoon. So, go home and pack a bag and crash here for the week. Get out of that *rustic* flat of yours."

My smile faded. Although I'd done my share of complaining, I liked my place now. I took my sparkling water and went with Cash to explore the five—yes, five—massive bedrooms and the fully-stocked bar on the terrace that looked eastward to the Thames and Vauxhall Bridge.

I went back to my place to pack a bag and was happy to breath in stale onion air. Had Cash and I changed that much in just six months? We felt oceans apart, not just in locations, but in economic standing too. When I returned to the Saint George's house, Cash had pizza and beer waiting for me. He handed me a beer as I walked in the door. "Clear your schedule, Lukey," Cash said. "We're drinking today."

Alright—maybe we hadn't changed *that* much.

***

The first few days of Cash's visit went better than expected. The first day, we drank at a bunch of pubs, then visited the Tate the next morning. That afternoon we did Churchill's War Rooms, then the British Museum the following morning, and the Natural History Museum in the afternoon.

Luckily, Cash's work picked up and I got some time for myself. But by day four, I felt myself being pulled between Cash and my past life and Shane and my new life. Shane tried to be understanding, but he was annoyed I was out of commission that week. "I understand he's your friend, mate, but we're leaving money on the table," Shane texted. "You're on double-time next week to make up for it."

By day five, the silences between Cash and I grew longer, so I invited Heath to meet us for drinks. "Should we do the American bar again?" Heath asked, over the phone.

"No!" I yelled. "That place got old, but we can do something near Uni, though. Meet after class?"

Heath met us at a pub called The Imperial, near Leicester Square. It was a proper pub, dripping in brass and dark-stained wood, and the floors were beautifully scuffed by centuries of drunken feet.

"Glad to finally put a face to the name," Heath told Cash.

Cash looked surprised. "Has he talked about me—hopefully good things?"

"Yeah, of course, mate," Heath sipped his beer. "But mostly, I've heard about you from Luke's manuscript—the fictionalized version of you."

Cash shot me a look. "Is that so?"

I gave Heath a slap on the back. "Loosely-based," I said. "A little bit of fiction goes a long way—so they say."

Cash raised a brow.

"Hey—" I said, abruptly. "Cash here is engaged. Heath and his girl, Bec, are super serious too."

Heath seemed to pick up on my topic change. "Uh, congratulations on your engagement," he said with a smile. "I've actually just bought a ring myself. I pick it up next week."

The three of us clinked glasses, but I was surprised to hear the news. All my friends who were settling down seemed to inform me after the fact. When we got back to the Saint George's house later, Cash brought me a beer as I scribbled furiously into my notebook. "Luke, are you good? Seemed like you checked out for the night after Heath and I talked about relationships."

I gave a reassuring smile. "I'm great, man." I cracked the beer. "Just don't have much to contribute to those conversations."

Cash squinted at me, then snapped his fingers. "Now, might be a good time to give you your birthday gift." He handed me a folded paper from his bag.

Inside was a first-class plane ticket, roundtrip from Heathrow to JFK. The date read, June fifteenth, returning June twenty-first. "What's this for?" I asked.

"June seventeenth is the day we set for the wedding," he said, smiling. "I want you to be my best man."

My eyes darted between him and the ticket. "Bro, I have assignments and shit during the summer. I can't just cut out for a week."

"It's still a way's out," he laughed. "Professors will understand. You're in the wedding after all."

That was a good point, but I wanted to fight it. "And this ticket, man." I held it up. "Feels like charity. I can pay my own way." I set the ticket on the counter.

"Sorry, I just figured as a student you wouldn't have airfare money laying around." He looked the ticket over. "Imagine my surprise, seeing you with mysterious stacks of cash on you," he chuckled.

Whoops. I didn't think he had noticed that. By day two, I was annoyed with him paying for everything, so I began picking up our tabs in cash.

"Where's that money coming from, anyway?" He studied me, as if waiting for a lie. "You had hundreds when you paid for the Churchill thing. Can't be student loan money, right?"

Think dammit! "Uh, I bartend—at The Rifleman in Catford."

"The pub with the cousin?"

"Yes, that's where Shane and those guys hang out. I get stories from them." I shrugged. "The money's legit, I swear."

Cash wasn't buying that. No bartender outside of Miami Beach makes that kind of money. I had to give him some truth with my lie. "I'm getting distinction level grades on my writing," I stated.

He opened his mouth, surprised.

"Being around those guys and hearing about their lives," I said. "It makes my work credible. My professors love my writing."

He cocked his head. "They love your writing?"

"They hate me, but seem to really dig my stories."

Cash laughed. I decided to make amends and got him a beer. We were quiet as we drank, until he said, "I'm sorry about the cousin thing. I just wanted to make sure you're making good decisions after Paris." He studied the San Miguel bottle in his hand and said, "You know, I've been seeing a therapist since I got back."

I set down my beer to listen.

"She thinks I might have post-traumatic stress disorder— after what happened," he said. "Don't worry, I didn't tell her things in exact detail, but you know—just take care of yourself."

As confidently as I could, I patted him on the shoulder. "Don't worry, bro," I said. "I have everything under control."

The day before my birthday, Cash and I were walking with a coffee near my uni. I should have known his inquisitive mind wouldn't rest, because just before I turned to go inside for class, he said, "Hey, let's hang out at The Rifleman tonight. Maybe I can meet Shane and your other characters—you know, since I'm sharing a space in literature with them."

Yeah, I was in control alright.

Chapter 35

Of all the pubs in all of London, Cash wanted to visit The Rifleman. I suggested other bars but he was adamant about meeting the people I'd been spending my time with. I decided to speak to Shane after class, and ask for his discretion about my involvement with the crew. Shane had been hunting for his leak for months with no luck and his mood could often shift without warning, so I was nervous about bothering him with my personal issues.

Shane sat alone at his corner table with ledger papers spread out in front of him, and although he was busy, he invited me to sit. I fidgeted for a moment, until I got the nerve to tell him how I was afraid Cash would no longer want to be my friend if he knew what I'd been up to in London.

Shane laughed. A little too hard if you ask me. "He was with you in Paris, right? Then you should be able to trust him. He ought to be taking your secrets to the grave."

"I'm not worried he'll turn me in," I said. "I'm worried he won't understand. That I'll lose him as a friend."

Shane nodded. "Is he the one who's marrying that bird you hate?"

I couldn't tell if I was more shocked by how much I'd drunkenly confessed to Shane or by how much he remembered. "Hate's a strong word—"

"When friends get married, they always promise things won't change, but it's a lie. He's got his future planned, while you're still sorting yours. You've got a lot of opportunity in London, between working for me and writing. Are you afraid he's starting to phase you out of his life?"

I clenched my hands, feeling a familiar pang of abandonment in my chest. "Well—I am now."

"That's how life works, mate. Doors opening, doors closing," Shane rolled a smoke. "Look, I'll speak to the boys for you—we'll keep business talk to a minimum while your mate's around. But as your friend, I want you to start thinking about what makes you happy. Not others."

"Thank you, Shane."

He gave me a fatherly pat on the arm. "That's what I'm here for. Now, be a good lad and do some runs with Stump. Earn your stories, mate." He grinned, showing his missing canine.

***

Stumpy and I were a half hour late getting to the pub, and when I texted Cash I was running behind, he responded with, *it's cool, I'm just hanging with your new pals.*

Shit. What was that conversation like?

Stumpy had barely put the BMW in park when I jumped out for the front door. The Rifleman was packed and I was hit with an invisible wall of beer breath. Daniel stood by the front door when I came in.

"Hello, good to see you," he shook my hand.

"Hey, Daniel," I looked past him for Cash. "The joint's packed tonight."

Cash sat at my spot at the corner table, between Shane and King. Cash waved while sipping his pint. Daniel pulled in a breath and looked at the cheery tables of drinkers enjoying his pub. "A full house, as they say," he said, beaming.

I was eager to get to intercept whatever incriminating information could be passed to Cash, but seeing Daniel gaze proudly at his hard work—the polished floors, painted walls, the repaired ceiling, I said, "You've done a great job with this place. The pub looks amazing."

Daniel ran a hand over his widow's peak. "I appreciate that, Luke. Thank you," but then he frowned. "I should probably warn you things may be changing round here—I won't go into detail now, but I thought you should know." My forehead crinkled, but before I could ask him to elaborate, he strode away.

I squeezed passed drinkers for my table. "What's up?" I said to everyone. The boys greeted me with a collective *happy birthday!* I smiled, trying to read Cash's face. "Thanks, boys. It's not official for a couple more hours, though."

Llanzo slid a chair in behind me. What a gent. I took my place with Shane wedged between Cash and me.

"Glad you could join us, mate," Shane smirked. "We're catching Corey up on all you've been doing this year."

"Ahh, that's not necessary—I've bored him enough with all that over the past few days."

"Nonsense," Shane shook his head. "You've had an eventful tenure here in the UK, son." He looked to Cash. "His writing is a testament to that. Brilliant writer, this one."

"Yeah!" Kieran leaned on Cash. "He's always writing, bruv. Always got a notebook and pen on him."

Cash smiled at Kieran, who had no concept of personal space. "He's a good writer," Cash agreed. "Haven't read any of the new stuff yet, though."

"One day," I said. "Needs some polishing. It's a little slow in the plot."

"Oh, I doubt that, mate." Shane shook his head. "Lots of action-packed stories around here."

I narrowed my eyes at Shane. Was he screwing with me?

"Luke writes good crime," Kieran said to Cash. "He could be a ghost writer for a rapper or somefin'. Hey—you're in business, right?"

Cash nodded. "Something like that, yeah."

"Perfect, 'cause I've got this rapper, right?" Kieran spilled some beer. "And I'm trying to break into talent management—"

"Kieran!" King said. "He don't wanna hear about that, fam. Give the man some space." King flashed a smile at me. He seemed to sense how awkward this was for me.

Cash chuckled at the onslaught. "Seems like you guys and Luke have quite the rapport." He drained his beer.

"We been through a lot, fam," Ibrahim said. "Like the show *Band of Brothers*, innit?"

Everyone at the table laughed, except me and Cash. He seemed to catch on that the boys and I were much closer than I let on. King dug into his pockets and handed me a tenner. "Happy birthday, Luke," he smiled. "Ten quid for you and Corey's next round."

God, I love that kid. I snatched the money and stood up. "I accept your gentlemanly offer, thank you. Cash—let's top you up."

Cash followed me to the bar, shaking his head. "Luke, what the hell?"

Sophie and Chiara watched us. My face felt hot. "Two IPA's, please." I handed Chiara the ten while Sophie pulled the pints. "Sophie, Chiara—this is my friend Corey Cash, from back home."

Chiara smiled at Cash. "Hello. It's lovely to meet you," she said.

"Nice to meet you, too," Cash waved.

Sophie handed him a pint. "You seem much too normal to be Luke's friend."

"I might have to agree with you," he said, eying me. I was growing frustrated, and my hands felt jittery. Cash set an elbow on the bar and leaned toward Chiara. "Tell me, is he a good bartender? He's had a lot of practice on this side of the bar, but never behind it."

Uh oh.

Chiara frowned. "Luke doesn't work here—"

"Luke doesn't work evenings with us," Sophie handed me a pint. "He takes the afternoon shifts. Hasn't been sacked yet, so he must do alright." She gave me the side eye.

I stared at her. Why would she help me? Maybe she doesn't completely hate me.

Chiara looked confused, but Cash bought it. "Hmm, I'll have to take your word for it—'cause the way the guys talked about him. Like he was another member of their gang."

Just as I went to speak a booming voice called from across the room. "May I have everyone's attention." It was Daniel, standing in the center of the pub. Everyone turned to listen.

I mouthed *thank you* to Sophie, but she just huffed.

"This will only take a second," Daniel continued, as the roar of conversation died. "It's been over a year since I took over Uncle Jerry's beloved Rifleman. And in that time, I've got to know most of you very well—some of you a bit too well," he said, to scattered laughs. "So, I wanted to take a moment to thank you for your patronage. Your support has meant a lot as I've worked to improve the place. And that's why it's bittersweet for me to tell you that as of this morning, I've sold the pub. Tomorrow evening will be my last."

The whole pub gasped, muttering to one another. My heart sunk. What would the pub or London be like without him?

When the murmurs died down, Daniel continued, "Fortunately, the pub will now be in the care of Catford's own, Tom Jernigan, who's just retired from the Metropolitan Police. He's excited to take on the pub in his retirement and to keep the old girl running as it's always been—a great place for friends."

Shane's face turned red across the room. Was this the first he'd heard of Daniel's plans to sell his unofficial headquarters? A serious looking man with gray hair and a bushy mustache stood up from a booth and waved to the room. There's no way a retired cop was going to let Shane have run of the place. As the regulars congratulated Daniel and Tom, Stumpy slipped through the front door and over to whisper in Shane's ear. Shane brooded, staring at a spot on the table in front of him. Behind me, Sophie and Chiara expressed their shock, asking themselves, *Do we still have jobs? Of course, we do—I think.* Shane looked the maddest I'd ever seen, and I worried he might hurt Daniel.

As soon as the thought came to my mind, Shane locked eye with me from across the room. He gestured toward the front door. Uh oh. "Be right back," I said to Cash.

I followed Shane and Stumpy outside, where Shane lit a spliff. "One of Charlie's disciples is at Caldera showing his money off. I need you and the boys to go and put him in his place."

I hadn't been to Caldera since the champagne incident. The boys had been back plenty of times to sell, but not me. "But Cash is here, man," I groaned.

"I'm not saying go and execute the man. Just wait for an opportune moment and confront the bastard," he took another drag.

"Shane, I really hoped to avoid this kind of work around Cash. This just feels risky."

"First Danny, and now you. Where's the bloody loyalty?" A cool breeze rushed between us, making me shudder. "After all the money I've put in your pockets, the stories I've let you write and I have to ask twice?"

The street was eerily silent as he and Stumpy stared at me. There was a deep chill in the breeze like God or nature warning me not to cave.

But I did.

Twenty minutes later, the six of us crammed into a big Uber for Soho. I told Cash we were going to Caldera to celebrate my birthday, a gesture from Shane.

"That's weirdly generous," Cash frowned. "I thought you hated clubs."

"I do," I opened his car door. "But he got us a VIP booth, so it's a bit more tolerable."

Cash went to get in but stopped to examine my hoodie and jeans. Then he pointed at the boys in their puffers, joggers and Air Max's. "We're not even dressed for a club," he slid into the back row. "This is going to be embarrassing."

"I agree," I said with a nod. "I don't foresee this going well at all."

Chapter 36

My heart raced as we piled out of the Uber for Caldera. King led us past the line of well-dressed, beautiful people waiting to get in. The eyes of the dejected pored over us for any signs of celebrity that could merit us jumping the line. *Who the bloody hell are they?* I heard scattered huffs as security ushered us inside.

A tall blonde woman with an earpiece led us to the same VIP booth as last time. The strobing lights and pounding bass hit me with that all-too-familiar sensory overload. My stomach turned and I knew champagne wasn't going to sooth my nerves, so I ordered a bottle of vodka and some mixers. I ignored Cash's glare when I flicked through a wad of bills to pay.

By my third screwdriver, I felt better and the club became bearable. King went looking for our target, some idiot named Bonez. Llanzo stood by the railing, keeping a watchful eye as King sifted through the crowd downstairs.

I poured myself and Cash another drink, then checked in with Llanzo. "Any sign?"

"Nah, mate," Llanzo said.

Cash came to the railing. "What are we looking at?"

"Uh, just scoping for chicks," I swallowed a gulp of vodka.

"Let me know if you find any prospects." Cash patted my back. "I'm a good wingman."

Cash *was* a good wingman, and an even better friend. I felt bad lying, and contemplated telling him the truth. Maybe he would just accept me as the flawed asshole I've always been?

Llanzo pointed to the far corner of the club. My drunk eyes scanned the masses below and by some miracle I spotted King through the flashing clips of light, waving us down.

I turned to our booth. "Hey, 'Brahim, wanna come with me and Llanzo for a minute?" I said. "And uh, Kieran—why don't you and Cash hang here? We'll see if we can bring up some ladies."

Kieran smoothed down the front of his shirt. "Oh, we see how it is." He put a lanky arm around Cash. "Leave the two taken men behind, then? Go on, fam. I've got to talk to Corey 'bout my business venture." Cash was a good sport and gave him a humoring pat on the arm.

The three of us slipped from the booth and downstairs to the dancefloor. Llanzo led us through, towering over the crowd to the far corner where King waited. King pointed down a long hallway to the restrooms. "I just seen mandem go to the bogs," he reported.

"How many?" I asked.

"Just two—Bonez got blond hair. Thinks he's a big man in a fancy gray suit," he said, grinning. "Other guy is in a blue button-up and ripped jeans."

The four of us pushed down the hallway, my heartrate matching the pulsing lights. It was crowded, but the club goers stepped aside as we filed past a line of women waiting for the bathroom. Their sugary perfume hung in the air. Llanzo shoved dudes out of the way. *Bugger off! What the hell!* They called out, but none of them stepped to us.

My fingers tingled as the club noise faded. The rush you feel before something like this is a drug in its own right. I felt like myself again after days of pretending not to be.

Llanzo burst through the bathroom door. "Everyone get the hell out!" His voice rumbled between the tiled walls. The room fell silent. A scared row of guys pissing into a urinal trough. Bonez and his friend zipped up their flies. Their eyes darting between us in the odd seconds of antebellum. They knew how this was going to go. Bystanders slipped from the room as the four of us rushed them. Llanzo hit ripped jeans guy. His head slammed into the tiled wall. He fell unconscious into the urinal.

Bonez took desperate swings at King. I took a cheap shot and rocked Bonez in the jaw. He rolled his ankle and fell on his face. We stuffed Bonez into the urinal next to his friend. His gray suit grew darker in the piss water. I flipped out my blade—CLICK—stuck it under his chin.

"You in the wrong ends, blud," King said. *Déjà vu—I'd heard that phrase before.*

"Naw, fam," Bonez shook his head. "Me and the boys just out for a dance."

The déjà vu was trippy. "Bullshit!" I said. "You think we're stupid?" I pressed the blade into his chin.

Bonez clenched his eyes shut in pain.

"Don't ever come back to this club, fam," King growled. Llanzo, Ibrahim and I loomed over him.

"Yeah, Sisqó," I said, pointing at Llanzo. "Or next time, big man will drown you in your own piss."

The words barely left my mouth before Cash called out behind me, "Luke, what the fuck?"

Caught. I spun around. Everyone in the bathroom froze. Cash stared at me with the same look of disappointment I'd seen my entire life. From Bill, my mother, teachers, girlfriends, Sophie. After twenty years, Cash finally saw what everyone else had always seen. He took a deep breath and exhaled two decades of brotherhood and left.

For a moment, there was only the sound of trickling piss water. Bonez sat patiently in the urinal, and I opened my mouth to finish my spiel, but nothing came. I wiped the blood from my knife onto his suit and followed after Cash.

A crowd had gathered outside the bathroom and a group of bouncers pushed through the people to calm the situation.

I dodged them, and fought through the dancefloor back up to VIP. Cash stood by the sofa, his coat in his arms and his face in his phone. His thumbs were a blur as he texted, presumably to Emma. The boys filed in sheepishly behind me as the music pounded. I peeked down into the crowd to see Bonez and his friend being escorted by security to the entrance. Bonez had his phone pressed to his ear. I knew it wouldn't be long before the bouncers kicked us out too.

I decided to break the silence. "You're not leaving, are you?"

Cash threw his coat on and glared at me. "Are you kidding? I am so tired of almost getting arrested with you—of course I'm leaving." He shouldered past me, just as the bouncers arrived at our booth.

"You were supposed to keep him here, Kier!" I shouted, as if any of this was his fault.

"Said he needed the toilet," Kieran shrugged. "He's a grown man, innit?"

The bouncers didn't have to say a word. The boys and I piled out of the booth and downstairs. It felt like Tower Bridge all over again, winding through the crowds after Cash. Brushing against strangers, the taste of their body odor and cologne in my mouth.

I caught up with Cash on the sidewalk outside, the boys and security team were hot on my heels. "Corey, you're my best friend," I said. "And I just didn't want you to think less of me."

He laughed. "Buddy, I couldn't think any less of you if I tried." He put a hand in the air for a cab.

"What the hell does that mean?"

He turned to face me. "It means, I've been defending you for years—telling everyone you're a good guy—that you'll work things out—that you've got *tons of potential*." He shook his head. "And that shit you just pulled in there makes me feel like a damn fool."

Shaking, I got in his face. "Why are you and *everyone* talking about me in the first place?"

"Because of shit like this, Luke!" he fired back. "If it's not fighting in bars on Glenwood South back home, it's holding someone at knife-point in a London club. Why that needs explaining is beyond me." He turned to the road for a cab.

The crowd waiting in line behind us fell silent. Spurred on by an audience, I was emboldened to fight back. "I gotta say, Corey, this talk sounds a lot like Emma and not so much like you."

He had fire in his eyes. "Are you kidding me? She's the reason I'm here! She's the reason I invited you to the wedding. *He's your best friend, Corey, you have to invite him to the wedding—he might be lonely, you should visit him for his birthday!*" He put a finger in my face. "Emma's about the only friend you've got back home. You ought to thank your lucky stars for her, asshole."

The boys groaned behind me and dispersed to give us space. Except Kieran, who stood next to me, still not big on social cues. I balled up my fist, angrier than I'd been since Profit. I wanted to break something.

"Jesus, dude," I said. "You live in New York and can't hail a goddamn cab?" I shoved past him, stepped out into the street and threw my hand in the air. "You have to be aggressive."

A cab waiting at the red light flashed his lights at me. Cash stared at me as Kieran stood next to him and held out his phone. "I k-know you're leaving, bruv," Kieran said. "But follow me on Instagram so we can talk business and all."

"Kieran, shut the fuck up!" I yelled at him.

There was a roar of an approaching engine in the street and the terrible screech of tires. A cold chill rocketed through me. I thought of Lambeth Bridge. And I don't know why, but I dropped to the ground. The line of waiting clubbers squealed.

"Yo, Cash!" a voice called from the street. It was the same black Mercedes from the bridge. The back window was down and inside was nothing but darkness.

Cash was still pissed. "What, asshole?" he yelled.

Gunshots rang out. So loud—as if the gun were inches away. Bullets fired for ages. My ears rang when it stopped. The scattering crowd screamed as Cash and Kieran fell in a tangle of limbs. A pink mist of blood hung in the bright lights of the club facade.

The Mercedes peeled off. The crowd collided and clambered over each other. I snapped out of it and lunged for Cash. His arms were clutched to his chest, writhing in pain. I pulled him from Kieran, whose neck was red and spurting blood.

King and Llanzo dropped down and grabbed Kieran. A blur of shouts and voices revolved around us. Cash groaned in my arms. "I'm so sorry," I kept repeating. "You're going to be okay."

I put my hands on Cash. Found a wound on his right pec muscle. Found another in his ribs. I clutched them. The warmth of his blood squeezed between my fingers. Kieran moaned next to us. His voice was hoarse as he began to cry.

"No, no, no—Kier," Llanzo said, as he held him.

Ibrahim stood over us with his phone pressed to his ear and tears in his eyes.

"Call 9-1-1!" I yelled, but that's not the UK number.

King gripped at Kieran's legs. They spasmed in his hands. "It's okay, Kier," he said. "It's okay, brudda, gonna be fine, fam. We'll get you sorted."

I held Cash tight, keeping his body together with my hands. Palming at his wounds to stop the blood from gushing.

Kieran cried out, "It hurts! It fucking hurts."

Cash silently gritted his teeth. Why was he so quiet? I shook him a little until I heard him groan. He struggled to breath. His eyes were clenched shut and there was red in the corners of his mouth.

Finally, the far-off whine of sirens. Happy to hear them for once.

"Stay with us, Kier!" King shouted. "Stay brudda!" he pleaded. The tremble in his voice broke my heart.

I braved a look at Kieran. His expression of pain was gone. Kieran's eyes were open and he looked at the city and sky above him with wonder. Like a baby, his blue eyes searched the world, as if seeing it for the first time.

"M-mum?" Kieran said, into the chaos of voices around him. Fear left his voice as he released Llanzo's pantleg. "Someone fetch my mum?"

My tears poured. Kieran's soul seemed to rise in a horizontal line from his motionless chest. It moved up his neck and left from the top of his head. As if he'd simply slipped below the surface of calm, cool waters into death. All that was left of Kieran now was our pain. I wept and held Cash close to me, desperate to keep him on the right side of life.

Chapter 37

The interrogation room at Charing Cross Police Station was freezing cold. I sat, shivering, at a table for hours, forced to stare at my stupid face in the one-way mirror. The glass was smudged with handprints, nose prints—whatever body parts detainees managed to smoosh against it.

In the movies, suspects always seemed to know that someone was watching them from behind the mirror, but sitting in the silence of that room, I knew I was alone. No one but me, my thoughts, and an encroaching hangover. The title of my third novel. And if I wanted someone to blame for how I'd gotten to that cold room, I didn't have to look any further than the guy staring back at me in the dick-smudged mirror.

***

When the EMTs couldn't revive Kieran, they sprang into action to save Cash. A second ambulance took Kieran away and the cops swarmed the street with flickering blue light. I pressed my nose against the back window of the ambulance, watching as they worked on Cash inside.

Llanzo touched my shoulder. "Your knife," he said. There were dried tears on his cheeks. "Can't have dat ting on ya, mate."

My mind worked slow, but eventually I slipped him my knife. Llanzo dropped it into a storm drain with a clank. He pulled another blade from his sock and dropped it in after mine. He said we could come back for them later, but I didn't want mine anymore.

The police encircled the four of us as we stood covered in our friend's blood. The cops assured me I wasn't under arrest as they guided me into a car. They said I should get checked out at the station and give a statement. From the backseat, I watched my boys get handcuffed. Guess a white face and an American passport still go a long way. The one guy they didn't cuff was the one who had escalated this violence into something unmanageable.

It was my fault, and mine alone.

Alone.

***

The interrogation room door swung open in the wee hours of the morning and a tall, young detective with a leather padfolio stepped in. He stood in the doorway texting. He was about thirty and was balding in a Prince William kinda way.

"Is my friend okay?" I said. "Corey Cash—the American who was shot—"

He put up a finger to finish his text. The detective clipped the phone to his belt, then waved in a dumpy officer in uniform, who handed me a long-sleeved white t-shirt and a clear evidence bag for my bloodstained hoodie. The two didn't say a word, they just left me to change in the cold silence.

When the detective returned a few minutes later, I asked again, "Please, have you heard anything about my friend?"

"I don't have that information, I'm sorry."

"Well, what hospital was he taken to?" I pleaded. "Maybe we can call and find out—"

"Unfortunately, that's not what I'm here to do." He pointed for me to sit, which I did. "I need to ask you some questions. After which, we may be able to look into the condition of your friend."

He handed me a bottle of water and sat across from me at the table. "I'm Detective Constable Alan Betts." He unfolded his padfolio. "And I'd like to get a better understanding of the incident at the club—Caldera."

Like a gag reflex, I had an urge to confess it all—starting with Madeleine in Paris, all the way up to this point. But as quickly as that feeling came, self-preservation stomped that idea to death.

"I—I have no idea," I said, sipping my water.

He raised a brow. "You have no idea how you, and your group, came to be attacked—your friend shot?"

I swallowed the water hard. "No."

"Any theories? Speculations?"

"Random act of violence?"

The detective sat back in his chair. "This isn't America. Gun violence isn't a common occurrence. And when it does happen, it's seldom random."

Think, Luke. My brain was too rattled to be clever. I gave the detective my best puppy dog eyes. "Do you think this was premeditated?"

"Lucas, my job is to find out what you think." He didn't miss a beat. "Two of your friends were shot tonight, you must have some theories as to why?"

There was something strange in his tone. This talk was more serious than filling in some details. The detective wanted someone to blame. He said Kieran was my friend, and if he thought the shooting was gang-related, then by association I was too. I'd have to denounce Kieran as my friend.

"I wouldn't say the other guy was my *friend*—just the American," I said, guiltily.

The detective studied me, then scribbled some notes. "We've reviewed Caldera's CCTV footage. You and your friend, Corey, seemed quite chummy with that group of young men. It's a strange mixing of sorts—I dare say."

I shrugged. "You can meet all types of people on a night out."

He looked up from his notes. "So, tonight was your first time meeting them?"

Shit. He was trying to box me in. I decided to backtrack—
no firm answers. "I mean, I'd seen them before tonight. I don't
remember where, but they're a hard group to miss—but yes,
tonight was the first time I'd hung out with them."

The only sound in the room came from the scratching of his
pen. The detective stopped abruptly, and placed an arrest photo
of Llanzo before me. "Do you know this man, Llanzo Jevaun
Abisai Henry?"

The arrest date read July. Two months before I met Llanzo.
"I mean, I don't know him, but he was there tonight," I quickly
added: "But he was a victim."

"Right—a *victim*," the detective said, leaving the photo on
the table. "Whilst applying for your visa to the UK, do you
remember having your fingerprints taken?"

My heart jumped in my chest. Talking about my fingerprints
can't be good. *Play it cool, Luke.* "Hmm," I looked at my fingers.
"Vaguely, yeah."

"Do you know where those fingerprints go, once they're
taken?"

I shook my head.

"They go into a shared database between our two countries,"
he said, his eyes not leaving mine. "And once you came in
tonight, we compared your prints against our own database
here at the Met, and do you know what we found?" He let the
question linger. "A match."

My chest rose and fell heavily. Thankfully my t-shirt was two
sizes too big for me. I gave him a pouty, confused expression.
"I don't understand."

The detective pointed to Llanzo's photo. "We found your
fingerprints at a crime scene in Camden Town, alongside
Mr Henry's. A trinket shop called Chaos. And months later, we
find you both at the scene of a gang-related murder. That's a bit
odd, isn't it?"

Sweat beaded across my forehead. I was caught. My story had found its bitter end. All the effort I'd invested, the time, the blood—Cash was more than likely dead—Kieran certainly was—it was going to end in this dingy room. All because some graveyard shift detective got lucky.

Just when I thought my heart would stop, it sputtered back to life as it did under the Thames. My story can't be over! It wasn't a good enough ending. There was a quiver in my throat as a voice inside me fought to be heard. *Duke*, my character, took control.

"That's a wonderful theory, detective, but back home we call that pissin' in the wind," I growled. "I'm here on an academic visa, which means I'm the kind of visitor the United Kingdom wants. And sitting here, accusing me of gang shit with no proof—"

"But your fingerprints—"

"My fingerprints?" I recoiled in disgust. "My prints are all over the Camden High Street—all over London. Why? Because I'm a tourist. Just tell me where the shop is and I could probably tell you when I was there. Maybe buying postcards."

The detective twirled his pen. Ten long seconds passed before he spoke, "Lucas, I can see that you're quite clever. But hyperbole doesn't supersede evidence in murder cases, and I believe there's more to this incident than what meets the eye."

Uh oh—stop talking, Luke. I took a deep breath. "Should I—call a lawyer or something?"

Detective Betts shook his head and collected his papers. "You're not being charged, but for the time being, you are being detained." He stood and crossed to the door. "I'll see if I can find out about your friend," he said, then left the room.

When the door shut behind him, I shoved my face into the evidence bag and vomited vodka and orange juice onto my hoodie. I slumped back into my chair and fought to compose myself, sensing that someone was now watching me from behind the glass.

Betts soon returned to inform me that Cash was in a stable condition at University College Hospital. I felt like I could finally breath again. Betts and the dumpy officer escorted me to a holding cell, which was even colder than the interrogation room. The acrid smell of cleaning chemicals nipped at my nostrils. I laid down on the padding they called a bed, but there was no chance of sleeping. I just stared at Cash's dried blood under my fingernails, too afraid to close my eyes and seeing Kieran's death all over again. Or hearing my last words to him, *shut the fuck up!*

***

Many hours passed until my cell door squealed open again. An older detective stood in the entryway. He had salt and pepper hair and squinty dark eyes, and a maroon paisley tie was looped around his broad neck. Next to him was a muscular officer in uniform, and glaring at me behind them was Detective Betts.

"Hello, Lucas," the older detective said. "I'm Detective Inspector Murphy. Please come with me."

I gave a dry swallow and followed him through the labyrinth of hallways and offices with the other two trailing behind me. At the front entrance the uniformed officer returned my belongings: phone, wallet, keys and shoelaces. I bit my lip and surveyed the waiting room of sad and mad faces before asking Detective Murphy, "That's it? I'm free to go?"

Detective Murphy gave a slow nod. I sighed and put a hand on the door. "There's one more thing," he said. "You're not a suspect at the moment, but something about this mess isn't sitting well with me or Detective Constable Betts. I'd like to advise you not to leave the Greater London area, until our investigation is concluded."

I was too tired to channel Duke again. "Whatever, man," I shoved open the front door.

I collapsed onto the front steps to lace up my shoes. My phone was dead and the sun was already low in the sky, and I guessed it was early afternoon—I'd been at the station over twelve hours. A cab cruised by the station and I bolted after it, pounding on the roof.

***

As a kid, I used to love the rare occasions I visited hospitals. There was something comforting about a place where people got fixed, but I never thought about how many people couldn't be saved—how many died in hospitals. I took a cramped elevator ride to the trauma unit with a stern-looking nurse with a crumpled patient in a wheelchair. The patient was wrapped up like a mummy, the edges of their gauze discolored, off-white, from whatever seeping carnage lay beneath. All that was visible were two glaring brown eyes, under shiny pink eyelids.

Scrambling from the elevator, I tried to prepare myself for whatever I might find. The hallway was long and white and humming from machinery and echoes of names called from the PA system. Curtains were draped in each doorway, giving almost-privacy to the tragedies behind them. My footsteps echoed across the buffed floor; this was a clean place meant to help people. And I was a dirty thing who had only ever caused harm to others.

The lights were off in Cash's room, save for the glow of a device that steadily pumped life into his veins and lungs. Shivering under a cold wave of grief, I pulled back the curtain and stepped inside. The smell of anti-bac chemicals rushed past me.

Cash's hair was matted down and his eyelids were closed and dark. There was a nest of wires running to and fro, an IV in his arm, and bandaging across his shoulder and chest.

Tears formed in my eyes. Cash was the only real family I had and I hurt him. I went to bury my face in my hands, but something moved in the corner of the room. My eyes adjusted to the dark and I saw two balloons, bobbing in an invisible breeze. *Get Well Soon!* and *I Love You!* And there were flowers next to his bed. Who in London would bring him those things? I gasped and backed into the hall, running smack into Emma.

Her face was makeup-less and her eyes looked tired from her red-eye flight. Her blonde hair was wound in a messy bun. She had a cup of coffee in her hand and on her finger was a big-ass diamond ring. Emma caught me looking at it and handed me her coffee. Like an idiot, I took her cup and she punched me in the face. I've always had trouble with lefties.

The cup fell and scalding coffee spilled across my giant white shirt.

"What are you doing here?" Emma whisper yelled.

"Emma, I'm sorry."

"Shh—" she yanked me away from Cash's room.

"I should have never brought him with me."

"This wasn't random?" she said. "Detectives have been here asking questions."

I looked at her with wet eyes. I wasn't going to incriminate myself to a chick who hated me. "It's hard to explain."

"What's hard to explain?" she asked. "Corey said you've been hanging out with a gang. Are you a moron?"

I fought back a sob. "Corey spoke to you? He's not in some kind of a coma?"

She stifled her anger as an elderly man in a hospital gown puttered past us. "No, he's not. He's doing okay now. He lost some blood, but they removed the bullets and he came through fairly well. He's on morphine for the pain."

"Thank you, God," I was happy, but I still wanted to cry.

"Amazing," she examined me. "Not a scratch on you. They said a boy died—nineteen years old. That's what you did," she cried.

Tears ran down my face.

"You've always been selfish," she said. "You leached from Corey. But I thought, hey—at least Corey has one true friend, Luke. So, what if it's a little one-sided? But that wasn't enough, you had to try and take his life too."

My vision blurred.

"What happened in Paris was bad," she continued. "But that was at least out of your control."

I shot her a look.

"He told me," she nodded. "I could kick myself, convincing him to give you another chance. You're not worth it."

"It's not your fault," I said. "It was my fault we were at that apartment."

"I know!" she snapped. Her hands were clenched, ready to hit me. "You don't get to play martyr. You're done."

"Are you going to tell the police?"

"I don't give a damn about the police! I care about Corey," she jabbed her finger into my chest. "You're never to see him again. He and I both agreed." Her words sunk like a dagger. The hall spun. "All you cause is *pain*."

Things went blurry. She hurled more insults—low class, redneck, white trash. Something about a trailer. She pointed down the hall for me to leave and the next thing I knew, I was standing in the cold shade of the hospital. My wet coffee shirt clinging to my chest.

I walked south to nowhere. Moving on autopilot, I shuffled through intersections and crosswalks, passed crowds of people in Piccadilly Circus like a ghost. No one seemed to notice me. No one managed to touch or brush past me. It had never been more apparent I was no one to anyone. My internal GPS led me to Lambeth Bridge. I stopped halfway across and prayed I'd be attacked again and thrown over. This time, I'd do everyone a favor and take a deep breath of brackish water and let the Thames have me.

When I reached the South Bank, I decided to keep walking in lieu of going home. Tired, hungry and thirsty, I ended up at a corner pub in Kennington, aptly named The Doghouse. I ordered a pint out of instinct, which was the first thing I'd consumed in fourteen hours and it went down quickly. I should have ordered food, but when the bartender asked if I wanted another, I agreed. The second pint filled my belly and the buzz made me feel better about ordering a third.

By the fourth pint, Cash, Emma and Kieran had all but slipped from my thoughts, and I was busy listening to three Australians argue about football. I was the only other person sitting at the bar, so they bought me a shot of whiskey, which I chased with a fifth pint. Before I knew it the sun went down, the place got crowded, and I was seven pints deep and crammed into the tiny pub bathroom doing key bumps of coke with the Aussies.

That's where things went black.

Chapter 38

I spent untold hours in a dark space where time no longer existed. Echoes of familiar voices visited me in the darkness. *I don't want to be around you right now, fam—Take a few days and pull yourself together, Luke.*

I was brought back to existence by the sound of a van door sliding open. The blue glow of morning poured into my eyes. I sat up and found myself in the backseat of a minivan. The front seat was empty, but through the windshield I discovered the van was parked on the side of an empty country road.

A cool breeze filtered through the open door, and beyond it was an endless pasture, rolling into dark green oblivion. I stumbled out of the van. My steamy breath hung in the crisp air.

"Didn't mean to wake you so soon," a voice said, from the rear of the vehicle. "We've still got a few minutes."

It was Daniel. Next to him was a guy my age. "Daniel?" my voice was hoarse. "Where are we? How—did I get here?"

He took a drag of his cigarette. "You got here by van."

"Why am I here?" I hobbled to the van. "Where is here?" I looked for road signs but saw only fence and pasture.

"You're headed to Bath," his voice was calm, fatherly. "To cool off from London. As you can see, it's taken its toll on you." He pointed at my feet.

Somehow, I'd lost my shoes and there were holes in the toes of my socks. I was still wearing the coffee-stained jail shirt, but mixed within the coffee were crusted blobs of what I hoped was my blood. My head hurt, trying to recall agreeing to Bath or meeting up with Daniel in the first place.

Daniel must have sensed my confusion. "You agreed that a few days in Bath with family would be good for you." He opened the van's back hatch. "And the few who remained at The Rifleman did too."

When did I go to The Rifleman? Daniel directed me to sit on the back bumper. The young man handed me a thermos and poured black coffee into the cup lid. "Thank you—I'm Luke," I said.

"Yeah, we met," he chuckled. "I'm Jon—Daniel's my uncle."

Daniel rolled me a smoke with my coffee and we sat quietly in the cool breeze. We watched the grass sway in the field and listened to the chatter of unseen birds in the distant trees. The orange morning sun rose from behind the woods, filling the cracks of sky between the clouds in a mosaic of burnt light.

"Now, look just there," Daniel pointed across the road.

I stood up and watched as the orange light unrolled across the grass and blanketed a ring of stone structures. "Oh, shit—Stonehenge," I gasped.

The monoliths stood a football field away, defiant against the open sky. Seeing them in person made me feel small and foolish, and I decided an escape from London might be what I needed.

**

I woke up in a bright room, under the covers of a plush bed. At the foot of the bed stood a bookshelf, packed floor to ceiling with novels from Austen to Yeats. A carriage clock ticked on the bedside—two in the afternoon. I sat up with the vague memory of being helped to bed by Daniel and Jon.

The staggered roofs of Bath lay outside my bedroom window. Georgian homes formed orderly lines and wound tight against the surrounding hills. My phone was busted to shit so I couldn't take a picture of the scene.

Great.

Clean clothes were folded on an armchair. They must have belonged to Daniel's son. I changed and crept into the silent hallway. It was small, but bright with a skylight above, and colorful paintings of west country cottages on the walls. In a hall mirror I discovered my lip was mysteriously busted, and Emma's diamond ring had slit my cheek and bruised up nicely.

I descended two levels in someone else's khakis and a Bath rugby sweatshirt. There were photos on the wall of Daniel, his wife Laura, their son and three daughters. Pictures of them skiing, or vacationing in French wine country and hiking the rugged mountains of Scotland. His son looked like Daniel, and his daughters, who were all a couple years apart in age, looked like his wife. But all of the kids had the same dark brown hair as their father.

Family photos intrigued me, since I never had many of my own. It was nice to see Daniel and his kids on the beach or smiling at family outings. He seemed like a good dad. I found Laura in the kitchen peeking at a roast in the oven. She smiled when she saw me, with a kind face and the slight crinkle of age in the corners of her big bright eyes. She looked familiar, like I'd met her before, but nevertheless I introduced myself.

"Hi, I'm Luke." I said, sitting at a stool at the counter.

She grinned. "We met before—at The Rifleman."

"Oh, God. I must have made a great first impression."

Laura hit the button on the first drip coffee maker I'd seen in six months. "You didn't do anything—too unpleasant. Just bad timing is all. Emotions ran high, and then you showed up very intoxicated. The little Italian girl didn't care for that."

My heart sunk. "Chiara," I said.

The night came back to me in pieces. Sophie was there, Chiara, King, Ibrahim, and Shane—everyone who knew Kieran had turned up. They were all mad at me, except Laura, who took a late train to commemorate Daniel's last night.

Laura poured me a cup of coffee and slid it across the counter. "Feisty thing, Chiara," she pointed to my face. "Gave you that fat lip."

I touched it. It was puffy and sore, and I remembered when she hit me, crying, *Bastardo! It should have been you!*

I took a gulp of hot coffee. "It's my fault," I said.

"You said that quite a lot that night."

"She was the second woman to hit me that day."

"You said that too." She wiped the counter with a tea towel.

"I'm sorry," I groaned. "It's very kind of you to take me in. I hope it's not too much trouble."

Laura looked up from her work. "I'm a mother of four," she said. "It's a job that toughens you, whilst softening your heart. There's no way Daniel and I were going to pour you into a taxi and just hope for the best." She shrugged. "Plus, I work in medicine, so I figured you'd be in good hands here."

My fat lip quivered. Why was she being so nice? "I'll try not to overstay my welcome," I said. "Maybe catch the train back to London in a day or so."

Laura draped the towel over her shoulder and shook her head. "Nonsense. It's Easter in a few days and the kids are here all week. We'd love the extra company."

Laura made me a ham and cheese sandwich with my black coffee, and after a moment said, "You're not my child, so I promise not to preach after this. But I'll tell you the same thing I tell my children; if you're truly sorry—then prove it. Are you sorry enough to change? To take responsibility for your actions, and not repeat the same mistakes?"

It was a damn good question, but I already knew the answer. "I don't have any other choice but to change. Can't keep doing what I've been doing."

"Good," she said. "Use this week to rest. And don't speak another word about overstaying your welcome. We all need a little family time."

A strange, warm feeling came over me. It was unfamiliar, but quenching. Like I'd needed water my whole life but never had the chance to drink. Laura went out into the garden and I cried into my coffee like a little bitch.

***

Daniel and his troupe filed through the front door, handing Waitrose bags to one another like a bucket brigade. They had a good system, so I stood out of the way and hovered with empty hands.

"Everyone, this is Luke," Daniel said.

They muttered *hello* as they worked. Eric, the oldest, was the spitting image of his father. He set an armful of groceries on the counter and shook my hand. "Eric," he said. "Nice to meet you, mate."

"You too," I said with a smile.

Once the groceries were stowed in their respective cupboards, Daniel introduced his daughters in descending order. "This is June, Samantha and Gabi," he said. Gabi, the youngest of about thirteen, curled her lip seeing my bruised face. "Now, who wants a coffee before the walk?"

Everyone's hands went up.

"The walk?" I asked.

"Yeah, down through town and up into the hills a bit," he said. "Are you up for it?"

The only thing I wanted was to climb back into bed, but the entire Ross family watched me. "Yeah, sounds good." I mustered as much enthusiasm as I could.

Within minutes I was wearing a pair of Eric's old hiking boots and one of Daniel's Barbour jackets, a sight the whole family got a kick out of—an American in British disguise. They even put a flat cap on me for a laugh. I clopped down Cavendish Road, the street slanted steeply under us. Beautifully tended Georgian homes lay to my left and a vast green hill to my right. Seeing Bath sprawled ahead made me happy I didn't go back to bed.

The Rosses took me to a phone repair shop near the Royal Crescent. The old man inside grimaced at my shattered phone, but assured me he could fix it in a few days. I tossed him the phone and rejoined the Rosses, glad to be rid of my only tether to the outside world.

We shimmied through crowds of tourists at the Roman Baths and the Abbey, trekking south beyond the train station and across the River Avon. We cut through Widcombe for the laborious climb up to Alexandra Park. My smoker's lungs burned all the way, and just when I thought I would collapse, the hill plateaued and the trees parted, offering a beautiful view of the entirety of Bath. It looked like a model train village.

Daniel and I took in the view while his kids explored the park. "Are you going to miss the pub?" I asked.

"Glad to be rid of it," he said. "I mean, the regulars were fine. Even you and the boys were entertaining—up to a point," he said with a grin. But soon his smile evaporated. "I shouldn't tell you this, but part of my decision to sell was so I didn't have to pay your employer a thousand pounds every two weeks. Just so Shane could use my pub for his headquarters. Bastard did the same to Uncle Jerry before me."

My body went cold. It was my job to collect from businesses, but Shane never had me collect from Daniel. He knew better. "I never knew that. Really, I didn't. I'm so sorry."

He waved a hand. "It's all done with now, but I'm sure there's a lot you don't know about that man. Shane is a disease. He manipulates those around him, and sucks the life out of those in his control. All for power, or money—what have you. But he's a bad person, and I regret ever pointing him out to you."

Ever since I came to London, I convinced myself I was the one in control of my destiny for once—writing my own story. And although my actions were mine alone, I was stunned by the insinuation I was being controlled by someone else after all.

***

I ate quietly during dinner, reflecting and listening to the family talk. They spoke about school and Uni, and Eric talked about his new job in London. I was afraid to speak, worried they'd judge the things I said. I felt like a stray dog on his first night indoors, waiting for a boot in the ass back into the cold.

But the boot never came.

Pieces of my last night at The Rifleman returned to me over the course of the week. King and Ibrahim blamed me for Kieran. Ibrahim was drunk, with tears in his eyes and refused to talk to me. King, however, wasn't afraid to speak his mind.

"They don't think Profit will ever walk without a cane, blud," he snarled. "You didn't think mandem would come for you?"

"I'm sorry, man," I pleaded. "I didn't—"

"You're sorry?" his voice, broke. "I protected Kier for years, until you came along and fucked it all. I don't want to be around you right now, fam."

Tossing and turning in the Ross's guest bed one night, I remembered what Shane said at The Rifleman. "Take a few days and pull yourself together—how do you think I feel? Kier's gone and Llanzo's nicked! I'm down two men when I need them most."

I sat up in a cold sweat—the bastard. The boys and I weren't his family, just numbers in his ranks. My hand ached for a pen, but my notebook and laptop were at Cash's company house. Maybe if I wrote the words well enough, I could convince Cash to be my friend again. Maybe people like King and Ibrahim would understand what I did it all for. And then maybe I wouldn't feel so alone.

***

After Easter dinner, I sat with the family in the living room while Eric shuffled through classic songs on the stereo. Eclectic hits from The Who, Elton John, Hall & Oates, and Marvin Gaye. The only good thing about Bill was his taste in music, so I hummed along with every song.

"Alright Carolina, got one for you," Eric grinned.

When he hit play, I heard a familiar jangle of acoustic guitar and James Taylor singing, 'In my mind I'm going to Carolina, can't you see the sunshine...' I hadn't heard *Carolina in My Mind* in years, and I chuckled when the family smiled at me. The melancholic words wafted through the room, and to my surprise once they reached me, I felt sad.

I was a stranger in the midst of a loving family, listening to a song about my home, thousands of miles away. And for the first time in my six-month absence, I felt homesick. Longing for a home I never had, and for a family that never was. Coupled with my guilt over Cash and Kieran, the tears came pouring as the whole Ross family watched.

The next morning, I sat on a bench in the garden, with half of my body in the shade of the roof and the other half in the warm sun. I flicked through the final pages of Jack Kerouac's *On the Road* and I thought back to September and how I'd hoped my own travels would stir a great awakening within me—and I was struck with a startling realization. What if Paris was my great awakening? A violent and volatile change had occurred within me, and maybe the reason it was so dangerous was because my metamorphosis wasn't complete.

I raised my hand from the shade into the sunlight and realized I needed to go back to London to face my other half. To kill the old me, and complete my awakening. I'd found a new family in the UK, and Shane was a disease that threatened them all. The Rosses were safe in Bath, but King and Ibrahim were my brothers and they needed my help.

I packed what little belongings I had and found Daniel in his study. He looked up from his laptop with a knowing look. "Heading back?" he asked. I nodded. Daniel sighed and pushed himself up from the desk. "Come say goodbye to the family and I'll give you a lift to the station."

The Rosses appeared from their respective nooks and assembled in the foyer and I gave everyone a hug, ending with Laura. "I've just realized I don't know much about your parents back home," she said. "But, whenever you're in England darling, Daniel and I can be your English parents."

I choked up, which made her do the same.

"Oh, Laura," Daniel laughed, rubbing her shoulders. "What have you done?"

"I didn't mean to!" she said, fanning her eyes.

We recovered with a laugh and I waved goodbye to the family from the van. We picked up my refurbished phone, but I didn't dare power it on. I wasn't ready to sift through a week's worth of notifications. The next train for London wasn't for another thirty minutes, so Daniel and I stopped for a final pint at the bar in the Royal Hotel across from the station.

"I'm not one to give unsolicited advice," Daniel said, eying his beer. "But I hope you'll avoid Shane when you return. I don't know what sort of trouble he may have got you into, but maybe it's time to consider returning to the States?" he said. I shot him a look. "I know that's not what you want to hear, with your course and all—but it might be the wisest choice."

There were a few restless nights that week where I'd considered fleeing the UK, but that wasn't the lesson I needed to learn. I needed to stop running for once, and face my problems head on.

"I feel stupid for how long it's taken me to see how manipulative Shane is," I said. "But I can't leave without trying to help King and Ibrahim. Maybe I can persuade them to leave him too."

"He won't take that lying down, you know," Daniel shrugged. "You may have a fight on your hands."

I chuckled, pointing to the fading cuts on my face. "Look at me—fighting is about all I'm good at."

He shook his head. "That's not true—I've read your writing. You've got more to offer than fighting. Truth be told, you remind me of myself as a young man. Always a knack for mischief, but I was lucky enough to have two strong parents to keep me in line. If not for them, I'd surely be in prison." He laughed into a sip of beer.

It was comforting to think I could turn out as well as Daniel, just as long as I had some direction. We finished our pints and stood at the corner by the station. Tourists shuffled past like the sheep herds on the surrounding hills.

"Good luck, son." Daniel shook my hand. "I know you're uncertain about a lot of things, but I'm confident when the time comes, you'll do the right thing."

"Thank you for everything, Daniel. I'm not sure how I can ever repay you, but I do hope I'll make you proud."

"Make yourself proud first, that's how you can repay me." He turned for the crosswalk and mingled into the crowd, a foot taller than the Chinese tourists, before disappearing around the corner.

It wasn't until I was on the platform that I realized that was the first time a man had called me *son* in a positive way. And I would have been sadder seeing Daniel go if there wasn't a voice in my head, reassuring me I would see him and the Ross family again someday.

When the train shoved off, I sat, brainstorming how to untangle myself and the boys from Shane. I slipped into a daze as the greenery rolled by my window, and it wasn't until Reading that I remembered having a working phone again.

The device came alive in a flurry of pings and buzzes— voicemails, texts, emails and missed calls. There were calls from Shane, King and Ibrahim, and multiple calls from an unknown London number. And finally, a text from Sophie that read:

"Don't come back to London. Do NOT meet up with Shane."

Chapter 39

Sophie's warning came too late—I was minutes from Paddington Station. I scanned through texts from King and Ibrahim for clues. Some asked where I was, and a couple mentioned Shane wanting to meet. Then I read Shane's texts, which started casual, *alright mate? When can we expect you back?* Then more invasive: *stopped by your flat. Latvian bloke said you've not been home in days. Where are you?*

And finally, downright aggressive, *Need to see you ASAP! You better not be avoiding me.* I figured it was best to call Sophie first, because I sure as hell wasn't going to meet up with Shane without a clear picture. Passengers surged past me on the Paddington platform. I was jittery as the phone dialed in my ear. "Hello?" she said, her voice still the sweetest thing.

"Hey, what's going on?" I asked. "What was your last text about?"

"Where are you? Who are you with?"

I stopped walking and some lady clipped my heel with her bike. "Who are *you* with?" I asked, not cut out for espionage.

A boarding announcement for Oxford chimed overhead. Sophie sighed. "You're at Paddington," she said. "I told you not to come back to London. Are you alone?"

"I live here, I had to come back," I said. "And yes, I'm alone, so please—Sophie, tell me what the hell is going on."

She paused. "I don't want to talk about it over the phone. Can we meet?"

"Sure." I nodded, as if she could see me. "Meet at my place?"

"No! Not there, um, do you remember when I fixed you up? The place you had your—*accident*. It's public. Let's meet there."

A line of people backed up behind me as I fumbled to scan my ticket through the turnstile. "Jesus, you're scaring me, woman."

"Just be there in forty-five minutes—alone."

We hung up and my stomach knotted. Paranoia I hadn't felt in a week came rushing back and I wanted a beer—something to take the edge off, but there was no time. I needed to face this now, and sober. I made for Lambeth Bridge and thought about what Daniel said about flying home. But what's home if it isn't a place filled with people you care about? Those people were Sophie, King, Ibrahim and Cash. Although, none of them wanted anything to do with me at the moment.

Post-lunch traffic swelled on the bridge, but I spotted Sophie at the South Bank. She didn't see me right away, so I stopped to watch her for a moment. It was warm out, but she wore a gray cardigan and black leggings. Her crystal blue eyes searched the passing traffic. She caught sight of me as I approached. She looked tired—worried.

"You're alone?" she scanned the bridge.

"You're never alone with Christ in your heart," I said with a smile. She just glared. "Yes, I'm alone. Please tell me what's going on?"

"It's Shane—he's found his leak," she said. I stared at her, unsure of what she meant. "He's found out who's been stealing, Luke!"

Relief washed over me. "That's it?" I laughed. "About damn time. Who is it?"

Sophie shivered in a breeze I couldn't feel. "It's not a good thing—and, I think for now it's better the less you know. It's less dangerous that way."

My head went back as I groaned. "Well, that's great. Speaking in code on a bridge like Cold War spies—really helpful, Soph," I crept toward the railing, feeling dizzy looking down at the Thames.

Sophie grabbed my arm. "Luke, this is serious."

"I'm sure it is," I said. "I'd hate to be the guy who gets caught stealing from Shane. The dude is super creepy about his money—real wrath of God shit is coming."

Her eyes suddenly filled with tears. "It's my fault," she sobbed.

I put a hand on her shoulder. "No, no—hey, we were all looking for the leak. So, whatever happens to this person will be on all of us, I guess."

Sophie cried harder, which broke my heart. She looked up at me. "Just promise me you won't meet up with Shane," she said. "He's a coward and he won't do it himself. But you're his golden boy—he'll get you to do it."

Somehow, I was still naive to gang stuff. "Do what?"

"Kill," she said, dropping the bomb. "He'll persuade you to do it. He's done it before. He'll pressure you to do it for him, so please, promise me if he asks you to take care of it for him—you won't."

All I could do was stare. *Kill?* Is that how far this had come? None of what I'd done for Shane up to that point, no matter how violent, was remotely close to murder.

I swallowed the lump in my throat. "Listen, I'm done with Shane," I said. "I've come back to London to tell him that. All I care about are the boys. I want to get them out of all of this and I'm sure as hell not going to kill anyone. This is *my* story, remember? I'm in control."

Sophie laughed at me. Her hands shook as she searched my eyes. "Do you honestly think you're the hero of this story? With all you've done. The game you've made of everyone's lives. Poor Kieran's dead. Chiara's gone back to Italy. Daniel's been run out of town—some shit story you've got."

There goes the pain she's always talking about. I looked down at my borrowed boots.

Maybe she felt bad, because she took my hand in hers. "But maybe you can fix the ending." Her grip was warm and soft. "Help the boys and don't kill for Shane. Can you do *some* good, please?"

Sophie's glare softened a bit with her pleading. Whatever was going on, it was apparent she was helpless to it. "Okay," I nodded. "I promise not to murder anyone." We stood quietly together, her hand still in mine. "This is the last time I'm going to see you, isn't it?"

"Probably, so."

I reached out and hugged her. And to my surprise, she held me tightly, nestling her forehead on mine. "Sophie, I'm sorry for all the trouble I've caused, really and truly."

When we separated, she looked up at me and for the first time, her blue eyes seemed to lose that x-ray vision. "In your own Luke way, I believe you mean that," she said, in that northern accent.

Sophie turned and walked east down the South Bank, and it hit me—*I knew where she was from.* "Hey, Soph!" I called out, over the traffic passing between us. She stopped and looked at me. "Manchester—right?"

She rolled those crystal blue eyes at me one last time, and nodded. "Yes. Finally."

Even through the sadness of knowing I'd never see her again, I couldn't help but give her a goofy grin. "Finally," I said.

Then I walked home alone.

***

London had blossomed into spring. There was something melancholic in the warm breeze rolling across the Thames and I wanted to savor my walk home, and take everything in from the city I loved. My phone rang, interrupting my moment. It was that London number again, but I let it go to voicemail. No time for spam calls. I needed to get the ball rolling on the ending for my London story, so I texted King to see if he and Ibrahim could meet.

"Yeah, where at?" King replied, rather quickly.

"My flat?"

"Bet."

He seemed pretty short with me, but why wouldn't he be? He blamed me for Kieran's death. As I walked home, I dreamed up an outlandish idea: King and Ibrahim should come to the States with me. They love American music and movies. We could see New York, Chicago and head west to Los Angeles, visit places like Yosemite, the Salt Flats and the Grand-goddamn-Canyon. Jack Kerouac style—I could write along the way and this could be the start of a whole new story!

I thought about my new plan all the way down Wandsworth Road to my building, until I stopped abruptly when I saw King. He was in all-black, mulling around my parking lot. I couldn't help but smile when I saw him.

"Hey, bro," I said.

"Alright, fam?" he asked, rubbing his hands together.

I was busy thinking about my newly-hatched idea and didn't notice he was a little fidgety. "Eh, I'm okay—you?"

King shrugged. It had only been a week since his best friend died, so I didn't expect him to be hunky dory. "We need to talk, Luke."

"Yes, we do," I nodded eagerly. "You and Brahim should come with me to the States. We'll road trip until things die down here. Hell—maybe you boys could claim asylum. You could say you're Haitian—Brahim could probably pass for Mexican," I blurted as my phone rang again.

King waved his hands like he wanted me to shut up. He groaned, and leaned against a bright blue construction van.

"Hold on," I said, seeing that London number calling again. "Hello?"

"Hello, is this Lucas?" A man asked on the other end.

"Yes, it is. What's up?"

The man cleared his throat. "This is Detective Inspector Murphy with the London Metropolitan Police. I've been trying all week to reach you," he said. My heartbeat pounded in my ears. "We need to ask you some follow-up questions concerning the incident at Caldera. Can you come round to the station this afternoon?"

Stumpy materialized to my left. His hat was down low and his beard was braided into some kind of Viking braid. "Lad," Stumpy said.

The door to the construction van slid open. Shane was sitting on the bench inside and Ibrahim was next to him. "Alright, Luke?" Shane asked.

What the hell was happening? The detective kept on in my ear, "...if transportation is an issue, we can arrange some officers to *collect* you," he said.

I hung up the phone. "I dunno, man," I said to Shane. "Am I alright?"

"Of course, mate," he grinned his big grin. "Hop in, and let's hear more about this American holiday while we take our own little road trip."

Both Shane and Stumpy carried guns, so I knew this was a command, not a request. With that detective wanting me to come in, it was an out of the pan and into the fire kind of scenario. Stumpy took a step toward me. My fight reflexes kicked in, but before I could react, I had the strange feeling like someone was watching me from across the street.

It was Mustafa in front of his kebab shop. He was squinting in the April sun with a stack of fliers in his hand. He looked happy and unmolested. I didn't think he recognized me, until he threw his hand into the air and waved. My urge to fight vanished and I couldn't help but smile and wave back.

Maybe, just maybe, I had actually helped someone in London. And if I played it cool and got into the van—maybe I could find a way to help King and Ibrahim too.

Chapter 40

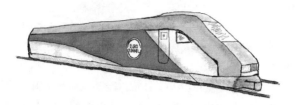

I found myself in another windowless van. It rumbled along as Shane, King, Ibrahim, and even Jamie and Swift, sat looking at me. Through the windshield, it looked as if we were headed to Catford, until we turned north of Lewisham through Deptford. We cut through the expanse of Greenwich Park, a greener side of London I had yet to see. There were people walking in the fields, playing soccer and biking—doing what people are supposed to do on a spring day, instead of whatever this was.

Shane grinned at me. He wasn't wearing his usual tailored suit, instead he wore an olive-green military style jacket, dark jeans and brown boots. Shane was dressed for war, or some rich guy's idea of war attire.

"Where've you been, Luke?" He broke the long silence. "We were worried—looked all over."

Didn't want to bring Daniel into this, so I lied. "Weston-super-Mare—wanted to be by the sea."

"Bollocks," he chuckled. "You'd have gone to Brighton for the sea. Danny took you to Bath, yeah? Posh little tourist trap." The calmer Shane looked, the scarier he was. His hands were in his lap and his head rested against the van wall.

"I didn't feel trapped in Bath," I said, copying his body language. "Feeling a little trapped now, though."

"Don't be silly, mate. We're all free men, here," he gestured to the sullen faces around him.

"Clearly—where are we going?"

"All will be revealed, my son," he smirked. "Just sit back and relax—there's travel pay in it for you."

The kidnapping nature of the ride and that call from the detective made me feel anything but relaxed. I searched the boys' faces and saw they were dressed in all-black—our uniform for tearing shit up. My mind raced. What if Shane thinks I'm the leak? He knows I've gotten close to Sophie, and if she knows who the culprit is, maybe he thinks I do too.

We passed through a lot of countryside on our drive east—a lot of pastures for my shallow grave. But after a while, the van slowed and the green country gave way to a long line of cars and lorries. We inched alongside a massive bed of train tracks and freight containers. It looked like some kind of train station, but ahead of us was a large bank of toll booths.

Stumpy put a bright sheet of pink paper in the windshield as we came to a booth. A red-faced man motioned us through without stopping. We pressed on through the industrial expanse of grimy girders and overhead wires. Diesel fumes seeped in through our air con. I was relieved we were taking a train. Trains are public, and Shane was too slick to murder me with an audience.

We waited in a long line of cars and utility vans like ours, creeping inch-by-inch, until we came alongside a massive train. The engine was blue and silver, and on the side read: *Eurotunnel*.

I lurched forward. "The Chunnel? We're going to France?"

"Well done, mate," Shane said. "Only took you an hour-and-a-half to put it together."

Why the hell were we going to France? Our van split from the line of lorries and joined in with a long line of other construction vans leaving customs. They were bright blue and identical to ours. They filed into the train car and things went dark as we puttered in behind them.

Stumpy killed the engine. King and the boys looked at me with wide eyes, mirroring my concern. Unlike Cash, I was deeply uncomfortable with going back to France, but here I was, being dragged back. A train worker knocked on Stumpy's window. A tall black dude with a hi-vis vest over his hoodie.

Shane stuffed a wad of cash into an empty coffee cup and passed it to Stumpy, who handed it to the worker. "You alright, Freddy?" Stumpy asked.

"Ye—alright," Freddy took his money and bailed.

"What's happening?" I asked Shane.

He chuckled smugly and lifted a floor panel between my feet, revealing a small compartment brimming with cash. Shane used the Chunnel to get cash out of the UK and drugs into it, then bribed whoever he needed to along the way. Simple but genius.

"Mate, it's details like this that make my organization a cut above the rest." He stomped the panel into place. "Imagine how I feel, hearing you no longer want to be a part of it."

Everyone looked at me. Even Stumpy turned in his seat. My heart began to thump loudly, or maybe it was the train revving up. I had hoped to avoid this conversation and just ghost Shane, like a true millennial.

"You're right, Shane—I don't," I said, coming clean. "After Kieran and spending a night in jail—it's sort of soured me on the whole thing."

Shane was quiet for a second. "Fine, give me your story. It's not yours anymore." He stuck out his hand.

"I, uh, don't have it on me," I stuttered. "Cash—maybe his fiancé could get it to me."

"If you don't have it, then you owe me," he said. "Which is why you're going to France. You're free when I say you are. But—" he put a finger in my face. "The boys work for me. They know I look out for them and they aren't going to the *bloody* States, do you understand?"

This was going to require some backbone, so I puffed out my chest. "And what if I don't want to do whatever we're doing in France?"

He flashed his awful grin. "That is entirely your choice, but I think I can persuade you." He pulled out another wad of cash. I rolled my eyes. He freed a newspaper clipping from the cash and handed it to me. "That's your payment."

The train lurched underneath us, turning my stomach. I knew what the clipping was without looking but I couldn't help myself—I looked down at it. There she was in black and white: Madeleine. She stared back at me, ghostly, from the Tottenham station.

"In forty minutes, this train will be on French soil," Shane said. "Paris is only three hours from there. *That* is your payment," he pointed to the clipping. "Do a good job and your secret stays a secret."

The boys scrunched their faces, confused. My body shook as I looked at Madeleine. Blackmailed again over the same poor girl, by another cunt looking to exploit her. "Fuck you, man," I said.

Shane laughed. "Is that a yes?"

My phone rang in my pocket, but I didn't dare pull it out. Shane didn't need any more leverage. "Yes," I said.

"Good," he nodded. "Now, who's phoning you?"

Dammit.

"Go on," he pointed. "Take it out." I pulled out my phone, and on the screen was the detective's number. Everyone stared as it stopped ringing. "Looks like a government number," Shane said, spot on.

The train hummed louder as it picked up speed. Shane and I stared at one another, playing some weird game of mental chess. I went to put the phone away and he grabbed my wrist. The phone dinged with a voicemail. "Play it," he said.

Everyone leaned forward to listen. "Hello, Lucas, this is Detective Inspector Murphy calling again," everyone sucked at the air. "I'm not sure if our previous call was dropped or was ended deliberately, but I want to make it clear that my request for your presence at Charing Cross Station was compulsory. We need to speak immed—"

Shane snatched my phone and held it to his ear.

"Fuckinell," Ibrahim, shook his head. "They must got a warrant for you, fam."

King looked to Jamie. "Same call your cuz got before his two-stretch, innit?"

Jamie gave a somber nod. Shane turned my phone off and slipped it into his jacket. "The phone stays off, and with me."

As the train picked up speed, my emotions spiked into fear, anger and sadness before dropping into a strange numbness. Too many emotions for one day, it was impossible to feel them all at once. The only thing I felt now was pain.

Daniel was wrong.

I'm incapable of doing the right thing. In fact, I was plopped smack in the middle of doing the wrong thing. And I was riding that son of a bitch all the way back to Paris.

Chapter 41

I shared a room with Stumpy at a roadside hotel in Calais. Luckily his sleep apnea drowned out the roar of the highway. Not that I could sleep anyway, with the probability of Shane killing me by the end of the excursion.

The next morning, everyone piled back into the construction van, where I watched Paris stream through the narrow view of the windshield. There was a flutter in my chest returning to that city—both the familiar and painful wadded into a tight ball in my diaphragm.

It felt like the last time I saw Bill. His hospice nurses called me to his place, said I should come immediately to see him and say goodbye. I didn't want to see him, but I sure as hell wanted to say goodbye. But when I got there, Bill had a final surge of energy and sat at the kitchen table, unhooked from his machines and smoking a cigarette.

"Hey, man," I rubbed my eyes in disbelief. "You're supposed to be dying. Get back in bed."

Bill glared at me, flicking ash onto the linoleum floor. Not like he'd be around to clean it. "They took my cigarettes," he said. "Had to dig out these old ones."

"Well, can you smoke in bed? If you die at the table, I'm leaving you for the next tenants to deal with."

Bill chuckled, followed by a long string of coughs. Figured, the one time I made the man laugh, it nearly killed him. He hobbled to his feet, and pushed me away when I went to help him. "Get your hands off me. I can do it."

He caned back to the hospital bed in the living room. I followed behind in case the bastard fell, and sure enough, he faltered when climbing into bed. I caught him and lifted him back to his feet. Bill was a raisin of the man he used to be, after all. He looked at me with that wild look in his eyes, the only thing truly left of him.

Maybe it was seeing his shitty life in the rearview—or coming to terms that his once-weak son was now much stronger than him. But the prick took a swing at me. A left hook in slow motion. I dodged it, and I know I shouldn't have given a shit, but come on! It was our last moments together. We didn't have to say our sorries but, Jesus—hit me?

White heat shot through me. I slapped Bill's spotted hands away and grabbed his leathery neck and squeezed.

***

Our van lurched to a stop on a long street of gothic rowhouses, pale and white. Endless doors leading to endless apartments. Stumpy parked us across from a long line of scooters and Shane clapped his hands together. "Luke. King—come with me." He slid the door open.

Morning light spilled into the cab. I squinted at the scooters and buildings—why did this street seem so familiar? King hopped out and I followed. His forehead crinkled with a worried expression I'd never seen on his ever-confident face. Although I was just as nervous, I gave him a comforting smile.

A dude on a scooter whizzed by and I recalled a night long-since passed. I studied the street again. The buildings and the apartment doors, until I landed on one massive door in particular, with a key-code box.

Rémy's flat.

"A return to the scene of the crime," Shane snickered, waving for us to follow him.

"Never seen Paris," King whispered to me. "Always wanted to."

"I've been here twice now," I said. "Both times sucked."

Stumpy joined the three of us at the massive front door. It was worn in the daylight; the finish dull and chipping. Shane punched a code into the box—69420. We stepped inside the narrow, tiled hallway. The echoes of our steps, the stench of old plaster—it all brought me back. I could practically smell Madeleine's shampoo still lingering in the air.

We labored up the stairs to the top floor. The hall was dark and the same buzzing bulb struggled to light the four of us on Rémy's landing. The camera above the door glared at us, with its all-seeing red light beaming into my soul. Shane pulled out a skeleton key with bright pink tape wrapped around the head, unbolted the door and stepped inside.

I peeked around Stumpy's big head down the long hallway. Light rained through the skylights, and standing at the end of the hall was Rémy. He was shirtless in a pair of jeans and smoking a blunt; a surprised look on his scraggly, bearded face. Rémy looked the same, except his hair was longer and tied up in a stupid manbun. I emitted something like a growl. Stumpy and King looked at me like I was insane.

"Shane. I didn't know you were in Paris," Rémy said, in perfect damn English.

Shane ran a finger across the sculptures in the hall. "Just popping in—is this a bad time?"

Rémy looked down his joint. "Non—give me a minute, I'll put on a shirt."

"Please, do," Shane said.

The rest of us filed into the apartment, and I shut the front door. I was having an out-of-body experience. The place looked the same, just as I'd seen it a thousand times in my head since September. Only this time without the awful purple light. Rémy reemerged from his bedroom, buttoning up a Hawaiian shirt.

"Where's George?" Shane asked.

"He's working, of course—" Rémy finally spotted me. His jaw dropped. "*You*—why are you here?"

I snapped. "Came here to kill you!" I charged at him.

Shane grabbed me, while Stumpy put me in a headlock. I kicked and writhed to free myself. "Leave it, lad!" Stumpy said. "Leave it!"

"Why bring this—animal—here?" Rémy backed away. "What is going on?"

I gargled. "I'll show you *animal*—"

Stumpy squeezed the air from my throat. Shane faced Rémy. "We're here for an emergency team meeting. I've got a place outside of town. It's quiet and private." Shane held out the palms of his hands. "All is well, Rémy—or it will be, rather. But we need everyone together. You know how I run my business— everyone has a stake and everyone should be present for big decisions. All we need is George now."

Shane put an arm around Rémy and they disappeared into the living room. Stumpy released me. I sucked in breath, hating myself for not killing Rémy in September. I looked for something to break. Maybe a statue or the camera above me, or—hey—my cigarette butt was still in the light fixture. The burn hole in the wall beneath it. This was all too weird. I needed out of there.

Shane returned and huddled me, King and Stumpy together. "George is at Le Perchoir Marais," he said. "You three go and collect him, while I have a talk with Rémy. Plus, if he and Luke are in the same room for much longer, there might be a mess to clean up," he laughed.

"You can bet your British ass," I said.

Shane grinned and shook me by the shoulder. "I'll need that enthusiasm when the time comes, but right now your job is to collect George."

It finally hit me. Rémy was the leak.

Shane was going to use my burning hatred for Rémy to solve his problem. And as I stood looking into the bedroom where I discovered Madeleine, I felt more open to the idea.

No! I thought. *Remember Daniel. I can do the right thing—right?*

***

The three of us came out to the street and into Rémy's silver Renault. Ibrahim, Jamie and Swift loitered by the van. I gave them a weak wave from the back seat—the same seat I sat with Madeleine, propped between Cash and me. We cruised the Fourth Arrondissement, a few blocks north of the Seine and beyond that, Notre Dame. Stumpy parked us on a narrow street of cafes and brunch goers. A sea of tables with smiling, coffee-sipping faces. I climbed out of the car, gawking at them. Why couldn't I be sitting there smoking and laughing with friends? Instead of running errands for a gangster with untold, nefarious ends.

"Come on," Stumpy nudged me. "It's not polite to stare, lad."

We followed Stumpy to a department store where there was a rooftop bar upstairs. Voices and laughter drifted down to us in the street. We wound through the store aisles for the elevator. The doors opened and the building opened up to a massive tented terrace. The place was fancy and we looked out of place. Women in smart dresses, men in sunny button-up shirts, while I wore hiking boots and a borrowed Bath rugby sweatshirt.

We moved through long rows of diners, gawping at the panoramic view of roofs and the Eiffel Tower in the distance. Amazing how even the view of tarnished copper roofs in Paris is breathtaking. King stepped on my heels and I ran into Stumpy when he stopped and pointed.

George sat in a plush corner booth, surrounded by the chatter of French voices. He wore a tan blazer and an open-collar shirt, sipping a brown drink. His table of beautiful men and women had erupted into laughter at something he'd just said. I wanted to be him. Well-dressed and handsome, with the Eiffel Tower propped over my shoulder. A waiter delivered them a tray of drinks when George looked up and saw us. His face contorted when he saw me.

We cast a literal shadow over the table and everyone glared at us. George said to his friends, "Everyone, these are my mates from London."

"Londres est ennuyeux," A blonde girl said, sipping her drink.

The table giggled at her brazenness. George smiled. "Oh, I can assure you, London is never boring with this lot. Luke— good to see you."

"You too, man," I said.

"Will you please excuse me for a moment?" George stood with his drink. He adjusted his suit and led us to the bar. "Why the hell are you here? And dressed like that?" George looked at me with searching eyes. Maybe he saw a flash of our ill-fated night long ago.

"Emergency team meeting," Stumpy stated.

"Can't it bloody wait?"

"Shane's the boss, lad. I just drive."

George looked over his shoulder at the table. "Well, I'm in the middle of a sale—and the Belgian bloke is a damn good customer."

Stumpy stroked his braided beard. "Can you close it in the next five minutes?"

"Seems I haven't much choice." George set his drink on the bar and returned to the table with Stumpy in tow.

King and I looked at one another as they collected the Belgian and disappeared around the corner. I grabbed George's drink and chugged it down. It was heavy on the rum.

"Can I get another one of these?" I called to the bartender, who looked down at me with his crooked nose. "Un autre verre, s'il vous plait—on that table's bill." I pointed to the corner.

"He's *you*," King said.

"He's what?" I sucked rum off an ice cube.

"George does the same job you do, just in Paris." King shrugged. "Drinks with people, winds them up to shot food. He's British you—in France."

Holy shit, King was right. Everything came circling back as I thought about that night. Was George working Cash and I? What would have happened if we'd never met him? That Madeleine business would have been someone else's problem—not mine.

"Yeah, well not anymore," I said, as the barman handed me a drink. I took another big gulp, and shot a look to the waiter. "Christ, there's so much rum, man." I grimaced, turning to King. "Look, I'm done with Shane, and you and Brahim should be too. Come with me to the States. I'll help you however I can."

King squinted out across the sunny rooftops. "Not that simple, bruv. Got my whole family in London. And I told Llanzo I'd check in on his mum and sis while he's away."

I signaled to the bartender for another. "Well, that's kind of you, but you need to look out for yourself. What about *your* future—football?"

He rolled his eyes. "Can't play Premier League if I'm in the States."

Ugh—so many obstacles in doing the right thing. "How did you guys get entangled with Shane in the first place?"

The sun slowly dipped behind the only cloud in the robin egg sky, blanketing everyone in a brief respite of shade. "He found us," King said.

There was a strange lull in the shaded voices around us. The bartender flared his French nostrils as he set another drink down. "Shane said he found Kieran shoplifting crisps and took him in," I sipped the rum and searched my pockets for a smoke.

"That ain't true, fam. Shane met all of us through that mayor's program."

"I don't understand." I lit a cigarette.

"We was all in the same program," he shrugged. "After school mentoring and shit, for like—at risk youth, innit," he said. My shoulders slumped in disbelief. "Like a program to keep us off the streets, and all that."

"Like a big brother program? Was Shane a mentor?"

"Exactly." he snapped his fingers. "That's how we all met."

It took a moment to compose my thoughts. "Let me get this straight—you were in a program designed to keep you off the streets. Shane joins as a mentor, and does the exact opposite—and puts you on the streets?"

King gritted his teeth. "It sounds bad when you put it like that. But we was just happy to make some Ps, man. We had a purpose—"

"I'm not blaming *you*," I said. "I blame Shane—Kieran is dead! That program could have kept y'all out of harm's way."

King's face contorted and he choked out a sob. I'd never seen him lose his cool exterior. "Worst part, bro," his voice straining. "We're going to miss the funeral tomorrow."

Forget Rémy. I wanted to kill Shane. What he had done to the boys was soulless. I lifted the rum, shakily, to my lips and swallowed a big gulp. There were too many hurdles getting the boys to the States, and with detectives waiting for me back in London, my options narrowed. Maybe killing Shane *was* me doing the right thing. Maybe I could live with that.

Stumpy and George finally returned. "Alright, lads," Stumpy said. "Let's go see Shane."

I threw back the rest of the rum drink and slammed the glass onto the bar. Nearby patrons scowled. "Hell yeah! Let's go see Shane," I shouted.

Chapter 42

I rode in Rémy's backseat with my head against the window, watching George bounce his knee in the front seat. Everyone in the car seemed nervous—except me. Either Rémy or Shane was going to die that day, and I looked forward to the coin toss.

Paris whizzed past my window and soon the scenery turned lush green. I would have paid more attention to where we were headed, but I was still reeling from the mentorship revelation. I was in YMCA youth programs for years until Bill stopped paying for them. What happened to King and the boys could have happened to me.

Stumpy stopped the car and we stepped out onto a gravel road, stained orange with tire tracks from some nearby clay. A dense wall of trees lined the road. The leaves rustled from above as if the trees were speaking to one another—or to me. *You shouldn't have come here.*

"Where are we?" I asked.

"We're in Bois du Bologne Park," Stumpy said.

Despite the remote location and the warning in the trees, I couldn't bring myself to fear that place. The sun shone through the shifting mosaic of green, which made me miss the longleaf pines back home. How they sing in the wind.

The four of us crunched down the gravel road for a short distance, until the path made a sharp left, ending at a clearing that was guarded by a tall fence. A sign on the gate informed visitors that the trail was closed for construction. Through the gate I could see a single-wide trailer, stacks of large concrete piping, and in the distance the arm of a massive backhoe. A tall black man in a hardhat came trudging through the muck toward us. Without a word, he unlocked the gate and dragged it open.

"Cheers," Stumpy said.

King, George and I stared at one another. "Shane's got a construction site?" I asked.

George sweat through his blazer. "The first I've heard of it."

We followed Stumpy, hopping puddles for dry gravel footholds. I waited for King to dig a pebble out his Air Max's, when I saw the construction worker fleeing down the path we'd just come from, disappearing around the corner.

That can't be good.

Stumpy motioned for us to hurry, and I thought about chasing after that construction worker for a ride back to town. But I couldn't leave—I was there for the boys. We rounded the trailer and discovered three more utility vans like the one we'd traveled in to France. They gave me the feeling it was always the plan for us to end up in these woods.

My heart pulsed in my throat following Stumpy to the backhoe, which was parked next to a massive trench. Its scoop was dug into a mound of brown-red dirt. Ibrahim stood at the edge of the trench with Swift and Jamie. They threw rocks at a long line of concrete piping that ran along the bottom. Me and King were just as relieved to see them as they were to see us.

Ibrahim threw his hands in the air. "Yo, what are we doing here, fam? Swear to God I've seen this place in a horror film."

I thought he was being dramatic until I reexamined the shovels, the machinery, the remoteness, and the trench—like a mass grave. This was the perfect place to kill someone. My knees almost gave out. Was Shane done with all of us? The boys and I could easily disappear in that hole, where he could return to that mayor's program and pick out a new litter of employees.

Speak of the Devil.

Shane came waltzing up the gravel with a confident stride. In the sun his green eyes looked cheery—vindicated. Wait a second.

He was alone.

"Where the hell is Rémy?" I blurted. "He's the leak, right?"

Shane raised a brow. "Er—I'm afraid Rémy couldn't join us."

"I want to see his body!"

I crept to the edge of the trench. Lose earth crumbled beneath my boots as I peered in. The trench ran for ages, dividing the sea of trees. But no Rémy. I looked at Shane, practically drooling with bloodlust.

Shane's broad shoulders rose and fell as he sighed. "I hate to disappoint you, Luke, but Rémy isn't our leak—is he, George?"

We all looked at George. "Now, Shane. Let's keep a cool head about this, mate." George put up his trembling hands. "We're family, after all."

"Family—" Shane marched across the gravel for him.

George stumbled back into the dirt mound behind him. Before he could jump back up, Shane took a powerful swing at him. The first blow stunned George. The second knocked him out cold. But Shane kept hitting him in the head and face.

The boys and I moved toward them, but Stumpy stepped between us. Shane kept pounding George's bloody face. I'd never seen Shane fight before. It was brutal. When Shane stopped, he threw his head back and roared. George was a mess of dirt and blood. He moaned, fighting to stay conscious.

It took George a moment to sit up. "Shane, you don't understand," he slurred. "I didn't have much choice."

"You're not leaving *me* much choice, are you Georgie?" Shane spat at his feet. "You said it yourself—we're family."

George rose shakily to his knees and clasped his hands together, pleading. "I had to look after mine, mate, and that's hard to do from another country." He was in tears. "Please, this was my idea, not hers! Take it out on me, not her."

I was still in shock that George was the leak, but what did he mean by *her*—Sophie? What did she have to do with any of this?

"Georgie, you're mad if you think I believe you put this together alone," he laughed. "She's the brains behind this."

Muddy tears streaked down George's cheeks. "Please, don't hurt her, Shane. I'll give it all back, mate. But don't kill me, I'm begging you!"

Were Sophie and George together? Adrenaline shot through me. Should I do something? I didn't want anything to happen to Sophie. George—I was caring less for, but I didn't want to see him die.

Shane silently regarded his bleeding cousin. "You're right." He patted George's head. "We are family, and I'd never be able to live with myself if I killed you." He pulled the old revolver from his jacket. "That's why I've brought the Yank."

That snapped me out of my daze. Shane and George looked at me. Hell, everyone did. "Why me?" I stepped back.

"To ensure your secret stays a secret, that's why," Shane said.

"Maybe if it was Rémy—but I ain't got beef with George, man."

Shane cocked his head. "Everything bad that's happened to you is because of him." He pointed at George, who was now crying. "You think you ended up in that apartment by accident, do you? That every door in Rémy's flat was locked except the room with the girl?"

I couldn't breathe. My mind couldn't work fast enough to understand.

"He's lying, Luke!" George pleaded. "I didn't know she was there!"

Shane grabbed George by the collar and threw him at my feet. I stared into George's blue eyes. "Look at me." Shane shook me. "They were shorthanded and needed to get rid of her fast. So, this bastard pulled you and your mate into the mix!"

George shook his head, sobbing. If that were true, I'd have never met Shane, never gotten entangled with Profit, and Cash and Kieran would have never been shot.

"And what about Sophie?" Shane asked. Our eyes met. "The girl you love is hung up on this sod. She chose *him* over you."

My shoulders slumped. So, George is her kid's father. He and I looked at one another. I really wanted to take the easy route and blame everything on George. Maybe with him out of the way, I could be with Sophie. I felt myself nodding along and just as I thought about putting a bullet between George's eyes, I remembered what Sophie said.

I'm not the hero of this story, but maybe I could fix the ending—*do some good.*

Seeing George like this made me realize how much I truly loved Sophie. I wanted to protect her, and by extension, that meant protecting George. Maybe Daniel was right about me doing the right thing. Ugh, I hate me.

"I'm sorry, Shane, but all my troubles belong to me alone," I said. "Plus, I'm from the south—we shoot our own cousins."

Shane clicked his tongue. "You bloody moron. Fine. You die too."

I locked eyes onto his pistol. "Yep, figured."

Instead of shooting me, Shane walked over to King, took his wrist and slapped the revolver into his palm. King looked down at the gun. "Me?"

"Hey, no way, man!" I said.

"You, shut your mouth," Shane yelled, then turned to King. "I want you to run Paris for me, son. You're ready for the challenge. And you'll do much better than George ever did."

The wheels seemed to turn in King's head. His eyes pored over George. I felt sick. I came back to London to get the boys out of Shane's grasp. Not fast track King's gangster career through murder. He's supposed to play for Chelsea. And Ibrahim is supposed to be on stage somewhere. They weren't murderers, they were good kids.

"King, what about soccer—er, football?" I shouted. He clenched his eyes shut. "You're a footballer, slick!"

Shane shoved me onto the jagged gravel. "Speak again and Stumpy will shoot you in the face."

"Fuck you, I don't care!" I sat up. "King, this isn't you!" Stumpy moved toward me. "King!" I called again.

George sobbed when King cocked the hammer on the revolver. Maybe King figured it was the only way out. Stumpy marched across the gravel for me and I went cold. I'd failed. There's no helping anyone if I'm dead.

Stumpy pulled his gun. One last try: "Oba, come on," I said. King looked at me and I smiled. "Ah, there we go."

Too late. Stumpy jammed his Springfield to my forehead. He pulled back the hammer. His finger hugged the trigger, but Shane shouted, "Brahim, no!"

WHACK. Ibrahim cracked Stumpy in the head with a shovel. Stumpy crumpled and shot himself in the thigh as he fell. My ears rang with the shot. Everyone froze. Shane went for King's pistol.

They fought for it.

If Shane gets that gun, I'm dead. Me and George in the hole. Sophie in another one. I charged for them. Shane punched King in the jaw—freeing the gun as I dove for him. Threw my shoulder into Shane's gut. He and I tumbled down into the trench. Shane landed on his back onto the concrete pipe. I landed at his feet in the dirt. I sprang up and leapt onto Shane. I threw a punch, but he clamped down on my arm. Then my other arm. A brief pause. He grinned then lifted me up. Effortlessly.

Uh oh. Shane was a lot stronger than me.

He rammed his knee into my gut. Knocking the air out of me. He threw me, rolling across the big pipe. Couldn't breath. But I had to keep moving. Your breath will come back. Just keep moving. A massive blur rocketed at me. Shane swung and barely missed my head as I dove into the dirt. But he didn't stop. He stomped through the trench and I shuffled away on my ass. He reached for my leg, but I kicked. Crunched his fingers.

"You bastard." He yanked my boot off.

I scrambled and dove for the pipe to put distance between us. He winged my boot at my face and I tumbled head first on the other side of the pipe.

"Get up, Luke! Get up!" King shouted.

"You've got him, come on!" Ibrahim added.

My breath hadn't returned, but encouragement was nice. I wobbled to my feet as Shane came swinging. I threw my hands up. Blocked his right, then his left. Each blow knocked my own fist into my skull. He swung like a mad man. Gravel jammed into my bare foot as I retreated. My foot—that's right! Forgot my own motto. *Fuck a fair fight.*

The boys shouted from the ledge as I backed away, letting Shane swing. He's got muscle, but does he have stamina? Finally, I faked a jab. He pulled his head back and I railed my heel into his gut. Haymaker to his cheek—contact. Now, hit him with a jab, and oh no—he caught it.

Shane punched me in the stomach again. I fell back, saw purple spots in the sky. Luckily, he was hurting too. Shane leaned against the pipe, wheezing through flared nostrils. He glared at me with his insane green eyes and took off his jacket.

Screw this. I'm out of here.

I tried clambering out of the trench. But the wall crumbled in my hands. I tore at the exposed roots but Shane yanked my sweater. I put my feet into the wall and pushed off. All my weight came down on him. He wrapped his arms around me and we fell back onto the pipe. The bastard squeezed the breath from my chest. I swung my torso, cracked him in the head with my elbow. The boys cheered, so I swung again. Hit him with my other elbow. Maybe, just maybe, I could win this fight.

Nope!

He growled in my ear, all teeth and anger. He swung my legs high into the air then slammed my head onto the concrete pipe. I bounced off and my chest landed on something solid in the dirt. The boys fell silent. My head spun, and the world dimmed.

Funny, I thought. How many years has it been since an American died in a trench in France? I tried to move, but nothing worked. I'd been playing cat and mouse with death for months and my luck had finally run out. I was never a good fighter. I was just meaner and had more to fight for than the other guy. Figures, the one time I fight for someone other than myself, I'd lose. The boys, Sophie and George—it was all for nothing. But wait—

Feeling tingled in my arms and hands. I felt breath in my lungs and my knees pressing into the gravel. The ground vibrated as Shane stood over me. His head blocked the sun. I felt the coolness of the shade and that thing pressing into my chest underneath me.

Shane lifted me like a child onto my feet. *My God, he's strong.* I'll never forget the look on his face when he saw what I had in my hands. I cracked him in the teeth with the handle of his own gun. Shane wobbled, stunned. The boys oohed from the ledge above. I saw a flash of Bill—my hands around his old neck. So, I hit Shane again. Shattered his two front teeth and remaining canine.

Shane fell onto his back on the pipe. My anger spewed like magma. Third times the charm. I cracked him senseless across the forehead—CLONK. His head bobbed and I jumped on top of him. Thought of Dieter in the yellow jacket. I shoved the barrel into Shane's bloody mouth. I put my hand around his throat and pulled back the hammer on the gun.

Maybe it was my head injury. Or the look of acceptance in Shane's eyes. But I saw Bill. My father. He was on the hospice bed, my hands around his neck. The anger faded from his hazel eyes, with an expression like—*just do it, pussy*. And I wanted to, so damn bad. All my life I wanted to beat Bill in a fight. Hurt him like he'd hurt my mother. How he'd hurt me. But not as some dying, shell of a man. I wanted Bill in his prime, while I was in mine. And with my hands around his neck, I realized that's not what people like Bill do. They don't hurt people as strong as them. They target the weak, the vulnerable. Seeing Bill on his death bed, I realized the tables had turned, and I let go of his throat. My eyes were wet as I stared at what was left of big, scary Bill.

I helped him back into bed. Lit us both cigarettes and sat quietly, until he looked at me and said the best three words he could have ever said.

Don't be me.

He died an hour later.

Blood poured from Shane's mouth. There were tears in my eyes as I grappled with it all. Everything told me to blow his brains out. Everything except Bill's dying words. *Don't be me.* So, I decided to be me, and I said something stupid with way too much southern drawl. "Ain't you purdy now, Shane?" I pulled the gun out of his mouth.

I gave him a proper slap across the face and rifled his pockets for my phone. I snagged Eric's hiking boot and, with the help of the four boys, I climbed out of my own grave.

King smiled that gap-toothed smile. "Fuckin' pitball, man," he laughed. "Every time I think you're done for—you pull it out the bag."

"You thought I was done for, slick?" I panted. "Just gonna let him kill me?"

"Naw, fam. We was spottin' you." He held up Stumpy's Springfield.

Great, I got my ass kicked for no reason. "You guys need to get the hell out of here," I pointed at the vans. "Get back to England. You know how to get to the Chunnel?"

He shrugged. "Google, innit? Wait, you not coming?"

I looked at George, who skulked beside me. "I've got some things to handle first. But I'll catch up—now go!"

King and Ibrahim had puppy dog eyes, like they didn't believe me. But King nodded and handed me Stumpy's gun. And before he turned to leave, King stopped and gave me a hug. The four of them, King, Ibrahim, Jamie and Swift, trotted across the gravel and cranked up the van. With King behind the wheel, they tore across the loose rocks through the open gate.

Shane was moving again. George and I watched him from the edge of the trench. The van disappeared around the corner and I felt a sinking feeling in my stomach. I missed them already. George breathed heavily. His face was swollen and he used the sleeve of his blazer to stop his eyebrow from bleeding.

"George, this is your mess, and I'm letting you clean it up," I said, watching Shane crawl on his hands and knees. "This Enfield has been in your family since the war." I handed him the revolver. "If you think Shane deserves to inherit it—go ahead and give it back to him. But if not, then you've got a decision to make."

George swallowed hard. "Right, yeah."

"Stumpy looks super dead, so I'm going to get the Renault keys from him and leave you to it. But I want two things from you." I poked his chest. "The first, go back to London and take care of Sophie and your kid. Be good to them. We need good fathers."

A tear rolled down George's cheek. "I will, I promise," he nodded. "And the second?"

***

I rolled down the Renault's windows and punched the directions into the GPS. My body throbbed as I watched the sun shimmer through the swaying trees. A single gunshot fired in the distance. No matter which cousin took the bullet, someone's idea of justice had been served. I started up the car and chugged down the gravel road, a cigarette dangling between my lips.

***

Rémy must have been anxious for how things would turn out in the woods, because he didn't seem to find it strange the single bulb lighting his hallway had burnt out. And in his haste to answer the knocking, he opened his door to a shadowy figure in the hall.

I hit Rémy in the mouth with Stumpy's gun, my new favorite move. He slid across the marble floor as blood poured from the stubs of his teeth. He wept as I dragged him down four flights of stairs by his manbun. I tugged him by the scalp to his Renault in the street, opening the trunk.

"Get in," I said.

Rémy cried and bled. His frantic eyes searched the quiet street for help that would never come.

"You wanted to put Madeleine in the trunk, remember?" I said.

"S'il vous plaît," he gargled. "Je ne comprend pas!"

I grabbed his throat and shoved him against the car. "I know you understand English, asshole! Now, get in."

It took a little cramming and crying from Rémy, but he eventually fit into his own tiny trunk. I googled police stations, but it was such a beautiful afternoon in Paris I decided to take the scenic route. I plugged some tunes into the stereo and rolled the windows down. *Carolina in My Mind* played as I passed the Louvre, regretting Cash and I never went. I felt foolish for the person I'd been, but decided regret would only bring pain—and

I was done with pain. I was ready to heal, and that meant paying for my actions. But before I did that, I decided it would be nice to sit down somewhere for a cup of Parisian coffee and to write.

I parked illegally in front of Le Bistrot Marguerite, which sat on the busy corner overlooking the Hotel De'Ville, the Seine, and beyond it, Pont Neuf. I sipped coffee and, with borrowed pen and paper, I let the words pour—unlike my first time in Paris. In just forty-five minutes, I wrote the opening chapters of this book, and as you can see, I didn't hold back any of the awful details. I'd finally gotten the brush with adventure I'd been looking for, and although most of it happened in London, what started in Paris would end in Paris.

When I finished, I folded up my papers into my pocket—both confession and the start of my magnum opus. I checked the time and rang my mother in California.

Her sunny voice came through on the second ring, "Hello, Luke," she said. It was nice to hear her voice.

"Hey, Mom—calling from Paris."

"Wow, what are you doing back there?"

"It's a long story, but I'm here tying up some loose ends," I said, eying the tourists who'd stopped to look at the Renault. "I just wanted to tell you I'm probably going away for a while. It'll be some time before you see me again."

"Going away?" she asked. "Are you traveling for the spring?"

"Eh, not quite," I said, watching Rémy's trunk rattle from the inside. A small crowd had gathered to look at it. "Look, Mom, you're going to hear a lot about me soon, and I wanted you to know—it's all true. Every word." I sighed. "I just don't want you to blame yourself. I could've dropped the hurt little boy thing a long time ago, but I didn't."

"Lu, you're kind of worrying me," she stammered. "Is everything okay?"

"I'm sorry, I didn't mean to scare you. Just wanted to call and say I love you, and yes, everything will soon be okay."

She was quiet for a moment. The pounding in the trunk grew louder and more people stopped to gawk, chattering among themselves. "I love you too. Always will."

It was nice to hear, and my eyes were wet. I went to hang up but stopped. "Oh, I need a favor!" I snapped my fingers. "Can you get Corey's New York address from Emma, and send him some flowers and a card?" I stood from my table, leaving behind a fat wad of British pounds.

I sauntered over to the car and tried shooing the crowd. They just stared at my busted-up face, so I lifted my sweater and flashed the gun in my pants. They all yelped and ran away. I took one last look at the lovely view and hopped into the driver's seat.

"Flowers, okay. And what should the card say?" my mother asked.

I started the engine and took a deep breath. Like before, the words came easy. "Have the card say: I'm sorry for hurting you. Thank you for always being my friend and trying to steer me in the right direction. It took me a while, but I found it. I'm truly thankful for you, and for the ugly, beautiful, terrifying and wonderful things I've discovered about this world and myself—

—by way of Paris."

The end.

About the Author

Christopher J. Newman was born and raised in North Carolina where he began writing stories from the back row of his high school math and science classes. What began as a hobby quickly turned into an obsession and Newman's passion for storytelling took on two specific forms: novel writing and filmmaking. He spent the next ten years working as a freelance filmmaker by day and writing novels by night.

In 2019, Newman decided to pursue writing further and moved to the United Kingdom to earn his master's degree in creative writing from Bath Spa University. His year-and-a-half spent abroad provided the inspiration for his debut novel, *By Way of Paris*. The novel served as his dissertation for his master's program and was awarded a distinction.

Newman currently works in marketing for a non-profit organization, moonlights as a freelance filmmaker, and works part-time as a university instructor, where he teaches storytelling through film.

You can connect with him on Instagram, Threads, Twitter and TikTok: @chrisjnewman

Or visit his website: christopherjamesnewman.com

ROUNDFIRE
BOOKS

FICTION

Put simply, we publish great stories. Whether it's literary or
popular, a gentle tale or a pulsating thriller, the connecting theme
in all Roundfire fiction titles is that once you pick them up you
won't want to put them down.
If you have enjoyed this book, why not tell other readers by
posting a review on your preferred book site.

Recent bestsellers from Roundfire are:

The Bookseller's Sonnets
Andi Rosenthal

The Bookseller's Sonnets intertwines three love stories
with a tale of religious identity and mystery spanning
five hundred years and three countries.
Paperback: 978-1-84694-342-3 ebook: 978-184694-626-4

Birds of the Nile
An Egyptian Adventure
N.E. David

Ex-diplomat Michael Blake wanted a quiet birding trip
up the Nile – he wasn't expecting a revolution.
Paperback: 978-1-78279-158-4 ebook: 978-1-78279-157-7

Blood Profit$
The Lithium Conspiracy
J. Victor Tomaszek, James N. Patrick, Sr.

The blood of the many for the profits of the few... *Blood Profit$*
will take you into the cigar-smoke-filled room where American
policy and laws are really made.
Paperback: 978-1-78279-483-7 ebook: 978-1-78279-277-2

The Burden
A Family Saga
N.E. David

Frank will do anything to keep his mother and father
apart. But he's carrying baggage – and it might
just weigh him down ...
Paperback: 978-1-78279-936-8 ebook: 978-1-78279-937-5

The Cause
Roderick Vincent
The second American Revolution will be a
fire lit from an internal spark.

Paperback: 978-1-78279-763-0 ebook: 978-1-78279-762-3

Don't Drink and Fly
The Story of Bernice O'Hanlon: Part One
Cathie Devitt
Bernice is a witch living in Glasgow. She loses her way
in her life and wanders off the beaten track looking for the
garden of enlightenment.

Paperback: 978-1-78279-016-7 ebook: 978-1-78279-015-0

Gag
Melissa Unger
One rainy afternoon in a Brooklyn diner, Peter Howland
punctures an egg with his fork. Repulsed, Peter pushes
the plate away and never eats again.

Paperback: 978-1-78279-564-3 ebook: 978-1-78279-563-6

The Master Yeshua
The Undiscovered Gospel of Joseph
Joyce Luck
Jesus is not who you think he is. The year is 75 CE. Joseph
ben Jude is frail and ailing, but he has a prophecy to fulfil ...

Paperback: 978-1-78279-974-0 ebook: 978-1-78279-975-7

On the Far Side, There's a Boy
Paula Coston
Martine Haslett, a thirty-something 1980s woman, plays hard
on the fringes of the London drag club scene until one night
which prompts her to sign up to a charity. She writes to a
young Sri Lankan boy, with consequences far and long.
Paperback: 978-1-78279-574-2 ebook: 978-1-78279-573-5

Tuareg
Alberto Vazquez-Figueroa
With over 5 million copies sold worldwide, *Tuareg* is a classic
adventure story from best-selling author Alberto Vazquez-
Figueroa, about honour, revenge and a clash of cultures.
Paperback: 978-1-84694-192-4

Readers of ebooks can buy or view any of these bestsellers by
clicking on the live link in the title. Most titles are published
in paperback and as an ebook. Paperbacks are available in
traditional bookshops. Both print and ebook formats are
available online.

Find more titles and sign up to our readers' newsletter at
www.collectiveinkbooks.com/fiction